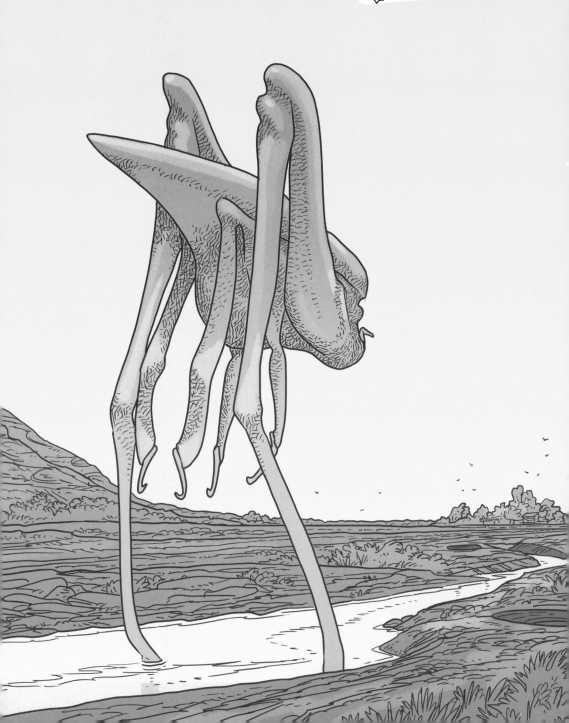

TO MY GRANDPA POTTER,
WHO TOLD ME THIS STORY

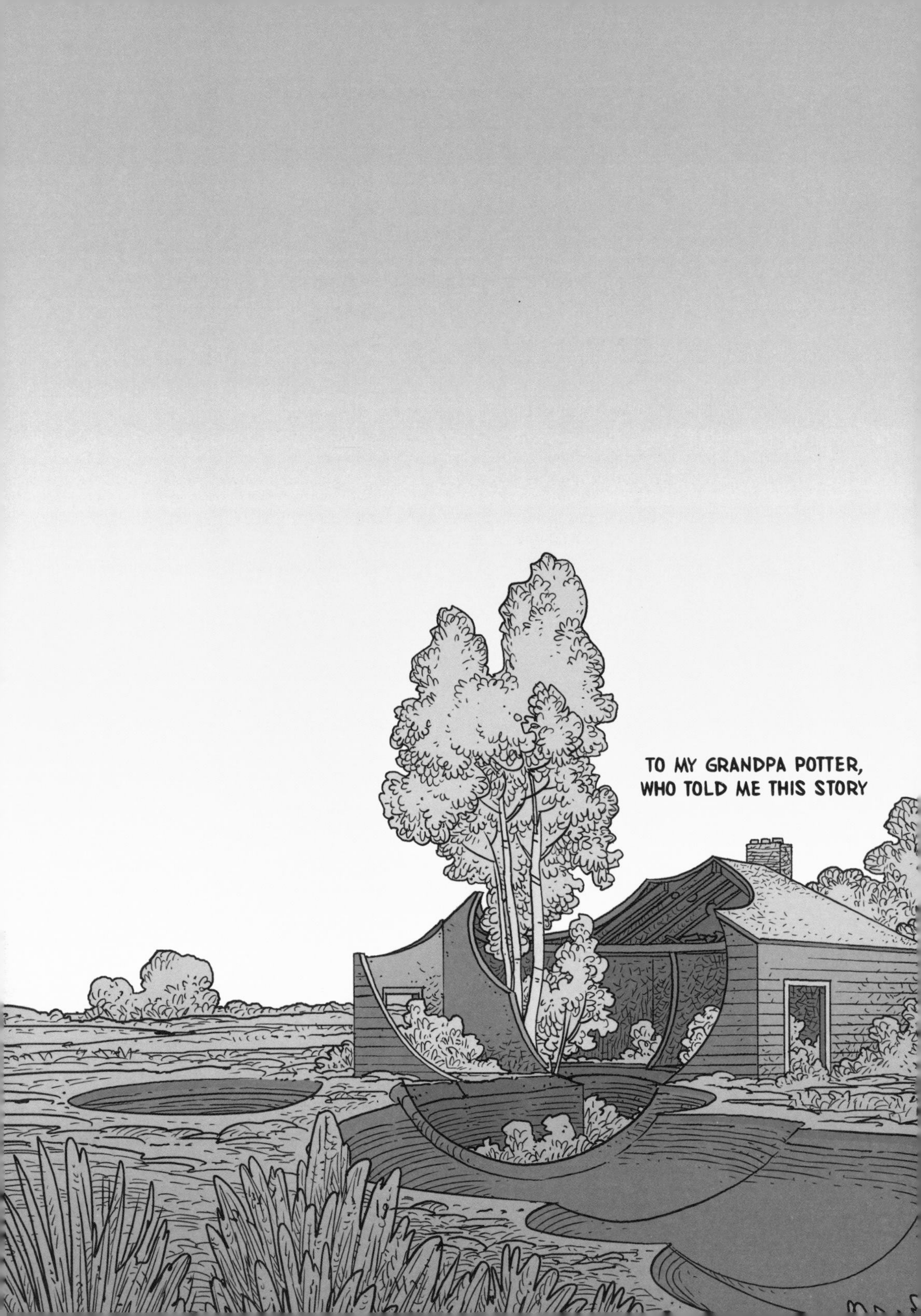

CATALOGING-IN-PUBLICATION DATA HAS BEEN APPLIED FOR
AND MAY BE OBTAINED FROM THE LIBRARY OF CONGRESS.

HARDCOVER ISBN: 978-1-4197-2128-1
PAPERBACK ISBN: 978-1-4197-2944-7

ORIGINALLY PUBLISHED IN HARDCOVER
BY AMULET BOOKS IN 2017.
TEXT AND ILLUSTRATIONS COPYRIGHT © 2017 NATHAN HALE
BOOK DESIGN BY NATHAN HALE AND CHAD W. BECKERMAN

PRINTED AND BOUND IN CHINA
10 9 8 7 6 5 4 3 2 1

AMULET BOOKS ARE AVAILABLE AT SPECIAL DISCOUNTS WHEN
PURCHASED IN QUANTITY FOR PREMIUMS AND PROMOTIONS
AS WELL AS FUNDRAISING OR EDUCATIONAL USE. SPECIAL
EDITIONS CAN ALSO BE CREATED TO SPECIFICATION. FOR
DETAILS, CONTACT SPECIALSALES@ABRAMSBOOKS.COM OR
THE ADDRESS BELOW.

ABRAMS The Art of Books
195 Broadway, New York, NY 10007
abramsbooks.com

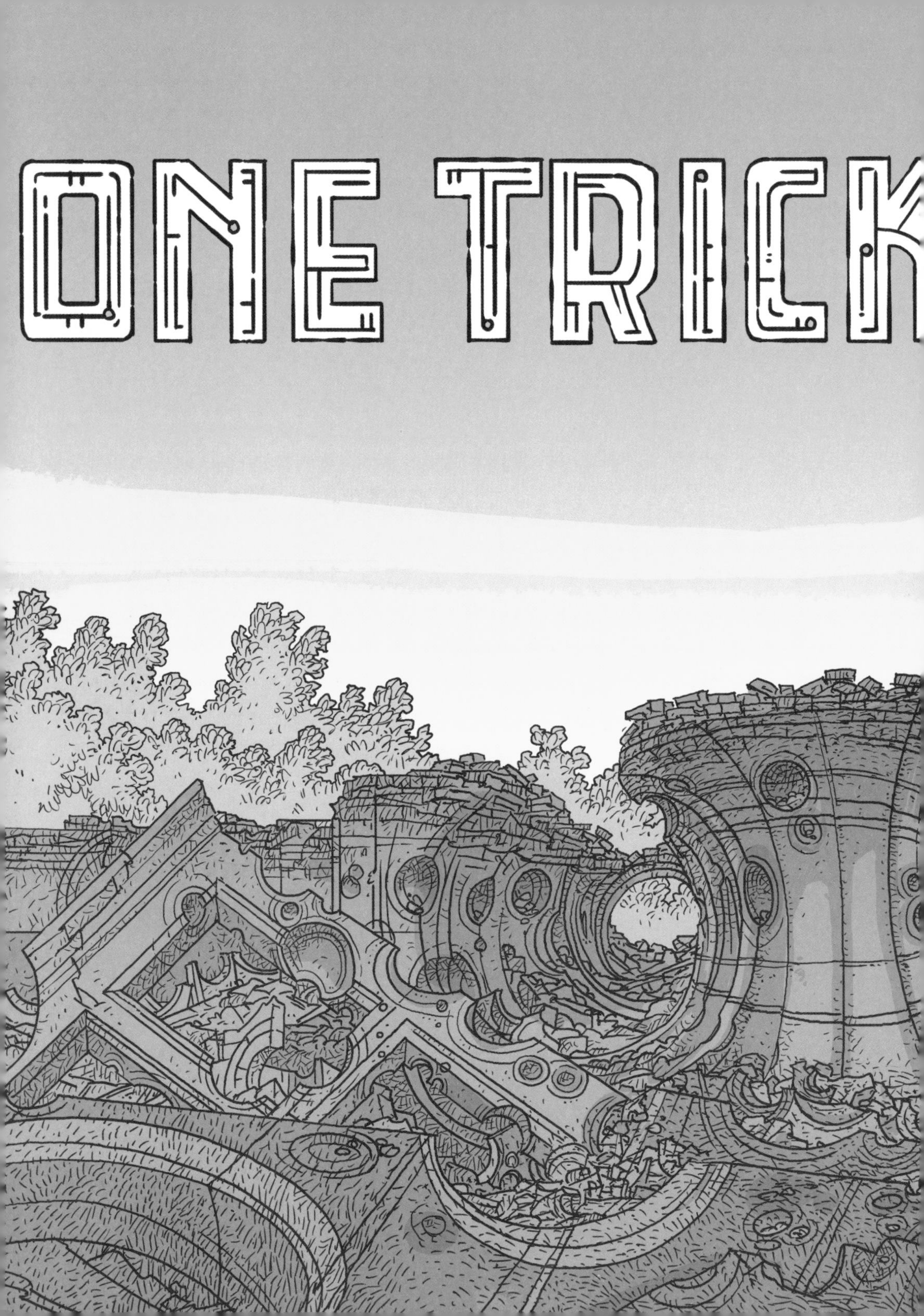
ONE TRICK

PONY

A GRAPHIC NOVEL BY

NATHAN HALE

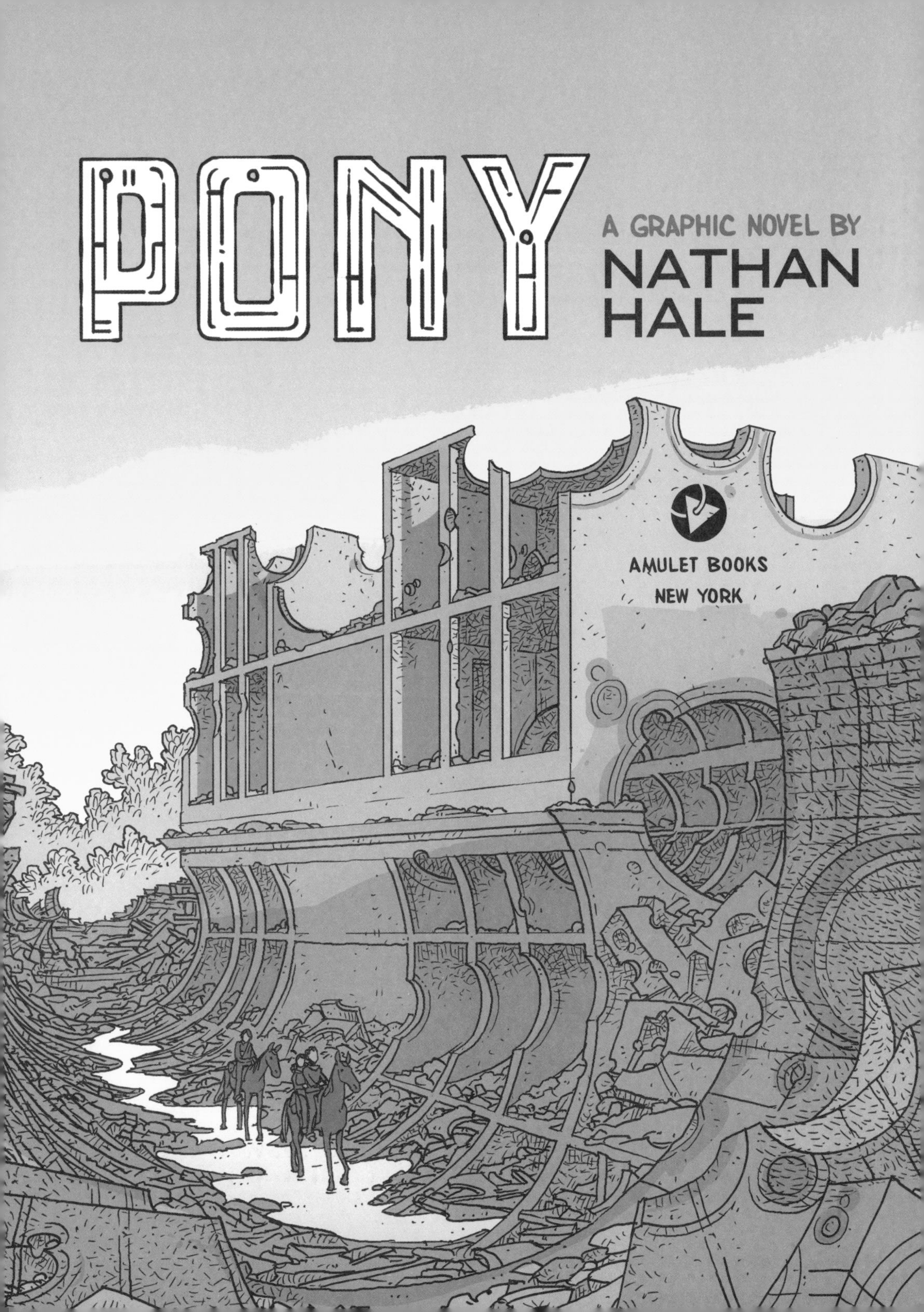
AMULET BOOKS
NEW YORK

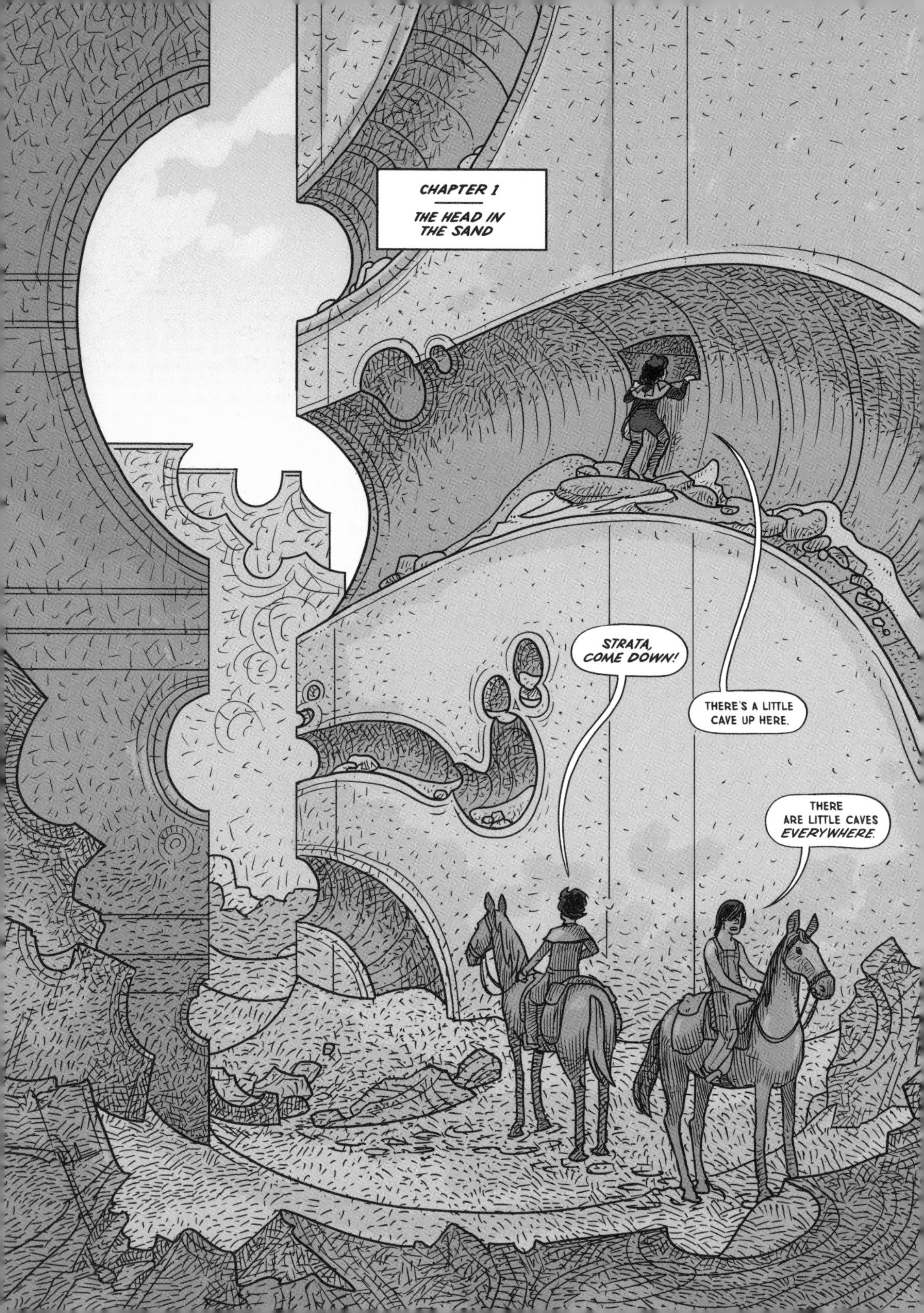
CHAPTER 1
THE HEAD IN THE SAND
THERE'S A LITTLE CAVE UP HERE.
STRATA, COME DOWN!
THERE ARE LITTLE CAVES EVERYWHERE.

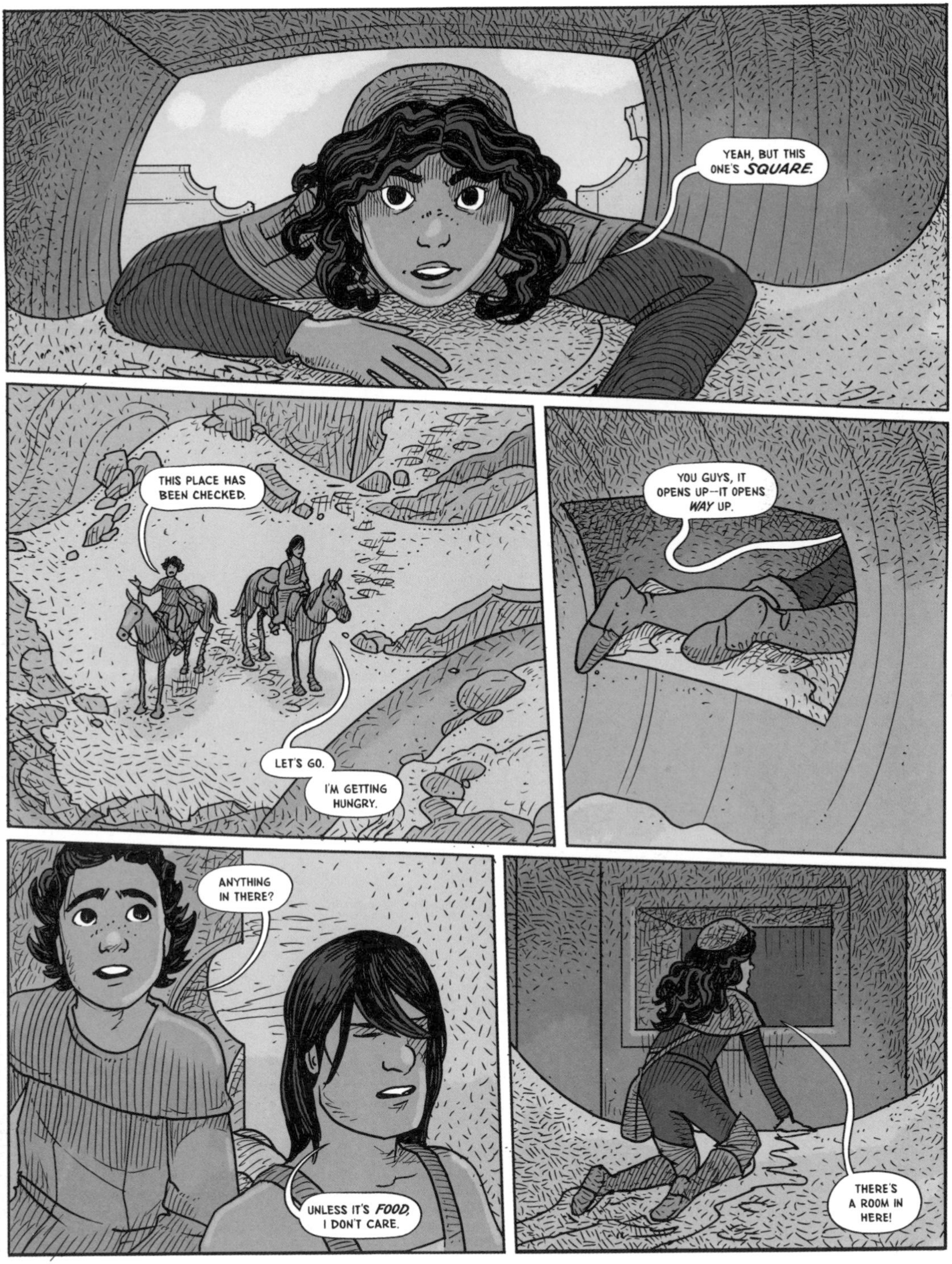
YEAH, BUT THIS ONE'S *SQUARE.*
THIS PLACE HAS BEEN CHECKED.
LET'S GO.
I'M GETTING HUNGRY.
YOU GUYS, IT OPENS UP--IT OPENS *WAY* UP.
ANYTHING IN THERE?
UNLESS IT'S *FOOD,* I DON'T CARE.
THERE'S A ROOM IN HERE!

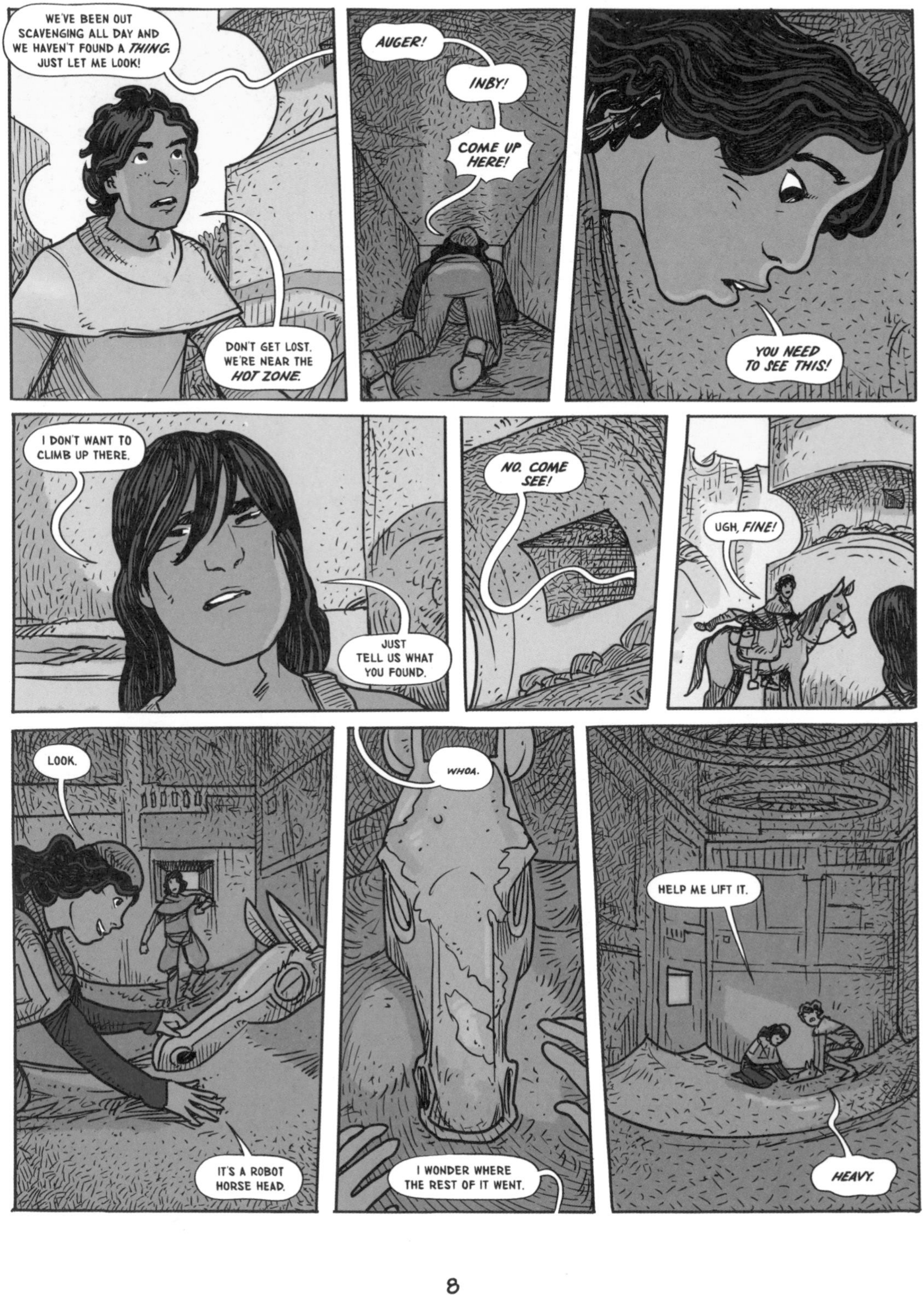
WE'VE BEEN OUT SCAVENGING ALL DAY AND WE HAVEN'T FOUND A *THING.* JUST LET ME LOOK!
DON'T GET LOST. WE'RE NEAR THE *HOT ZONE.*
AUGER!
INBY!
COME UP HERE!
YOU NEED TO SEE THIS!
I DON'T WANT TO CLIMB UP THERE.
JUST TELL US WHAT YOU FOUND.
NO. COME SEE!
UGH, *FINE!*
LOOK.
IT'S A ROBOT HORSE HEAD.
WHOA.
I WONDER WHERE THE REST OF IT WENT.
HELP ME LIFT IT.
HEAVY.

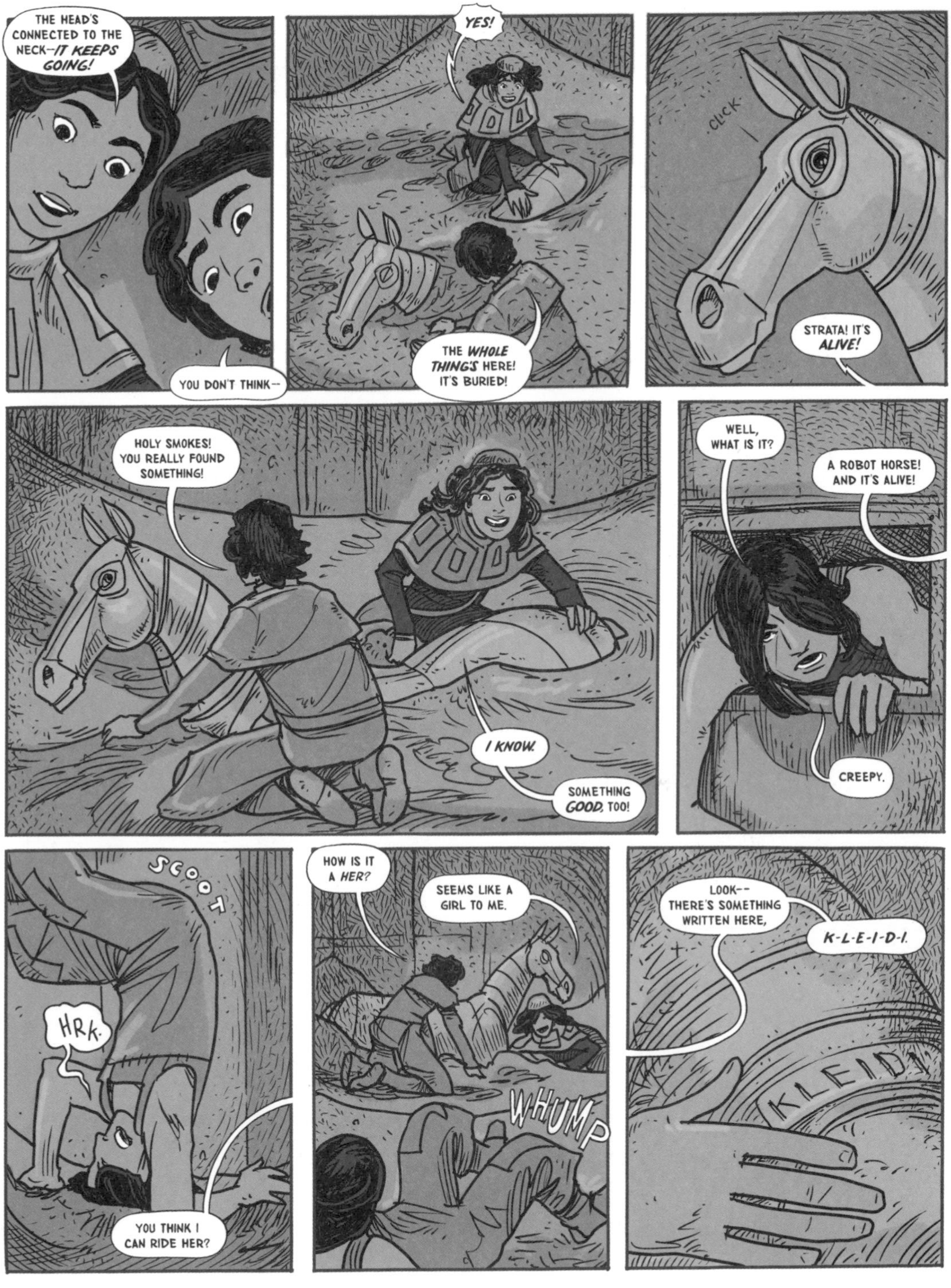
THE HEAD'S CONNECTED TO THE NECK--IT KEEPS GOING!
YOU DON'T THINK--
YES!
THE WHOLE THING'S HERE! IT'S BURIED!
CLICK
STRATA! IT'S ALIVE!
HOLY SMOKES! YOU REALLY FOUND SOMETHING!
I KNOW.
SOMETHING GOOD, TOO!
WELL, WHAT IS IT?
A ROBOT HORSE! AND IT'S ALIVE!
CREEPY.
SCOOT
HRK.
YOU THINK I CAN RIDE HER?
HOW IS IT A HER?
SEEMS LIKE A GIRL TO ME.
WHUMP
LOOK-- THERE'S SOMETHING WRITTEN HERE,
K-L-E-I-D-I.
KLEIDI

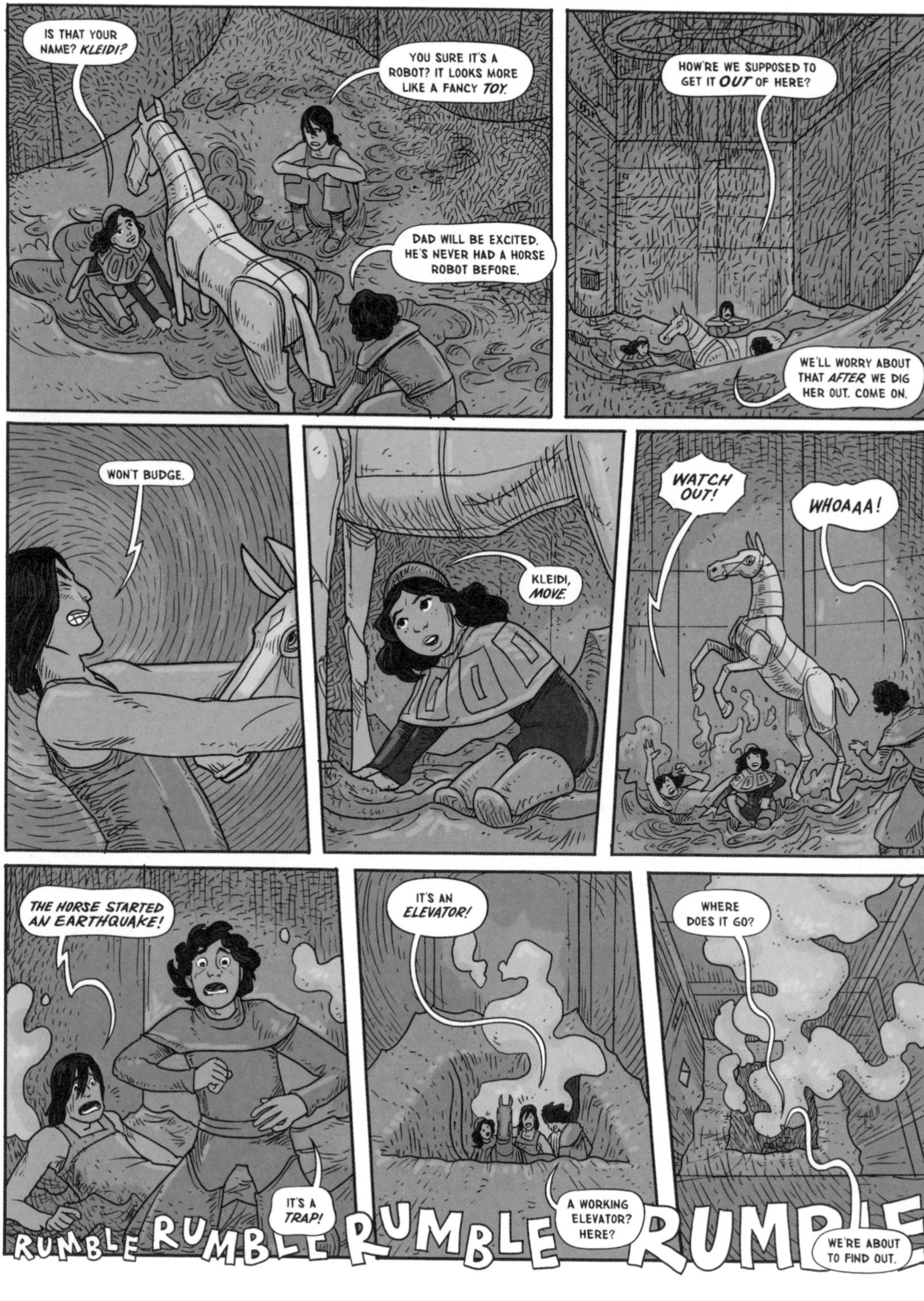
IS THAT YOUR NAME? *KLEIDI?*
YOU SURE IT'S A ROBOT? IT LOOKS MORE LIKE A FANCY *TOY.*
DAD WILL BE EXCITED. HE'S NEVER HAD A HORSE ROBOT BEFORE.
HOW'RE WE SUPPOSED TO GET IT *OUT* OF HERE?
WE'LL WORRY ABOUT THAT *AFTER* WE DIG HER OUT. COME ON.
WON'T BUDGE.
KLEIDI, *MOVE.*
WATCH OUT!
WHOAAA!
THE HORSE STARTED AN EARTHQUAKE!
IT'S A *TRAP!*
IT'S AN *ELEVATOR!*
A WORKING ELEVATOR? HERE?
WHERE DOES IT GO?
WE'RE ABOUT TO FIND OUT.
RUMBLE RUMBLE RUMBLE RUMBLE

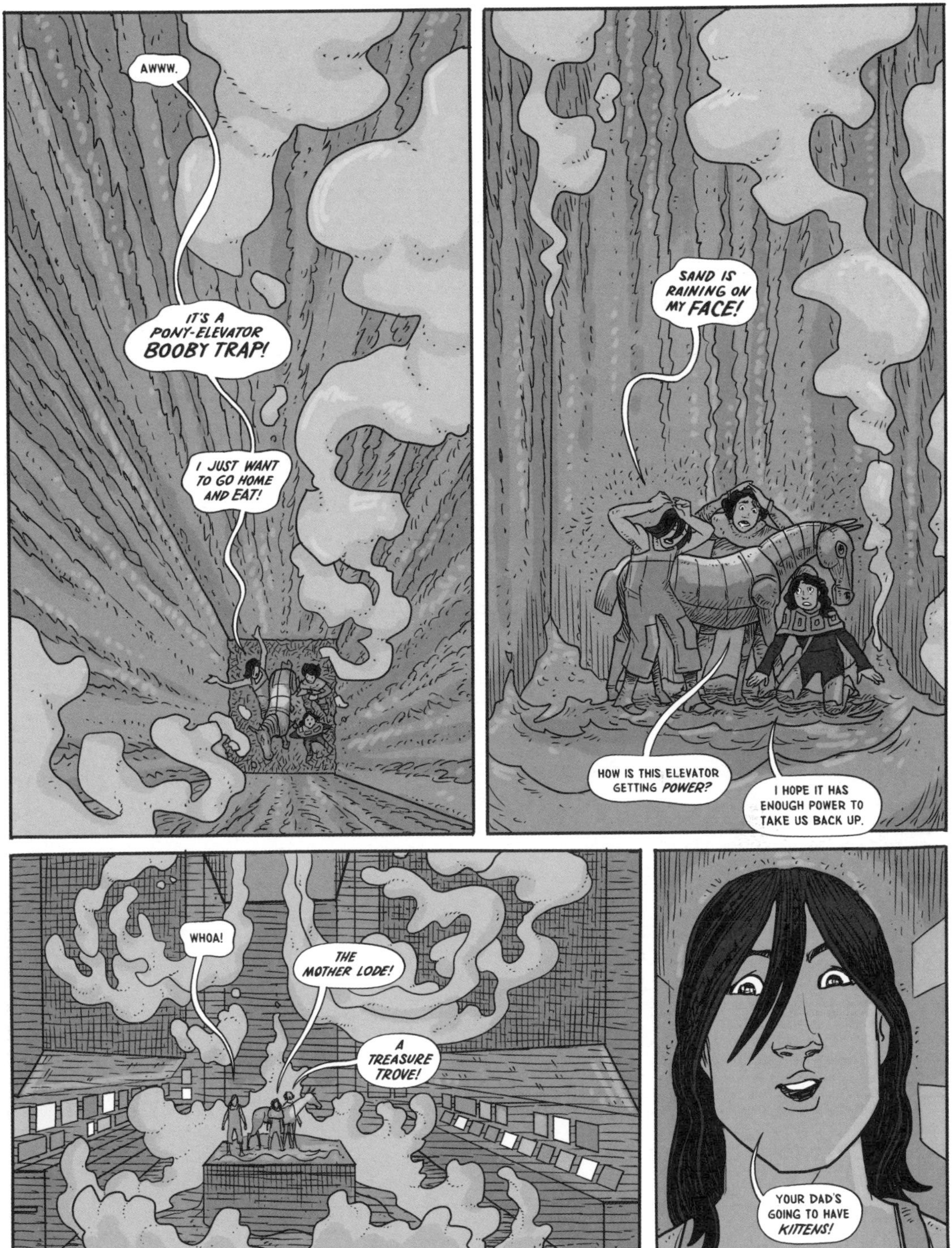
AWWW.
IT'S A PONY-ELEVATOR BOOBY TRAP!
I JUST WANT TO GO HOME AND EAT!
SAND IS RAINING ON MY FACE!
HOW IS THIS ELEVATOR GETTING POWER?
I HOPE IT HAS ENOUGH POWER TO TAKE US BACK UP.
WHOA!
THE MOTHER LODE!
A TREASURE TROVE!
YOUR DAD'S GOING TO HAVE KITTENS!

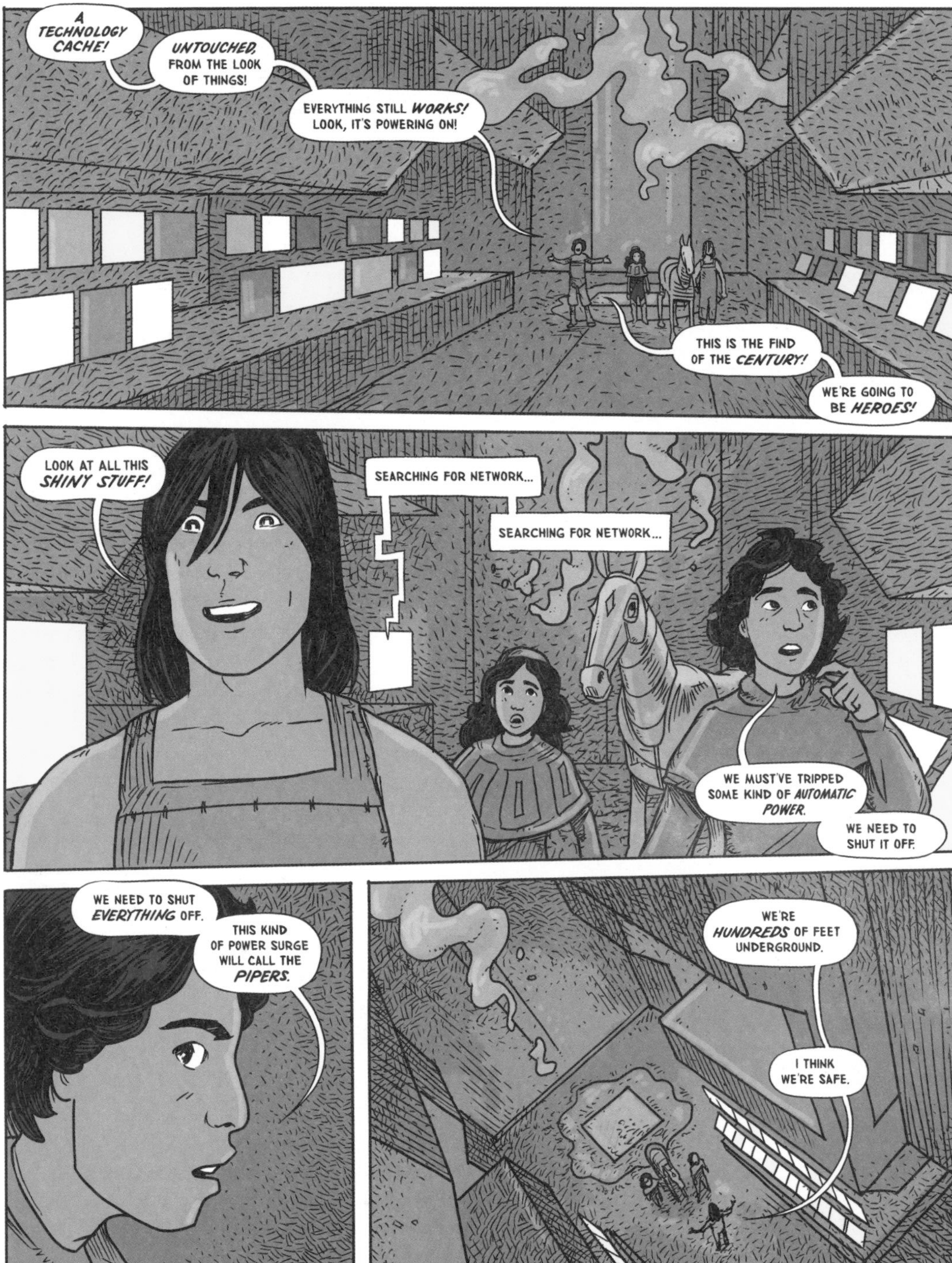
A TECHNOLOGY CACHE!
UNTOUCHED, FROM THE LOOK OF THINGS!
EVERYTHING STILL WORKS! LOOK, IT'S POWERING ON!
THIS IS THE FIND OF THE CENTURY!
WE'RE GOING TO BE HEROES!
LOOK AT ALL THIS SHINY STUFF!
SEARCHING FOR NETWORK...
SEARCHING FOR NETWORK...
WE MUST'VE TRIPPED SOME KIND OF AUTOMATIC POWER.
WE NEED TO SHUT IT OFF.
WE NEED TO SHUT EVERYTHING OFF.
THIS KIND OF POWER SURGE WILL CALL THE PIPERS.
WE'RE HUNDREDS OF FEET UNDERGROUND.
I THINK WE'RE SAFE.

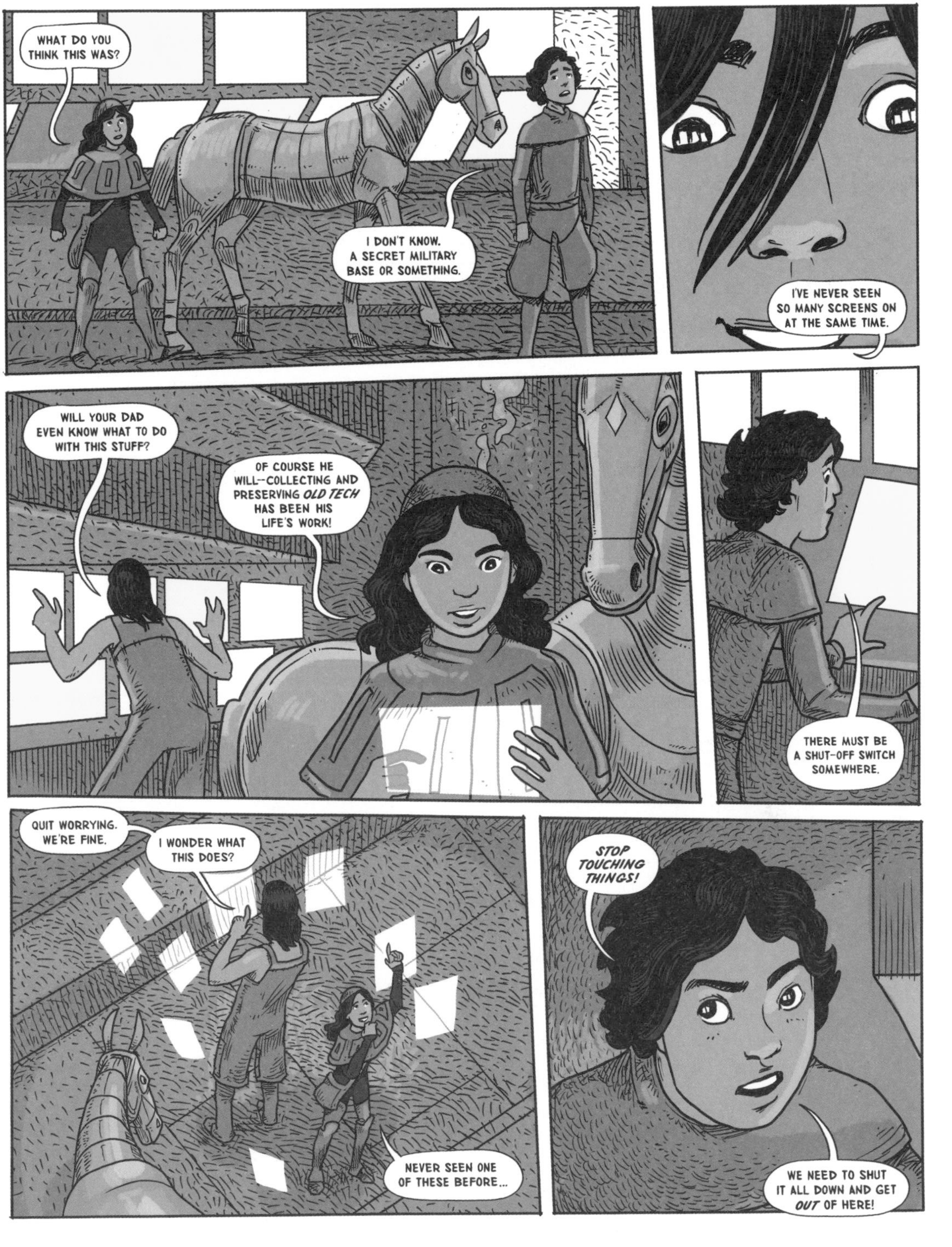
WHAT DO YOU THINK THIS WAS?
I DON'T KNOW. A SECRET MILITARY BASE OR SOMETHING.
I'VE NEVER SEEN SO MANY SCREENS ON AT THE SAME TIME.
WILL YOUR DAD EVEN KNOW WHAT TO DO WITH THIS STUFF?
OF COURSE HE WILL--COLLECTING AND PRESERVING *OLD TECH* HAS BEEN HIS LIFE'S WORK!
THERE MUST BE A SHUT-OFF SWITCH SOMEWHERE.
QUIT WORRYING. WE'RE FINE.
I WONDER WHAT THIS DOES?
NEVER SEEN ONE OF THESE BEFORE...
STOP TOUCHING THINGS!
WE NEED TO SHUT IT ALL DOWN AND GET *OUT* OF HERE!

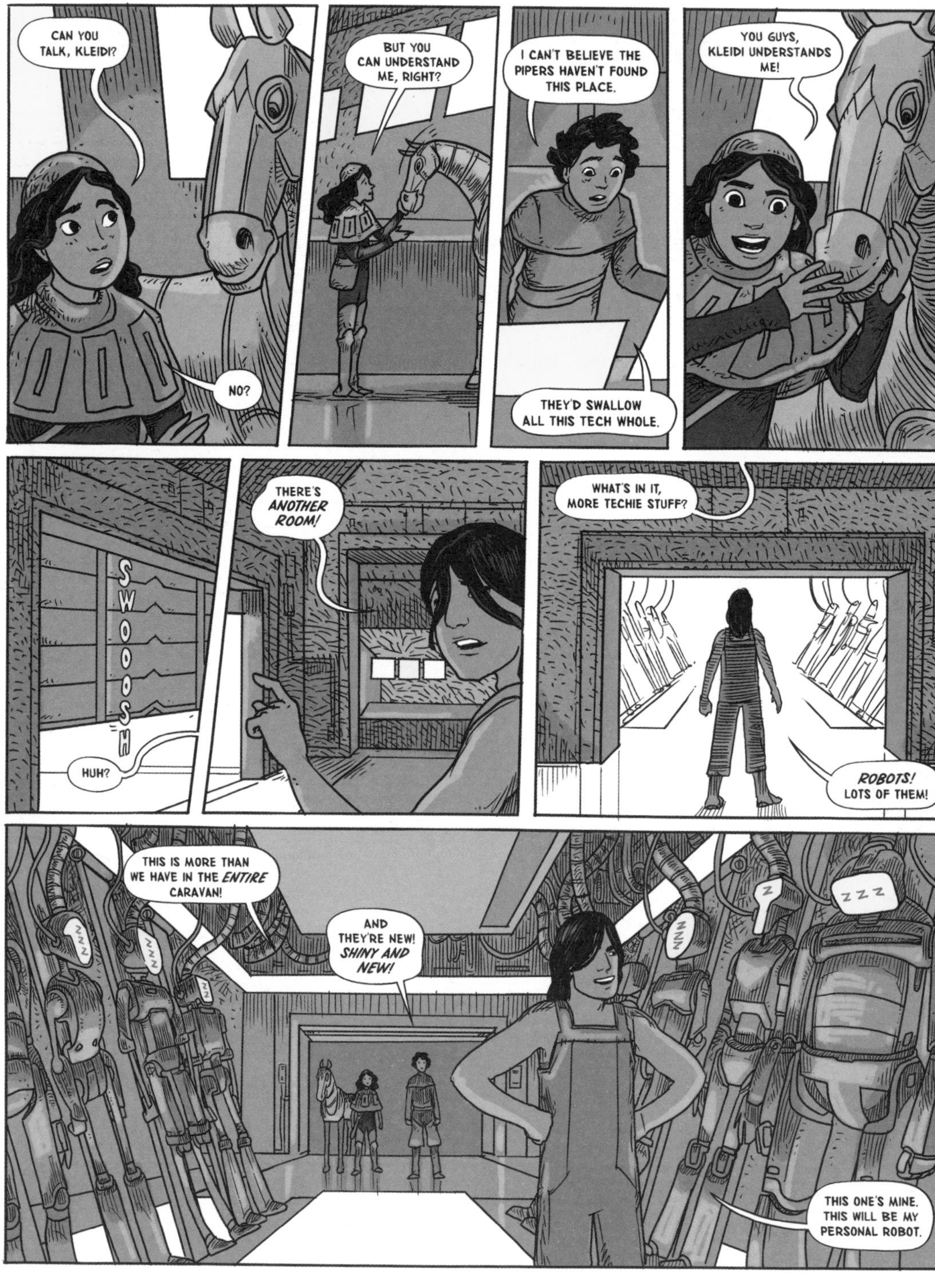
CAN YOU TALK, KLEIDI?
NO?
BUT YOU CAN UNDERSTAND ME, RIGHT?
I CAN'T BELIEVE THE PIPERS HAVEN'T FOUND THIS PLACE.
THEY'D SWALLOW ALL THIS TECH WHOLE.
YOU GUYS, KLEIDI UNDERSTANDS ME!
SWOOOSH
HUH?
THERE'S *ANOTHER ROOM!*
WHAT'S IN IT, MORE TECHIE STUFF?
ROBOTS! LOTS OF THEM!
THIS IS MORE THAN WE HAVE IN THE *ENTIRE* CARAVAN!
AND THEY'RE NEW! *SHINY AND NEW!*
THIS ONE'S MINE. THIS WILL BE MY PERSONAL ROBOT.

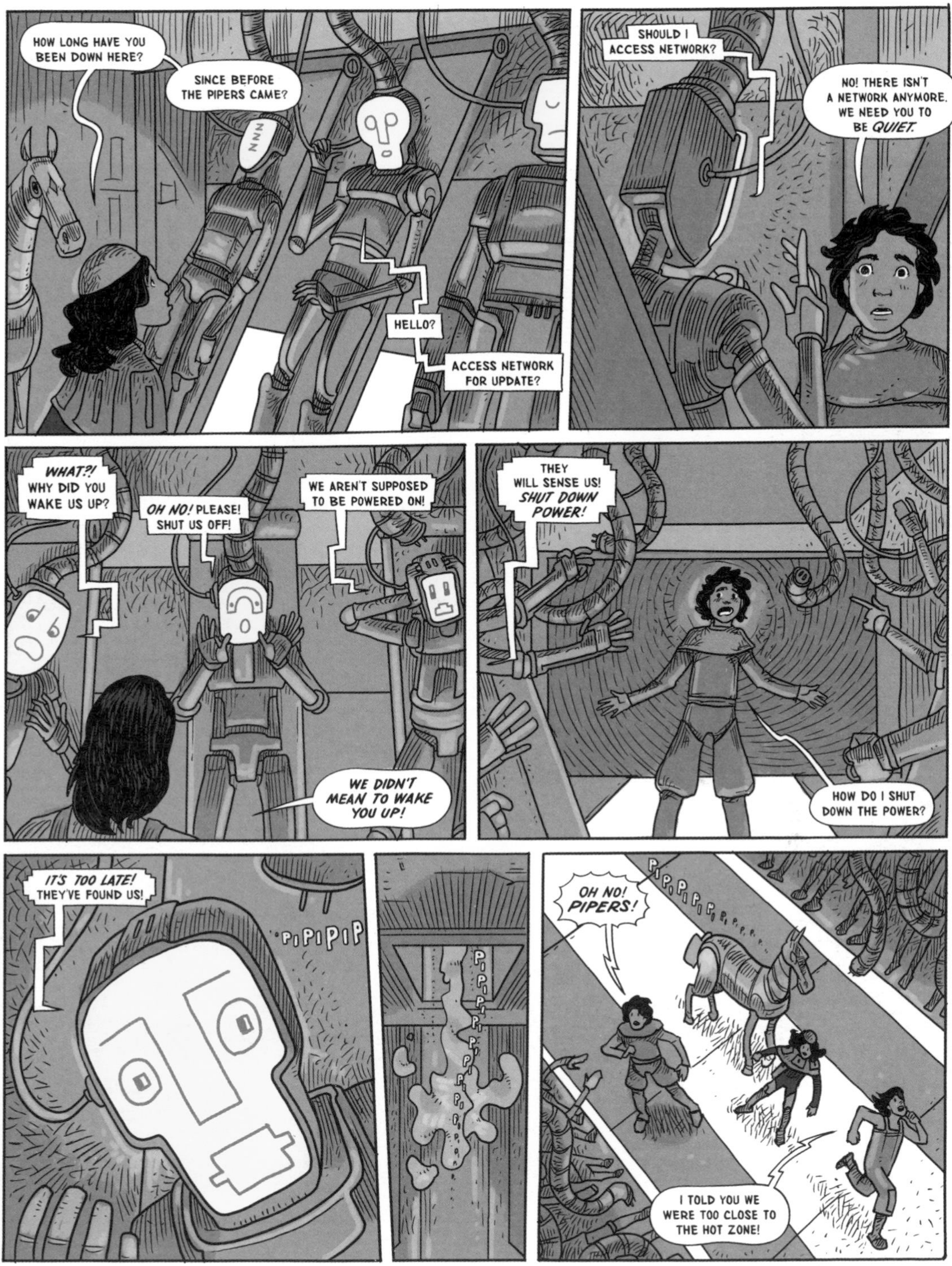
HOW LONG HAVE YOU BEEN DOWN HERE?
SINCE BEFORE THE PIPERS CAME?
ZZZ
HELLO?
ACCESS NETWORK FOR UPDATE?
SHOULD I ACCESS NETWORK?
NO! THERE ISN'T A NETWORK ANYMORE. WE NEED YOU TO BE QUIET.
WHAT?! WHY DID YOU WAKE US UP?
OH NO! PLEASE! SHUT US OFF!
WE AREN'T SUPPOSED TO BE POWERED ON!
WE DIDN'T MEAN TO WAKE YOU UP!
THEY WILL SENSE US! SHUT DOWN POWER!
HOW DO I SHUT DOWN THE POWER?
IT'S TOO LATE! THEY'VE FOUND US!
PIPIPIP
PIPIPIPIPIPIPIP
OH NO! PIPERS!
PIPIPIPIPIPIPIPIP
I TOLD YOU WE WERE TOO CLOSE TO THE HOT ZONE!

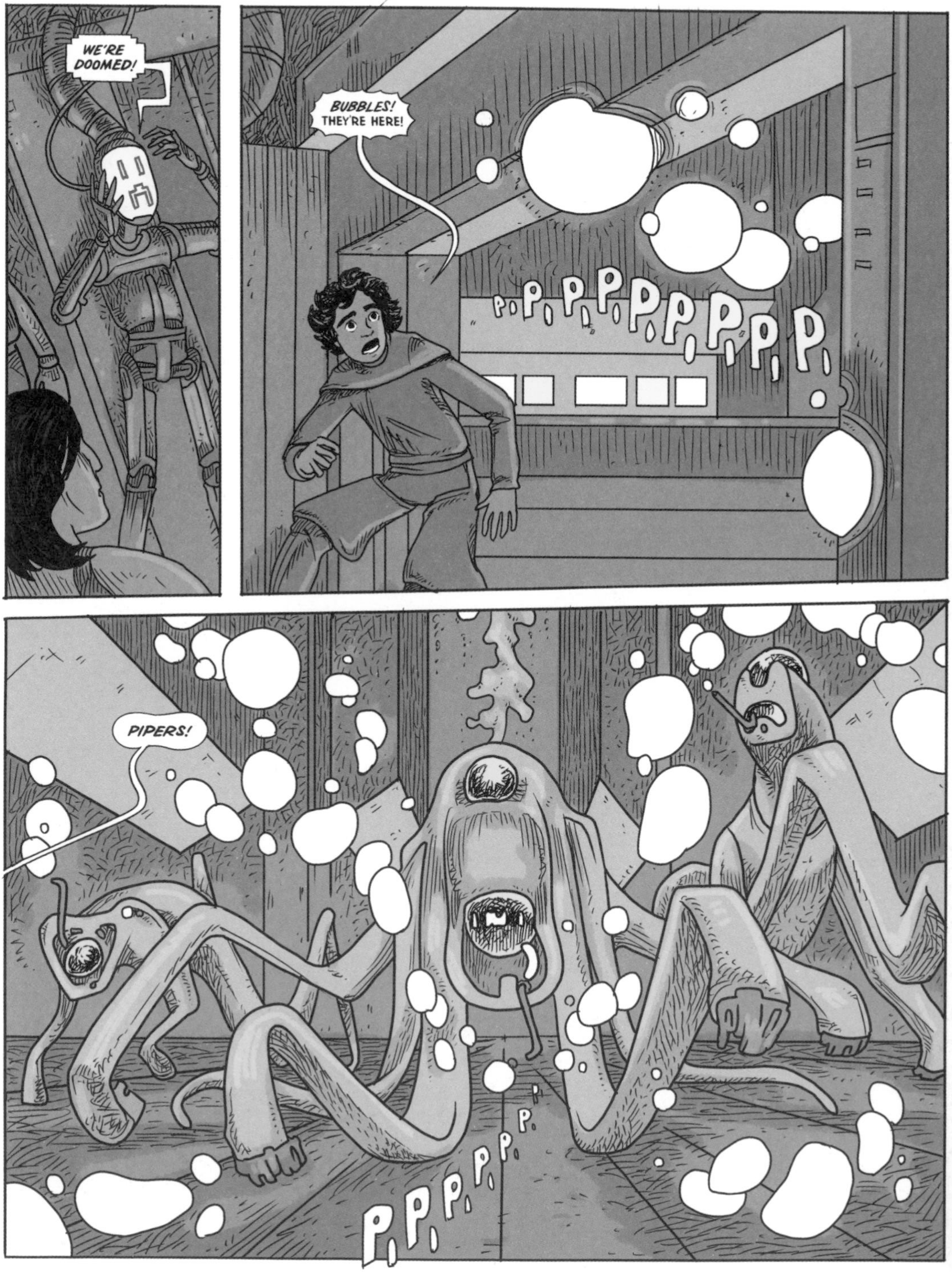

WE'RE DOOMED!
BUBBLES! THEY'RE HERE!
PPPPPPPPPP
PIPERS!
PPPPPPP

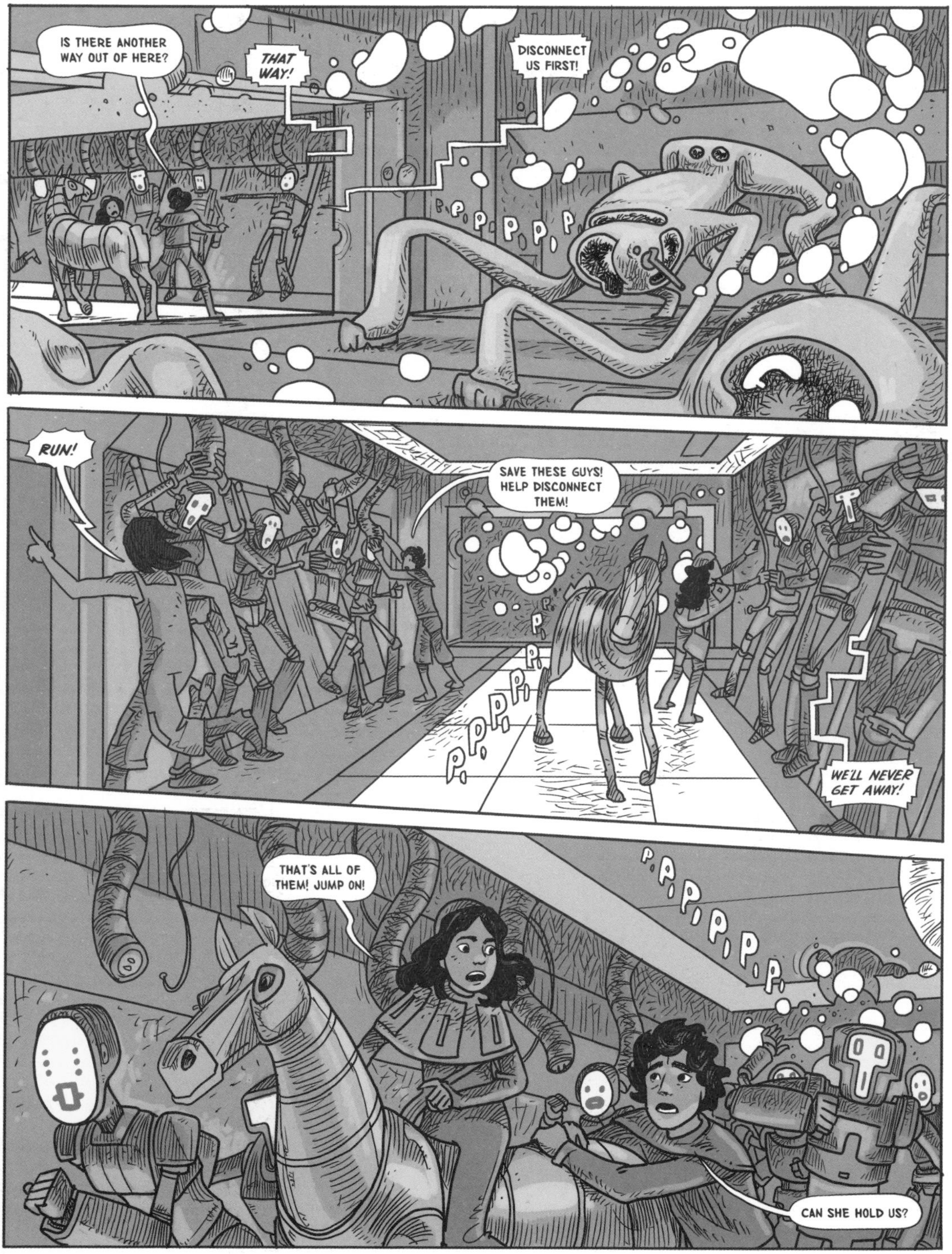
IS THERE ANOTHER WAY OUT OF HERE?
THAT WAY!
DISCONNECT US FIRST!
RUN!
SAVE THESE GUYS! HELP DISCONNECT THEM!
WE'LL NEVER GET AWAY!
THAT'S ALL OF THEM! JUMP ON!
CAN SHE HOLD US?

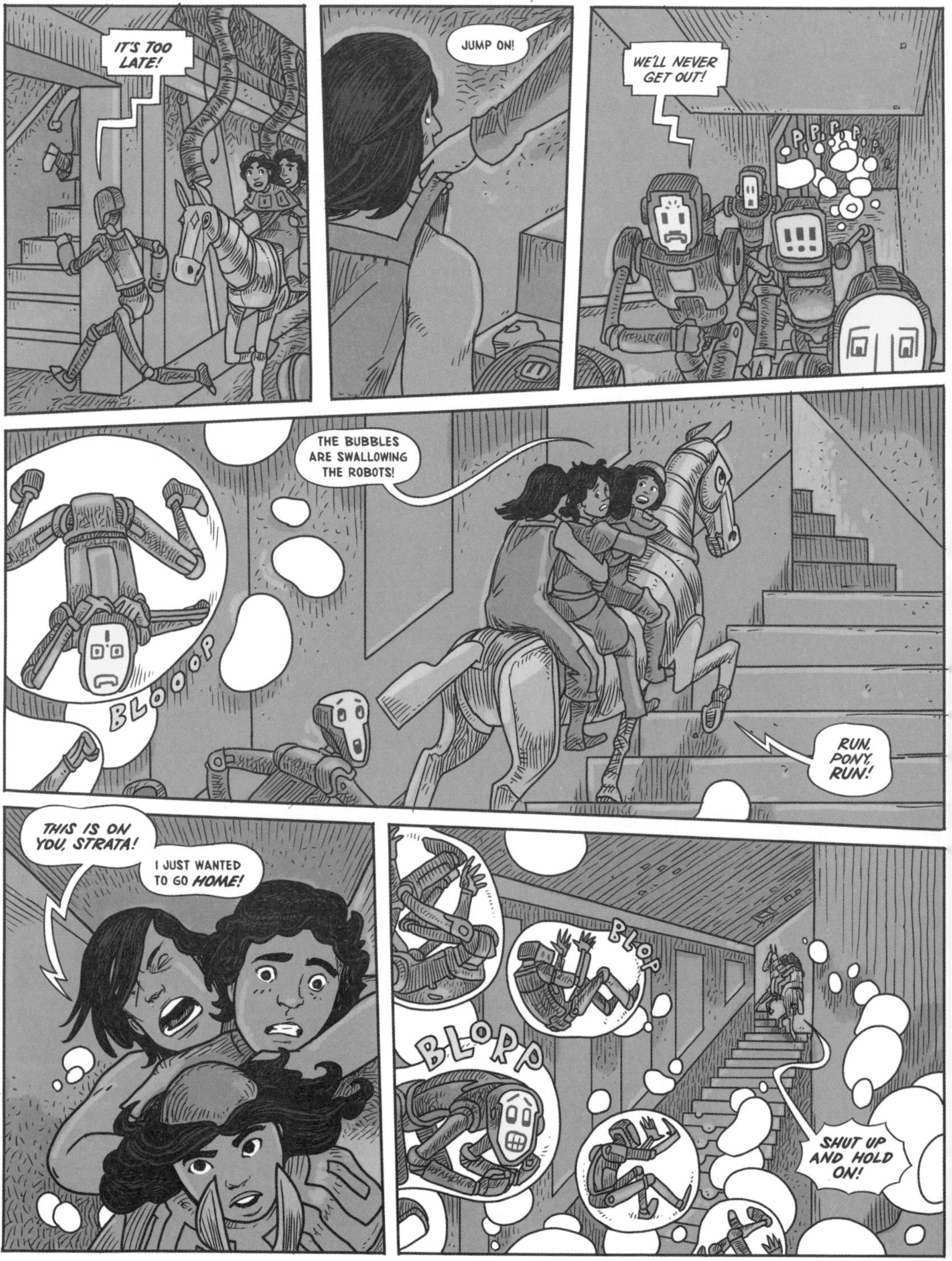

IT'S TOO LATE!
JUMP ON!
WE'LL NEVER GET OUT!
THE BUBBLES ARE SWALLOWING THE ROBOTS!
BLOOOP
RUN, PONY, RUN!
THIS IS ON YOU, STRATA!
I JUST WANTED TO GO *HOME!*
BLOP
BLORP
SHUT UP AND HOLD ON!

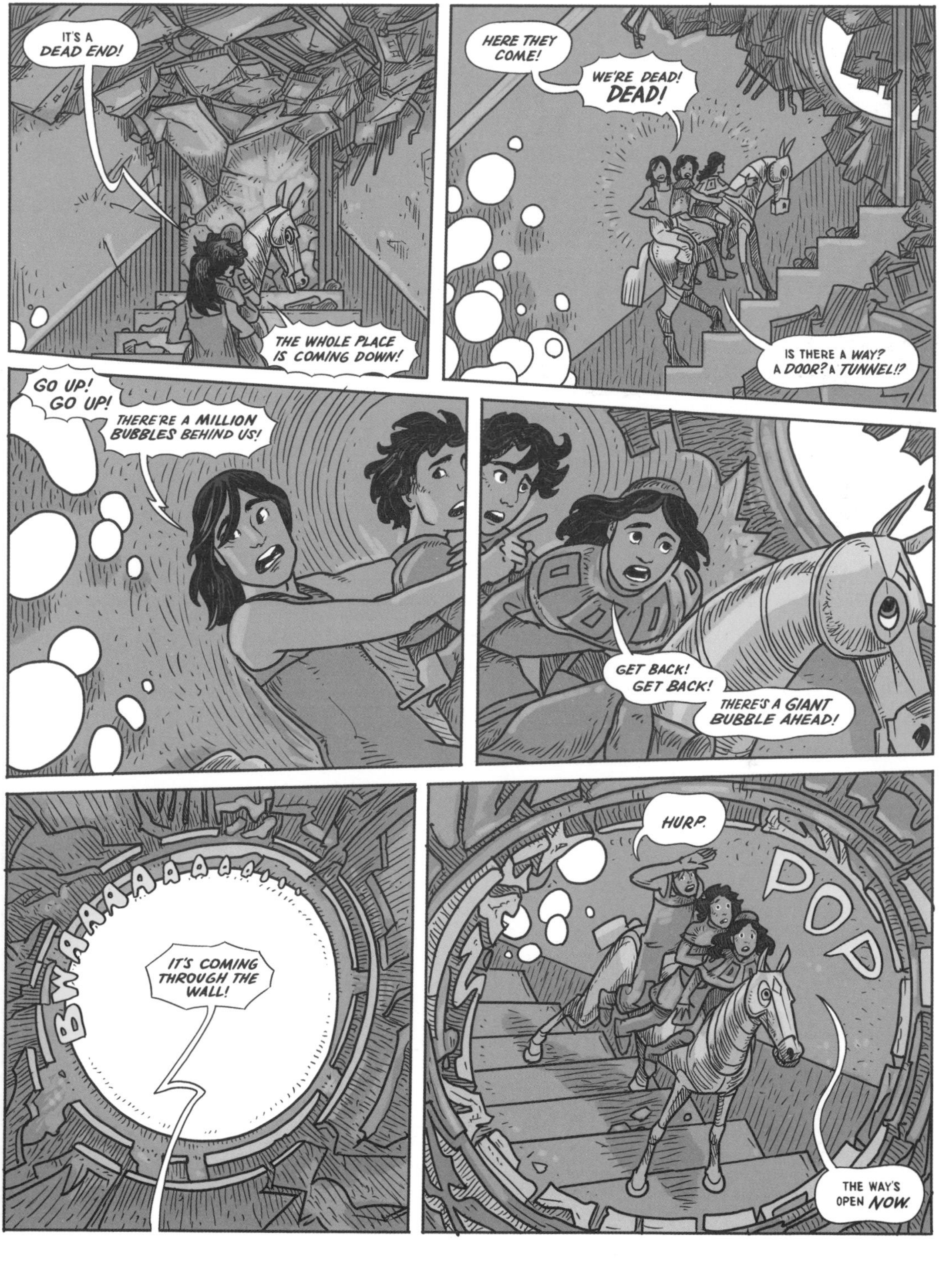
IT'S A DEAD END!
THE WHOLE PLACE IS COMING DOWN!
HERE THEY COME!
WE'RE DEAD! DEAD!
IS THERE A WAY? A DOOR? A TUNNEL!?
GO UP! GO UP!
THERE'RE A MILLION BUBBLES BEHIND US!
GET BACK! GET BACK!
THERE'S A GIANT BUBBLE AHEAD!
BWAAAAAAAAA......
IT'S COMING THROUGH THE WALL!
HURP.
POP
THE WAY'S OPEN NOW.

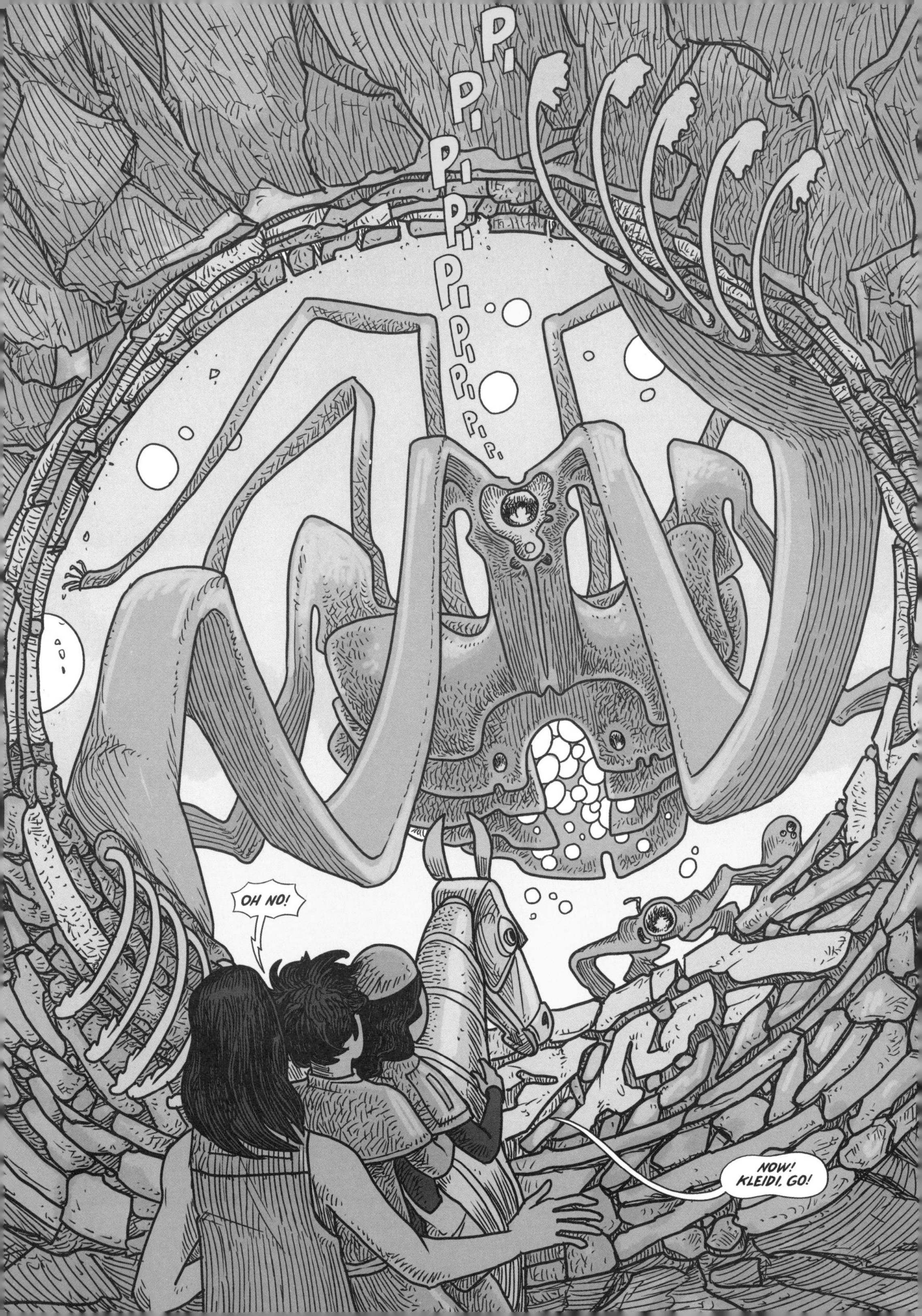
PI PI PI PI PI PI PI PI PI PI
OH NO!
NOW! KLEIDI, GO!

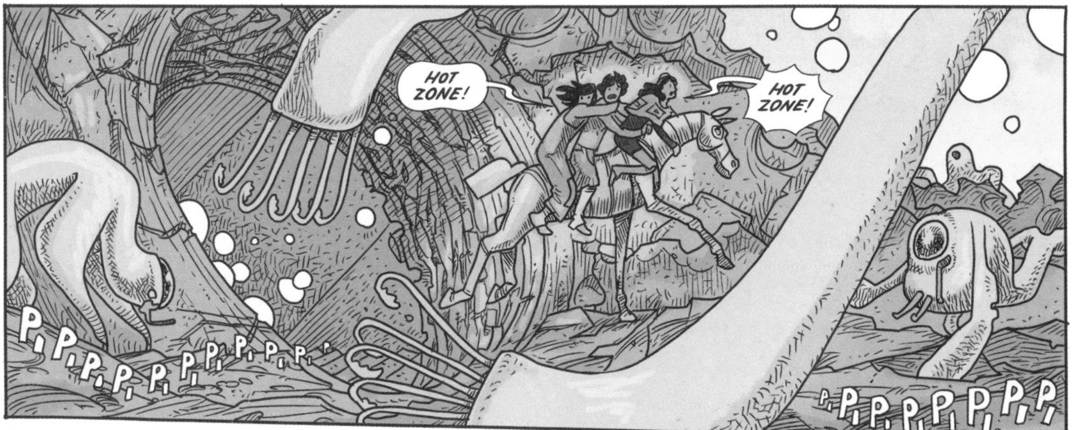
HOT ZONE!
HOT ZONE!

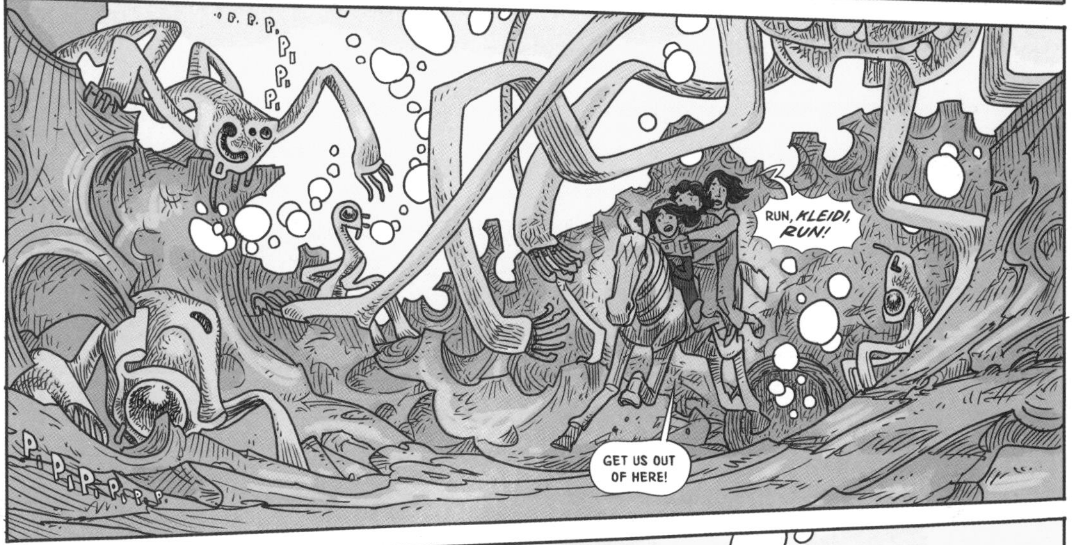
RUN, KLEIDI, RUN!
GET US OUT OF HERE!

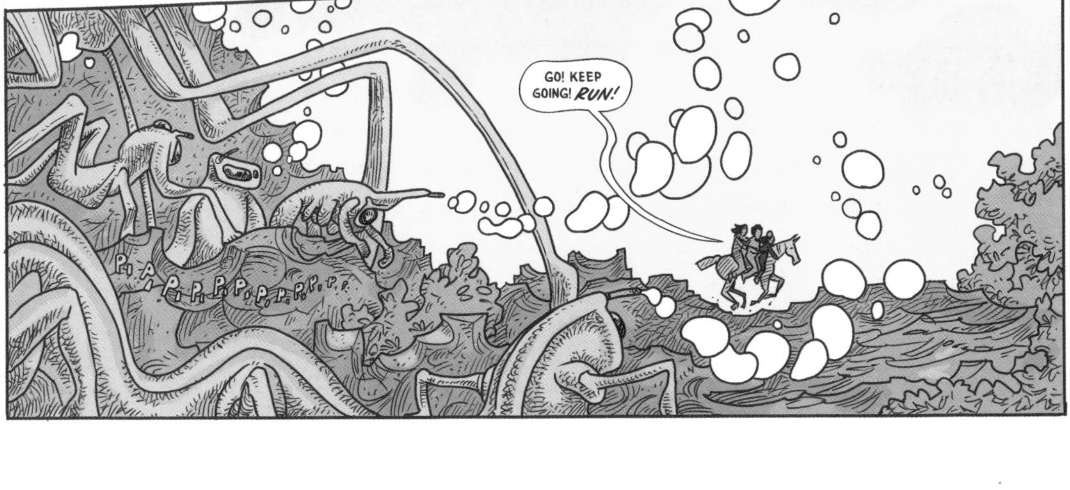
GO! KEEP GOING! RUN!

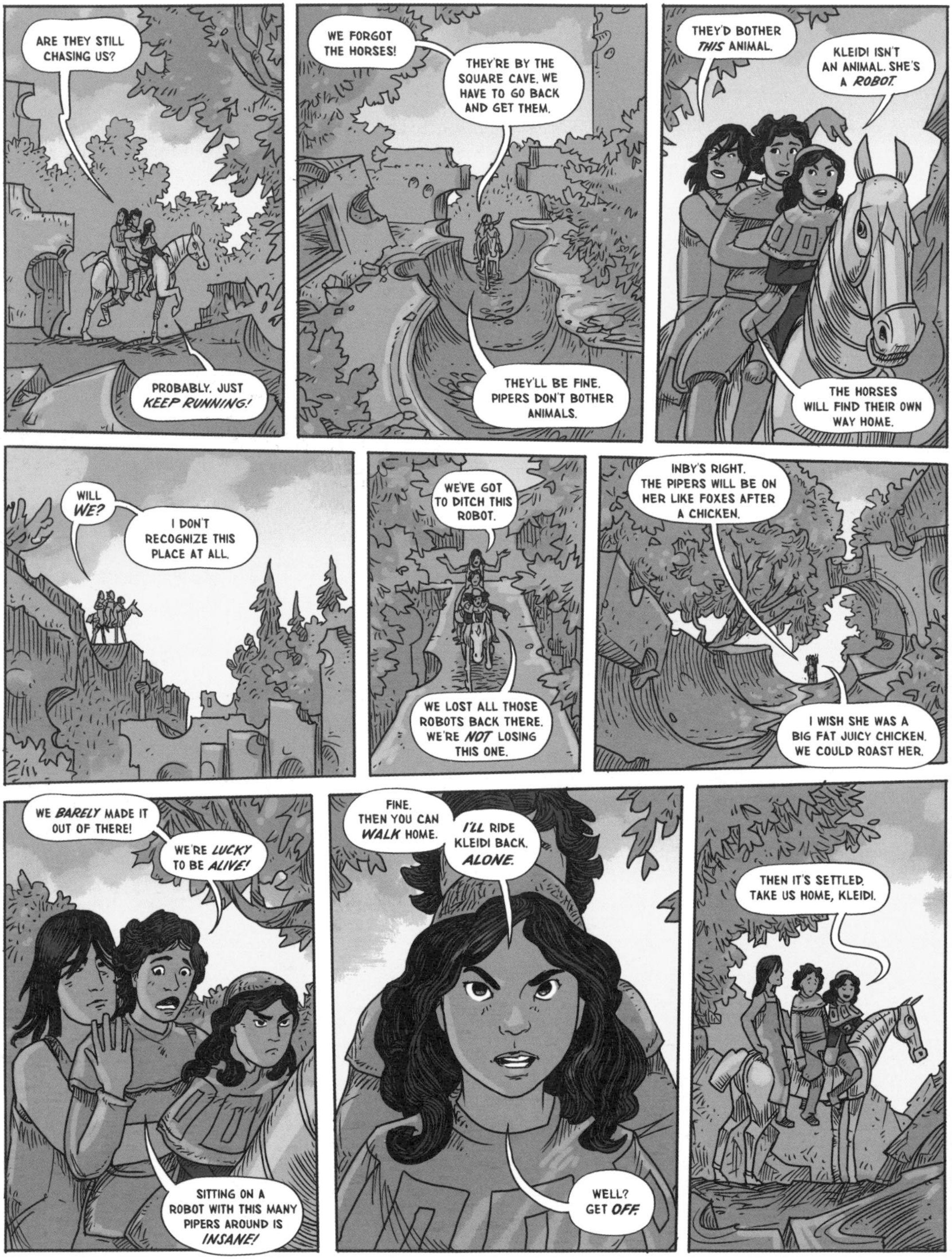
ARE THEY STILL CHASING US?
PROBABLY. JUST KEEP RUNNING!
WE FORGOT THE HORSES!
THEY'RE BY THE SQUARE CAVE. WE HAVE TO GO BACK AND GET THEM.
THEY'LL BE FINE. PIPERS DON'T BOTHER ANIMALS.
THEY'D BOTHER THIS ANIMAL.
KLEIDI ISN'T AN ANIMAL. SHE'S A ROBOT.
THE HORSES WILL FIND THEIR OWN WAY HOME.
WILL WE?
I DON'T RECOGNIZE THIS PLACE AT ALL.
WE'VE GOT TO DITCH THIS ROBOT.
WE LOST ALL THOSE ROBOTS BACK THERE. WE'RE NOT LOSING THIS ONE.
INBY'S RIGHT. THE PIPERS WILL BE ON HER LIKE FOXES AFTER A CHICKEN.
I WISH SHE WAS A BIG FAT JUICY CHICKEN. WE COULD ROAST HER.
WE BARELY MADE IT OUT OF THERE!
WE'RE LUCKY TO BE ALIVE!
SITTING ON A ROBOT WITH THIS MANY PIPERS AROUND IS INSANE!
FINE. THEN YOU CAN WALK HOME.
I'LL RIDE KLEIDI BACK. ALONE.
WELL? GET OFF.
THEN IT'S SETTLED. TAKE US HOME, KLEIDI.

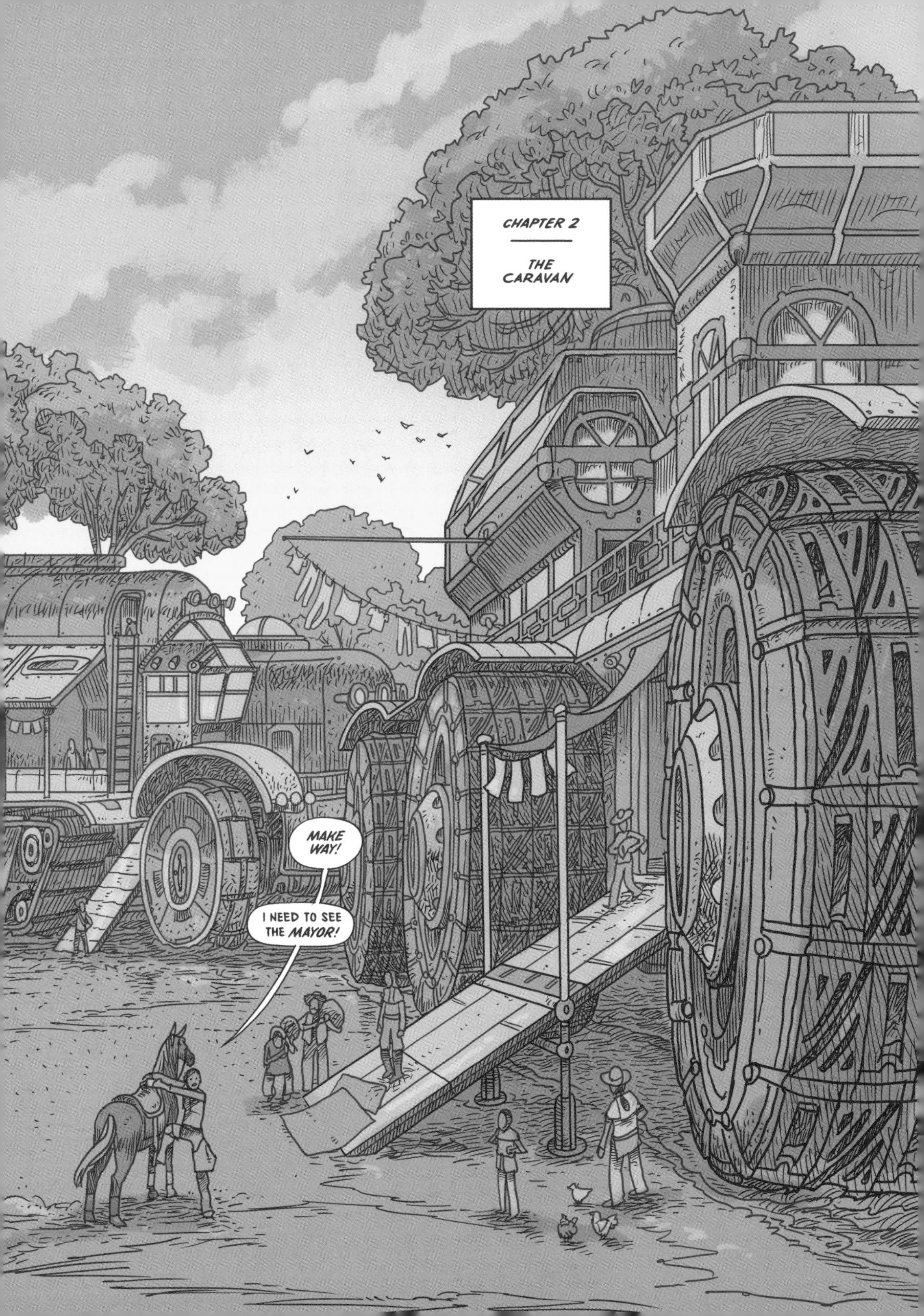
CHAPTER 2
THE CARAVAN
MAKE WAY!
I NEED TO SEE THE MAYOR!

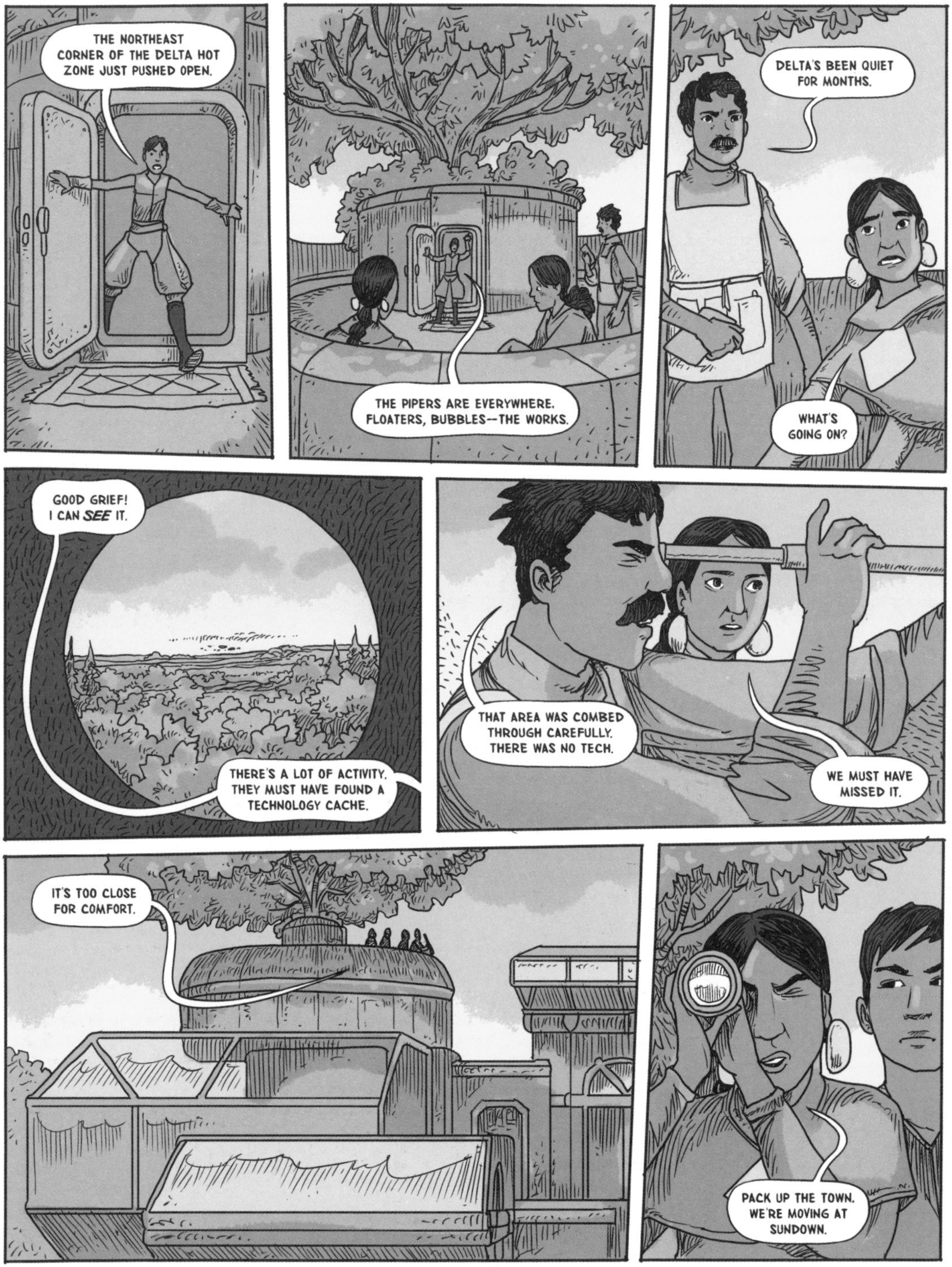

THE NORTHEAST CORNER OF THE DELTA HOT ZONE JUST PUSHED OPEN.
THE PIPERS ARE EVERYWHERE. FLOATERS, BUBBLES--THE WORKS.
DELTA'S BEEN QUIET FOR MONTHS.
WHAT'S GOING ON?
GOOD GRIEF! I CAN *SEE* IT.
THERE'S A LOT OF ACTIVITY. THEY MUST HAVE FOUND A TECHNOLOGY CACHE.
THAT AREA WAS COMBED THROUGH CAREFULLY. THERE WAS NO TECH.
WE MUST HAVE MISSED IT.
IT'S TOO CLOSE FOR COMFORT.
PACK UP THE TOWN. WE'RE MOVING AT SUNDOWN.

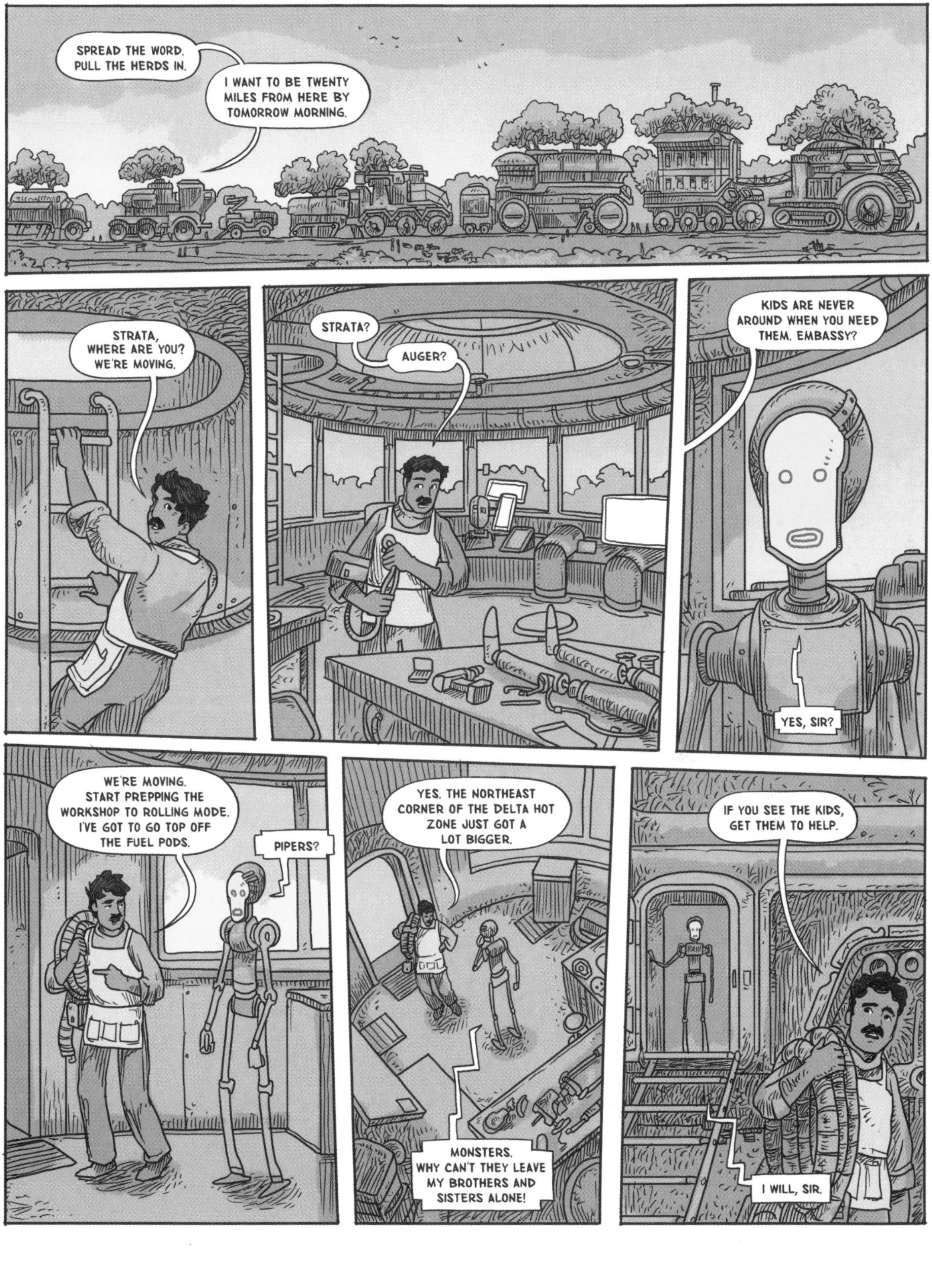
SPREAD THE WORD. PULL THE HERDS IN.
I WANT TO BE TWENTY MILES FROM HERE BY TOMORROW MORNING.
STRATA, WHERE ARE YOU? WE'RE MOVING.
STRATA?
AUGER?
KIDS ARE NEVER AROUND WHEN YOU NEED THEM. EMBASSY?
YES, SIR?
WE'RE MOVING. START PREPPING THE WORKSHOP TO ROLLING MODE. I'VE GOT TO GO TOP OFF THE FUEL PODS.
PIPERS?
YES. THE NORTHEAST CORNER OF THE DELTA HOT ZONE JUST GOT A LOT BIGGER.
MONSTERS. WHY CAN'T THEY LEAVE MY BROTHERS AND SISTERS ALONE!
IF YOU SEE THE KIDS, GET THEM TO HELP.
I WILL, SIR.

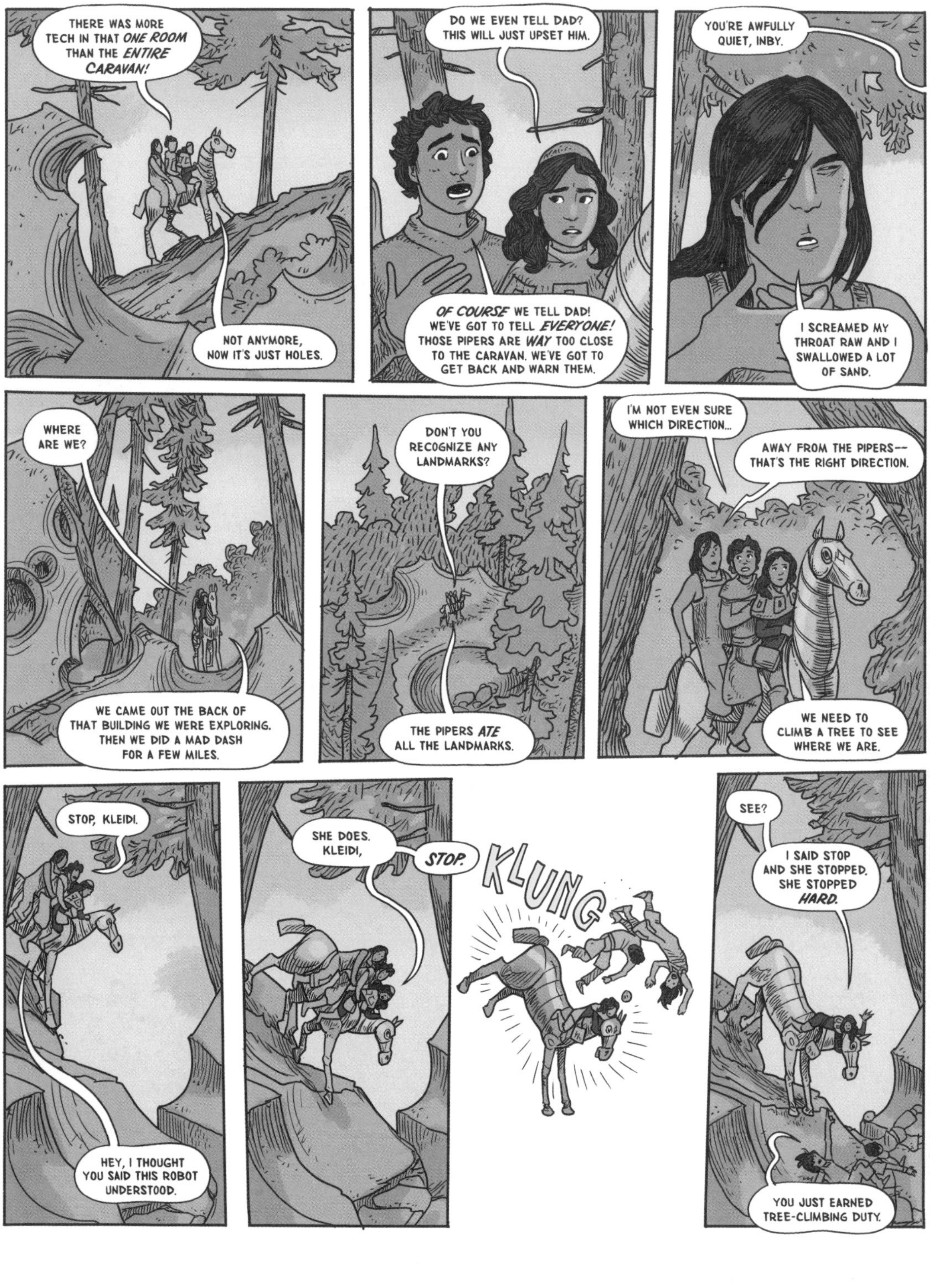
THERE WAS MORE TECH IN THAT ONE ROOM THAN THE ENTIRE CARAVAN!
NOT ANYMORE, NOW IT'S JUST HOLES.
DO WE EVEN TELL DAD? THIS WILL JUST UPSET HIM.
OF COURSE WE TELL DAD! WE'VE GOT TO TELL EVERYONE! THOSE PIPERS ARE WAY TOO CLOSE TO THE CARAVAN. WE'VE GOT TO GET BACK AND WARN THEM.
YOU'RE AWFULLY QUIET, INBY.
I SCREAMED MY THROAT RAW AND I SWALLOWED A LOT OF SAND.
WHERE ARE WE?
WE CAME OUT THE BACK OF THAT BUILDING WE WERE EXPLORING. THEN WE DID A MAD DASH FOR A FEW MILES.
DON'T YOU RECOGNIZE ANY LANDMARKS?
THE PIPERS ATE ALL THE LANDMARKS.
I'M NOT EVEN SURE WHICH DIRECTION...
AWAY FROM THE PIPERS-- THAT'S THE RIGHT DIRECTION.
WE NEED TO CLIMB A TREE TO SEE WHERE WE ARE.
STOP, KLEIDI.
HEY, I THOUGHT YOU SAID THIS ROBOT UNDERSTOOD.
SHE DOES. KLEIDI,
STOP.
KLUNG
SEE?
I SAID STOP AND SHE STOPPED. SHE STOPPED HARD.
YOU JUST EARNED TREE-CLIMBING DUTY.

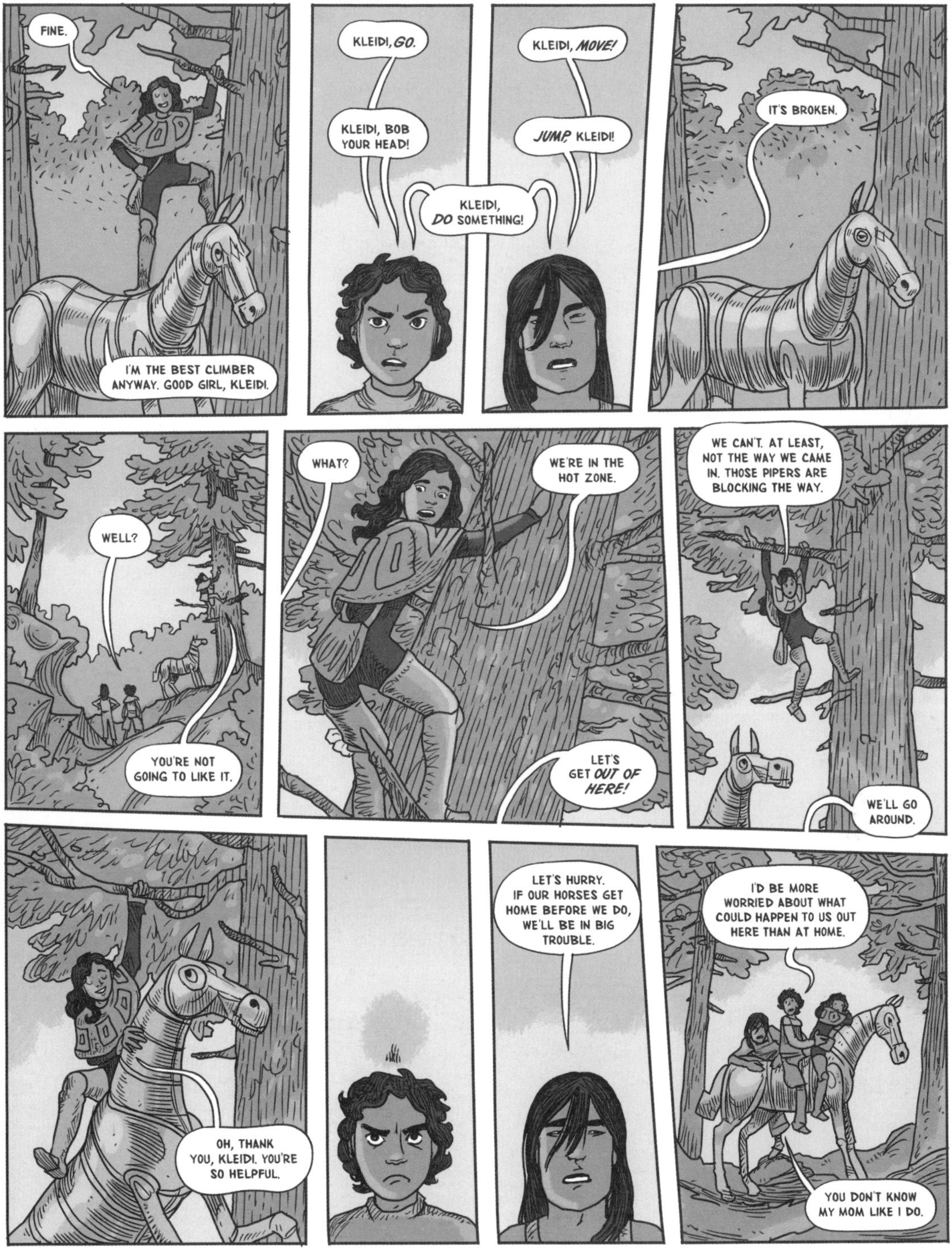
FINE.
I'M THE BEST CLIMBER ANYWAY. GOOD GIRL, KLEIDI.
KLEIDI, GO.
KLEIDI, BOB YOUR HEAD!
KLEIDI, MOVE!
JUMP, KLEIDI!
KLEIDI, DO SOMETHING!
IT'S BROKEN.
WELL?
YOU'RE NOT GOING TO LIKE IT.
WHAT?
WE'RE IN THE HOT ZONE.
LET'S GET OUT OF HERE!
WE CAN'T. AT LEAST, NOT THE WAY WE CAME IN. THOSE PIPERS ARE BLOCKING THE WAY.
WE'LL GO AROUND.
OH, THANK YOU, KLEIDI. YOU'RE SO HELPFUL.
LET'S HURRY. IF OUR HORSES GET HOME BEFORE WE DO, WE'LL BE IN BIG TROUBLE.
I'D BE MORE WORRIED ABOUT WHAT COULD HAPPEN TO US OUT HERE THAN AT HOME.
YOU DON'T KNOW MY MOM LIKE I DO.

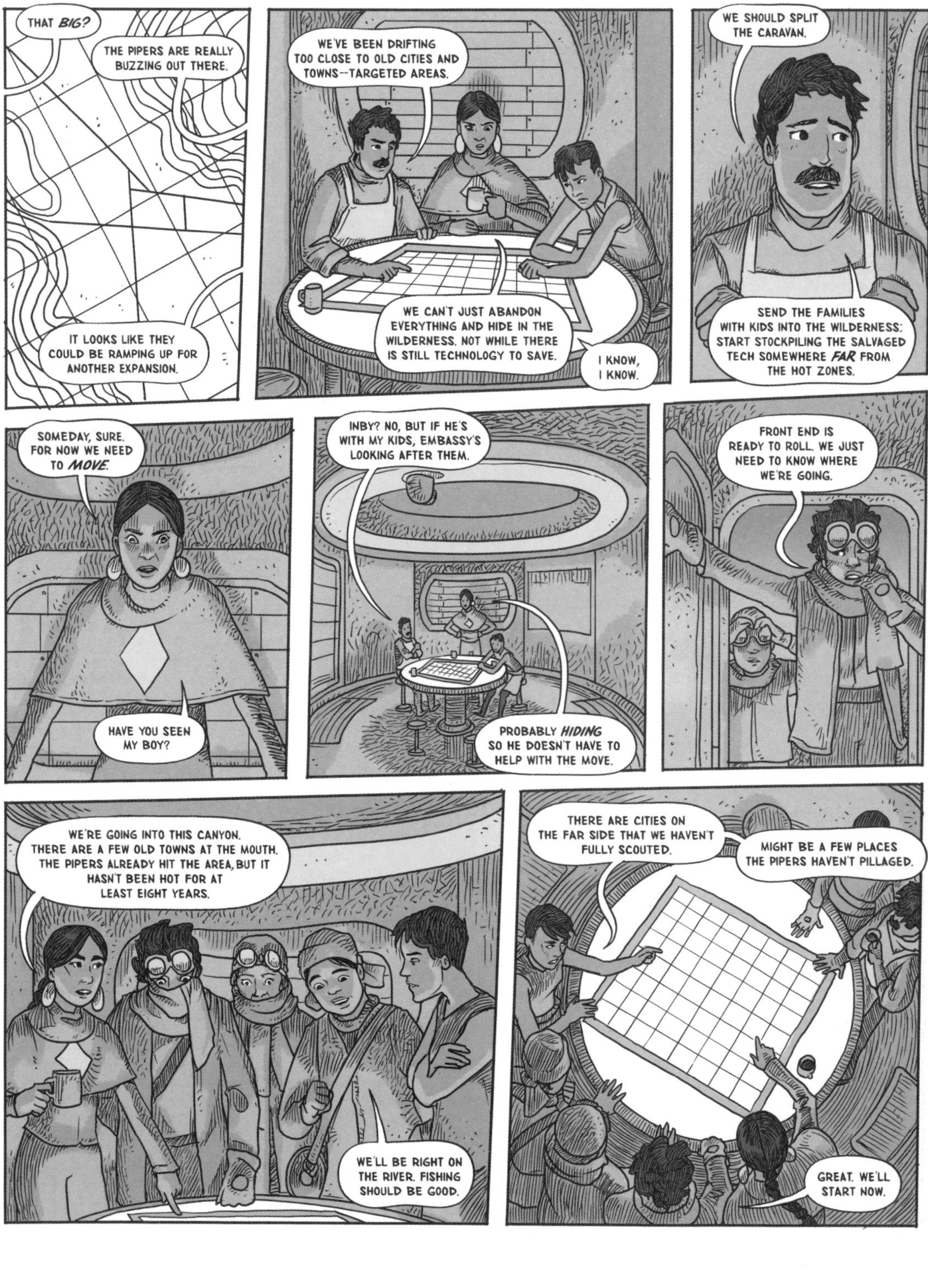
THAT *BIG?*
THE PIPERS ARE REALLY BUZZING OUT THERE.
IT LOOKS LIKE THEY COULD BE RAMPING UP FOR ANOTHER EXPANSION.
WE'VE BEEN DRIFTING TOO CLOSE TO OLD CITIES AND TOWNS--TARGETED AREAS.
WE CAN'T JUST ABANDON EVERYTHING AND HIDE IN THE WILDERNESS. NOT WHILE THERE IS STILL TECHNOLOGY TO SAVE.
I KNOW, I KNOW.
WE SHOULD SPLIT THE CARAVAN.
SEND THE FAMILIES WITH KIDS INTO THE WILDERNESS; START STOCKPILING THE SALVAGED TECH SOMEWHERE *FAR* FROM THE HOT ZONES.
SOMEDAY, SURE. FOR NOW WE NEED TO *MOVE.*
HAVE YOU SEEN MY BOY?
INBY? NO, BUT IF HE'S WITH MY KIDS, EMBASSY'S LOOKING AFTER THEM.
PROBABLY *HIDING* SO HE DOESN'T HAVE TO HELP WITH THE MOVE.
FRONT END IS READY TO ROLL. WE JUST NEED TO KNOW WHERE WE'RE GOING.
WE'RE GOING INTO THIS CANYON. THERE ARE A FEW OLD TOWNS AT THE MOUTH. THE PIPERS ALREADY HIT THE AREA, BUT IT HASN'T BEEN HOT FOR AT LEAST EIGHT YEARS.
WE'LL BE RIGHT ON THE RIVER. FISHING SHOULD BE GOOD.
THERE ARE CITIES ON THE FAR SIDE THAT WE HAVEN'T FULLY SCOUTED.
MIGHT BE A FEW PLACES THE PIPERS HAVEN'T PILLAGED.
GREAT. WE'LL START NOW.

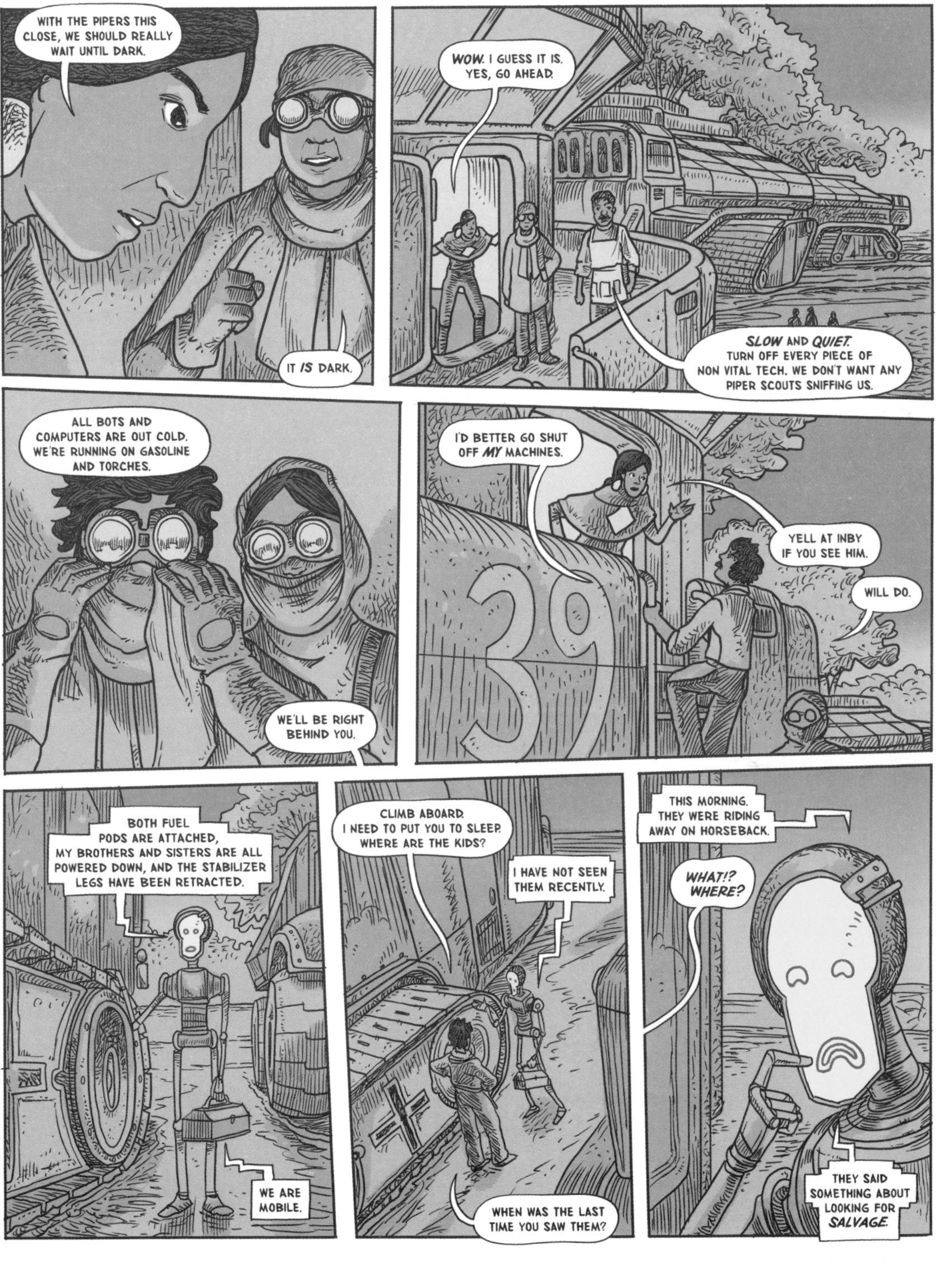
WITH THE PIPERS THIS CLOSE, WE SHOULD REALLY WAIT UNTIL DARK.
IT IS DARK.
WOW. I GUESS IT IS. YES, GO AHEAD.
SLOW AND QUIET. TURN OFF EVERY PIECE OF NON VITAL TECH. WE DON'T WANT ANY PIPER SCOUTS SNIFFING US.
ALL BOTS AND COMPUTERS ARE OUT COLD. WE'RE RUNNING ON GASOLINE AND TORCHES.
WE'LL BE RIGHT BEHIND YOU.
I'D BETTER GO SHUT OFF MY MACHINES.
YELL AT INBY IF YOU SEE HIM.
WILL DO.
39
BOTH FUEL PODS ARE ATTACHED, MY BROTHERS AND SISTERS ARE ALL POWERED DOWN, AND THE STABILIZER LEGS HAVE BEEN RETRACTED.
WE ARE MOBILE.
CLIMB ABOARD. I NEED TO PUT YOU TO SLEEP. WHERE ARE THE KIDS?
I HAVE NOT SEEN THEM RECENTLY.
WHEN WAS THE LAST TIME YOU SAW THEM?
THIS MORNING. THEY WERE RIDING AWAY ON HORSEBACK.
WHAT!? WHERE?
THEY SAID SOMETHING ABOUT LOOKING FOR SALVAGE.

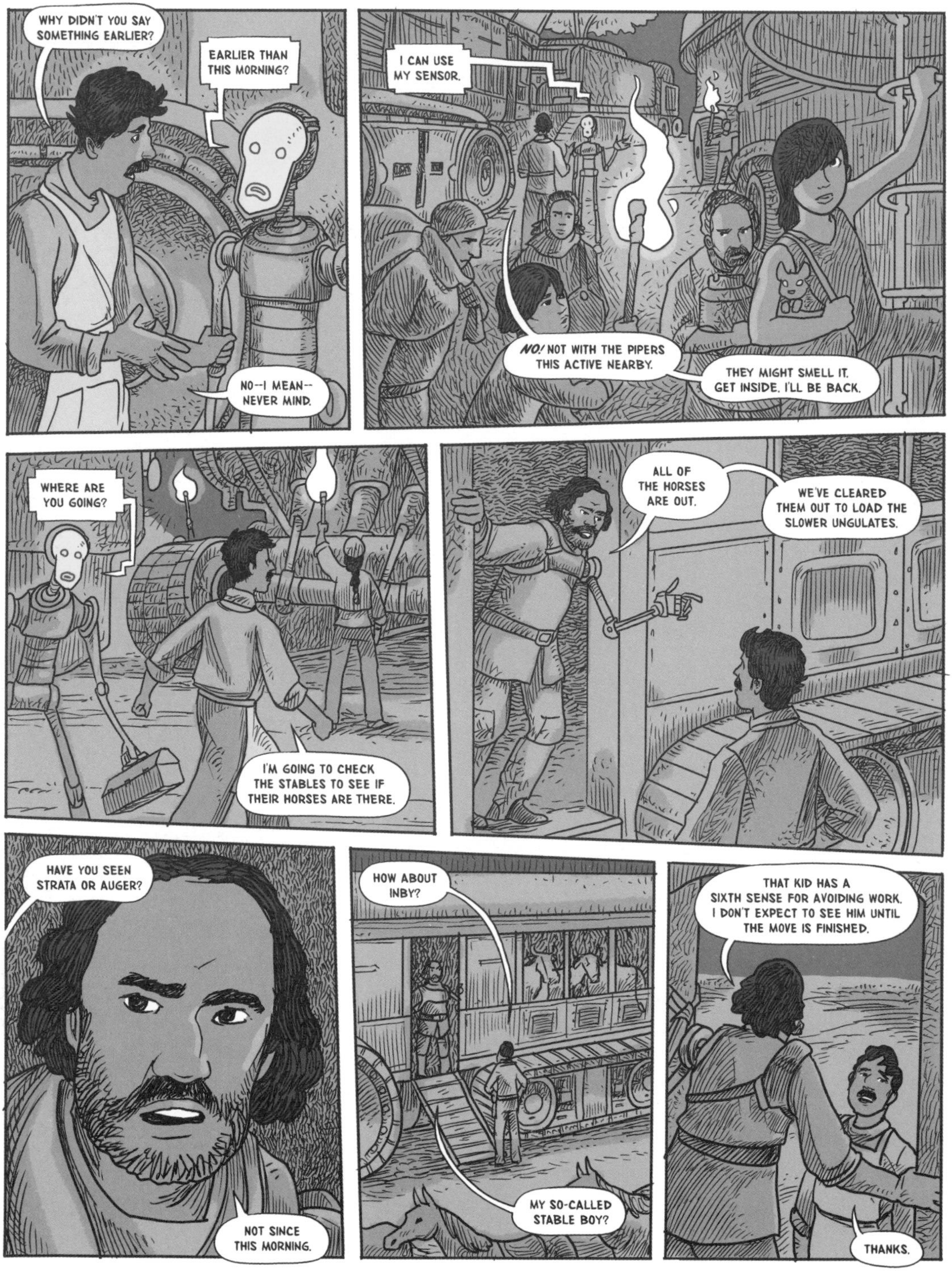
WHY DIDN'T YOU SAY SOMETHING EARLIER?
EARLIER THAN THIS MORNING?
NO--I MEAN-- NEVER MIND.
I CAN USE MY SENSOR.
NO! NOT WITH THE PIPERS THIS ACTIVE NEARBY.
THEY MIGHT SMELL IT. GET INSIDE. I'LL BE BACK.
WHERE ARE YOU GOING?
I'M GOING TO CHECK THE STABLES TO SEE IF THEIR HORSES ARE THERE.
ALL OF THE HORSES ARE OUT.
WE'VE CLEARED THEM OUT TO LOAD THE SLOWER UNGULATES.
HAVE YOU SEEN STRATA OR AUGER?
NOT SINCE THIS MORNING.
HOW ABOUT INBY?
MY SO-CALLED STABLE BOY?
THAT KID HAS A SIXTH SENSE FOR AVOIDING WORK. I DON'T EXPECT TO SEE HIM UNTIL THE MOVE IS FINISHED.
THANKS.

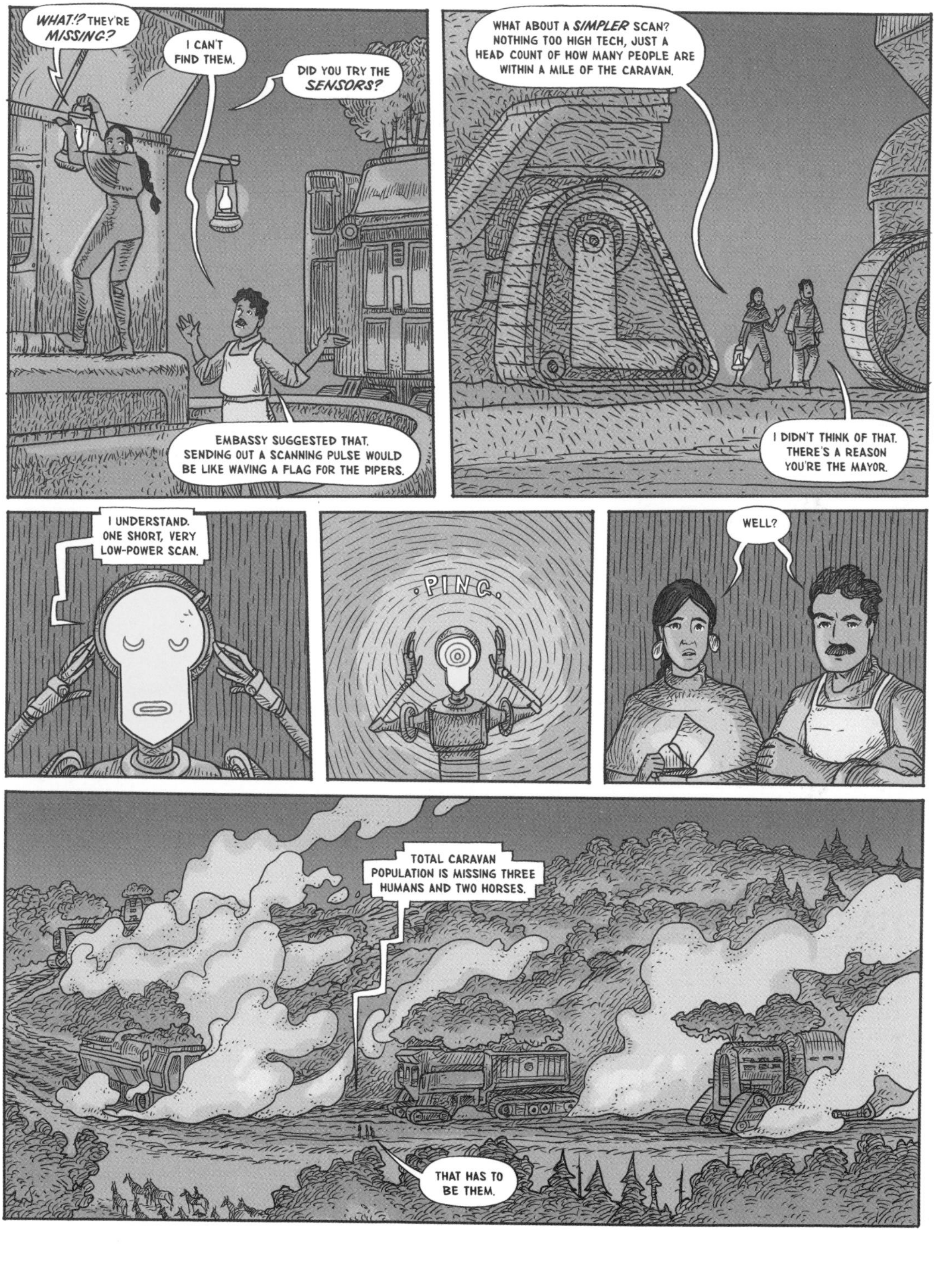

WHAT!? THEY'RE MISSING?
I CAN'T FIND THEM.
DID YOU TRY THE SENSORS?
EMBASSY SUGGESTED THAT. SENDING OUT A SCANNING PULSE WOULD BE LIKE WAVING A FLAG FOR THE PIPERS.
WHAT ABOUT A SIMPLER SCAN? NOTHING TOO HIGH TECH, JUST A HEAD COUNT OF HOW MANY PEOPLE ARE WITHIN A MILE OF THE CARAVAN.
I DIDN'T THINK OF THAT. THERE'S A REASON YOU'RE THE MAYOR.
I UNDERSTAND. ONE SHORT, VERY LOW-POWER SCAN.
PING.
WELL?
TOTAL CARAVAN POPULATION IS MISSING THREE HUMANS AND TWO HORSES.
THAT HAS TO BE THEM.

I JUST HAD A *HORRIBLE* THOUGHT.

WHAT'S THAT?

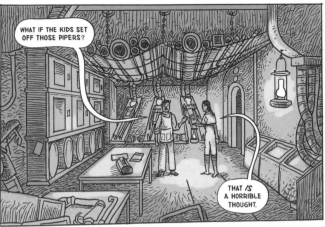

WHAT IF THE KIDS SET OFF THOSE PIPERS?

THAT *IS* A HORRIBLE THOUGHT.

TAKE A SEARCH PARTY. GO GET THEM.

I'M ON MY WAY.

YOUR KIDS ARE *SMART,* RIGHT?

I HOPE SO.

GOOD, BECAUSE I KNOW FOR A FACT MINE *ISN'T.*

THEY ALL KNOW PIPER PROTOCOL. IF THEY AVOID HOT ZONES AND STAY CLEAR OF TECHNOLOGY, THEY'LL BE FINE.

KNOWING INBY, THEY'RE PROBABLY PARADING AROUND THE HOT ZONE WITH A ROBOT.

32

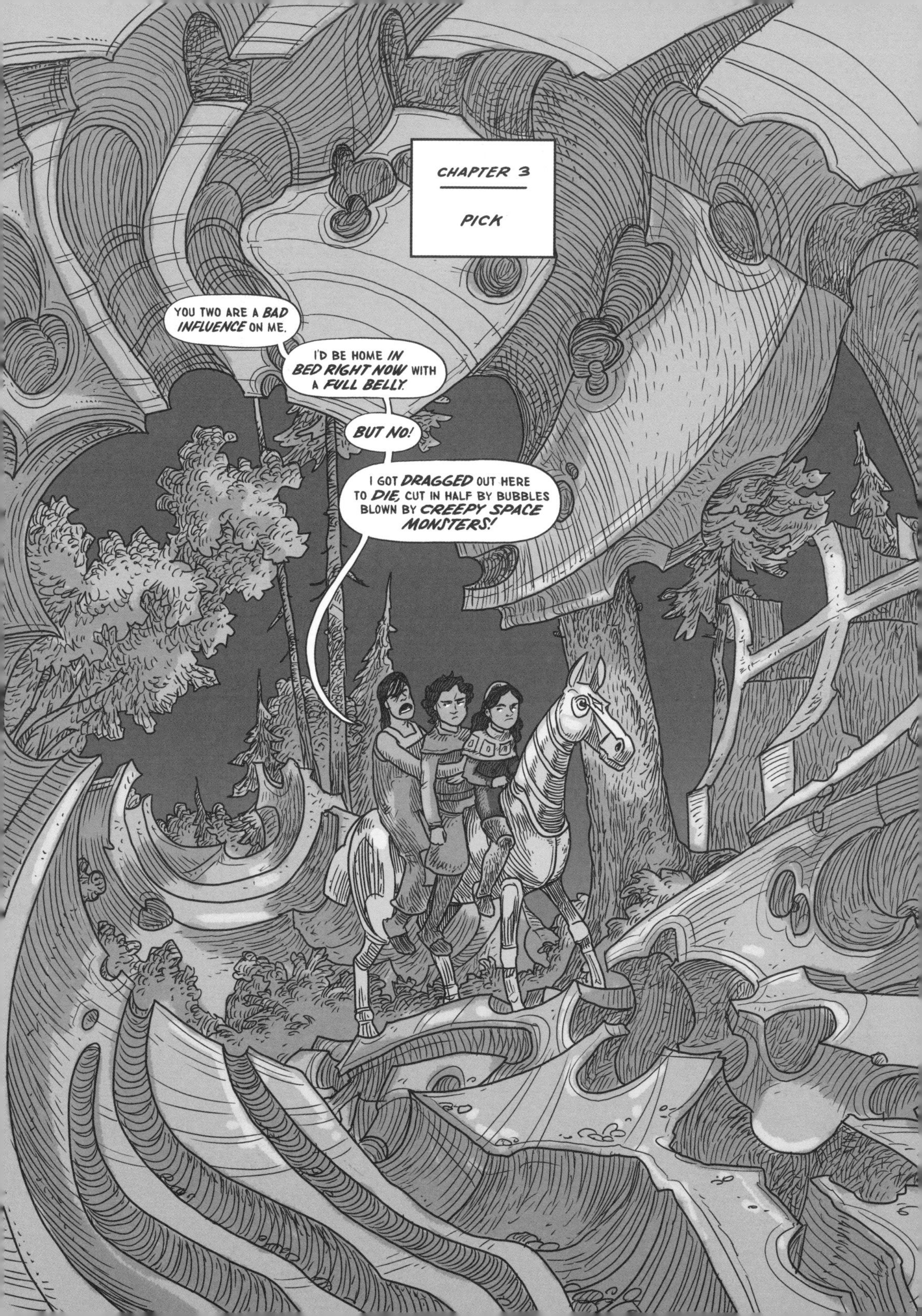
CHAPTER 3
PICK
YOU TWO ARE A BAD INFLUENCE ON ME.
I'D BE HOME IN BED RIGHT NOW WITH A FULL BELLY.
BUT NO!
I GOT DRAGGED OUT HERE TO DIE, CUT IN HALF BY BUBBLES BLOWN BY CREEPY SPACE MONSTERS!

DO THE BUBBLES REALLY *CUT* PEOPLE?

YEAH. HAVEN'T YOU SEEN THE STABLE MASTER'S MISSING ARM?

IT WAS ZAPPED *CLEAN OFF* WHEN HE GOT BETWEEN A PIPER AND SOME OLD COMPUTERS.

THE BUBBLE TURNED HIS ARM INTO SAND!

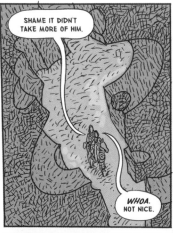

SHAME IT DIDN'T TAKE MORE OF HIM.

WHOA. NOT NICE.

YOU DON'T HAVE TO WORK FOR HIM.

THERE ARE *LIGHTS* UP AHEAD. KLEIDI, STOP.

KLUNG

MAYBE NEXT TIME YOU COULD SAY, KLEIDI, *STOP SLOWLY.*

OW!

I CAN'T HELP IT IF SHE OBEYS ME PERFECTLY.

I SEE THE LIGHTS. *SOMETHING'S COMING* TOWARD US!

HIDE! WE NEED TO HIDE!

NO! WE SHOULD RUN!

RUN! GO BACK THE OTHER WAY!

WE CAN'T KEEP TURNING AROUND, WE'LL *NEVER* GET HOME.

WE NEED TO HIDE.

TAKE US UP THERE, KLEIDI.

DO PIPERS EVEN USE LIGHTS?

I DON'T KNOW. HAVE YOU EVER SEEN ONE AT NIGHT?

NO, AND I DON'T WANT TO!

THEY'RE SCARY ENOUGH DURING THE DAYTIME!

THOSE ARE TORCHES. I THINK IT'S *PEOPLE!*

FROM THE CARAVAN? *WE'RE SAVED! HEY!*

SSSH!

I'M FINE WITH PEOPLE—*ANY PEOPLE!*

SSSH!

I DON'T RECOGNIZE THEM.

FERALS!?

OH, WAIT. I *DON'T* LIKE FERALS.

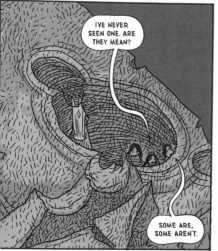

I'VE NEVER SEEN ONE. ARE THEY MEAN?

SOME ARE, SOME AREN'T.

HOW CAN YOU TELL WHICH ONES ARE WHICH?

WHO SAID THAT?

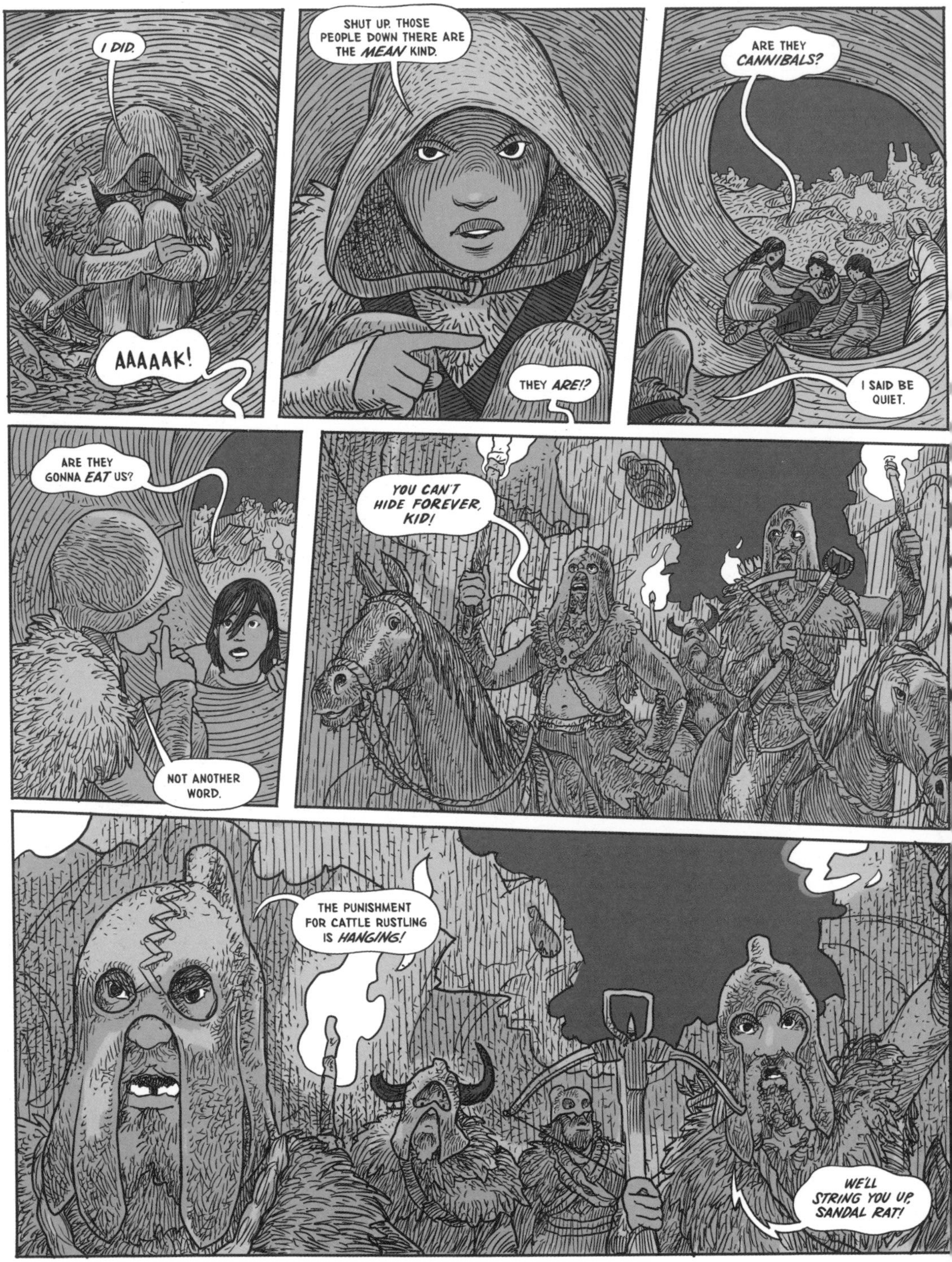
I DID.
AAAAAK!
SHUT UP. THOSE PEOPLE DOWN THERE ARE THE MEAN KIND.
THEY ARE!?
ARE THEY CANNIBALS?
I SAID BE QUIET.
ARE THEY GONNA EAT US?
NOT ANOTHER WORD.
YOU CAN'T HIDE FOREVER, KID!
THE PUNISHMENT FOR CATTLE RUSTLING IS HANGING!
WE'LL STRING YOU UP, SANDAL RAT!

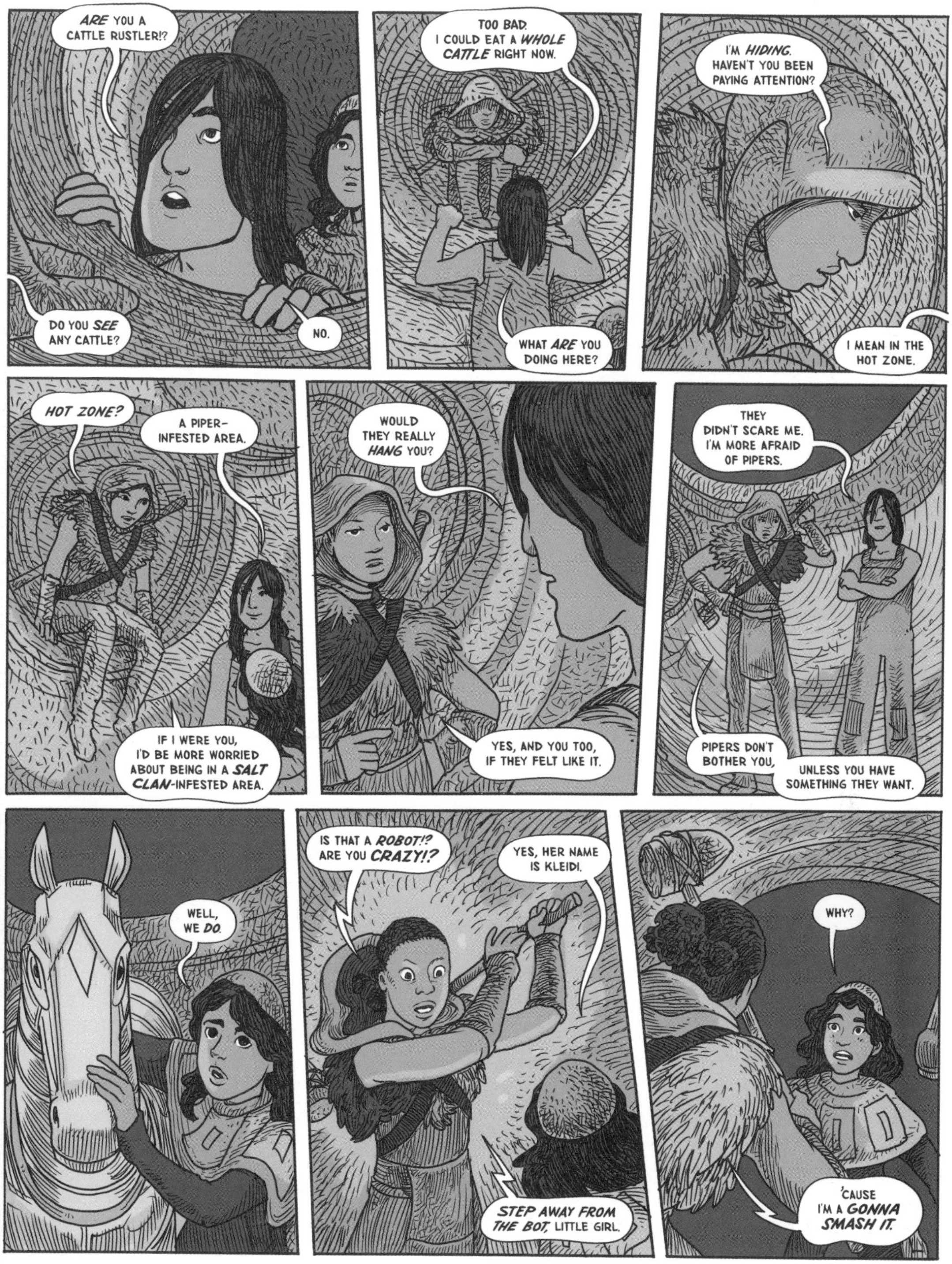
ARE YOU A CATTLE RUSTLER!?
DO YOU SEE ANY CATTLE?
NO.
TOO BAD. I COULD EAT A WHOLE CATTLE RIGHT NOW.
WHAT ARE YOU DOING HERE?
I'M HIDING. HAVEN'T YOU BEEN PAYING ATTENTION?
I MEAN IN THE HOT ZONE.
HOT ZONE?
A PIPER-INFESTED AREA.
IF I WERE YOU, I'D BE MORE WORRIED ABOUT BEING IN A SALT CLAN-INFESTED AREA.
WOULD THEY REALLY HANG YOU?
YES, AND YOU TOO, IF THEY FELT LIKE IT.
THEY DIDN'T SCARE ME. I'M MORE AFRAID OF PIPERS.
PIPERS DON'T BOTHER YOU,
UNLESS YOU HAVE SOMETHING THEY WANT.
WELL, WE DO.
IS THAT A ROBOT!? ARE YOU CRAZY!?
YES, HER NAME IS KLEIDI.
STEP AWAY FROM THE BOT, LITTLE GIRL.
WHY?
'CAUSE I'M A GONNA SMASH IT.

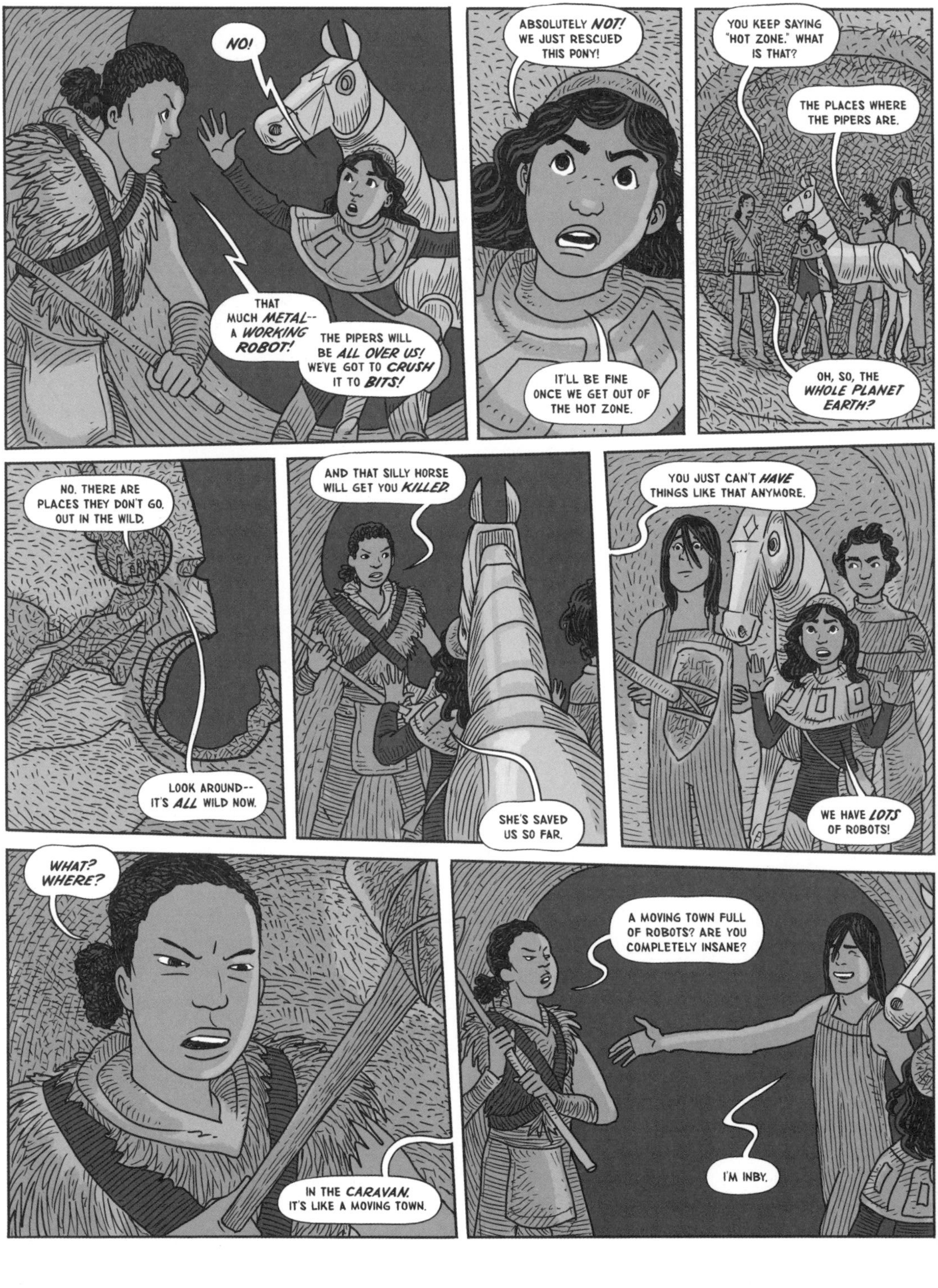
NO!
THAT MUCH METAL-- A WORKING ROBOT!
THE PIPERS WILL BE ALL OVER US! WE'VE GOT TO CRUSH IT TO BITS!
ABSOLUTELY NOT! WE JUST RESCUED THIS PONY!
IT'LL BE FINE ONCE WE GET OUT OF THE HOT ZONE.
YOU KEEP SAYING "HOT ZONE." WHAT IS THAT?
THE PLACES WHERE THE PIPERS ARE.
OH, SO, THE WHOLE PLANET EARTH?
NO. THERE ARE PLACES THEY DON'T GO. OUT IN THE WILD.
LOOK AROUND-- IT'S ALL WILD NOW.
AND THAT SILLY HORSE WILL GET YOU KILLED.
SHE'S SAVED US SO FAR.
YOU JUST CAN'T HAVE THINGS LIKE THAT ANYMORE.
WE HAVE LOTS OF ROBOTS!
WHAT? WHERE?
IN THE CARAVAN. IT'S LIKE A MOVING TOWN.
A MOVING TOWN FULL OF ROBOTS? ARE YOU COMPLETELY INSANE?
I'M INBY.

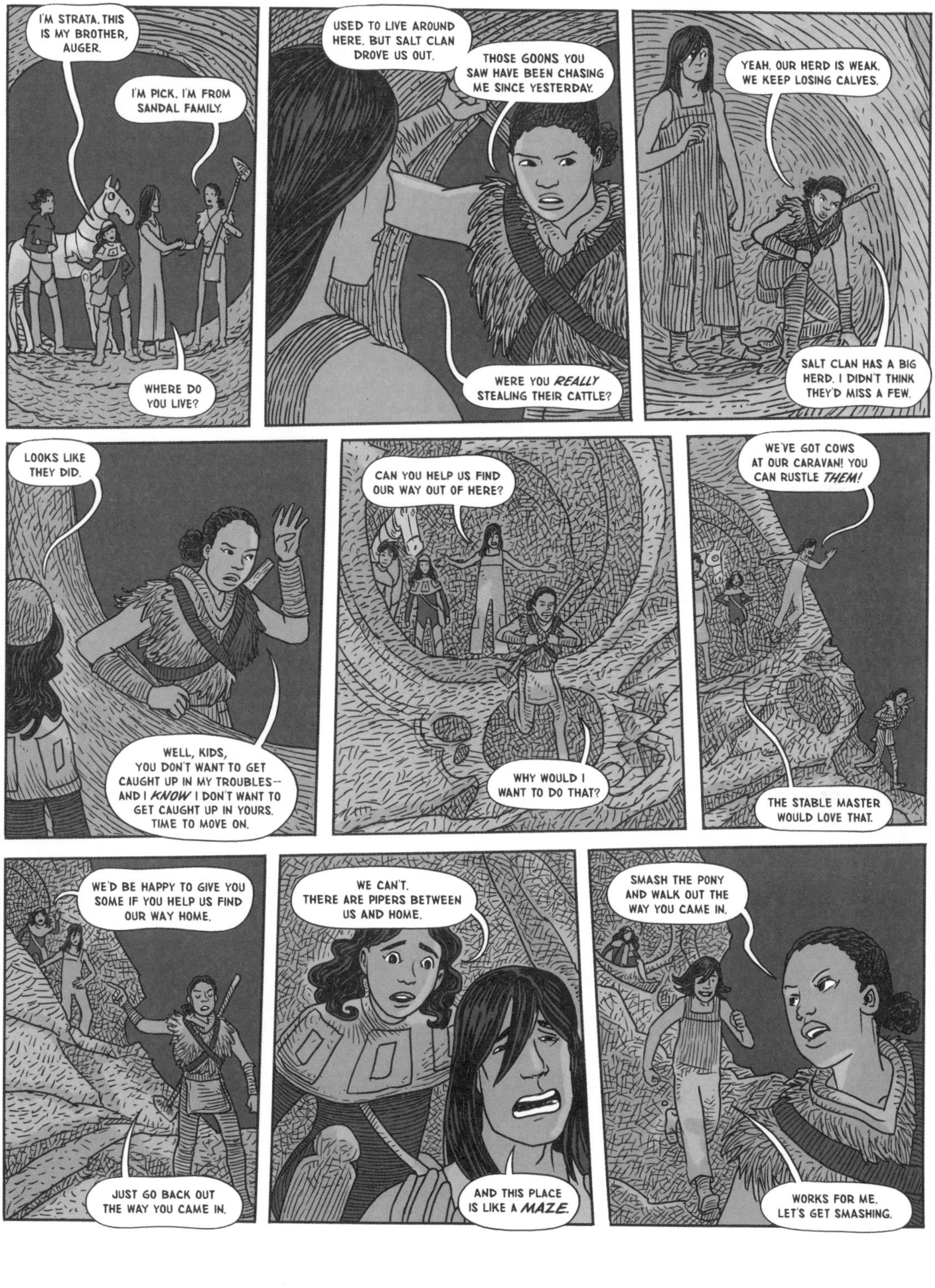
I'M STRATA. THIS IS MY BROTHER, AUGER.
I'M PICK. I'M FROM SANDAL FAMILY.
WHERE DO YOU LIVE?
USED TO LIVE AROUND HERE. BUT SALT CLAN DROVE US OUT.
THOSE GOONS YOU SAW HAVE BEEN CHASING ME SINCE YESTERDAY.
WERE YOU *REALLY* STEALING THEIR CATTLE?
YEAH. OUR HERD IS WEAK. WE KEEP LOSING CALVES.
SALT CLAN HAS A BIG HERD. I DIDN'T THINK THEY'D MISS A FEW.
LOOKS LIKE THEY DID.
WELL, KIDS, YOU DON'T WANT TO GET CAUGHT UP IN MY TROUBLES-- AND I *KNOW* I DON'T WANT TO GET CAUGHT UP IN YOURS. TIME TO MOVE ON.
CAN YOU HELP US FIND OUR WAY OUT OF HERE?
WHY WOULD I WANT TO DO THAT?
WE'VE GOT COWS AT OUR CARAVAN! YOU CAN RUSTLE *THEM!*
THE STABLE MASTER WOULD LOVE THAT.
WE'D BE HAPPY TO GIVE YOU SOME IF YOU HELP US FIND OUR WAY HOME.
JUST GO BACK OUT THE WAY YOU CAME IN.
WE CAN'T. THERE ARE PIPERS BETWEEN US AND HOME.
AND THIS PLACE IS LIKE A *MAZE.*
SMASH THE PONY AND WALK OUT THE WAY YOU CAME IN.
WORKS FOR ME. LET'S GET SMASHING.

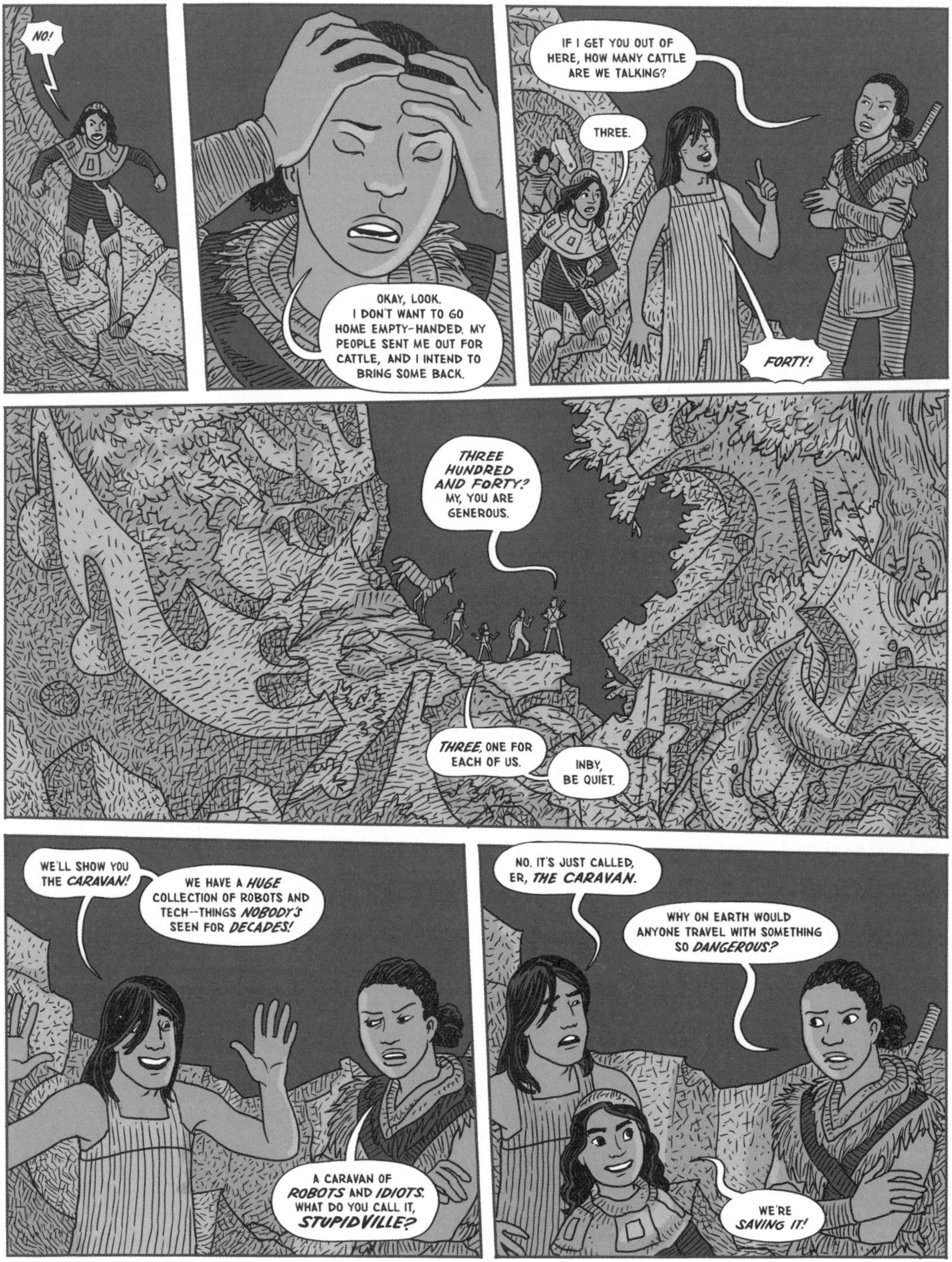
NO!
OKAY, LOOK. I DON'T WANT TO GO HOME EMPTY-HANDED. MY PEOPLE SENT ME OUT FOR CATTLE, AND I INTEND TO BRING SOME BACK.
IF I GET YOU OUT OF HERE, HOW MANY CATTLE ARE WE TALKING?
THREE.
FORTY!
THREE HUNDRED AND FORTY? MY, YOU ARE GENEROUS.
THREE, ONE FOR EACH OF US.
INBY, BE QUIET.
WE'LL SHOW YOU THE CARAVAN!
WE HAVE A HUGE COLLECTION OF ROBOTS AND TECH--THINGS NOBODY'S SEEN FOR DECADES!
A CARAVAN OF ROBOTS AND IDIOTS. WHAT DO YOU CALL IT, STUPIDVILLE?
NO. IT'S JUST CALLED, ER, THE CARAVAN.
WHY ON EARTH WOULD ANYONE TRAVEL WITH SOMETHING SO DANGEROUS?
WE'RE SAVING IT!

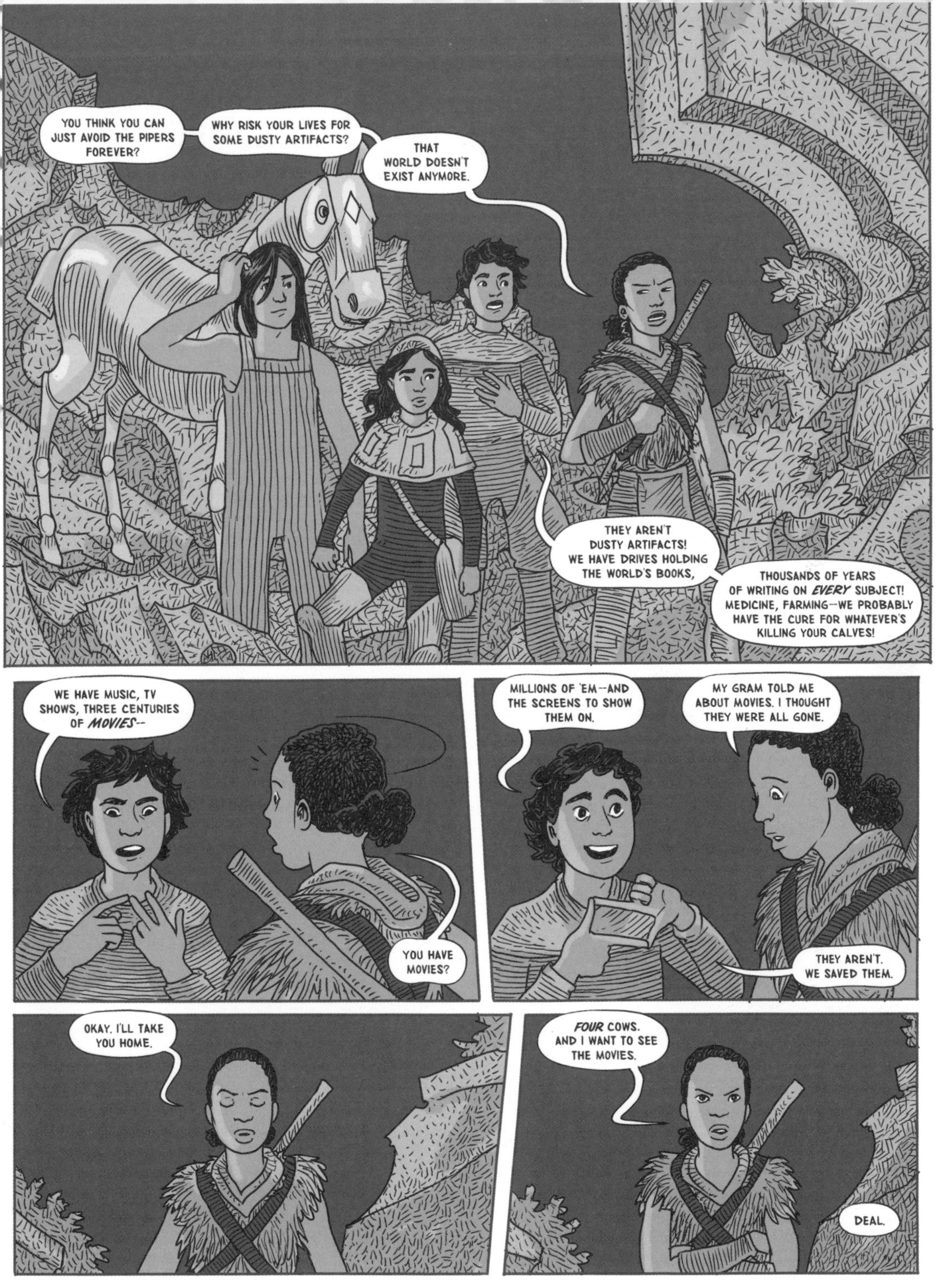
YOU THINK YOU CAN JUST AVOID THE PIPERS FOREVER?
WHY RISK YOUR LIVES FOR SOME DUSTY ARTIFACTS?
THAT WORLD DOESN'T EXIST ANYMORE.
THEY AREN'T DUSTY ARTIFACTS! WE HAVE DRIVES HOLDING THE WORLD'S BOOKS,
THOUSANDS OF YEARS OF WRITING ON *EVERY* SUBJECT! MEDICINE, FARMING--WE PROBABLY HAVE THE CURE FOR WHATEVER'S KILLING YOUR CALVES!
WE HAVE MUSIC, TV SHOWS, THREE CENTURIES OF *MOVIES*--
YOU HAVE MOVIES?
MILLIONS OF 'EM--AND THE SCREENS TO SHOW THEM ON.
MY GRAM TOLD ME ABOUT MOVIES. I THOUGHT THEY WERE ALL GONE.
THEY AREN'T. WE SAVED THEM.
OKAY. I'LL TAKE YOU HOME.
FOUR COWS. AND I WANT TO SEE THE MOVIES.
DEAL.

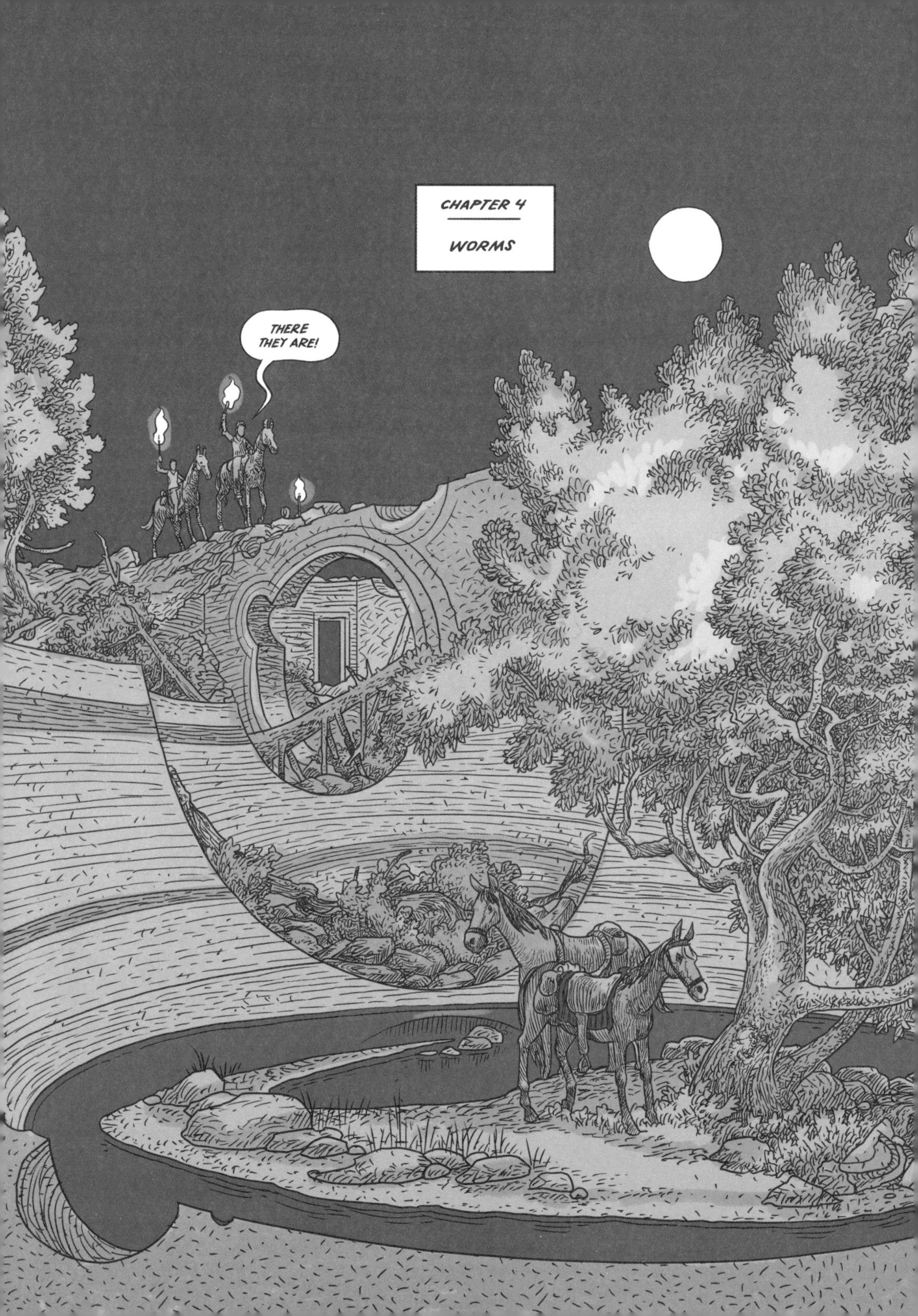
CHAPTER 4
WORMS
THERE THEY ARE!

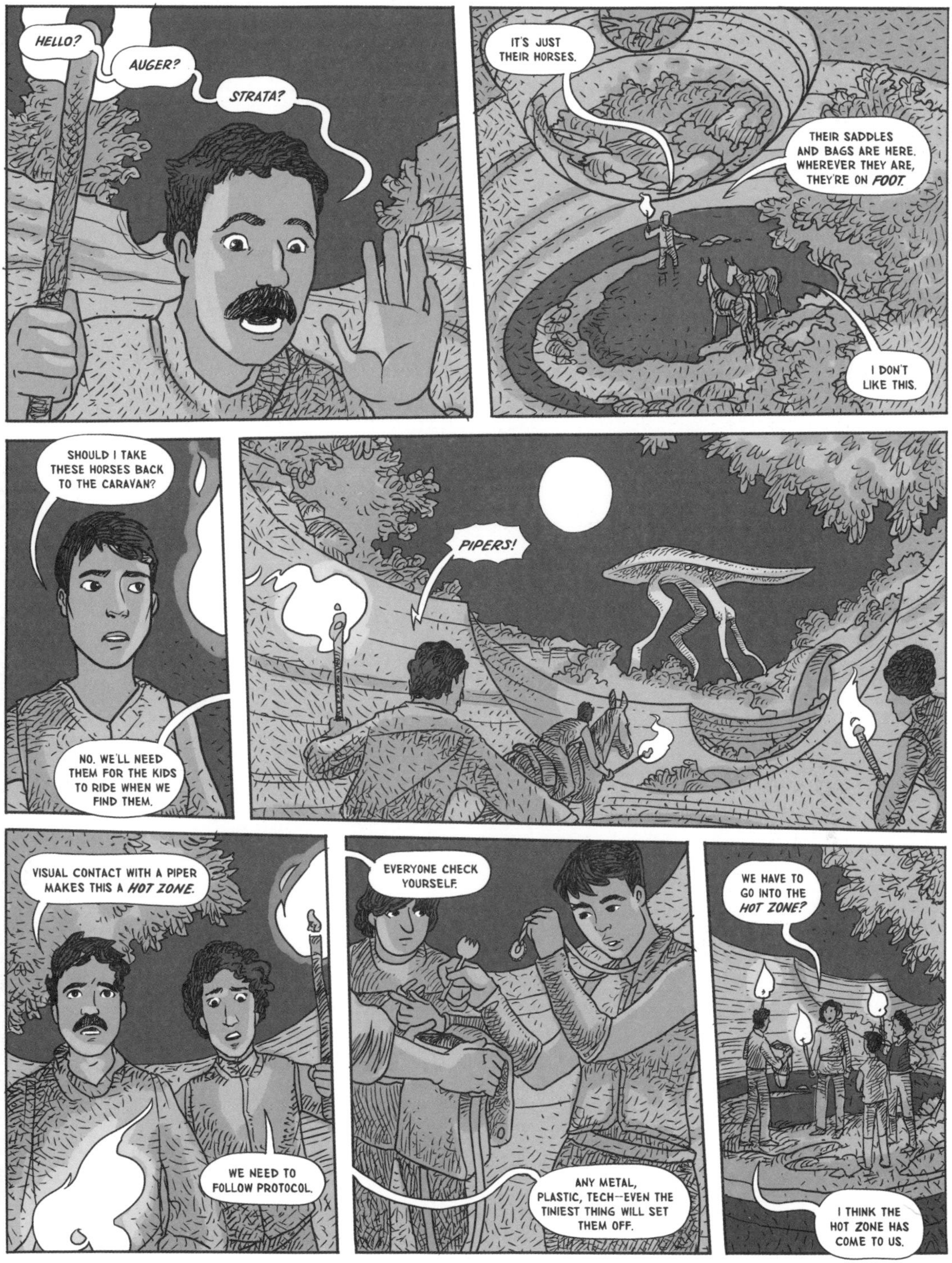
HELLO?
AUGER?
STRATA?
IT'S JUST THEIR HORSES.
THEIR SADDLES AND BAGS ARE HERE. WHEREVER THEY ARE, THEY'RE ON *FOOT*.
I DON'T LIKE THIS.
SHOULD I TAKE THESE HORSES BACK TO THE CARAVAN?
NO. WE'LL NEED THEM FOR THE KIDS TO RIDE WHEN WE FIND THEM.
PIPERS!
VISUAL CONTACT WITH A PIPER MAKES THIS A *HOT ZONE*.
WE NEED TO FOLLOW PROTOCOL.
EVERYONE CHECK YOURSELF.
ANY METAL, PLASTIC, TECH--EVEN THE TINIEST THING WILL SET THEM OFF.
WE HAVE TO GO INTO THE *HOT ZONE?*
I THINK THE HOT ZONE HAS COME TO US.

I'LL HANG IT ON THIS BRANCH.

THIS TREE SHOULD BE EASY TO SPOT ON OUR RETURN.

I'LL TIE THIS BANDANA ON SO WE DON'T MISS IT.

OKAY, LET'S GO.

PIPIPIPIPIPIPiPi

PiPiPi

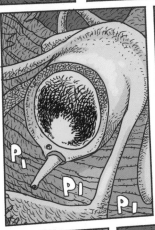

Pi

Pi

Pi

BWAB

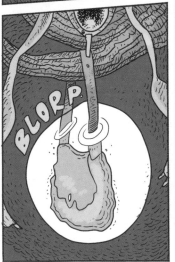

BLORP.

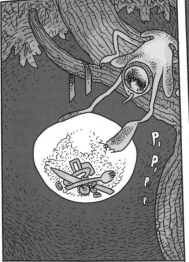

PiPiPiPi

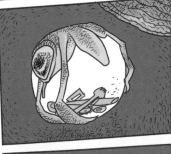

PiPiPiPiPi

44

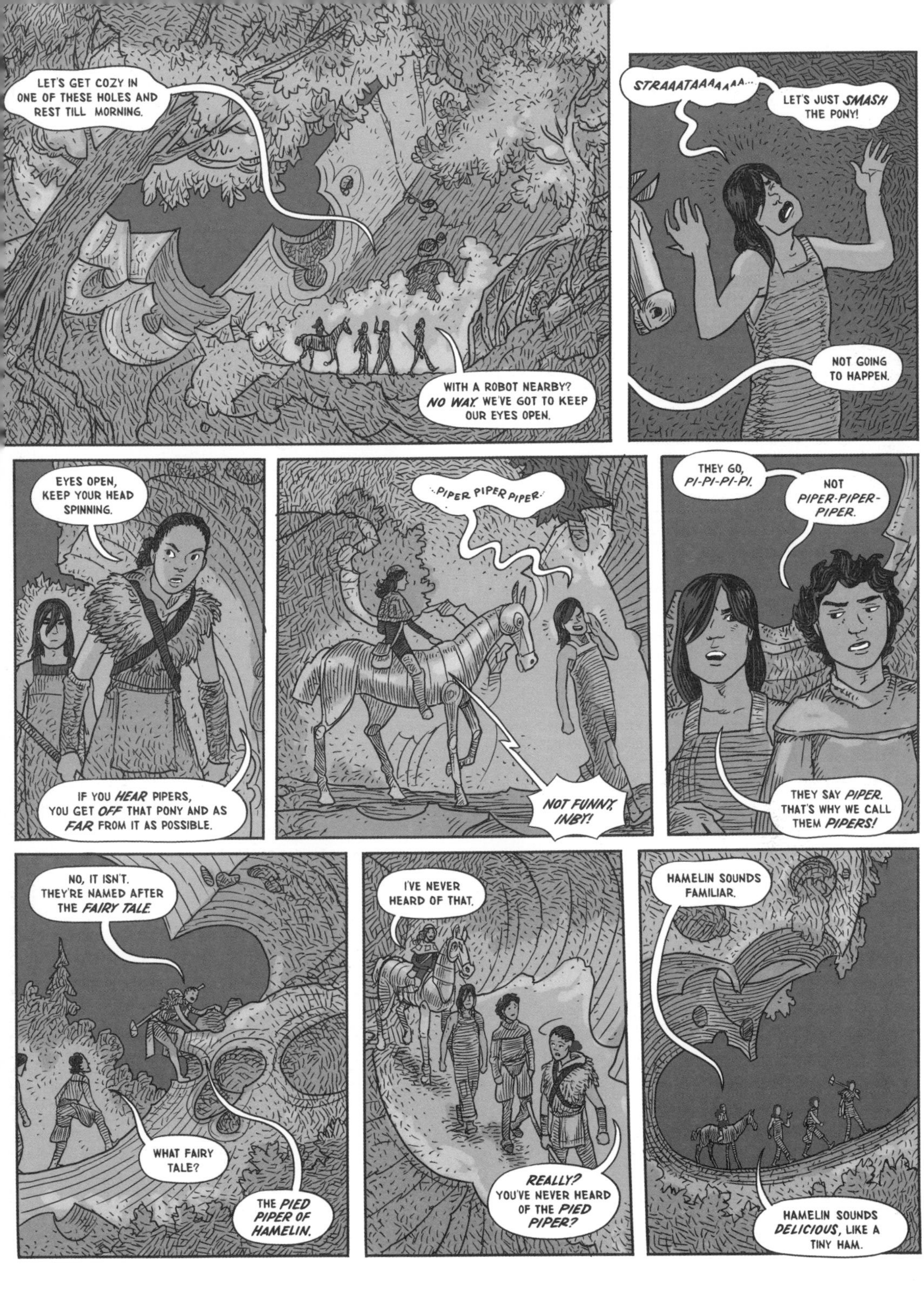
LET'S GET COZY IN ONE OF THESE HOLES AND REST TILL MORNING.
WITH A ROBOT NEARBY? NO WAY. WE'VE GOT TO KEEP OUR EYES OPEN.
STRAAATAAAAAAA...
LET'S JUST SMASH THE PONY!
NOT GOING TO HAPPEN.
EYES OPEN, KEEP YOUR HEAD SPINNING.
IF YOU HEAR PIPERS, YOU GET OFF THAT PONY AND AS FAR FROM IT AS POSSIBLE.
PIPER PIPER PIPER
NOT FUNNY, INBY!
THEY GO, PI-PI-PI-PI.
NOT PIPER-PIPER-PIPER.
THEY SAY PIPER. THAT'S WHY WE CALL THEM PIPERS!
NO, IT ISN'T. THEY'RE NAMED AFTER THE FAIRY TALE.
WHAT FAIRY TALE?
THE PIED PIPER OF HAMELIN.
I'VE NEVER HEARD OF THAT.
REALLY? YOU'VE NEVER HEARD OF THE PIED PIPER?
HAMELIN SOUNDS FAMILIAR.
HAMELIN SOUNDS DELICIOUS, LIKE A TINY HAM.

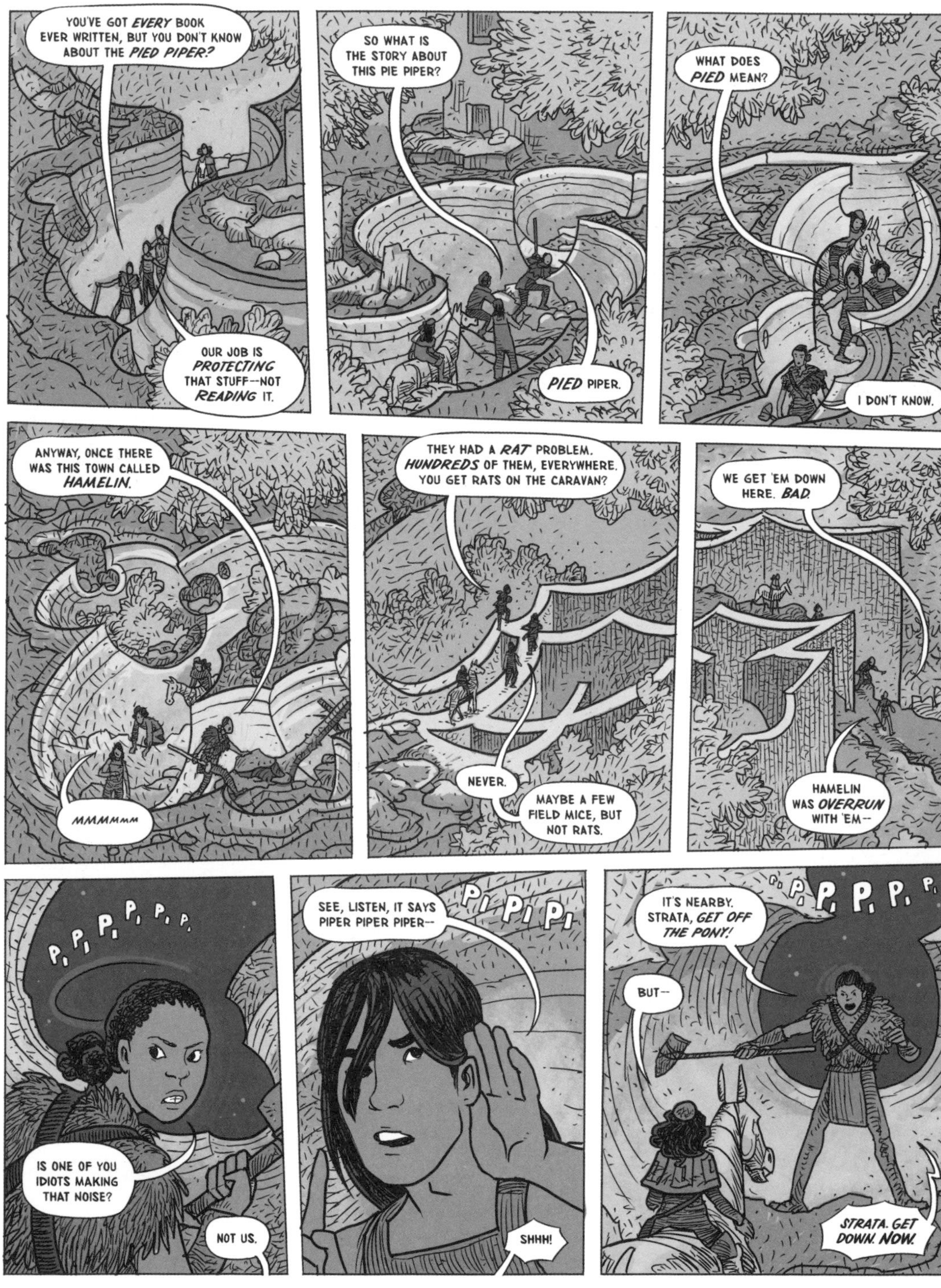
YOU'VE GOT EVERY BOOK EVER WRITTEN, BUT YOU DON'T KNOW ABOUT THE PIED PIPER?
OUR JOB IS PROTECTING THAT STUFF--NOT READING IT.
SO WHAT IS THE STORY ABOUT THIS PIE PIPER?
PIED PIPER.
WHAT DOES PIED MEAN?
I DON'T KNOW.
ANYWAY, ONCE THERE WAS THIS TOWN CALLED HAMELIN.
MMMMMM
THEY HAD A RAT PROBLEM. HUNDREDS OF THEM, EVERYWHERE. YOU GET RATS ON THE CARAVAN?
NEVER.
MAYBE A FEW FIELD MICE, BUT NOT RATS.
WE GET 'EM DOWN HERE. BAD.
HAMELIN WAS OVERRUN WITH 'EM--
P P P P P P
IS ONE OF YOU IDIOTS MAKING THAT NOISE?
NOT US.
SEE, LISTEN, IT SAYS PIPER PIPER PIPER--
PI PI PI
SHHH!
P P P P P P
IT'S NEARBY. STRATA, GET OFF THE PONY!
BUT--
STRATA. GET DOWN. NOW.

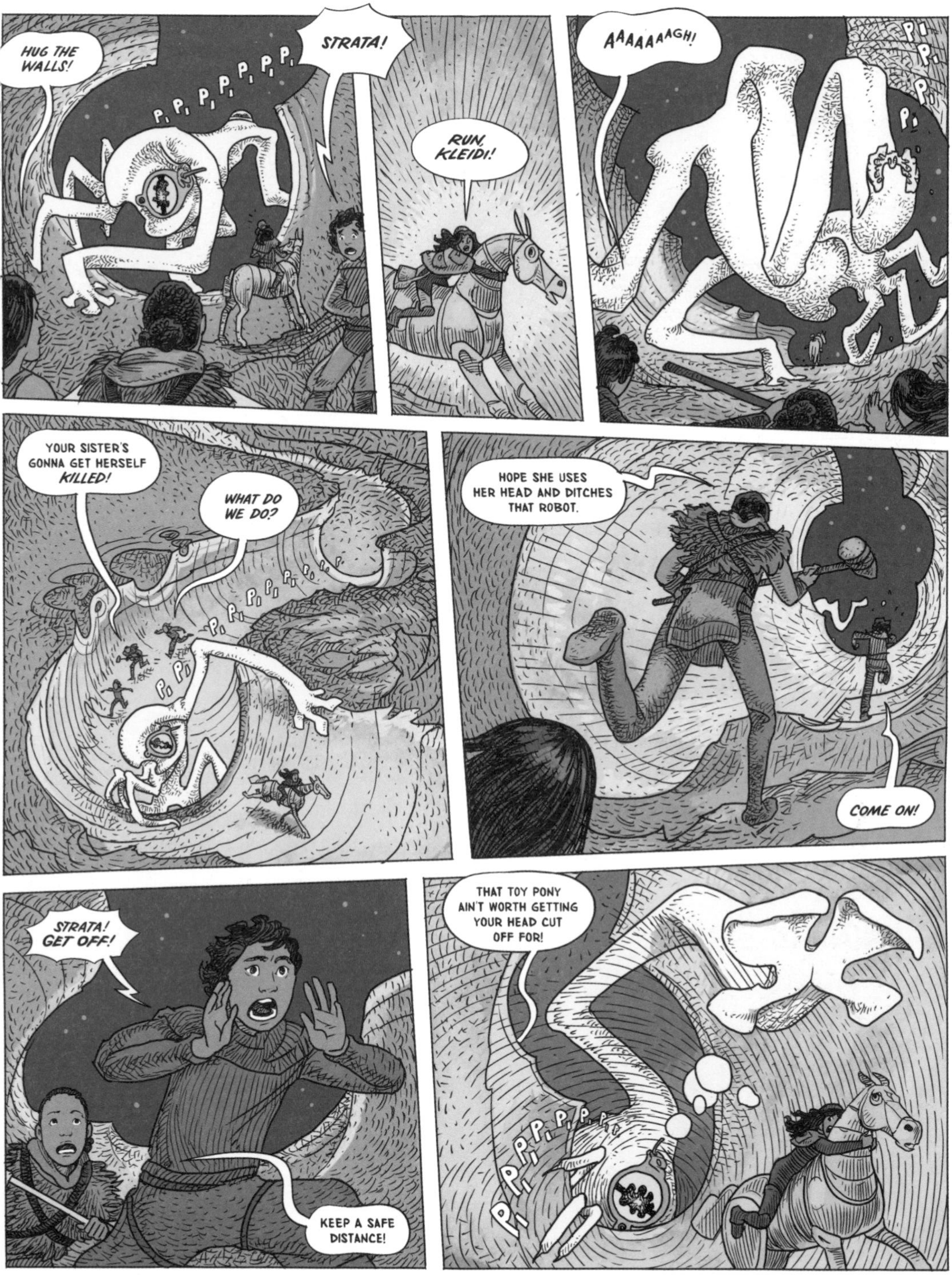

HUG THE WALLS!
P P P P P P P P
STRATA!
RUN, KLEIDI!
AAAAAAAGH!
P P P P
YOUR SISTER'S GONNA GET HERSELF KILLED!
WHAT DO WE DO?
HOPE SHE USES HER HEAD AND DITCHES THAT ROBOT.
COME ON!
STRATA! GET OFF!
KEEP A SAFE DISTANCE!
THAT TOY PONY AIN'T WORTH GETTING YOUR HEAD CUT OFF FOR!

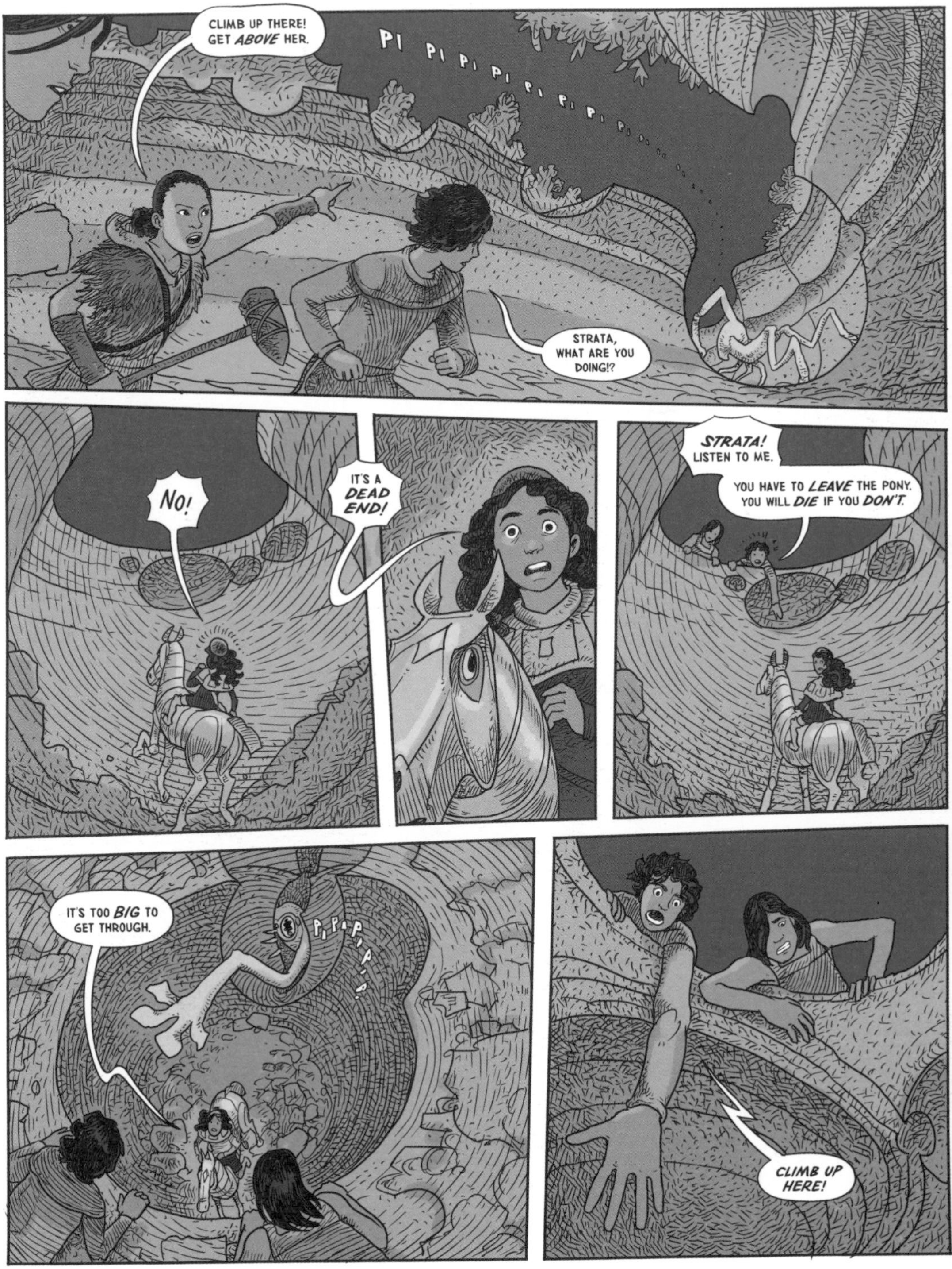

CLIMB UP THERE! GET *ABOVE* HER.
PI PI PI PI PI PI PI PI PI PI...
STRATA, WHAT ARE YOU DOING!?
NO!
IT'S A *DEAD END!*
STRATA! LISTEN TO ME.
YOU HAVE TO *LEAVE* THE PONY. YOU WILL *DIE* IF YOU *DON'T.*
IT'S TOO *BIG* TO GET THROUGH.
CLIMB UP HERE!

IT'S MAKING BUBBLES!
PIPIPIPPPPP
IT'S COMING THROUGH!
BWAP
BWAP
BWAAAAP
CLIMB UP! IT'S COMING!
YOU'RE ALMOST THERE.
I CAN'T REACH!
I'M SO SORRY, KLEIDI!
I THOUGHT WE COULD GET AWAY!
CRUMP
OOOF!

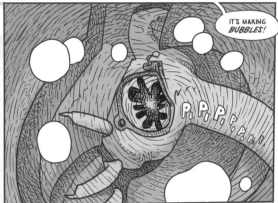

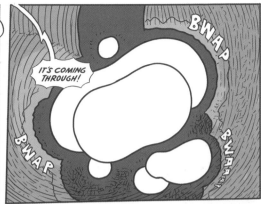

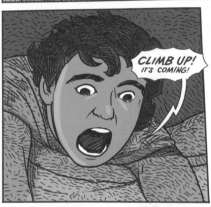

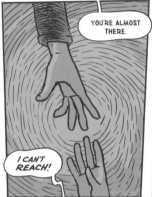

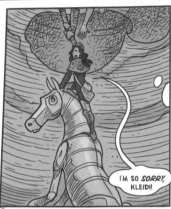

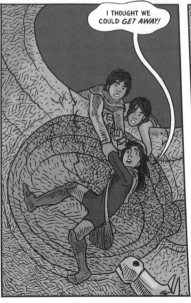

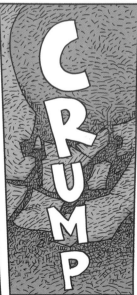

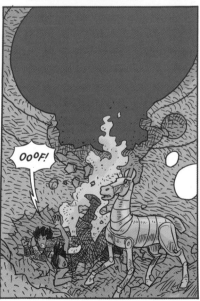

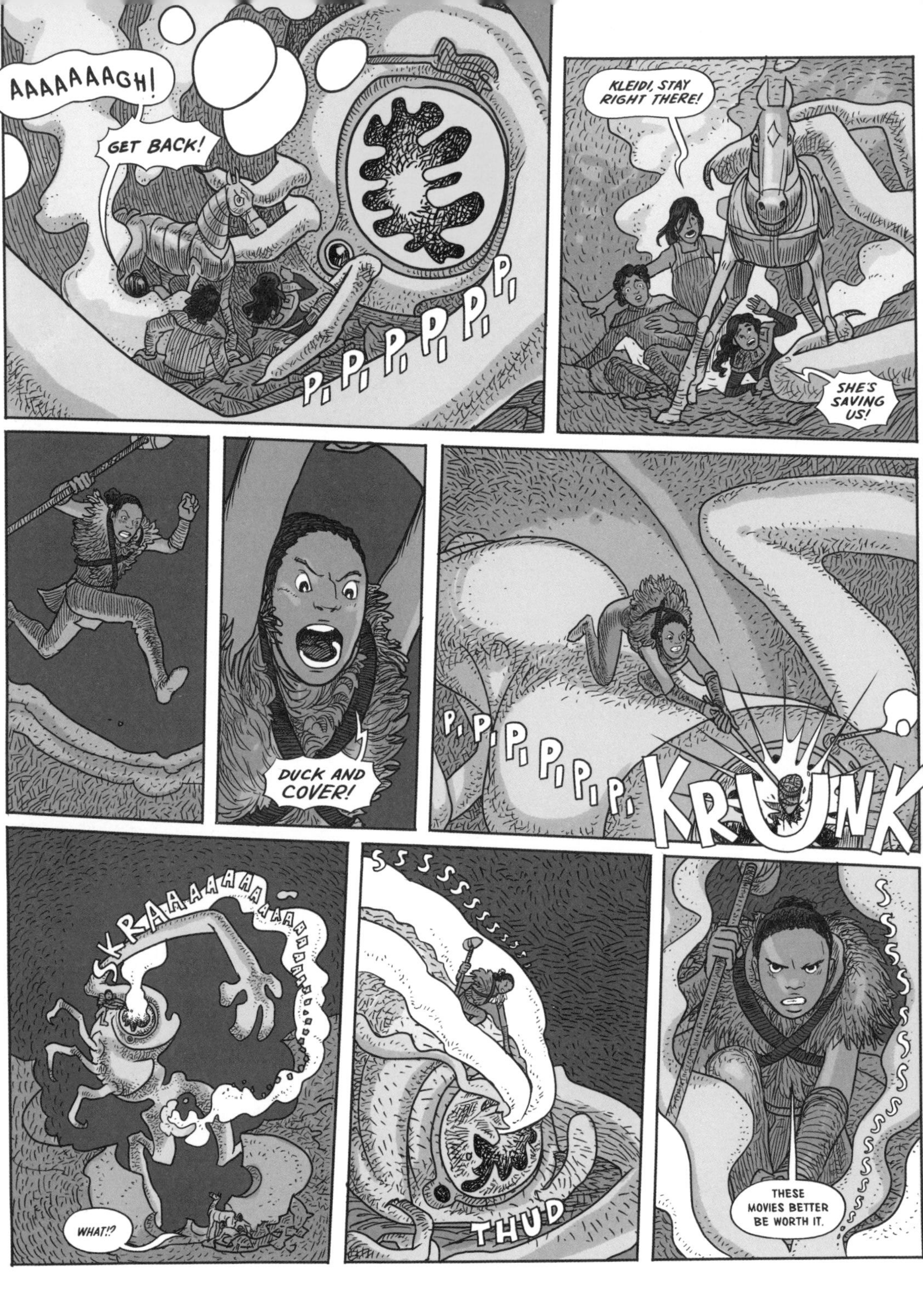
AAAAAAAGH!
GET BACK!
P, P, P, P, P, P, P,
KLEIDI, STAY RIGHT THERE!
SHE'S SAVING US!
DUCK AND COVER!
P, P, P, P, P, P, P, P,
KRUNK
SKRAAAAAAAAAAAAAAAAA
WHAT!?
SSSSSSSSSSSS
THUD
SSSSSSSSSSSSSSSS
THESE MOVIES BETTER BE WORTH IT.

HOLY CATS! YOU *KILLED* A *PIPER!*

STAY WHERE YOU ARE!

HOLD STILL!

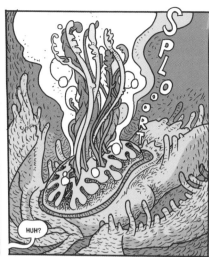

HUH?

SPLOORT

WHAT?

BLOORP

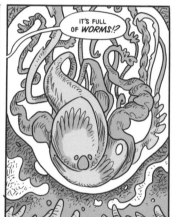

IT'S FULL OF *WORMS!?*

STAY BACK! THE PIPER'S DOWN, BUT THAT BUBBLE'S STILL *DEADLY!*

WORMS?!

IS IT THEIR *GUTS?*

NO, PIPERS ARE *MACHINES.* THOSE WORMY THINGS ARE WHAT'S DRIVING THEM.

YOU SAVED US!

NOT QUITE YET.

WE'LL BE *SAFE* WHEN THAT PONY'S IN *PIECES.*

NO!

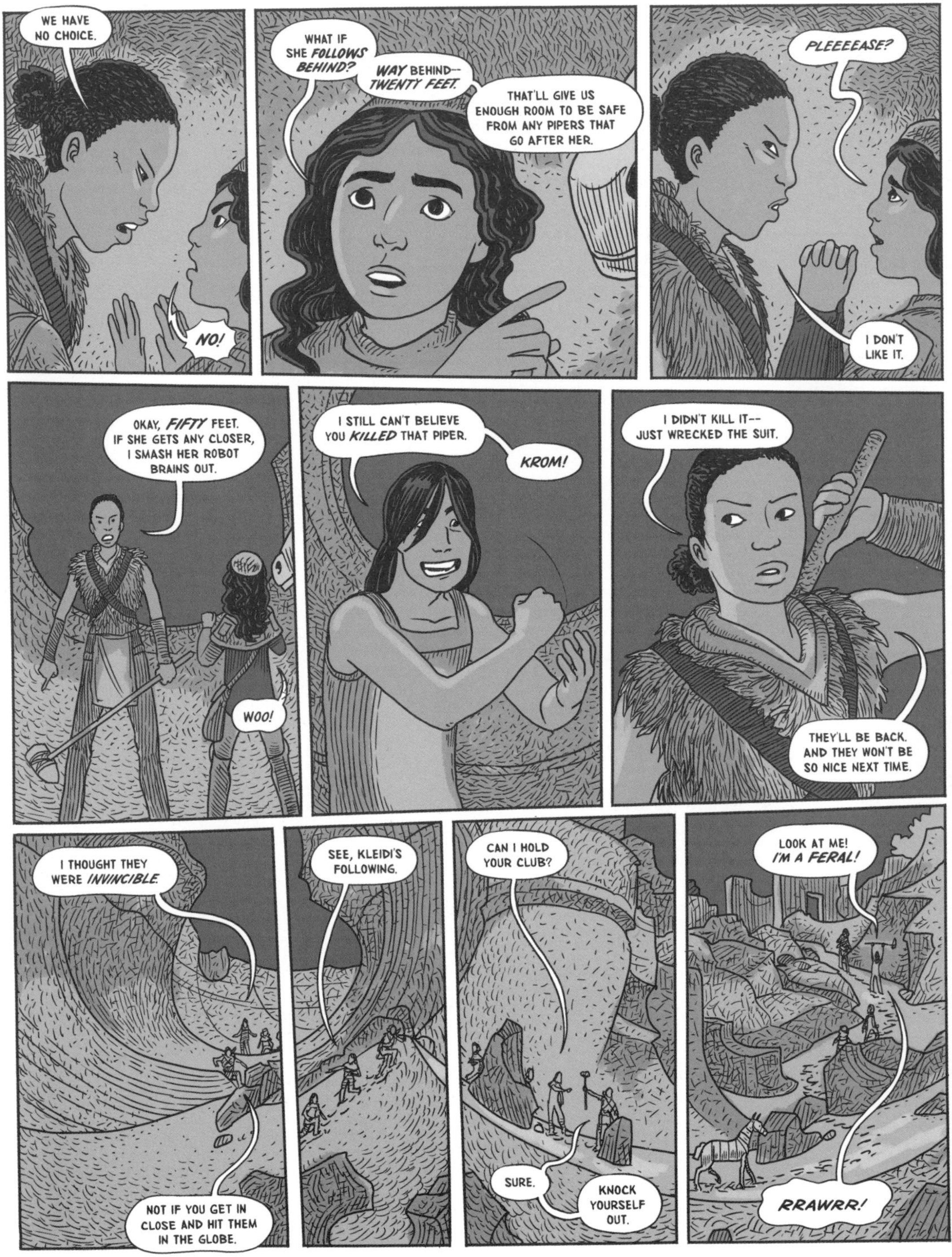
WE HAVE NO CHOICE.
NO!
WHAT IF SHE FOLLOWS BEHIND?
WAY BEHIND-- TWENTY FEET.
THAT'LL GIVE US ENOUGH ROOM TO BE SAFE FROM ANY PIPERS THAT GO AFTER HER.
PLEEEEASE?
I DON'T LIKE IT.
OKAY, FIFTY FEET. IF SHE GETS ANY CLOSER, I SMASH HER ROBOT BRAINS OUT.
WOO!
I STILL CAN'T BELIEVE YOU KILLED THAT PIPER.
KROM!
I DIDN'T KILL IT-- JUST WRECKED THE SUIT.
THEY'LL BE BACK. AND THEY WON'T BE SO NICE NEXT TIME.
I THOUGHT THEY WERE INVINCIBLE.
NOT IF YOU GET IN CLOSE AND HIT THEM IN THE GLOBE.
SEE, KLEIDI'S FOLLOWING.
CAN I HOLD YOUR CLUB?
SURE.
KNOCK YOURSELF OUT.
LOOK AT ME! I'M A FERAL!
RRAWRR!

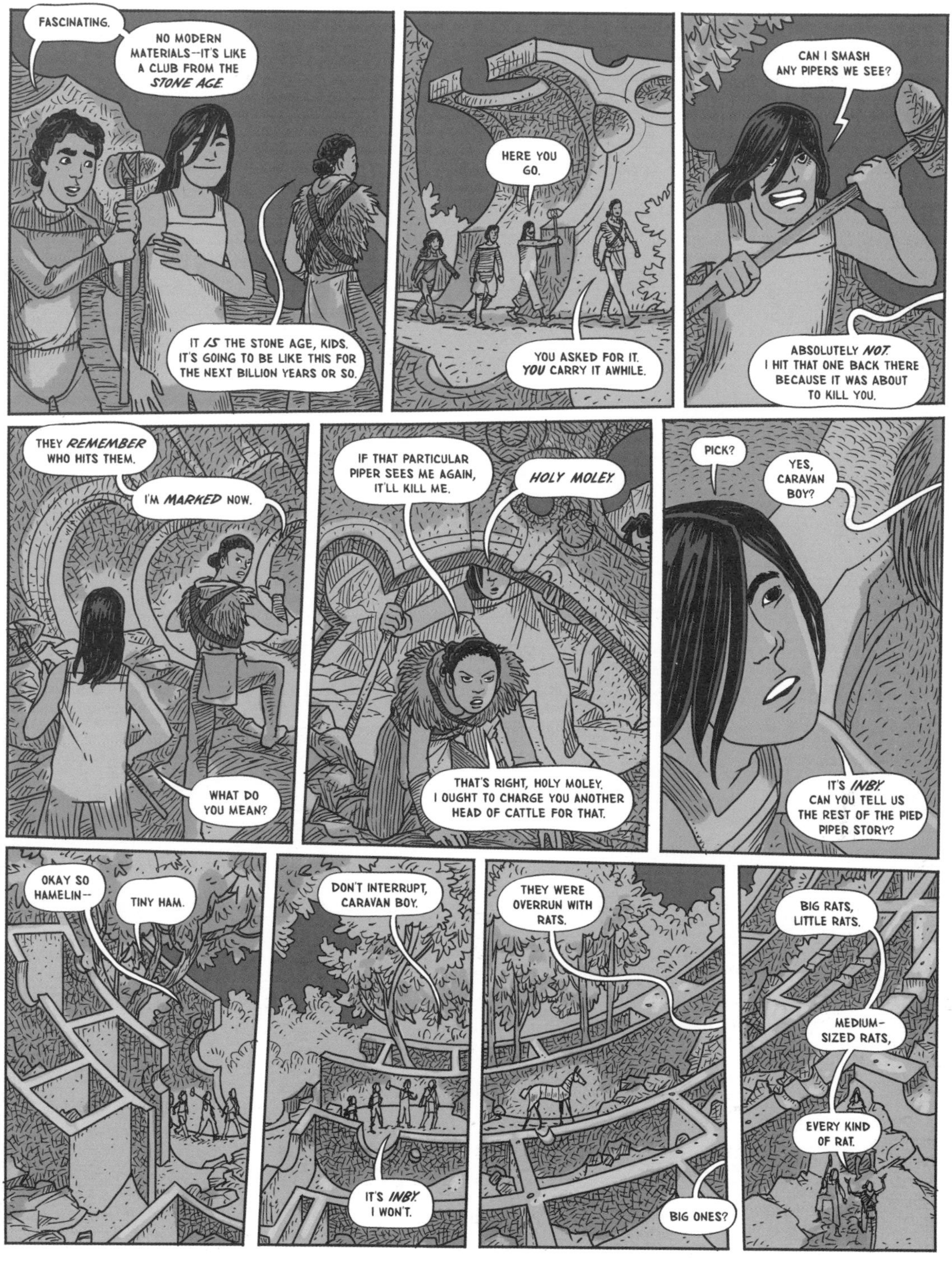
FASCINATING.
NO MODERN MATERIALS--IT'S LIKE A CLUB FROM THE STONE AGE.
IT IS THE STONE AGE, KIDS. IT'S GOING TO BE LIKE THIS FOR THE NEXT BILLION YEARS OR SO.
HERE YOU GO.
YOU ASKED FOR IT. YOU CARRY IT AWHILE.
CAN I SMASH ANY PIPERS WE SEE?
ABSOLUTELY NOT. I HIT THAT ONE BACK THERE BECAUSE IT WAS ABOUT TO KILL YOU.
THEY REMEMBER WHO HITS THEM.
I'M MARKED NOW.
WHAT DO YOU MEAN?
IF THAT PARTICULAR PIPER SEES ME AGAIN, IT'LL KILL ME.
HOLY MOLEY.
THAT'S RIGHT, HOLY MOLEY. I OUGHT TO CHARGE YOU ANOTHER HEAD OF CATTLE FOR THAT.
PICK?
YES, CARAVAN BOY?
IT'S INBY. CAN YOU TELL US THE REST OF THE PIED PIPER STORY?
OKAY SO HAMELIN--
TINY HAM.
DON'T INTERRUPT, CARAVAN BOY.
IT'S INBY. I WON'T.
THEY WERE OVERRUN WITH RATS.
BIG ONES?
BIG RATS, LITTLE RATS.
MEDIUM-SIZED RATS,
EVERY KIND OF RAT.

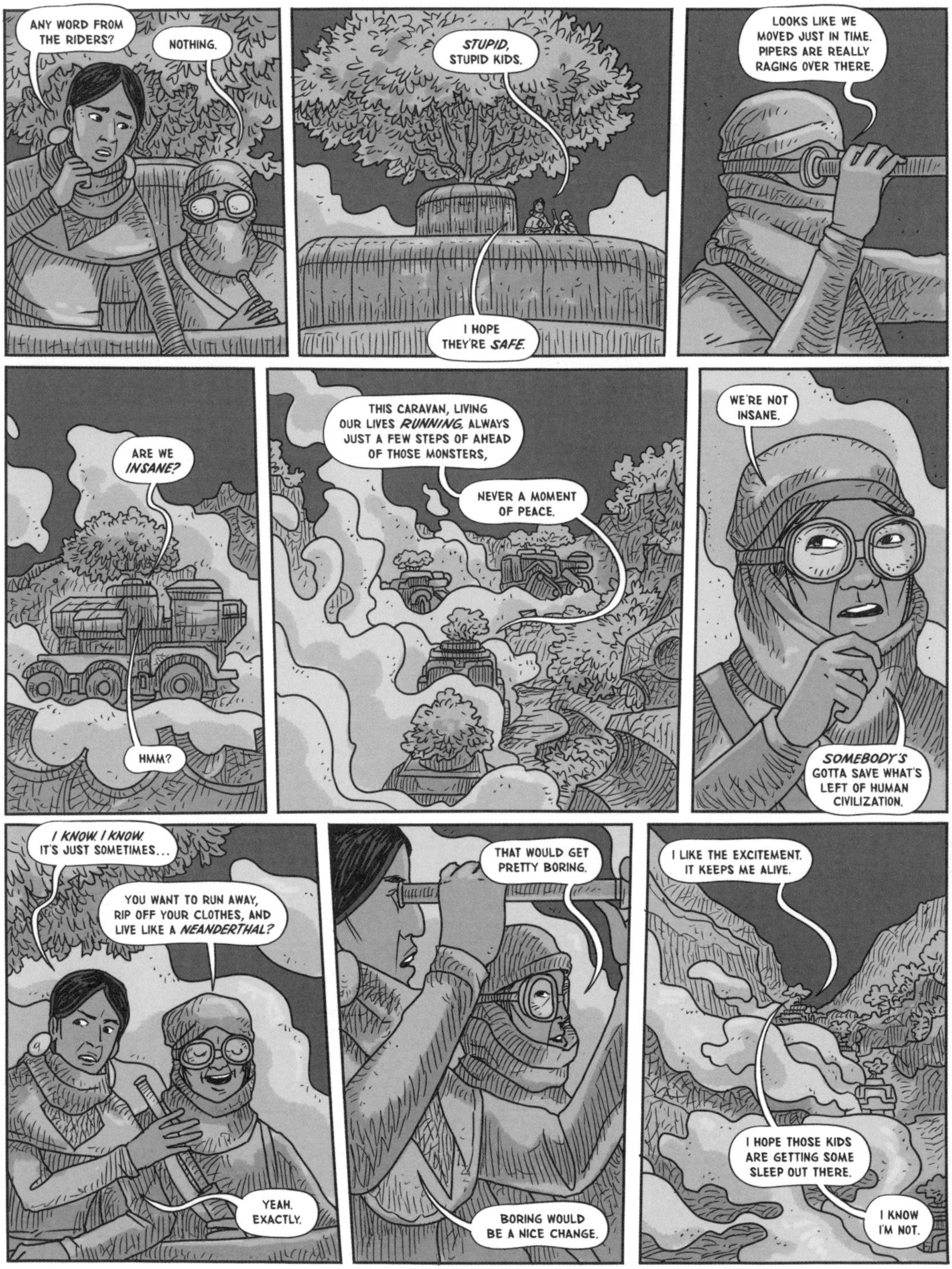

ANY WORD FROM THE RIDERS?
NOTHING.
STUPID, STUPID KIDS.
I HOPE THEY'RE SAFE.
LOOKS LIKE WE MOVED JUST IN TIME. PIPERS ARE REALLY RAGING OVER THERE.
ARE WE INSANE?
HMM?
THIS CARAVAN, LIVING OUR LIVES RUNNING, ALWAYS JUST A FEW STEPS OF AHEAD OF THOSE MONSTERS,
NEVER A MOMENT OF PEACE.
WE'RE NOT INSANE.
SOMEBODY'S GOTTA SAVE WHAT'S LEFT OF HUMAN CIVILIZATION.
I KNOW. I KNOW. IT'S JUST SOMETIMES...
YOU WANT TO RUN AWAY, RIP OFF YOUR CLOTHES, AND LIVE LIKE A NEANDERTHAL?
YEAH. EXACTLY.
THAT WOULD GET PRETTY BORING.
BORING WOULD BE A NICE CHANGE.
I LIKE THE EXCITEMENT. IT KEEPS ME ALIVE.
I HOPE THOSE KIDS ARE GETTING SOME SLEEP OUT THERE.
I KNOW I'M NOT.

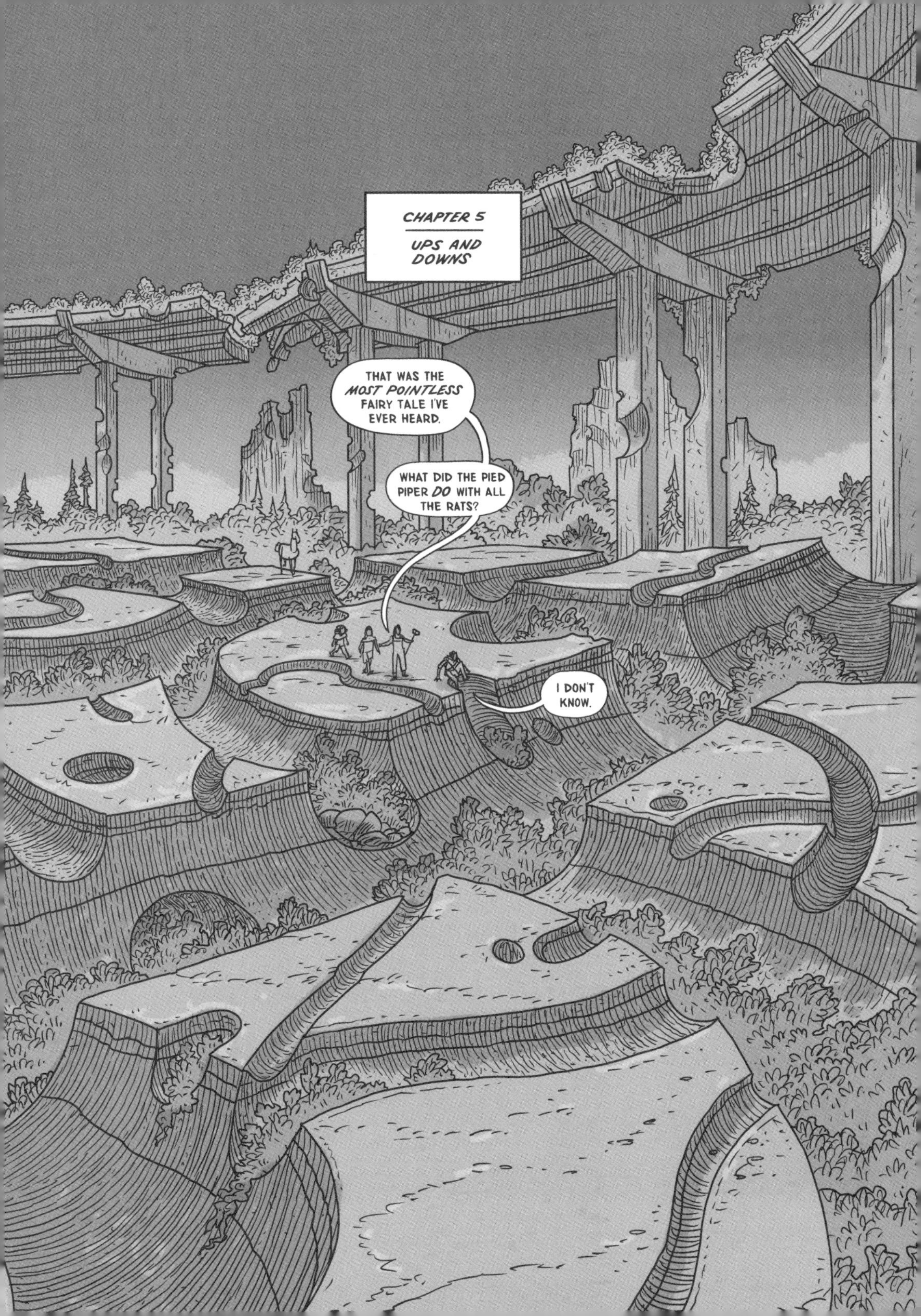
CHAPTER 5
UPS AND DOWNS
THAT WAS THE MOST POINTLESS FAIRY TALE I'VE EVER HEARD.
WHAT DID THE PIED PIPER DO WITH ALL THE RATS?
I DON'T KNOW.

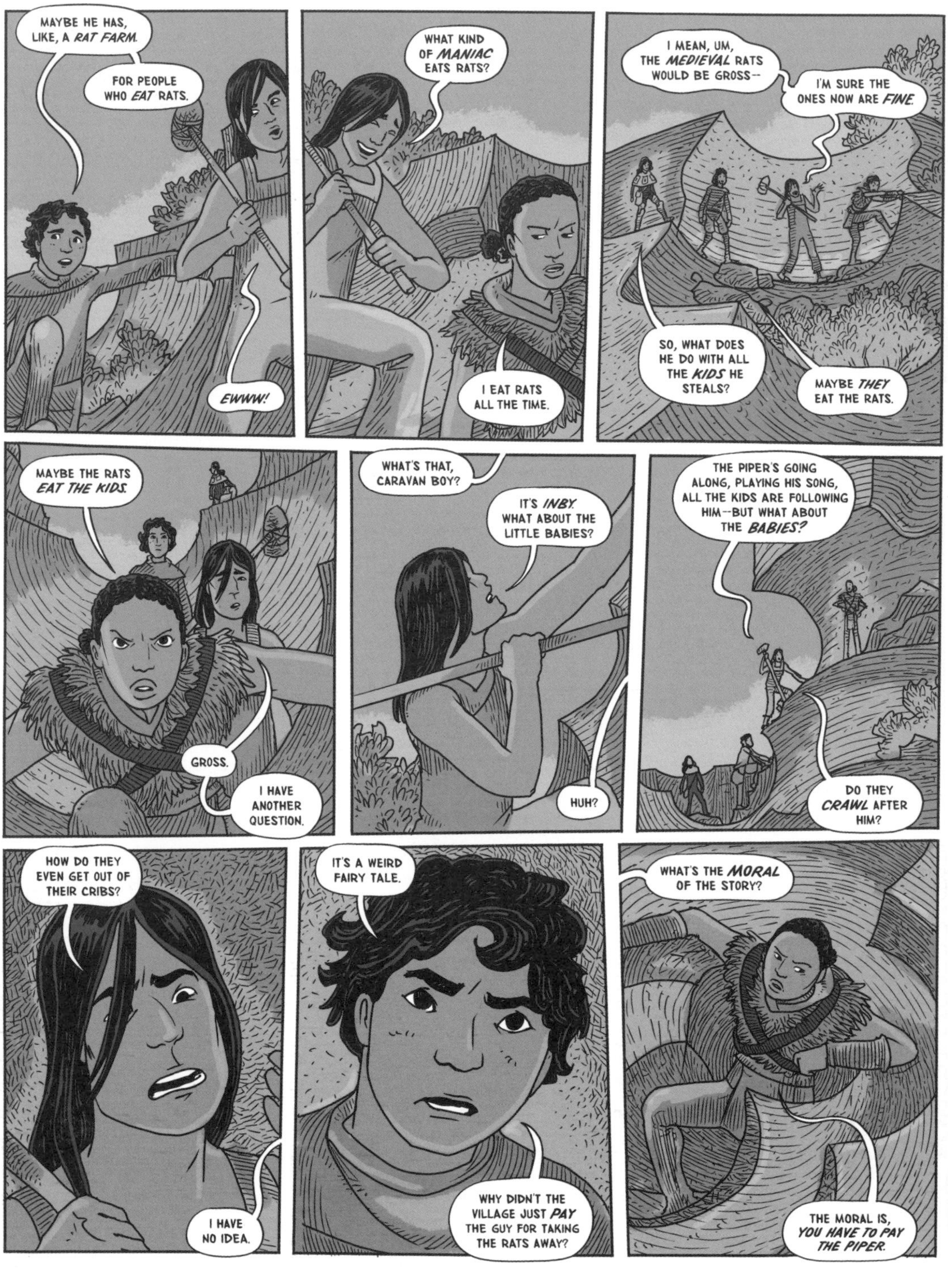
MAYBE HE HAS, LIKE, A RAT FARM.
FOR PEOPLE WHO EAT RATS.
EWWW!
WHAT KIND OF MANIAC EATS RATS?
I EAT RATS ALL THE TIME.
I MEAN, UM, THE MEDIEVAL RATS WOULD BE GROSS--
I'M SURE THE ONES NOW ARE FINE.
SO, WHAT DOES HE DO WITH ALL THE KIDS HE STEALS?
MAYBE THEY EAT THE RATS.
MAYBE THE RATS EAT THE KIDS.
GROSS.
I HAVE ANOTHER QUESTION.
WHAT'S THAT, CARAVAN BOY?
IT'S INBY. WHAT ABOUT THE LITTLE BABIES?
HUH?
THE PIPER'S GOING ALONG, PLAYING HIS SONG, ALL THE KIDS ARE FOLLOWING HIM--BUT WHAT ABOUT THE BABIES?
DO THEY CRAWL AFTER HIM?
HOW DO THEY EVEN GET OUT OF THEIR CRIBS?
I HAVE NO IDEA.
IT'S A WEIRD FAIRY TALE.
WHY DIDN'T THE VILLAGE JUST PAY THE GUY FOR TAKING THE RATS AWAY?
WHAT'S THE MORAL OF THE STORY?
THE MORAL IS, YOU HAVE TO PAY THE PIPER.

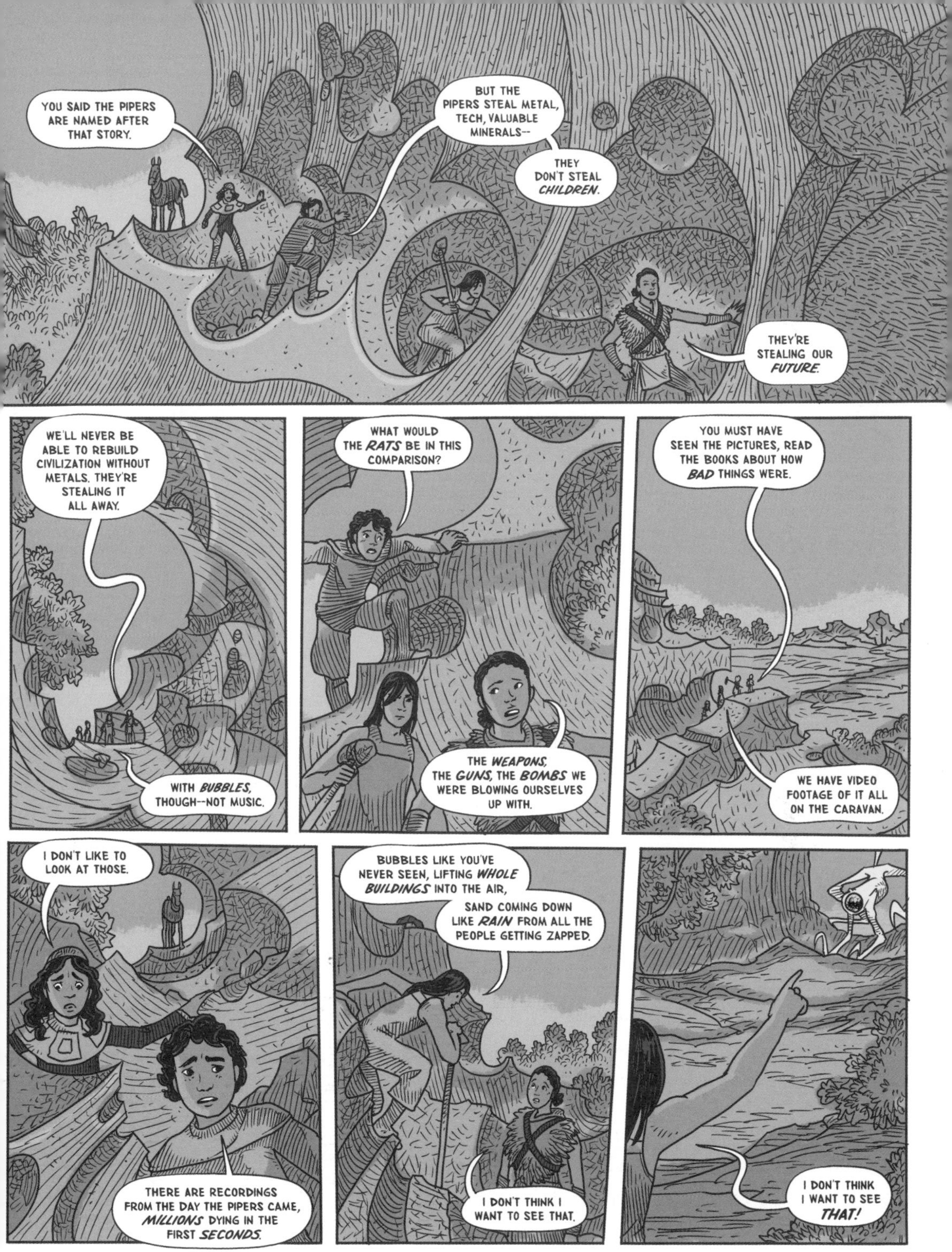
YOU SAID THE PIPERS ARE NAMED AFTER THAT STORY.
BUT THE PIPERS STEAL METAL, TECH, VALUABLE MINERALS--
THEY DON'T STEAL *CHILDREN.*
THEY'RE STEALING OUR *FUTURE.*
WE'LL NEVER BE ABLE TO REBUILD CIVILIZATION WITHOUT METALS. THEY'RE STEALING IT ALL AWAY.
WITH *BUBBLES,* THOUGH--NOT MUSIC.
WHAT WOULD THE *RATS* BE IN THIS COMPARISON?
THE *WEAPONS,* THE *GUNS,* THE *BOMBS* WE WERE BLOWING OURSELVES UP WITH.
YOU MUST HAVE SEEN THE PICTURES, READ THE BOOKS ABOUT HOW *BAD* THINGS WERE.
WE HAVE VIDEO FOOTAGE OF IT ALL ON THE CARAVAN.
I DON'T LIKE TO LOOK AT THOSE.
THERE ARE RECORDINGS FROM THE DAY THE PIPERS CAME, *MILLIONS* DYING IN THE FIRST *SECONDS.*
BUBBLES LIKE YOU'VE NEVER SEEN, LIFTING *WHOLE BUILDINGS* INTO THE AIR,
SAND COMING DOWN LIKE *RAIN* FROM ALL THE PEOPLE GETTING ZAPPED.
I DON'T THINK I WANT TO SEE THAT.
I DON'T THINK I WANT TO SEE *THAT!*

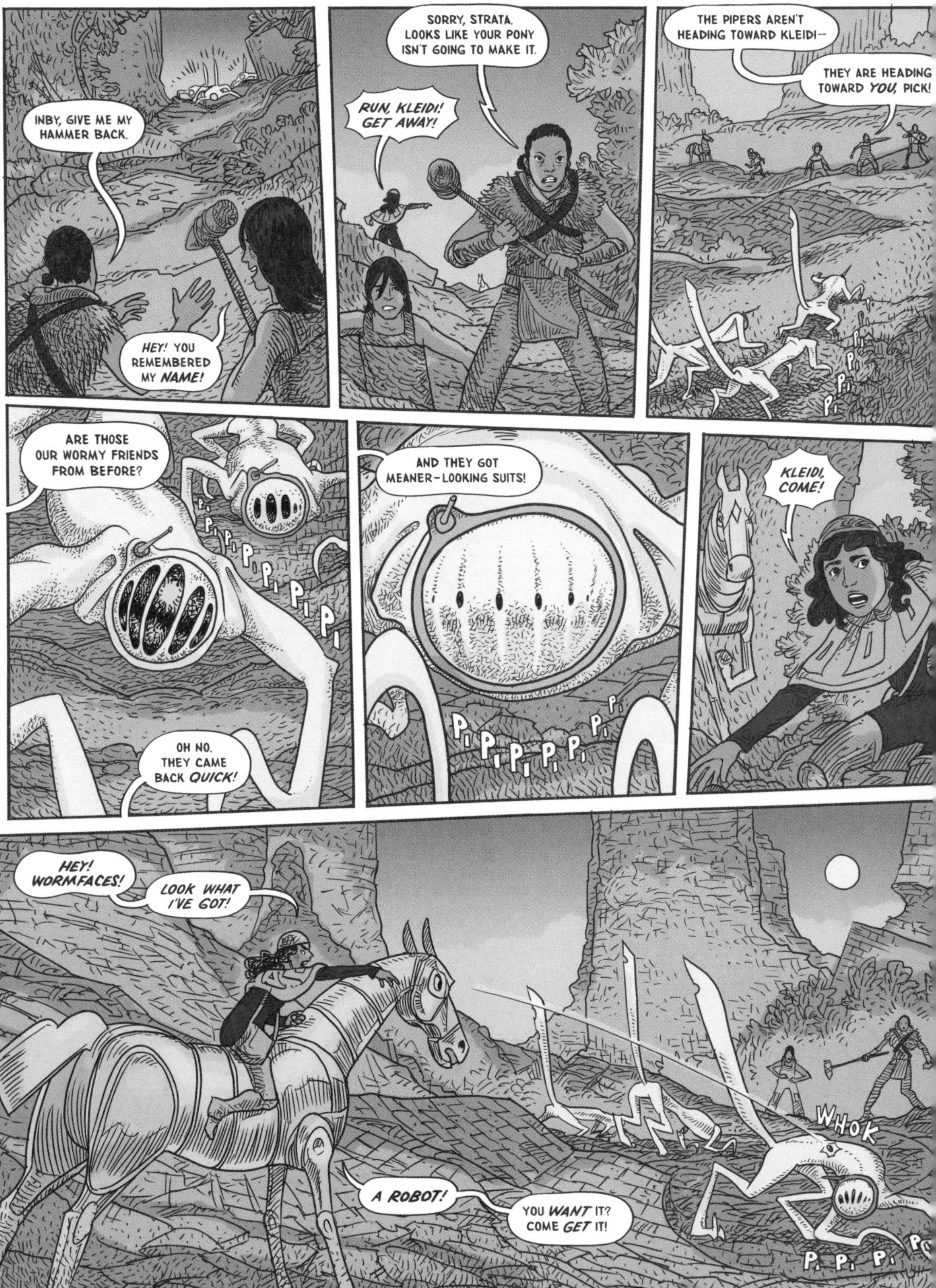
INBY, GIVE ME MY HAMMER BACK.
HEY! YOU REMEMBERED MY NAME!
SORRY, STRATA. LOOKS LIKE YOUR PONY ISN'T GOING TO MAKE IT.
RUN, KLEIDI! GET AWAY!
THE PIPERS AREN'T HEADING TOWARD KLEIDI--
THEY ARE HEADING TOWARD YOU, PICK!
PI PI PI PI
ARE THOSE OUR WORMY FRIENDS FROM BEFORE?
PI PI PI PI PI PI PI
OH NO. THEY CAME BACK QUICK!
AND THEY GOT MEANER-LOOKING SUITS!
PI PI PI PI PI PI
KLEIDI, COME!
HEY! WORMFACES!
LOOK WHAT I'VE GOT!
WHOK
A ROBOT!
YOU WANT IT? COME GET IT!
PI PI PI PO

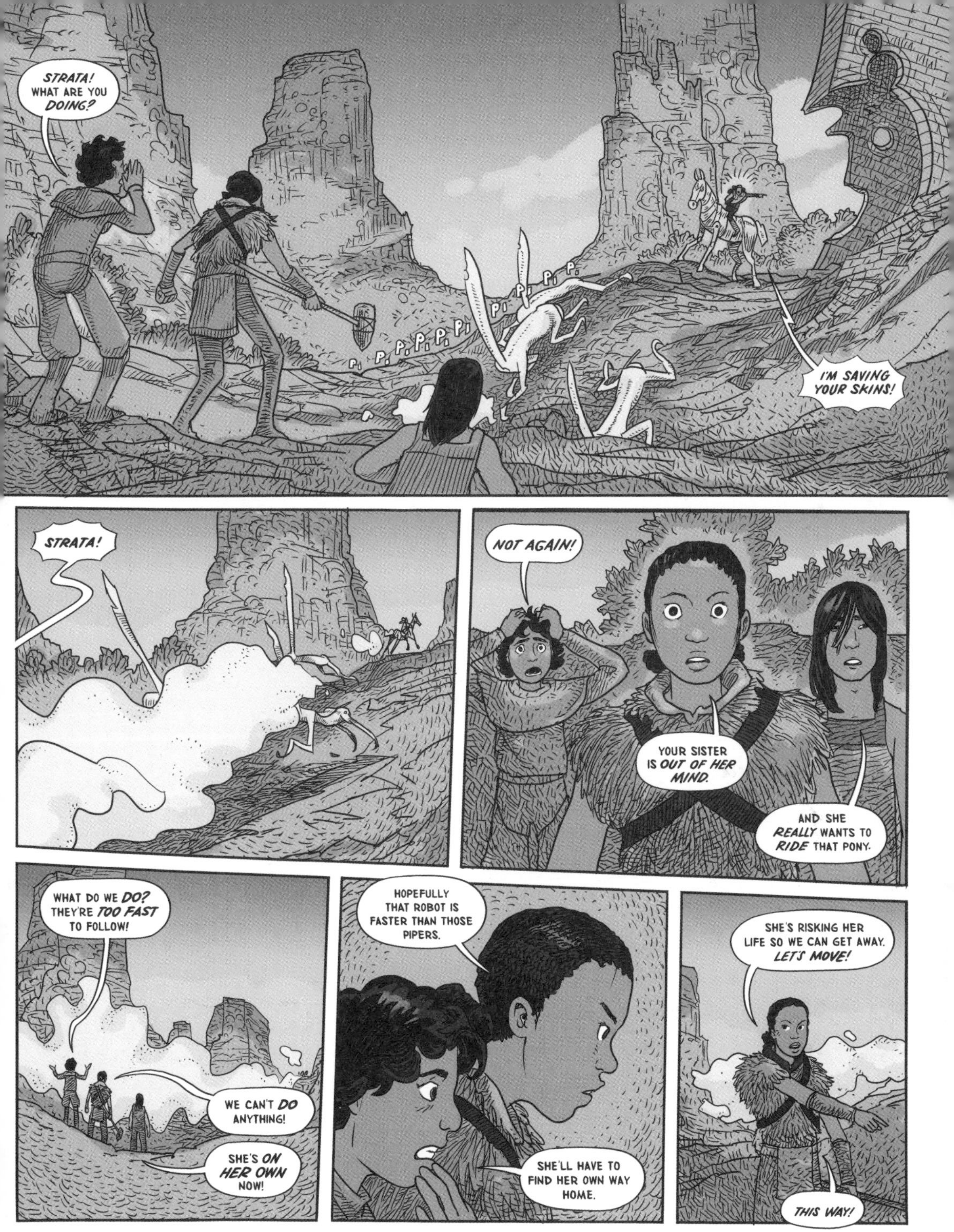
STRATA! WHAT ARE YOU DOING?
I'M SAVING YOUR SKINS!
STRATA!
NOT AGAIN!
YOUR SISTER IS OUT OF HER MIND.
AND SHE REALLY WANTS TO RIDE THAT PONY.
WHAT DO WE DO? THEY'RE TOO FAST TO FOLLOW!
WE CAN'T DO ANYTHING!
SHE'S ON HER OWN NOW!
HOPEFULLY THAT ROBOT IS FASTER THAN THOSE PIPERS.
SHE'LL HAVE TO FIND HER OWN WAY HOME.
SHE'S RISKING HER LIFE SO WE CAN GET AWAY. LET'S MOVE!
THIS WAY!

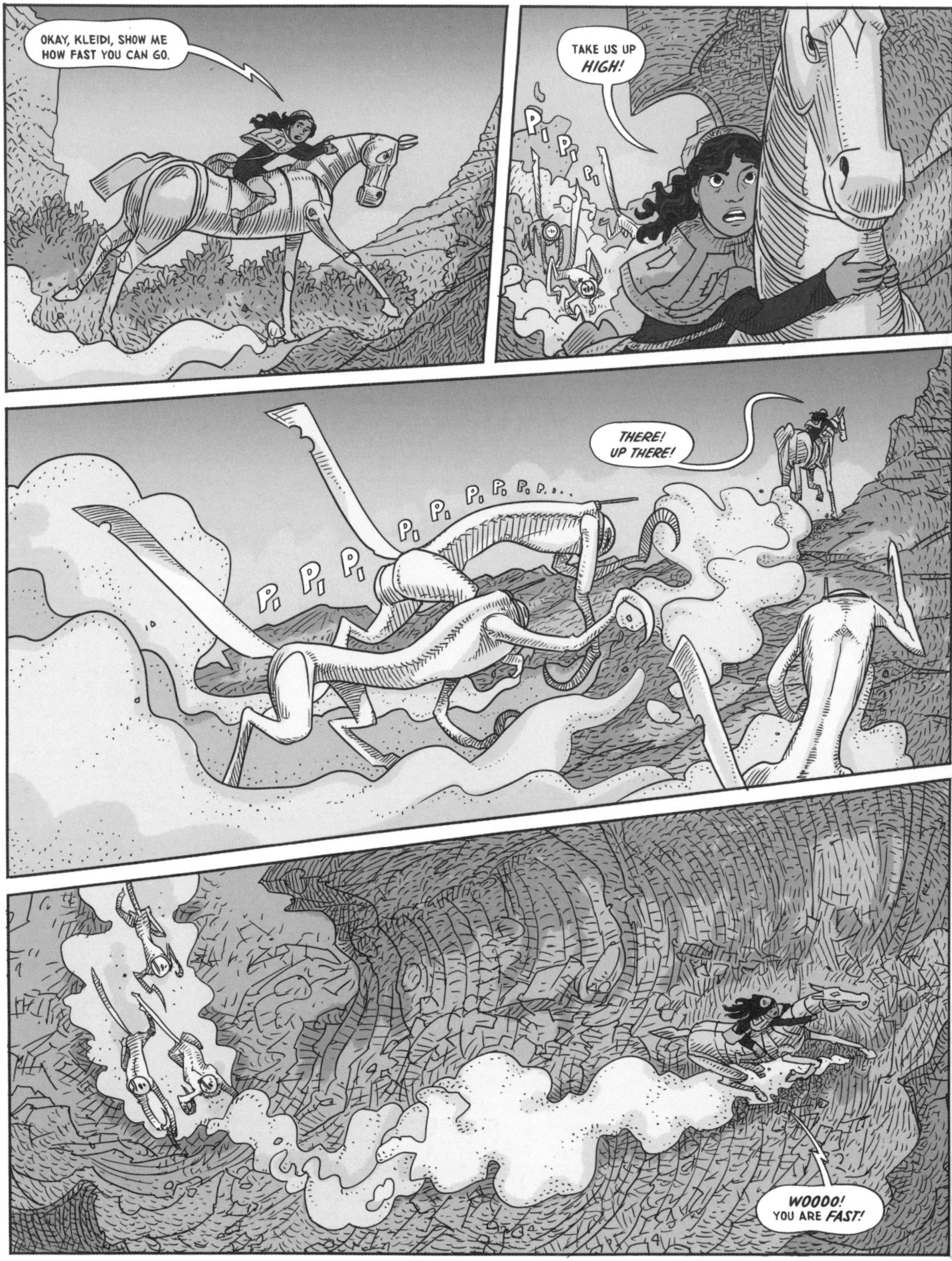
OKAY, KLEIDI, SHOW ME HOW FAST YOU CAN GO.
TAKE US UP HIGH!
PI PI PI PI
THERE! UP THERE!
PI PI PI PI PI PI PI PI PI PI...
WOOOO! YOU ARE FAST!

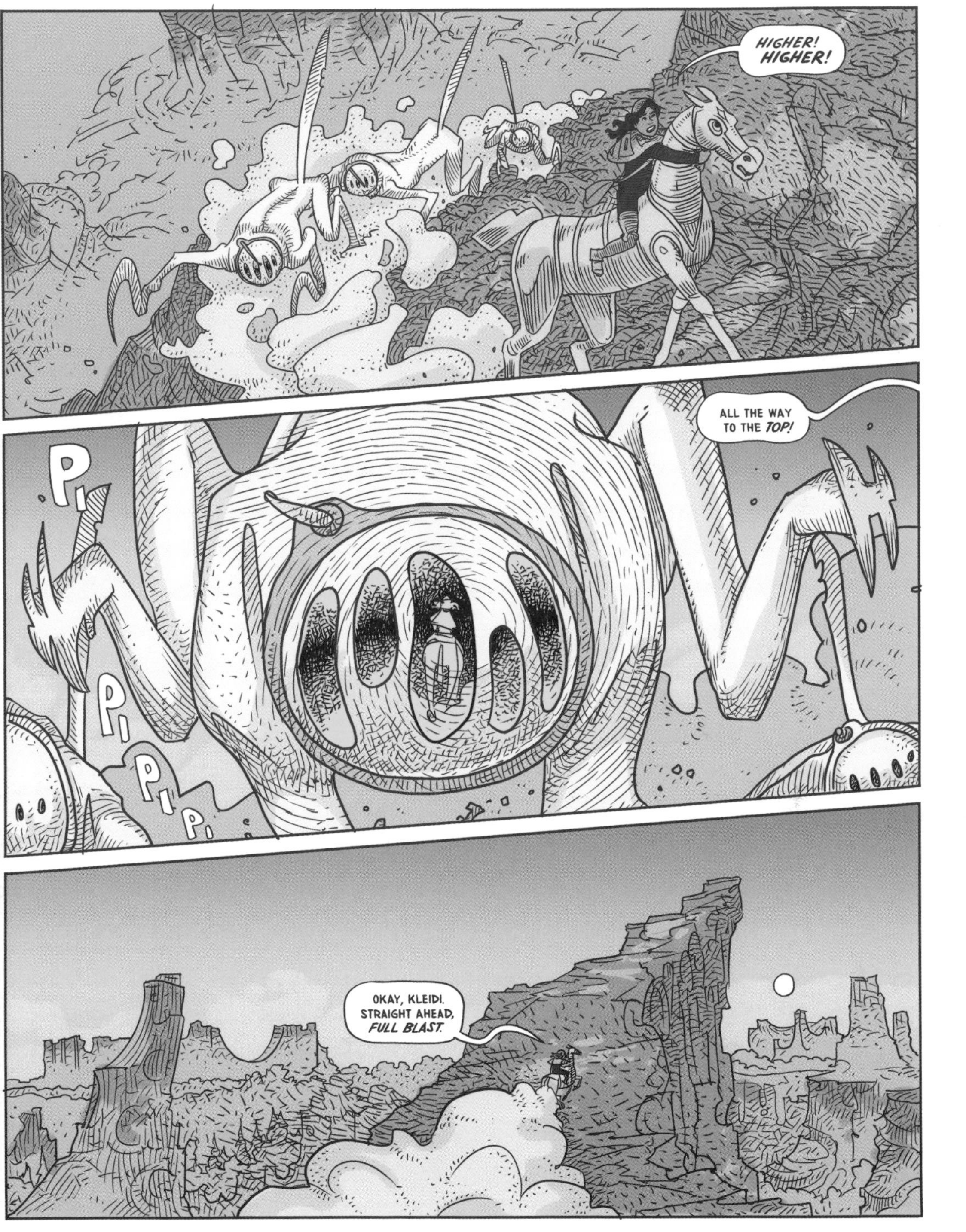
HIGHER! HIGHER!
ALL THE WAY TO THE TOP!
PI PI PI PI PI
OKAY, KLEIDI. STRAIGHT AHEAD, FULL BLAST.

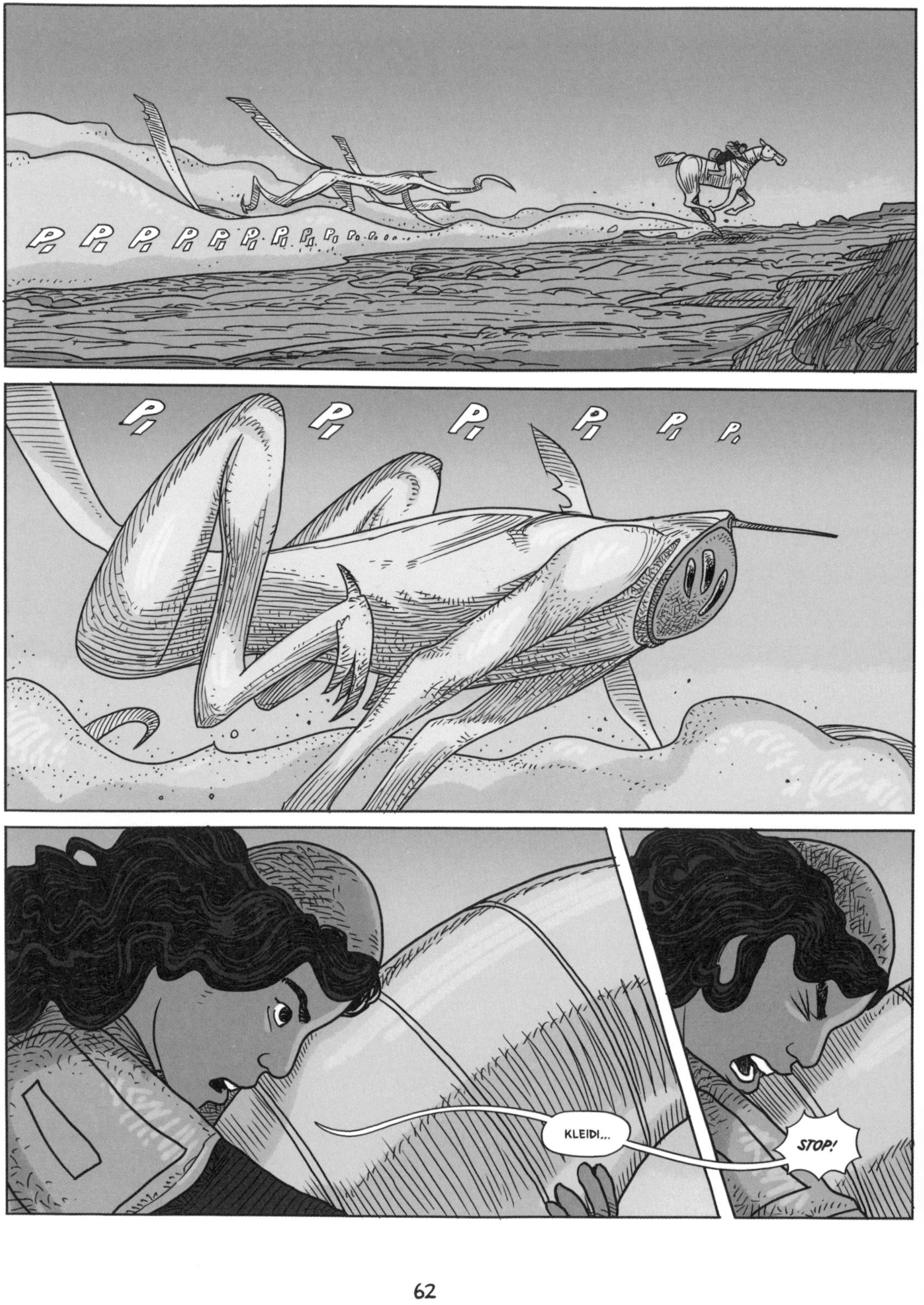
PI PI PI PI PI PI PI PI PI
PI PI PI PI PI PI
KLEIDI...
STOP!

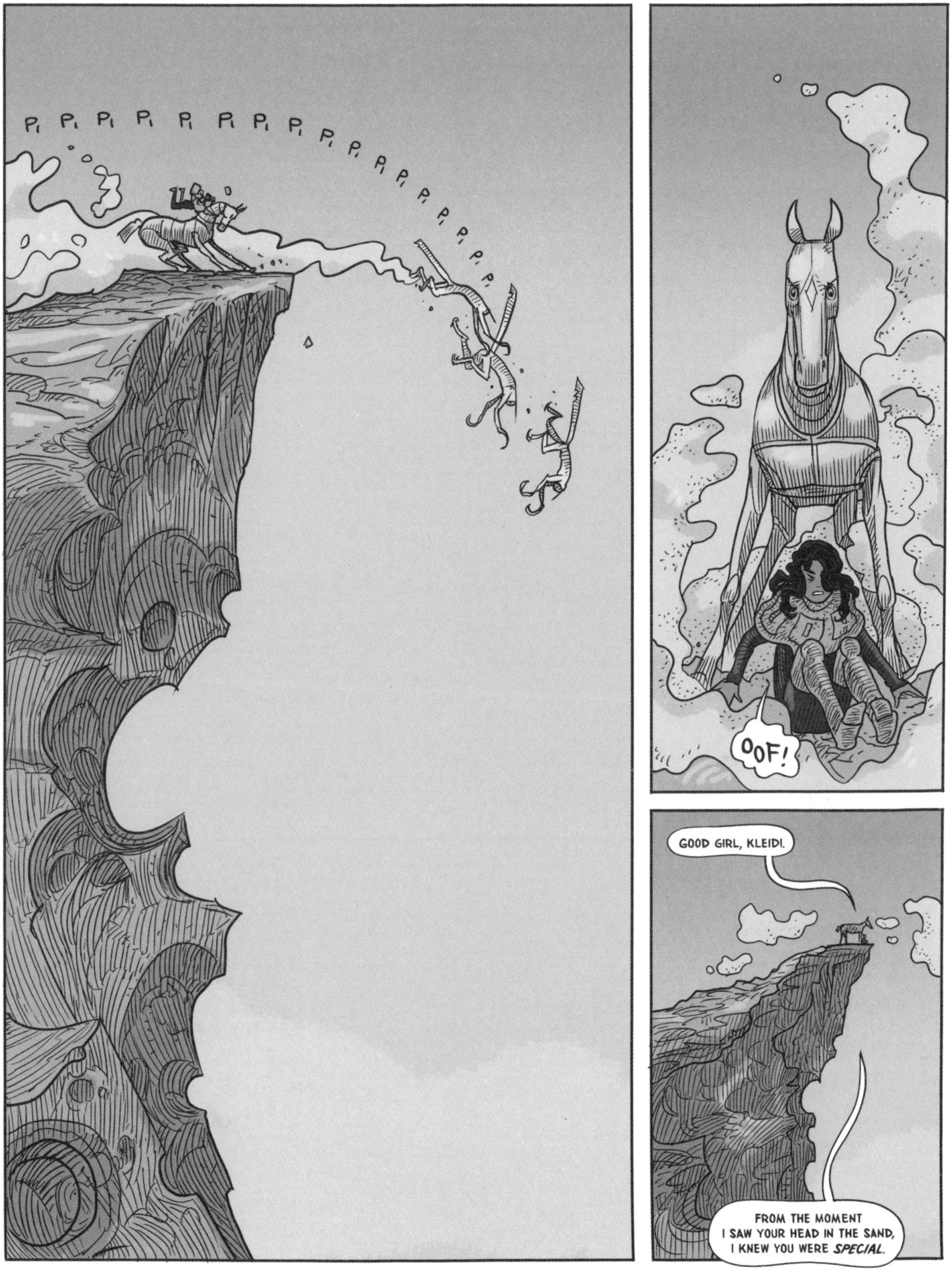

P P P P P P P P P P P P P P P P P P P
OOF!
GOOD GIRL, KLEIDI.
FROM THE MOMENT I SAW YOUR HEAD IN THE SAND, I KNEW YOU WERE *SPECIAL*.

SHH! *FREEZE.*

PIPERS?

RIDERS?

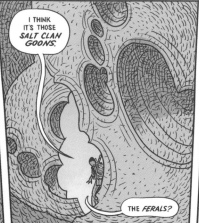

I THINK IT'S THOSE *SALT CLAN GOONS.*

THE *FERALS?*

IS THERE ANYTHING OUT HERE THAT *ISN'T* TRYING TO KILL YOU?

COME ON. *QUIETLY.*

SHH!

DO YOU HEAR *THAT?*

WHAT?

SOUNDED LIKE *VOICES.*

IT'S ALL THE ECHOES IN HERE. C'MON.

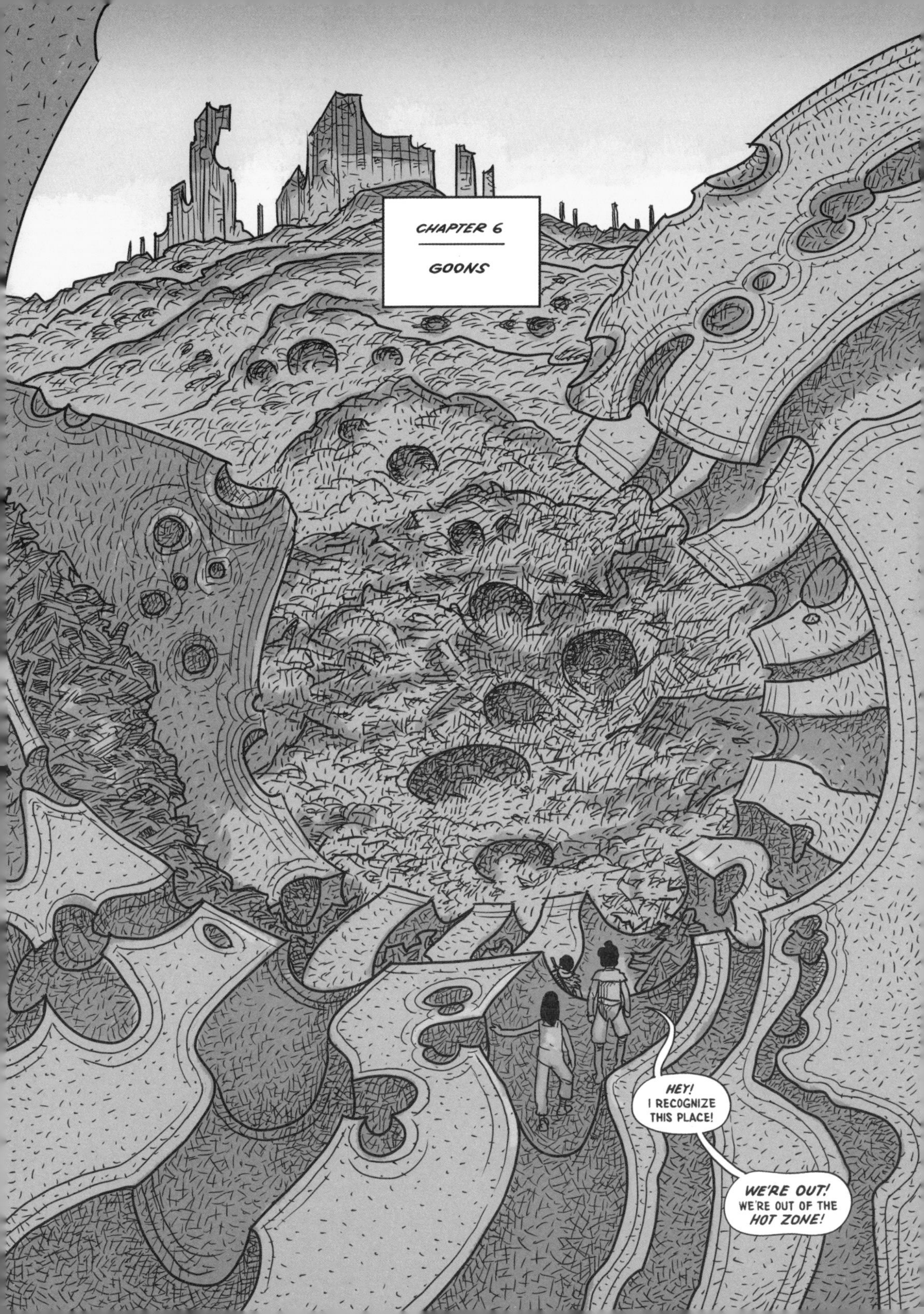
CHAPTER 6
GOONS
HEY! I RECOGNIZE THIS PLACE!
WE'RE OUT! WE'RE OUT OF THE HOT ZONE!

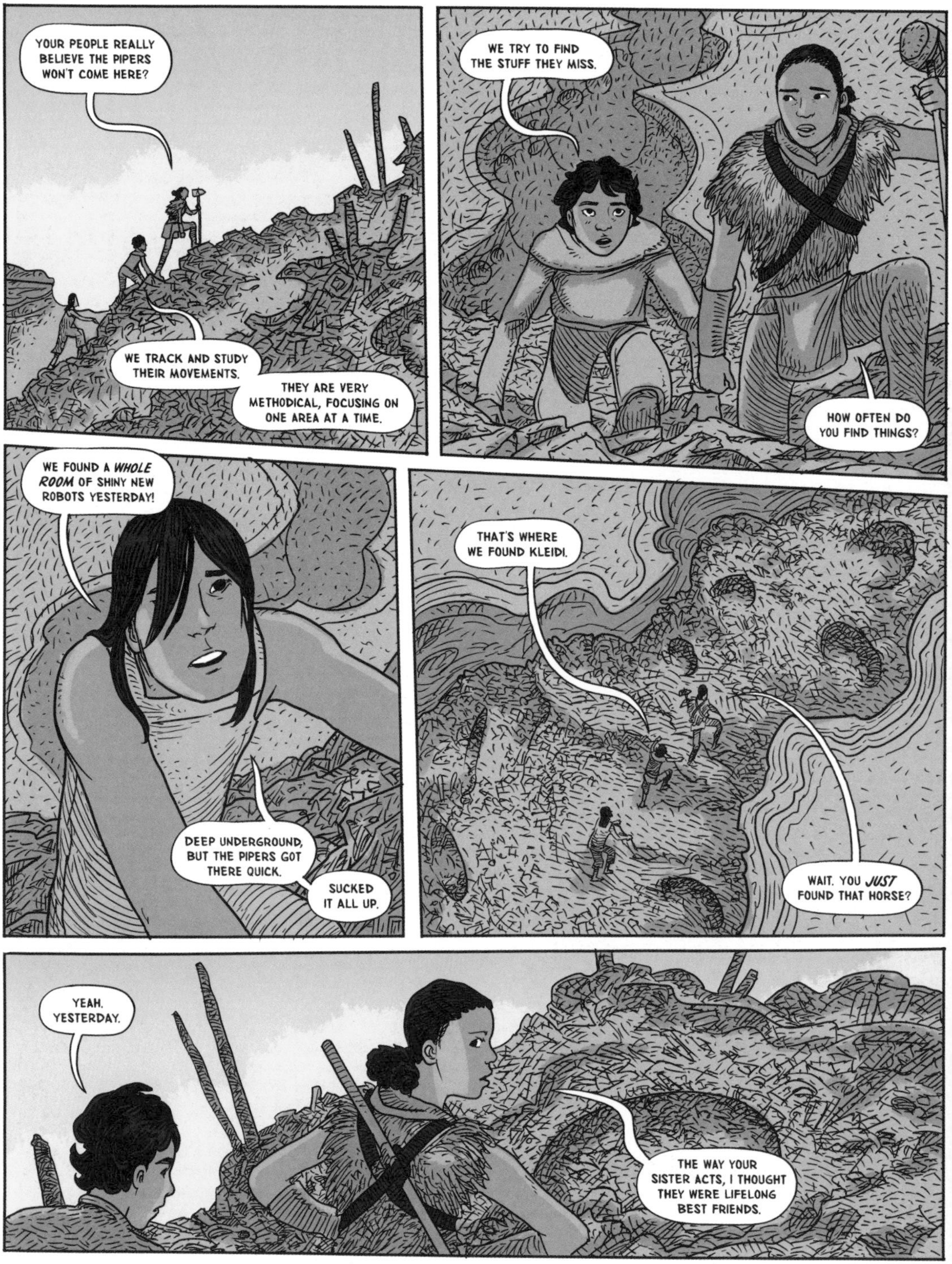
YOUR PEOPLE REALLY BELIEVE THE PIPERS WON'T COME HERE?
WE TRACK AND STUDY THEIR MOVEMENTS.
THEY ARE VERY METHODICAL, FOCUSING ON ONE AREA AT A TIME.
WE TRY TO FIND THE STUFF THEY MISS.
HOW OFTEN DO YOU FIND THINGS?
WE FOUND A *WHOLE ROOM* OF SHINY NEW ROBOTS YESTERDAY!
DEEP UNDERGROUND, BUT THE PIPERS GOT THERE QUICK.
SUCKED IT ALL UP.
THAT'S WHERE WE FOUND KLEIDI.
WAIT. YOU *JUST* FOUND THAT HORSE?
YEAH. YESTERDAY.
THE WAY YOUR SISTER ACTS, I THOUGHT THEY WERE LIFELONG BEST FRIENDS.

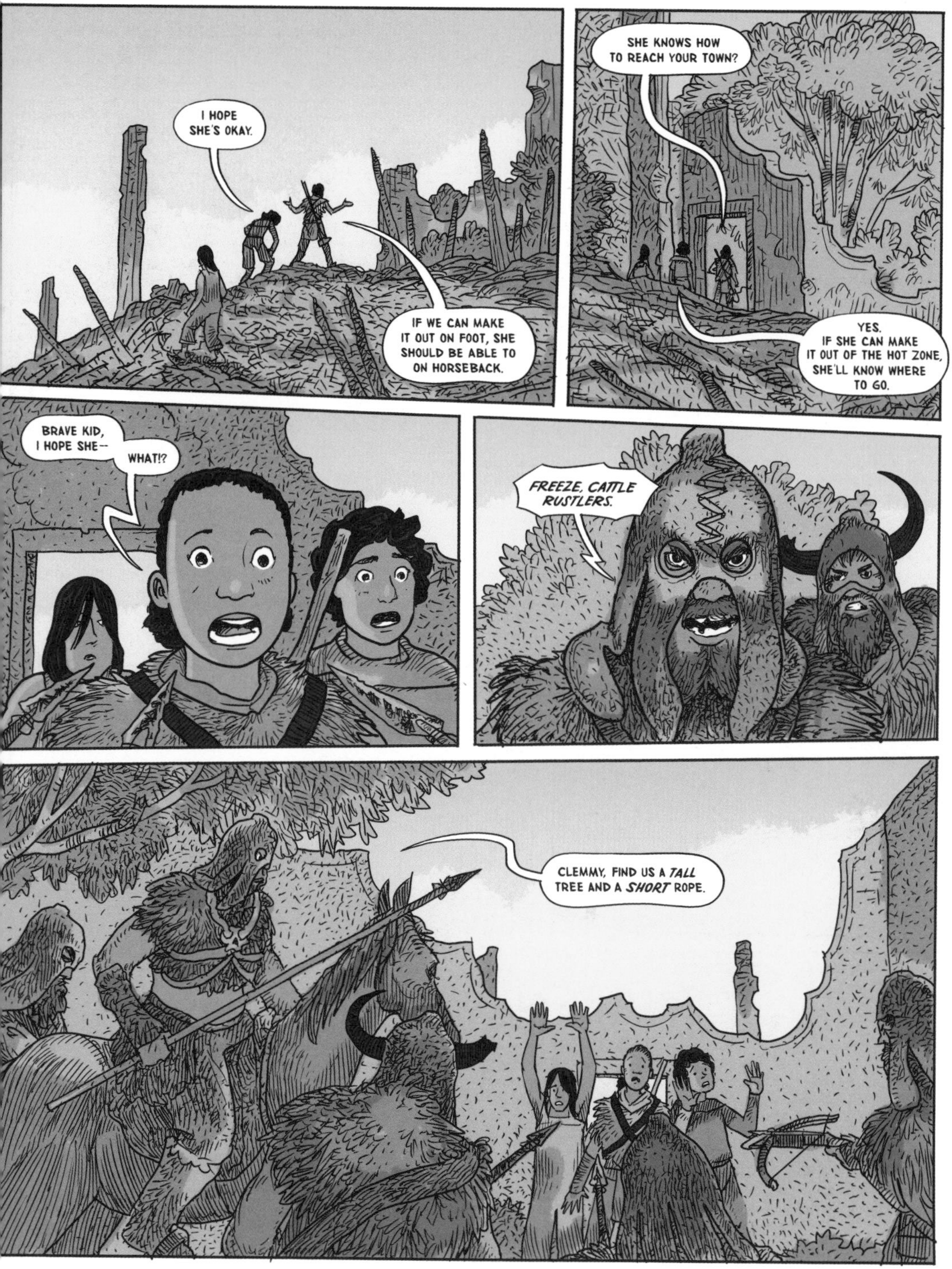
I HOPE SHE'S OKAY.
IF WE CAN MAKE IT OUT ON FOOT, SHE SHOULD BE ABLE TO ON HORSEBACK.
SHE KNOWS HOW TO REACH YOUR TOWN?
YES. IF SHE CAN MAKE IT OUT OF THE HOT ZONE, SHE'LL KNOW WHERE TO GO.
BRAVE KID, I HOPE SHE--
WHAT!?
FREEZE, CATTLE RUSTLERS.
CLEMMY, FIND US A TALL TREE AND A SHORT ROPE.

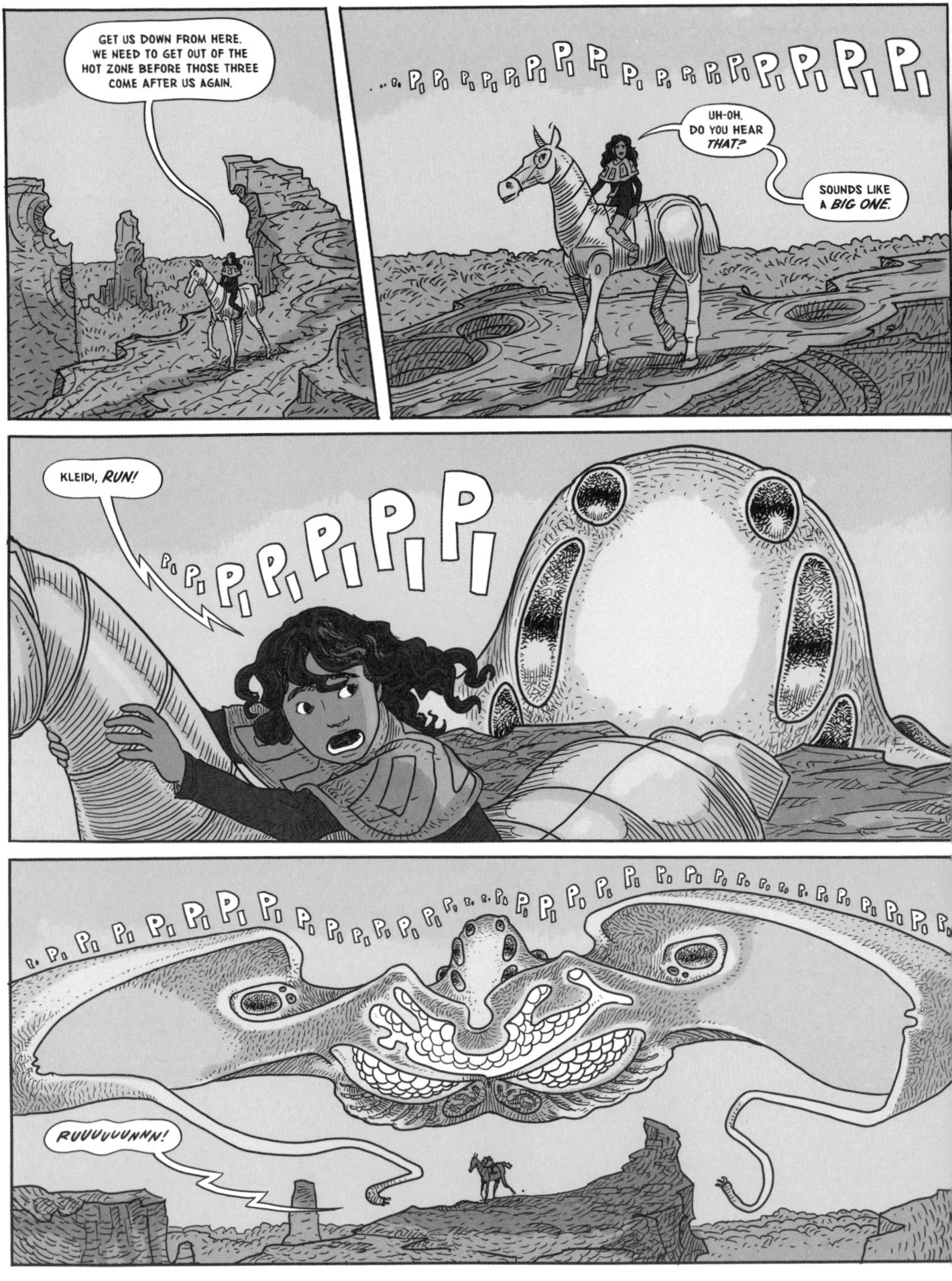

GET US DOWN FROM HERE. WE NEED TO GET OUT OF THE HOT ZONE BEFORE THOSE THREE COME AFTER US AGAIN.
...PI PI PI PI PI PI PI PI PI PI PI PI PI PI PI PI PI PI
UH-OH. DO YOU HEAR *THAT?*
SOUNDS LIKE A *BIG ONE.*
KLEIDI, *RUN!*
PI PI PI PI PI PI PI PI PI
PI PI PI PI PI PI PI PI PI PI PI PI PI PI PI PI PI PI PI PI PI PI PI PI PI PI PI PI PI PI PI PI PI PI PI
RUUUUUUNNN!

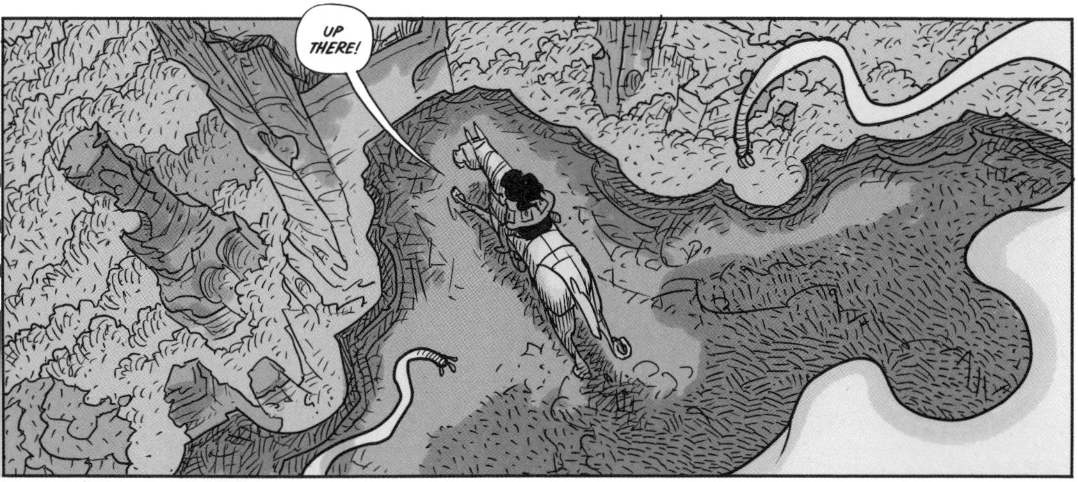
UP THERE!

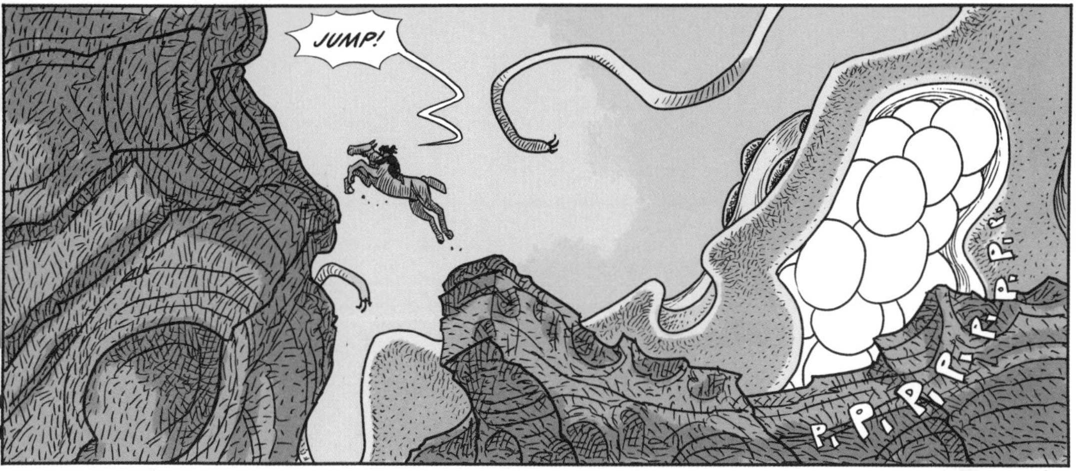
JUMP!
PI PI PI PI PI PI

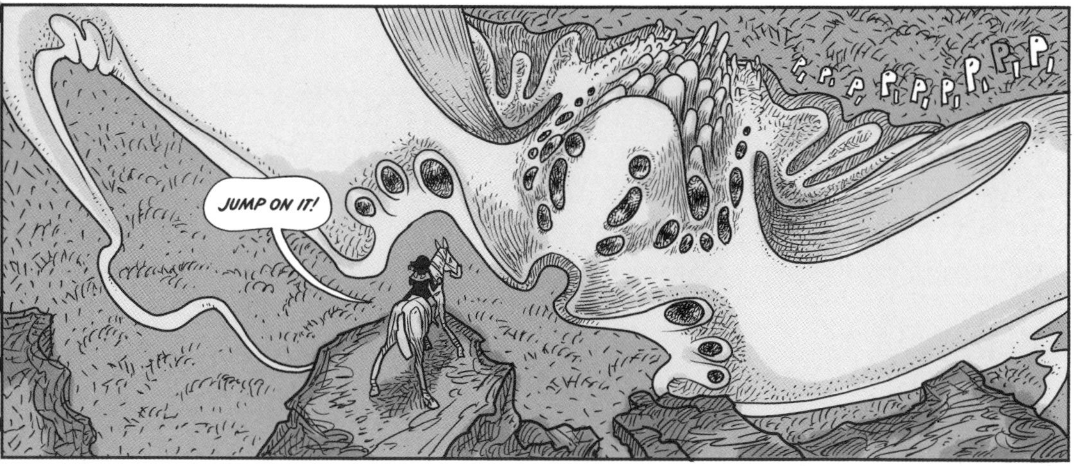
PI PI PI PI PI PI PI PI PI
JUMP ON IT!

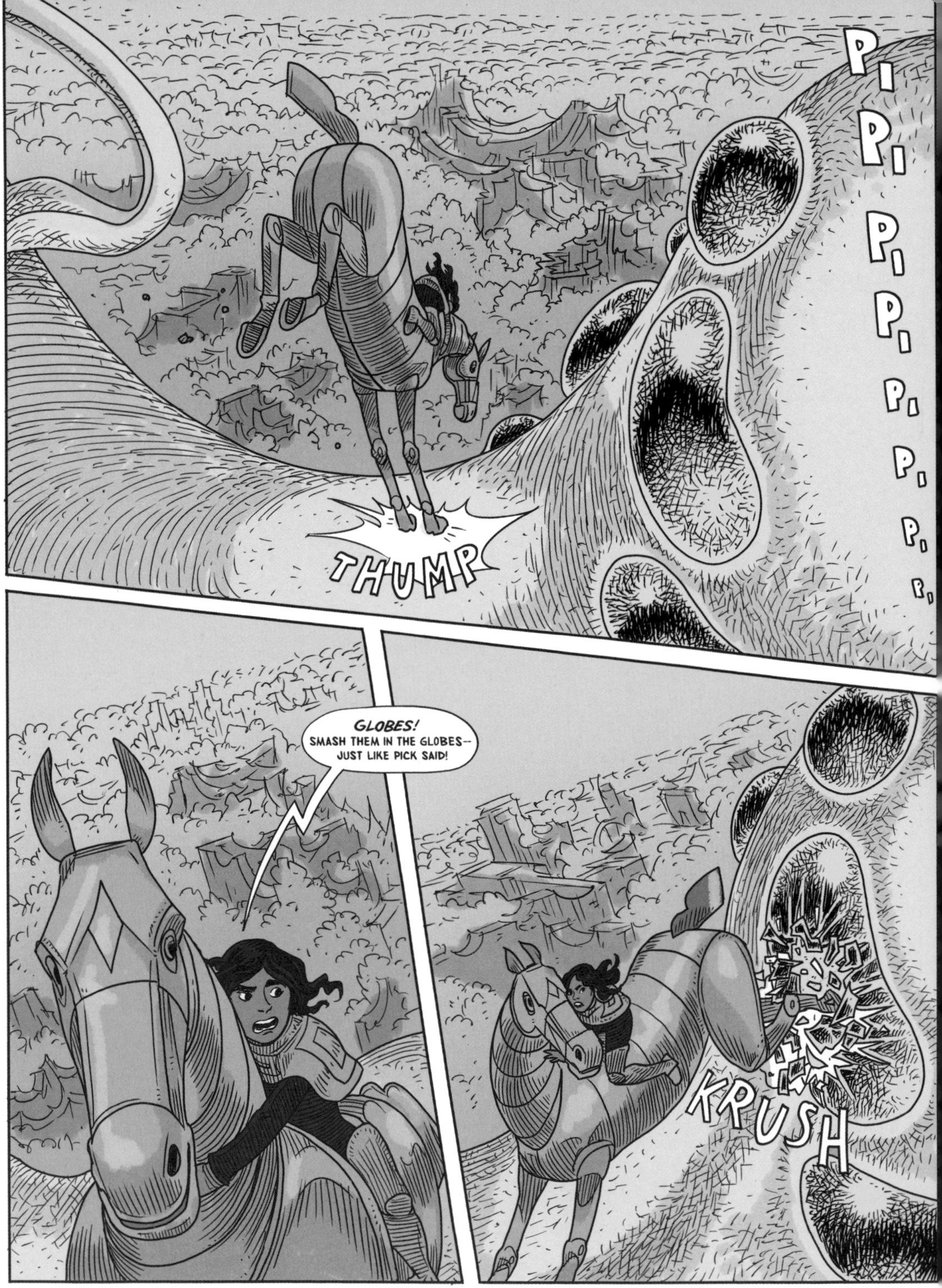
PI PI PI PI PI PI PI PI
THUMP
GLOBES!
SMASH THEM IN THE GLOBES--
JUST LIKE PICK SAID!
KRUSH

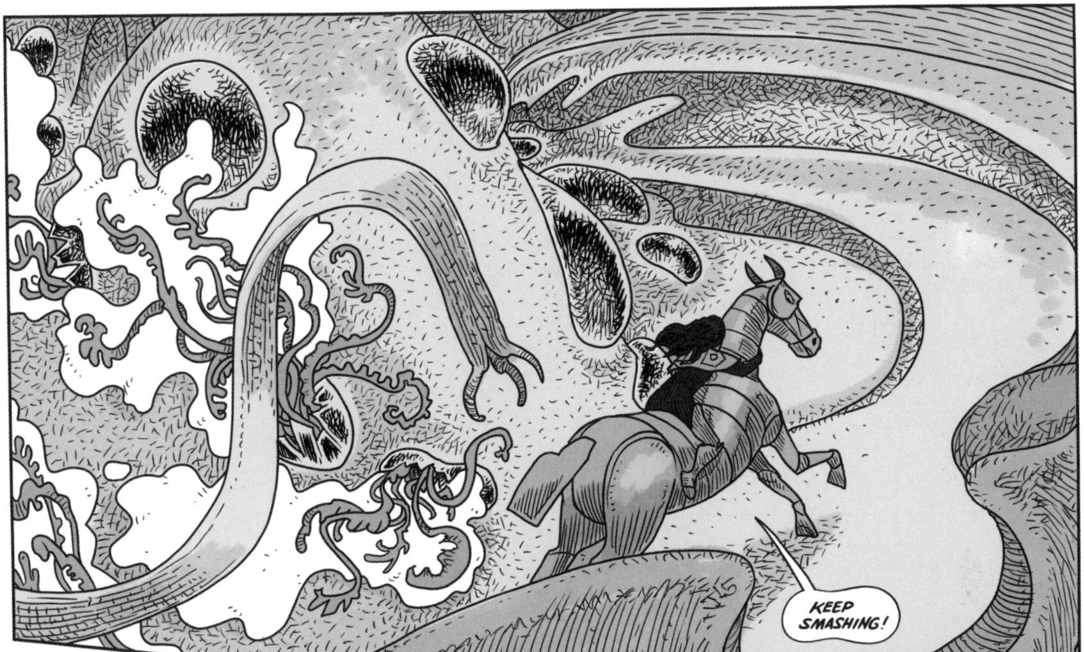
KEEP SMASHING!

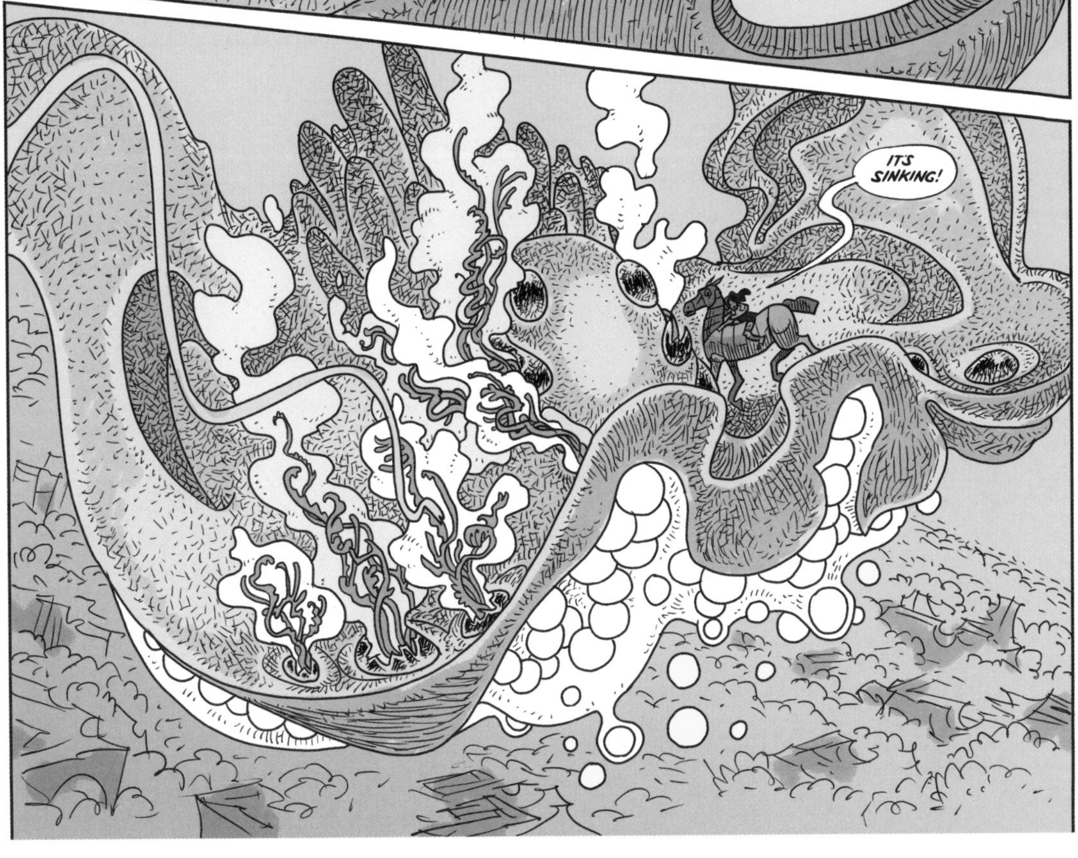
IT'S SINKING!

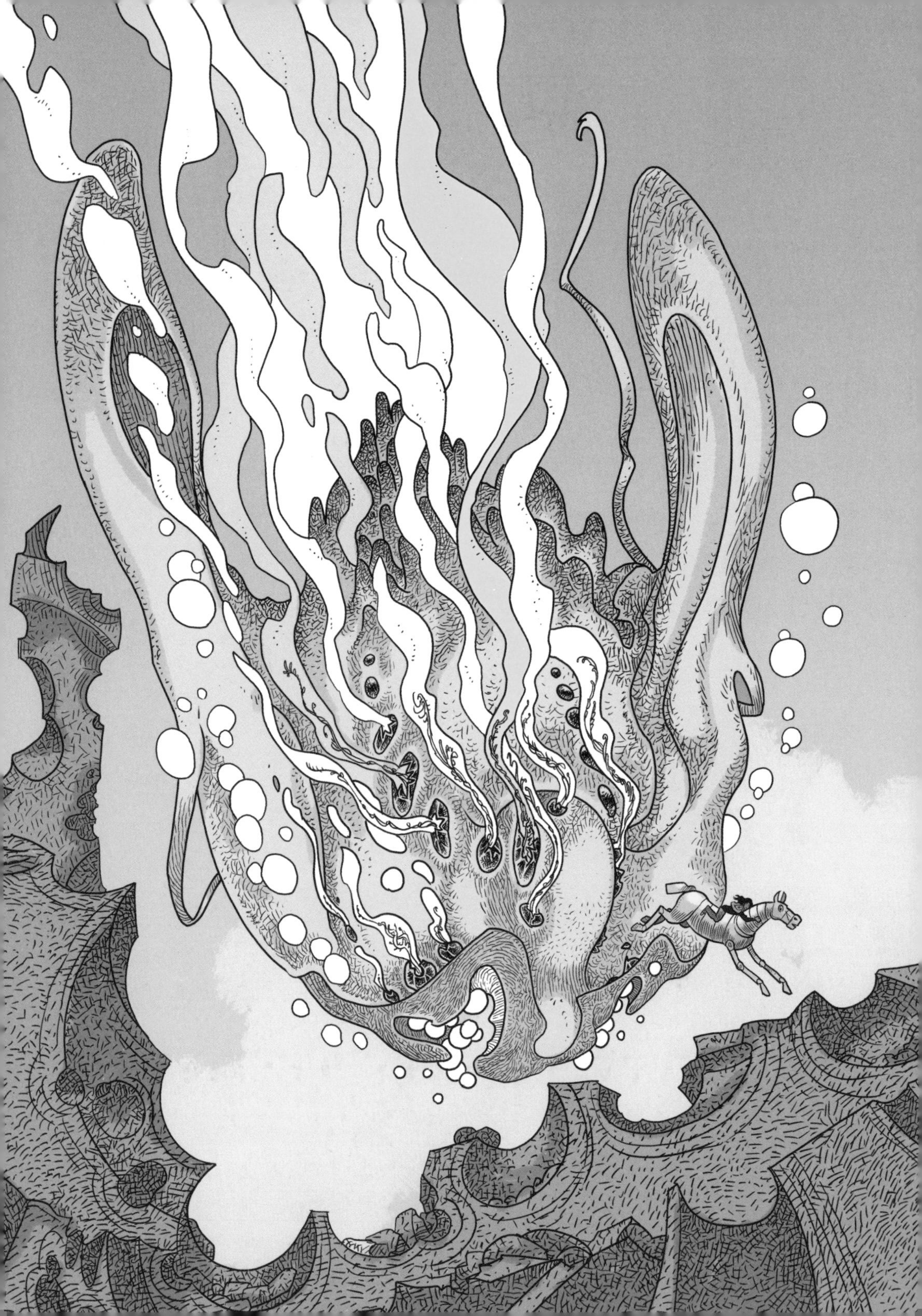

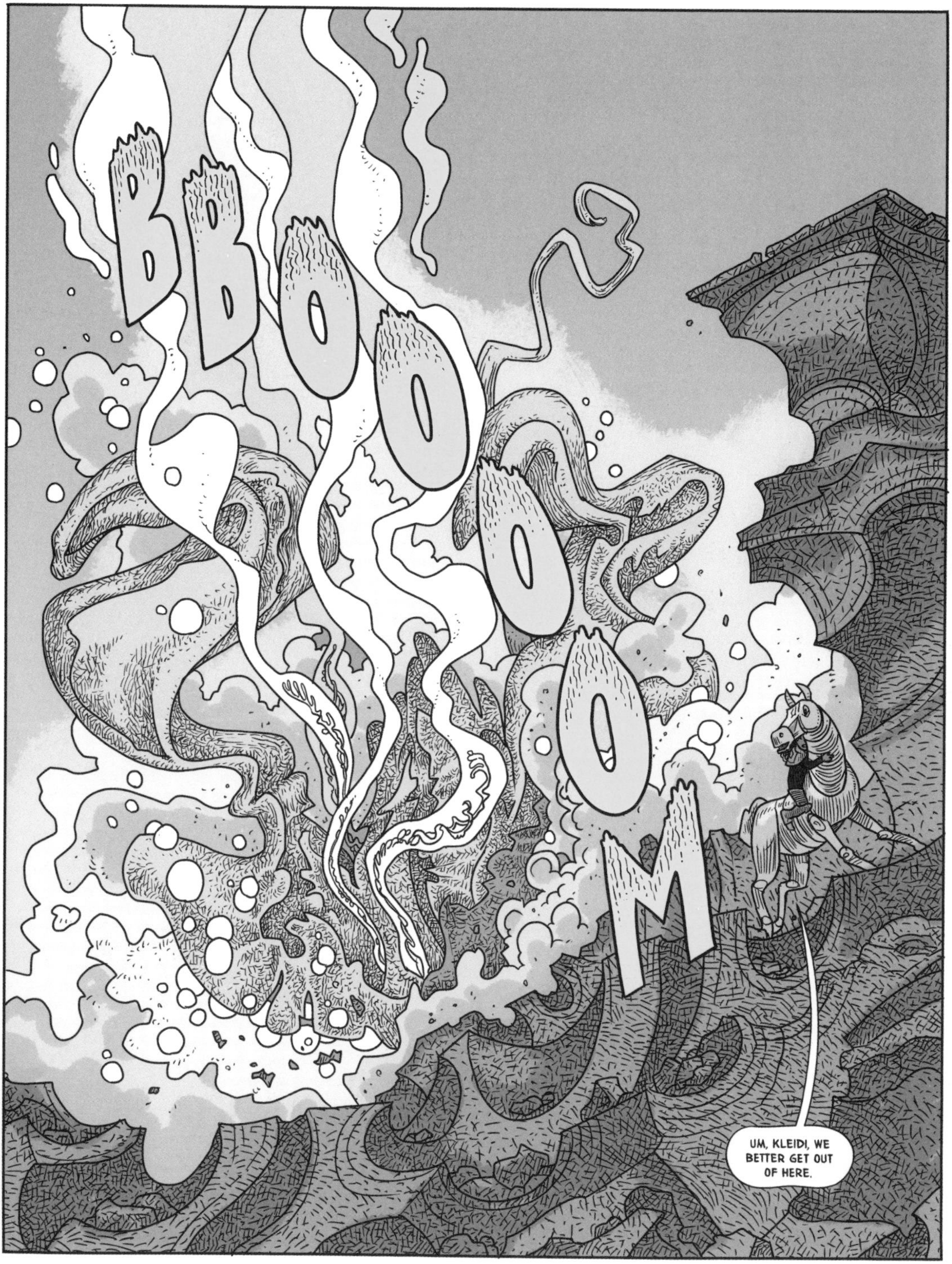
BBOOOOOM
UM, KLEIDI, WE BETTER GET OUT OF HERE.

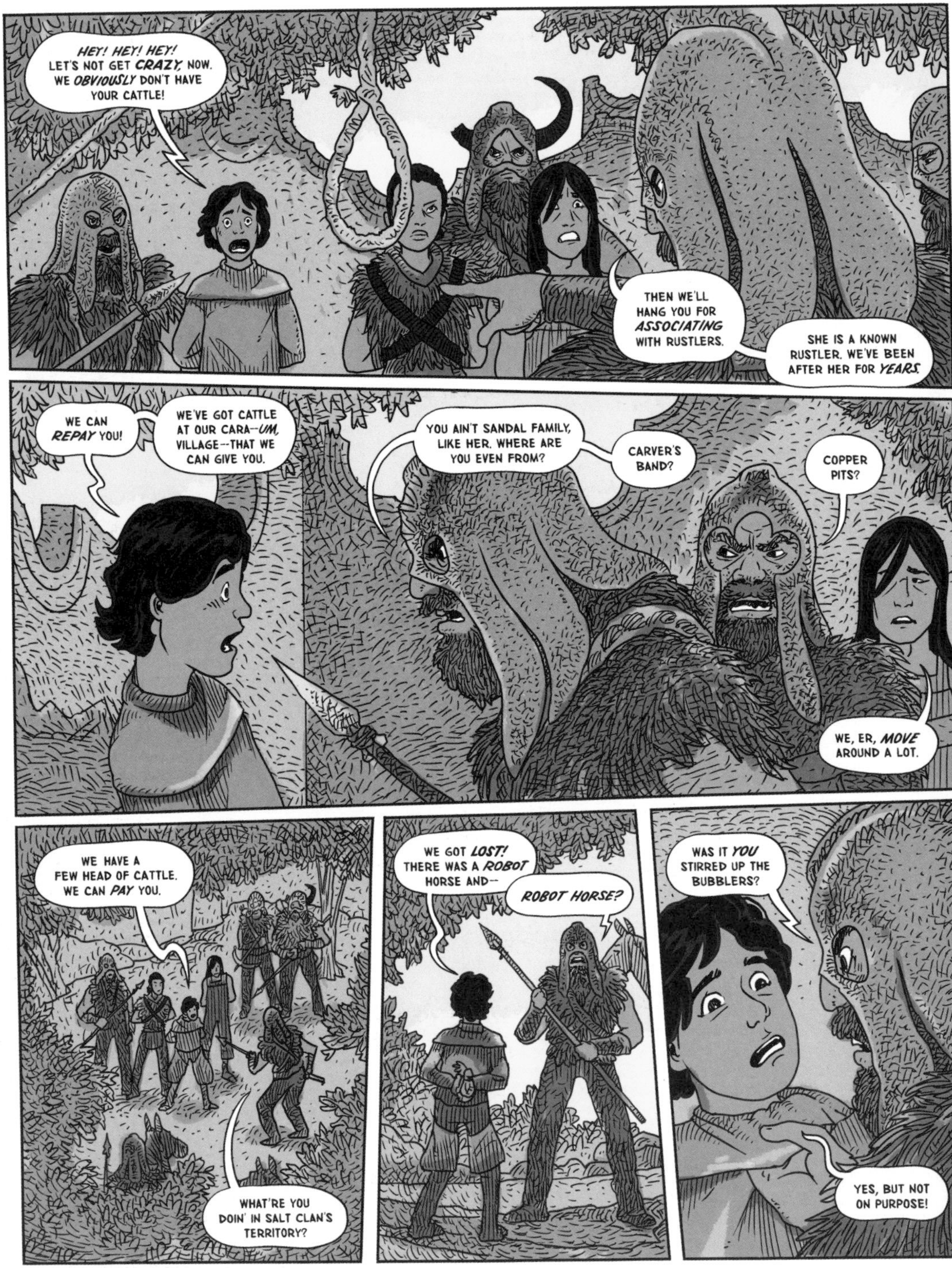
HEY! HEY! HEY! LET'S NOT GET CRAZY, NOW. WE OBVIOUSLY DON'T HAVE YOUR CATTLE!
THEN WE'LL HANG YOU FOR ASSOCIATING WITH RUSTLERS.
SHE IS A KNOWN RUSTLER. WE'VE BEEN AFTER HER FOR YEARS.
WE CAN REPAY YOU!
WE'VE GOT CATTLE AT OUR CARA--UM, VILLAGE--THAT WE CAN GIVE YOU.
YOU AIN'T SANDAL FAMILY, LIKE HER. WHERE ARE YOU EVEN FROM?
CARVER'S BAND?
COPPER PITS?
WE, ER, MOVE AROUND A LOT.
WE HAVE A FEW HEAD OF CATTLE. WE CAN PAY YOU.
WHAT'RE YOU DOIN' IN SALT CLAN'S TERRITORY?
WE GOT LOST! THERE WAS A ROBOT HORSE AND--
ROBOT HORSE?
WAS IT YOU STIRRED UP THE BUBBLERS?
YES, BUT NOT ON PURPOSE!

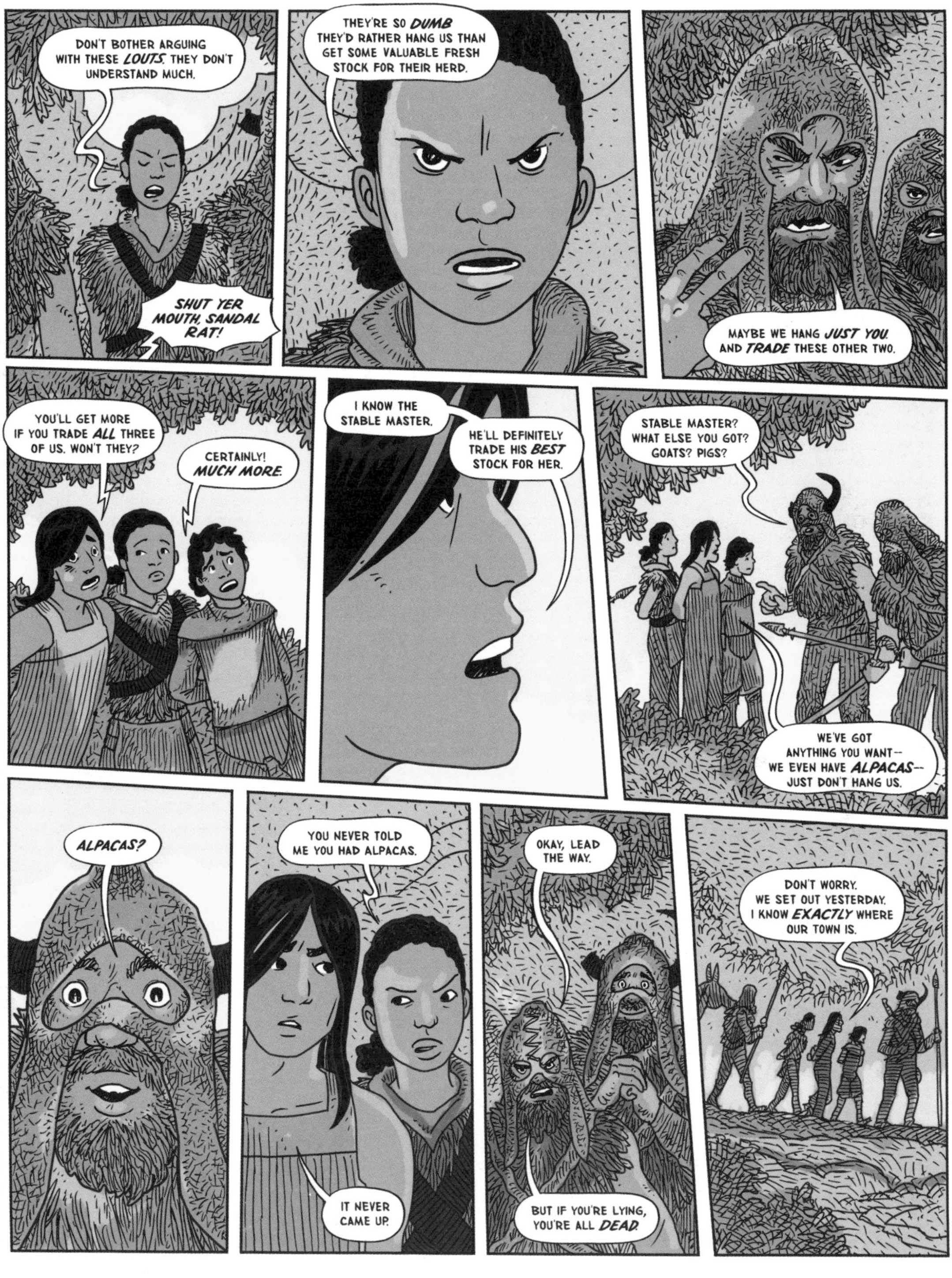
DON'T BOTHER ARGUING WITH THESE LOUTS. THEY DON'T UNDERSTAND MUCH.
SHUT YER MOUTH, SANDAL RAT!
THEY'RE SO DUMB THEY'D RATHER HANG US THAN GET SOME VALUABLE FRESH STOCK FOR THEIR HERD.
MAYBE WE HANG JUST YOU. AND TRADE THESE OTHER TWO.
YOU'LL GET MORE IF YOU TRADE ALL THREE OF US. WON'T THEY?
CERTAINLY! MUCH MORE.
I KNOW THE STABLE MASTER.
HE'LL DEFINITELY TRADE HIS BEST STOCK FOR HER.
STABLE MASTER? WHAT ELSE YOU GOT? GOATS? PIGS?
WE'VE GOT ANYTHING YOU WANT-- WE EVEN HAVE ALPACAS-- JUST DON'T HANG US.
ALPACAS?
YOU NEVER TOLD ME YOU HAD ALPACAS.
IT NEVER CAME UP.
OKAY, LEAD THE WAY.
BUT IF YOU'RE LYING, YOU'RE ALL DEAD.
DON'T WORRY. WE SET OUT YESTERDAY. I KNOW EXACTLY WHERE OUR TOWN IS.

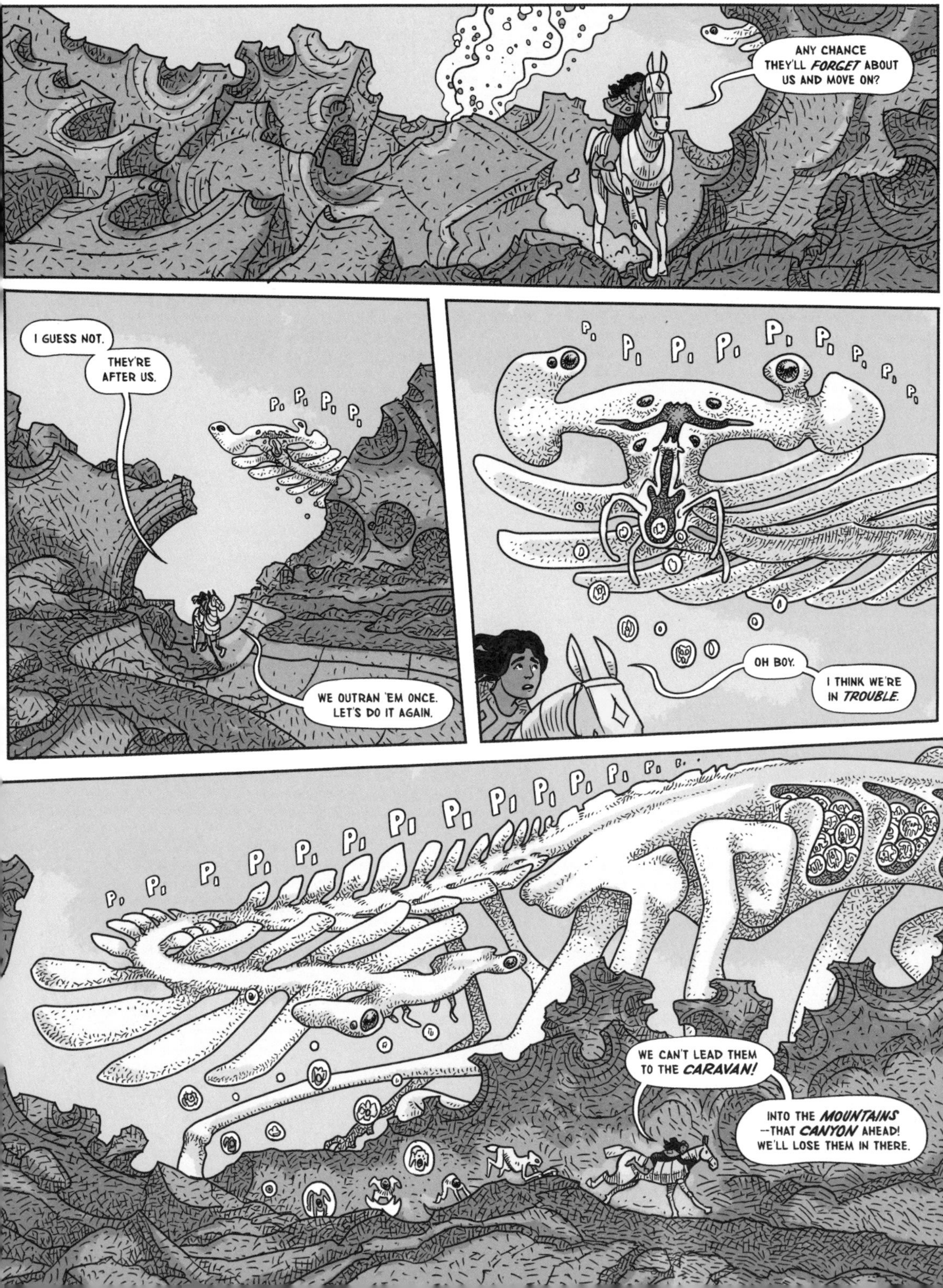
ANY CHANCE THEY'LL *FORGET* ABOUT US AND MOVE ON?
I GUESS NOT.
THEY'RE AFTER US.
P P P P
WE OUTRAN 'EM ONCE. LET'S DO IT AGAIN.
P P P P P P P P P P
OH BOY.
I THINK WE'RE IN *TROUBLE*.
P P P P P P P P P P P P P P P P P P . .
WE CAN'T LEAD THEM TO THE *CARAVAN!*
INTO THE *MOUNTAINS* --THAT *CANYON* AHEAD! WE'LL LOSE THEM IN THERE.

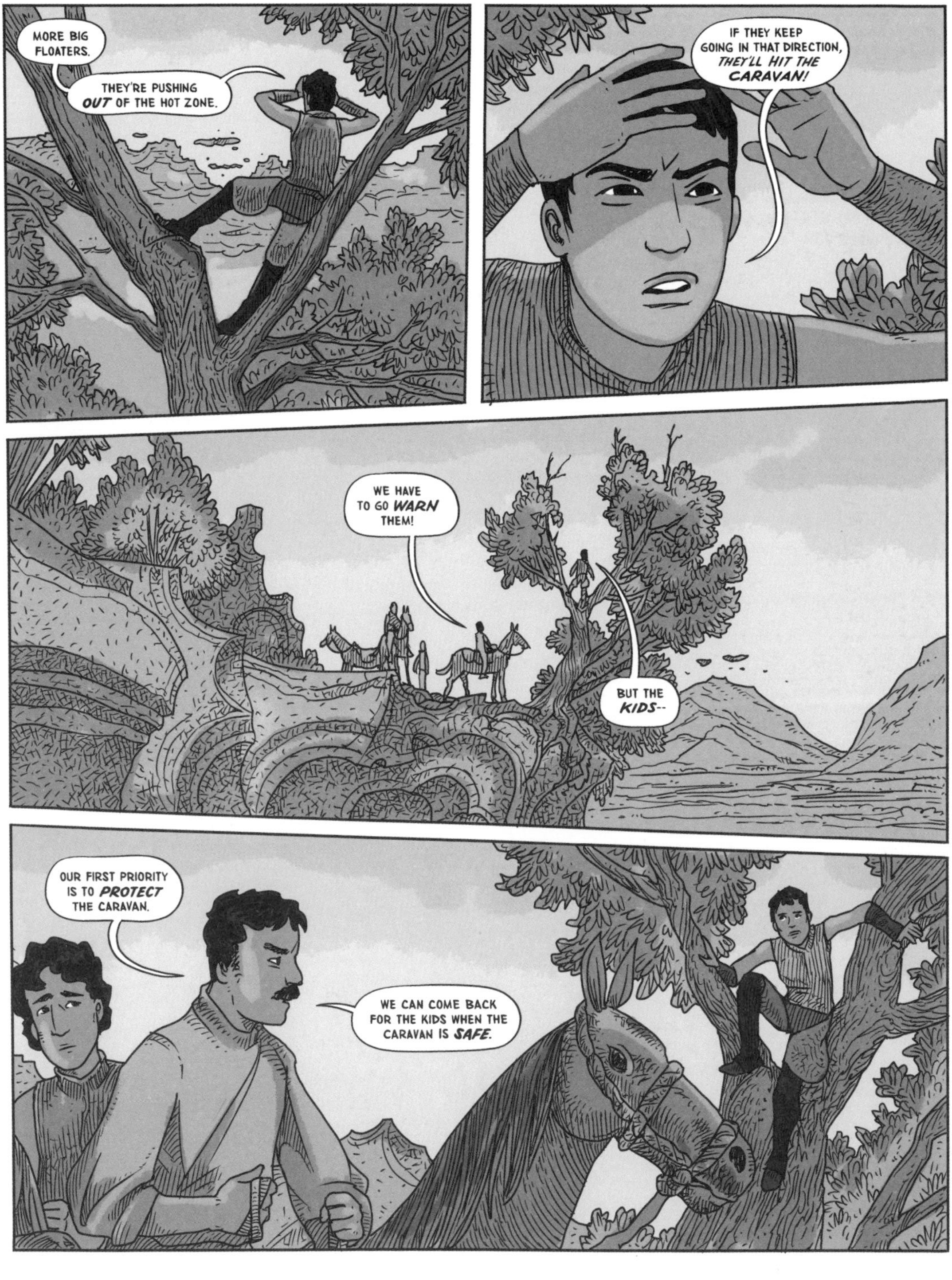

MORE BIG FLOATERS.
THEY'RE PUSHING *OUT* OF THE HOT ZONE.
IF THEY KEEP GOING IN THAT DIRECTION, *THEY'LL HIT THE CARAVAN!*
WE HAVE TO GO *WARN* THEM!
BUT THE *KIDS*--
OUR FIRST PRIORITY IS TO *PROTECT* THE CARAVAN.
WE CAN COME BACK FOR THE KIDS WHEN THE CARAVAN IS *SAFE*.

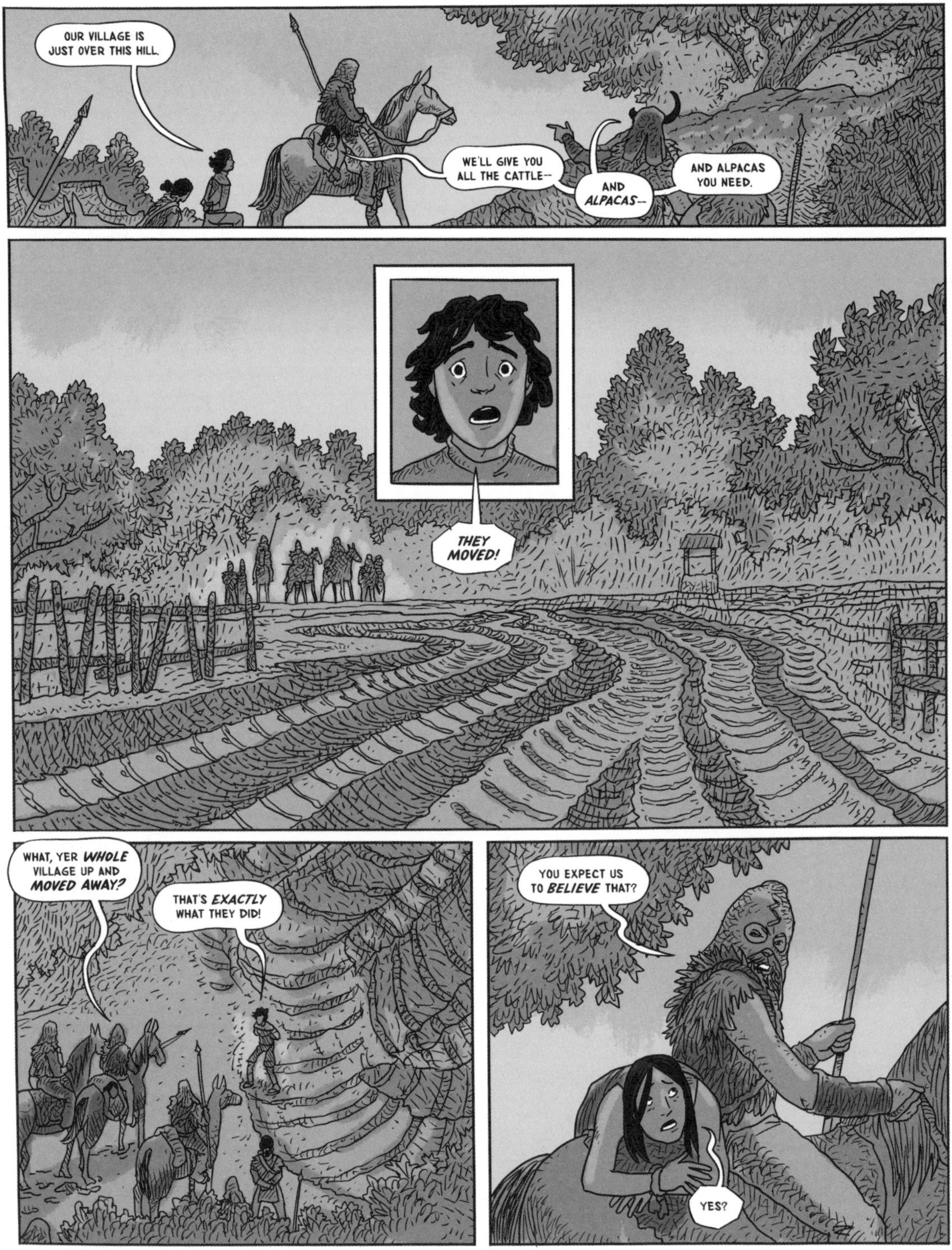
OUR VILLAGE IS JUST OVER THIS HILL.
WE'LL GIVE YOU ALL THE CATTLE--
AND *ALPACAS*--
AND ALPACAS YOU NEED.
THEY MOVED!
WHAT, YER ***WHOLE*** VILLAGE UP AND ***MOVED AWAY?***
THAT'S *EXACTLY* WHAT THEY DID!
YOU EXPECT US TO ***BELIEVE*** THAT?
YES?

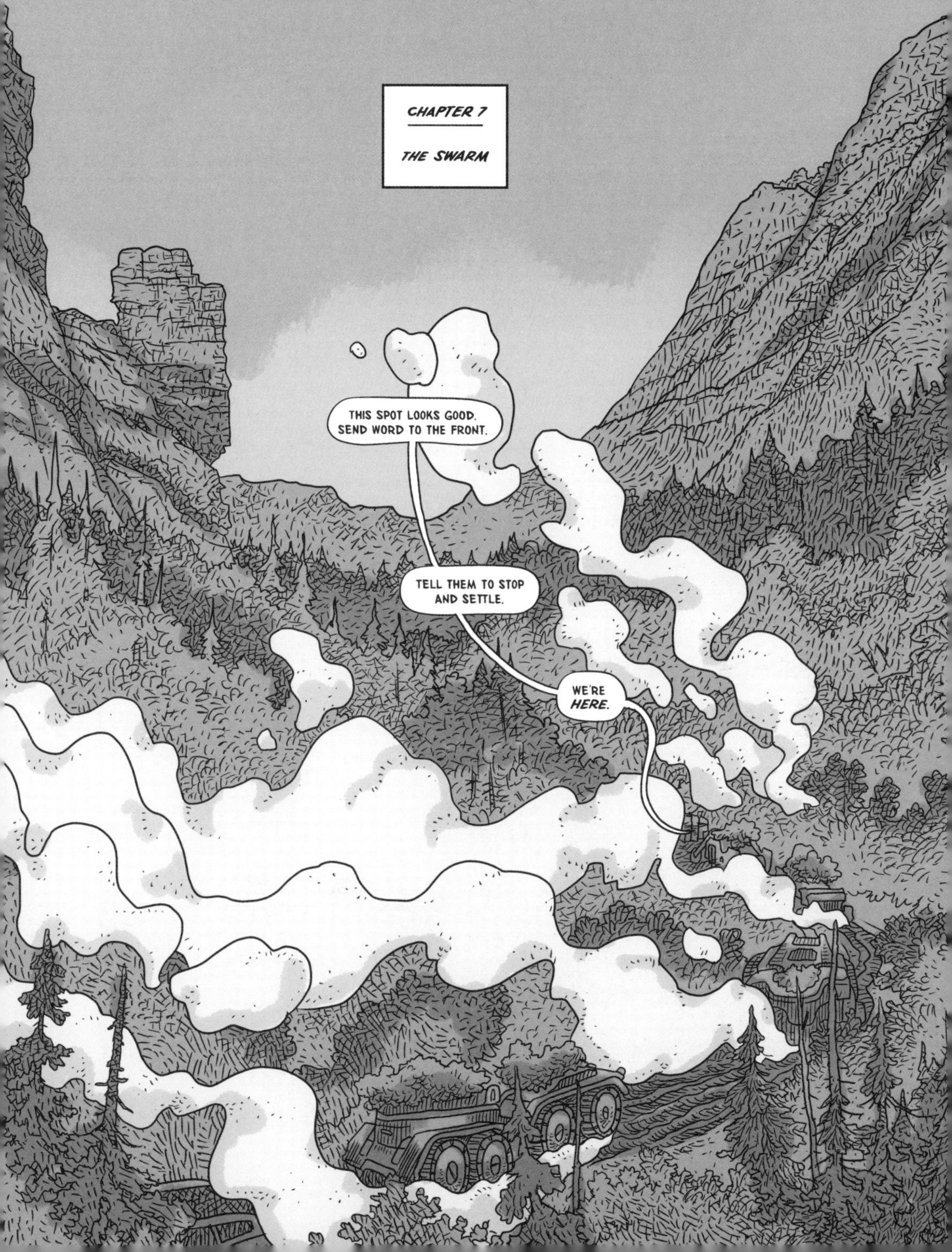
CHAPTER 7
THE SWARM
THIS SPOT LOOKS GOOD. SEND WORD TO THE FRONT.
TELL THEM TO STOP AND SETTLE.
WE'RE HERE.

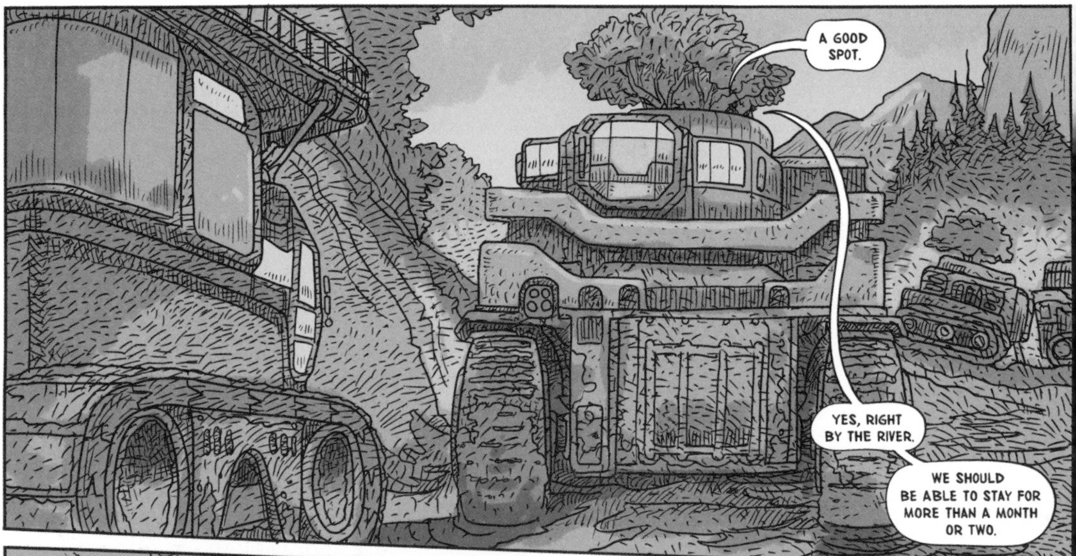
A GOOD SPOT.
YES, RIGHT BY THE RIVER.
WE SHOULD BE ABLE TO STAY FOR MORE THAN A MONTH OR TWO.

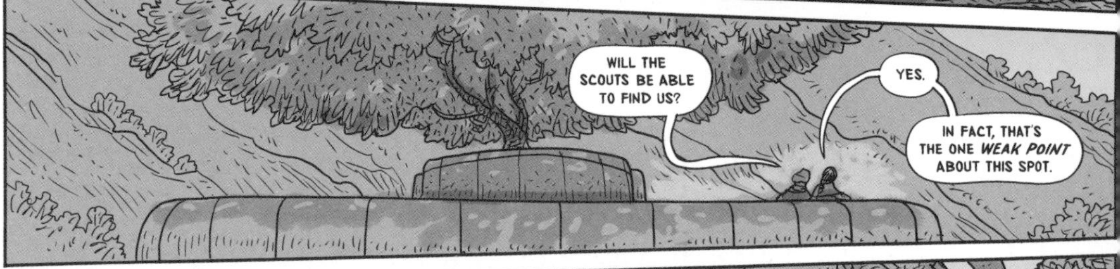
WILL THE SCOUTS BE ABLE TO FIND US?
YES.
IN FACT, THAT'S THE ONE *WEAK POINT* ABOUT THIS SPOT.

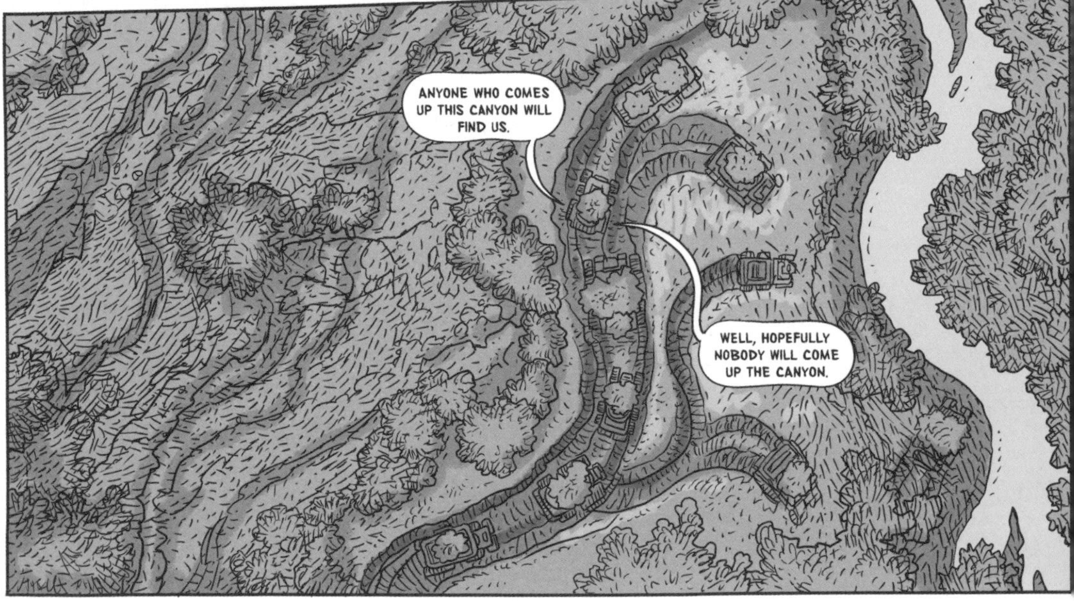
ANYONE WHO COMES UP THIS CANYON WILL FIND US.
WELL, HOPEFULLY NOBODY WILL COME UP THE CANYON.

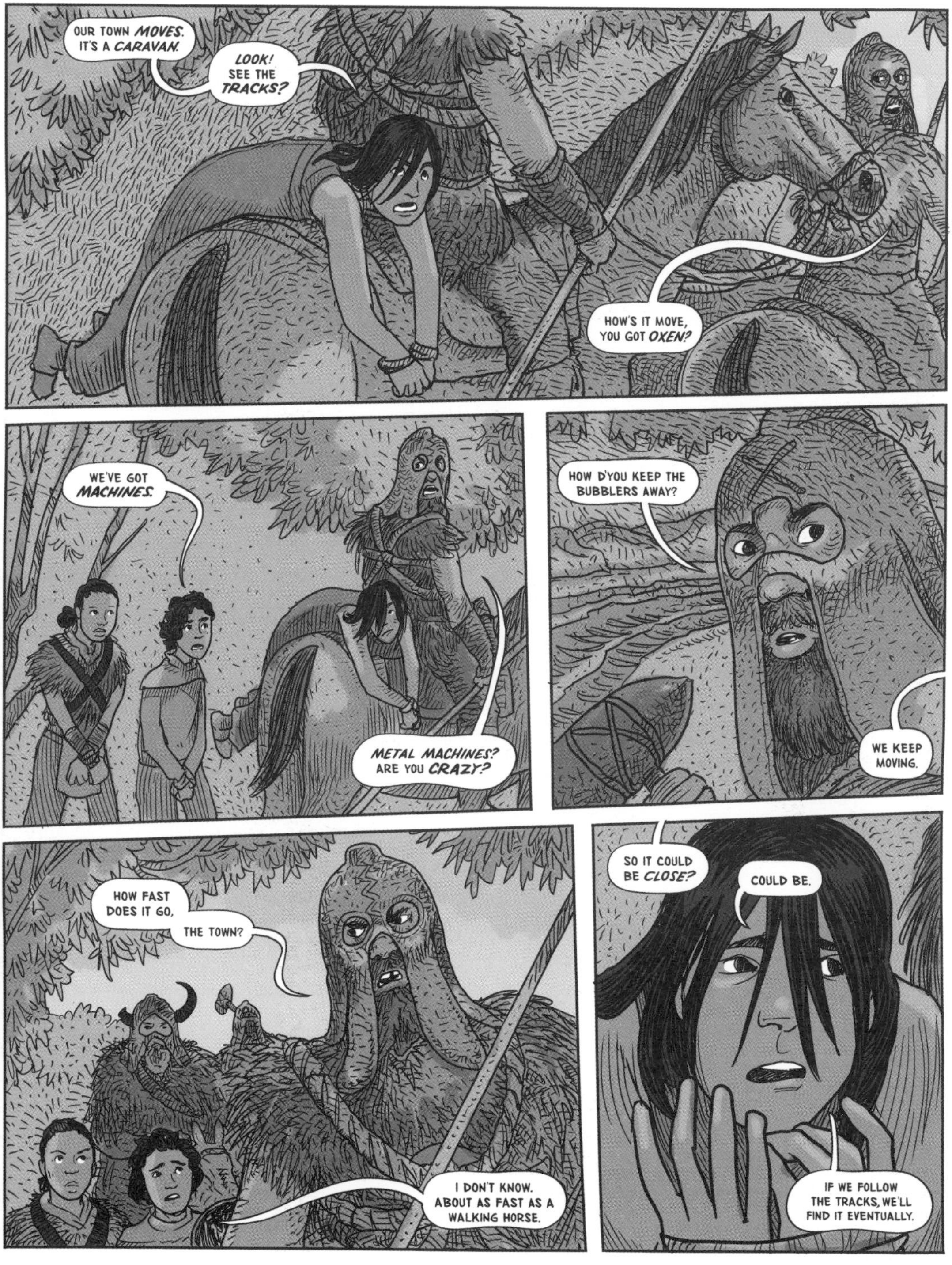
OUR TOWN MOVES. IT'S A CARAVAN.
LOOK! SEE THE TRACKS?
HOW'S IT MOVE, YOU GOT OXEN?
WE'VE GOT MACHINES.
METAL MACHINES? ARE YOU CRAZY?
HOW D'YOU KEEP THE BUBBLERS AWAY?
WE KEEP MOVING.
HOW FAST DOES IT GO,
THE TOWN?
I DON'T KNOW. ABOUT AS FAST AS A WALKING HORSE.
SO IT COULD BE CLOSE?
COULD BE.
IF WE FOLLOW THE TRACKS, WE'LL FIND IT EVENTUALLY.

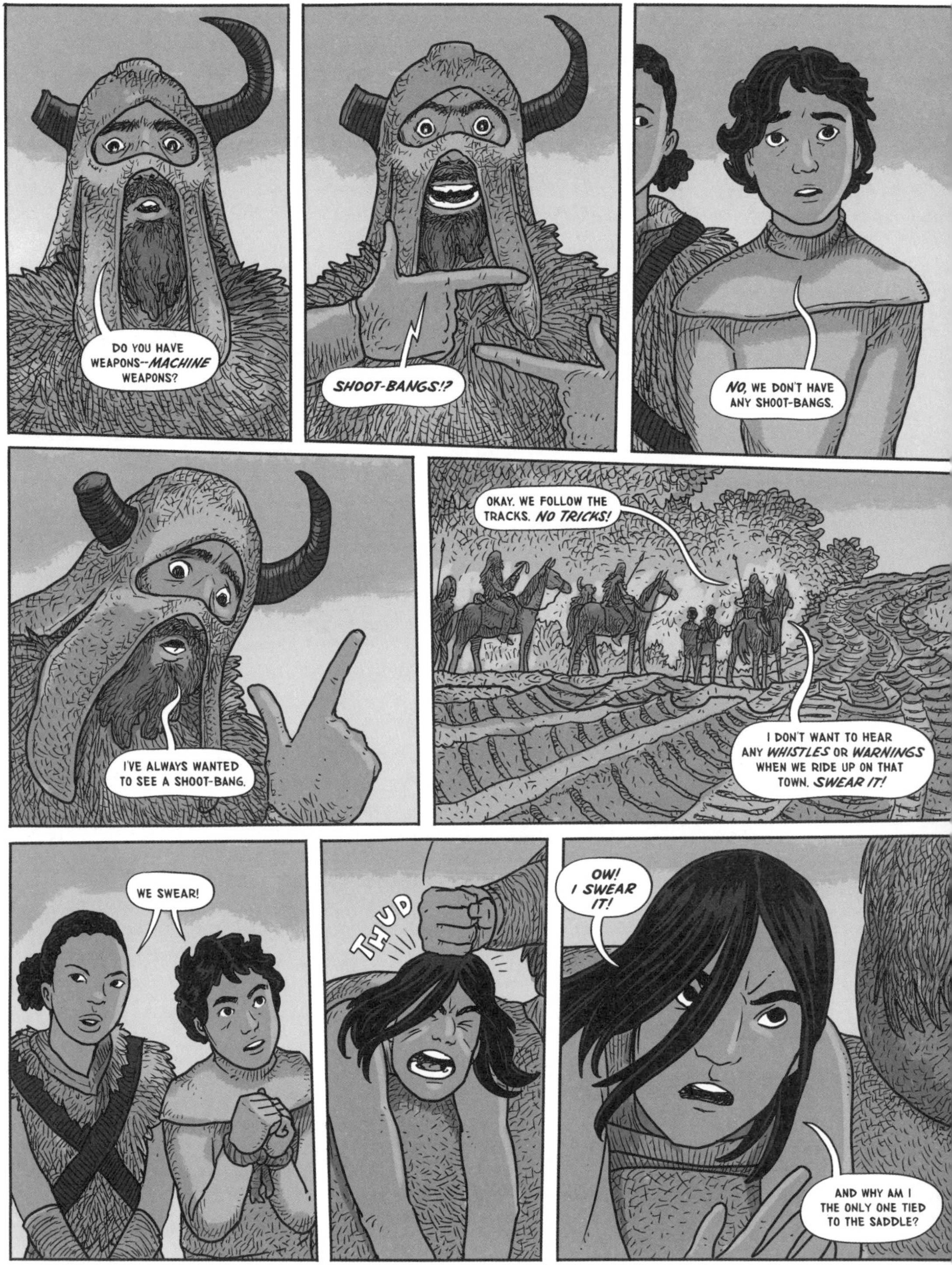
DO YOU HAVE WEAPONS--MACHINE WEAPONS?
SHOOT-BANGS!?
NO, WE DON'T HAVE ANY SHOOT-BANGS.
I'VE ALWAYS WANTED TO SEE A SHOOT-BANG.
OKAY. WE FOLLOW THE TRACKS. NO TRICKS!
I DON'T WANT TO HEAR ANY WHISTLES OR WARNINGS WHEN WE RIDE UP ON THAT TOWN. SWEAR IT!
WE SWEAR!
THUD
OW! I SWEAR IT!
AND WHY AM I THE ONLY ONE TIED TO THE SADDLE?

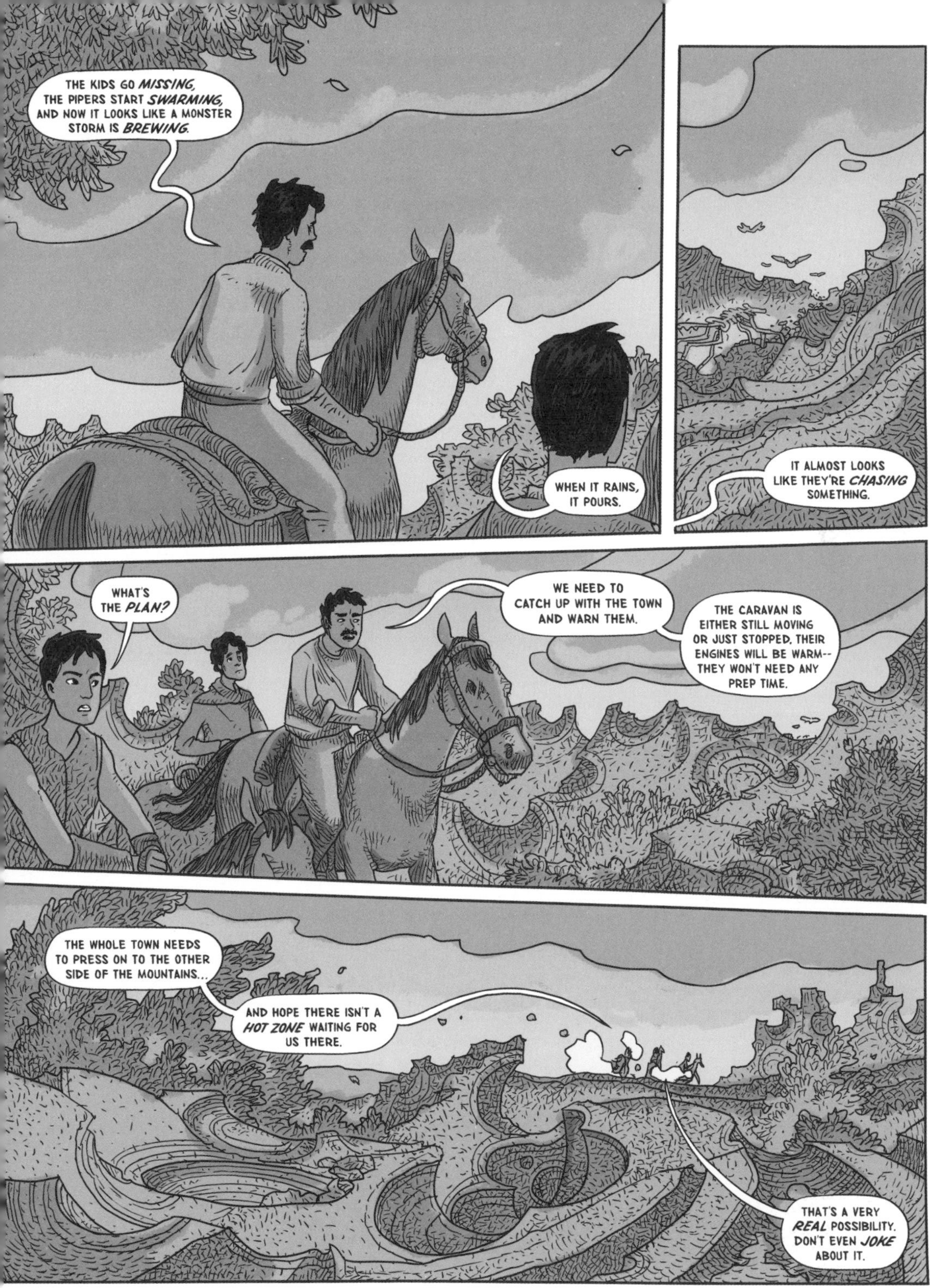
THE KIDS GO MISSING, THE PIPERS START SWARMING, AND NOW IT LOOKS LIKE A MONSTER STORM IS BREWING.
WHEN IT RAINS, IT POURS.
IT ALMOST LOOKS LIKE THEY'RE CHASING SOMETHING.
WHAT'S THE PLAN?
WE NEED TO CATCH UP WITH THE TOWN AND WARN THEM.
THE CARAVAN IS EITHER STILL MOVING OR JUST STOPPED. THEIR ENGINES WILL BE WARM-- THEY WON'T NEED ANY PREP TIME.
THE WHOLE TOWN NEEDS TO PRESS ON TO THE OTHER SIDE OF THE MOUNTAINS...
AND HOPE THERE ISN'T A HOT ZONE WAITING FOR US THERE.
THAT'S A VERY REAL POSSIBILITY. DON'T EVEN JOKE ABOUT IT.

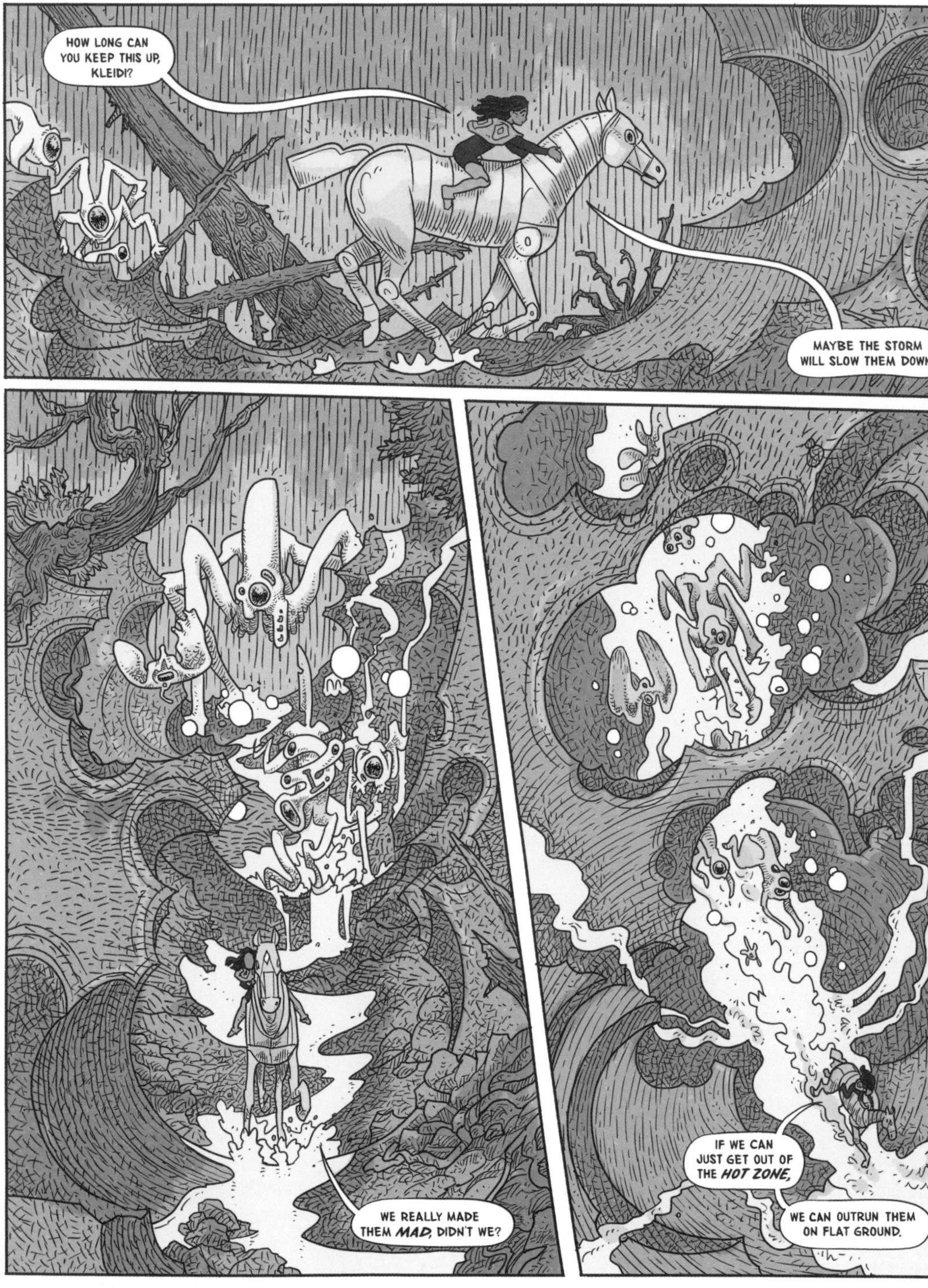
HOW LONG CAN YOU KEEP THIS UP, KLEIDI?
MAYBE THE STORM WILL SLOW THEM DOWN.
WE REALLY MADE THEM MAD, DIDN'T WE?
IF WE CAN JUST GET OUT OF THE HOT ZONE,
WE CAN OUTRUN THEM ON FLAT GROUND.

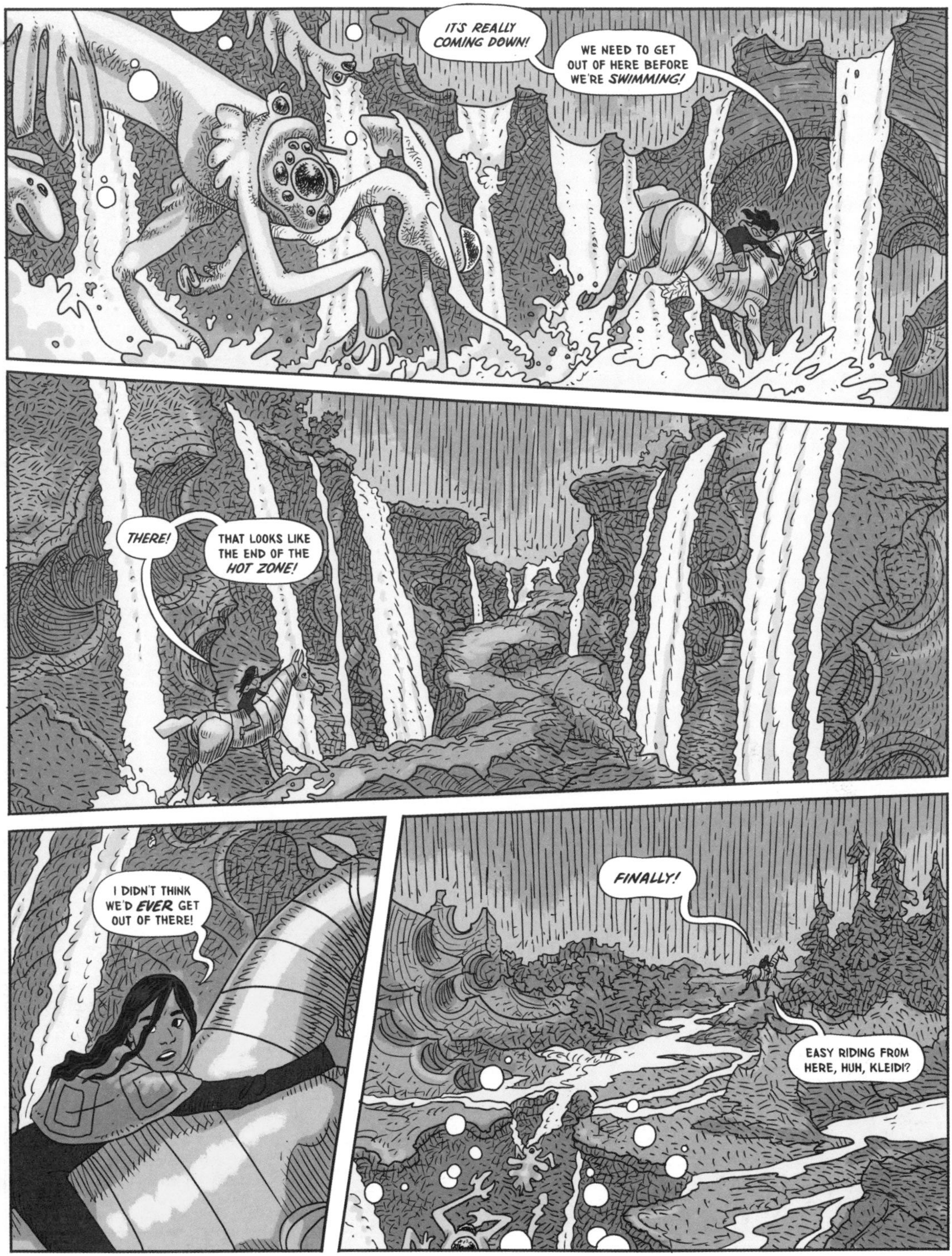
IT'S REALLY COMING DOWN!
WE NEED TO GET OUT OF HERE BEFORE WE'RE SWIMMING!
THERE!
THAT LOOKS LIKE THE END OF THE HOT ZONE!
I DIDN'T THINK WE'D EVER GET OUT OF THERE!
FINALLY!
EASY RIDING FROM HERE, HUH, KLEIDI?

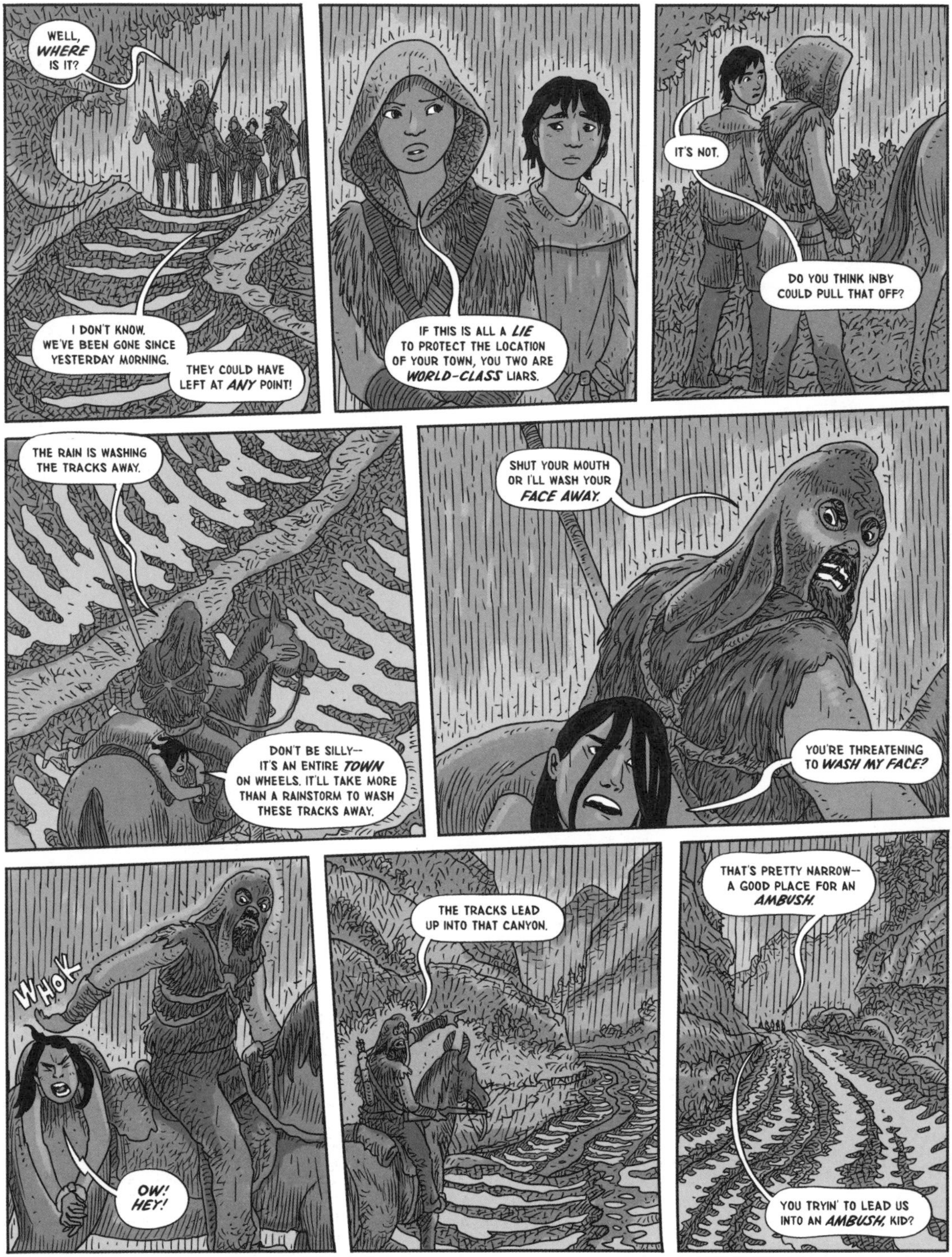
WELL, WHERE IS IT?
I DON'T KNOW. WE'VE BEEN GONE SINCE YESTERDAY MORNING.
THEY COULD HAVE LEFT AT ANY POINT!
IF THIS IS ALL A LIE TO PROTECT THE LOCATION OF YOUR TOWN, YOU TWO ARE WORLD-CLASS LIARS.
IT'S NOT.
DO YOU THINK INBY COULD PULL THAT OFF?
THE RAIN IS WASHING THE TRACKS AWAY.
DON'T BE SILLY-- IT'S AN ENTIRE TOWN ON WHEELS. IT'LL TAKE MORE THAN A RAINSTORM TO WASH THESE TRACKS AWAY.
SHUT YOUR MOUTH OR I'LL WASH YOUR FACE AWAY.
YOU'RE THREATENING TO WASH MY FACE?
WHOK
OW! HEY!
THE TRACKS LEAD UP INTO THAT CANYON.
THAT'S PRETTY NARROW-- A GOOD PLACE FOR AN AMBUSH.
YOU TRYIN' TO LEAD US INTO AN AMBUSH, KID?

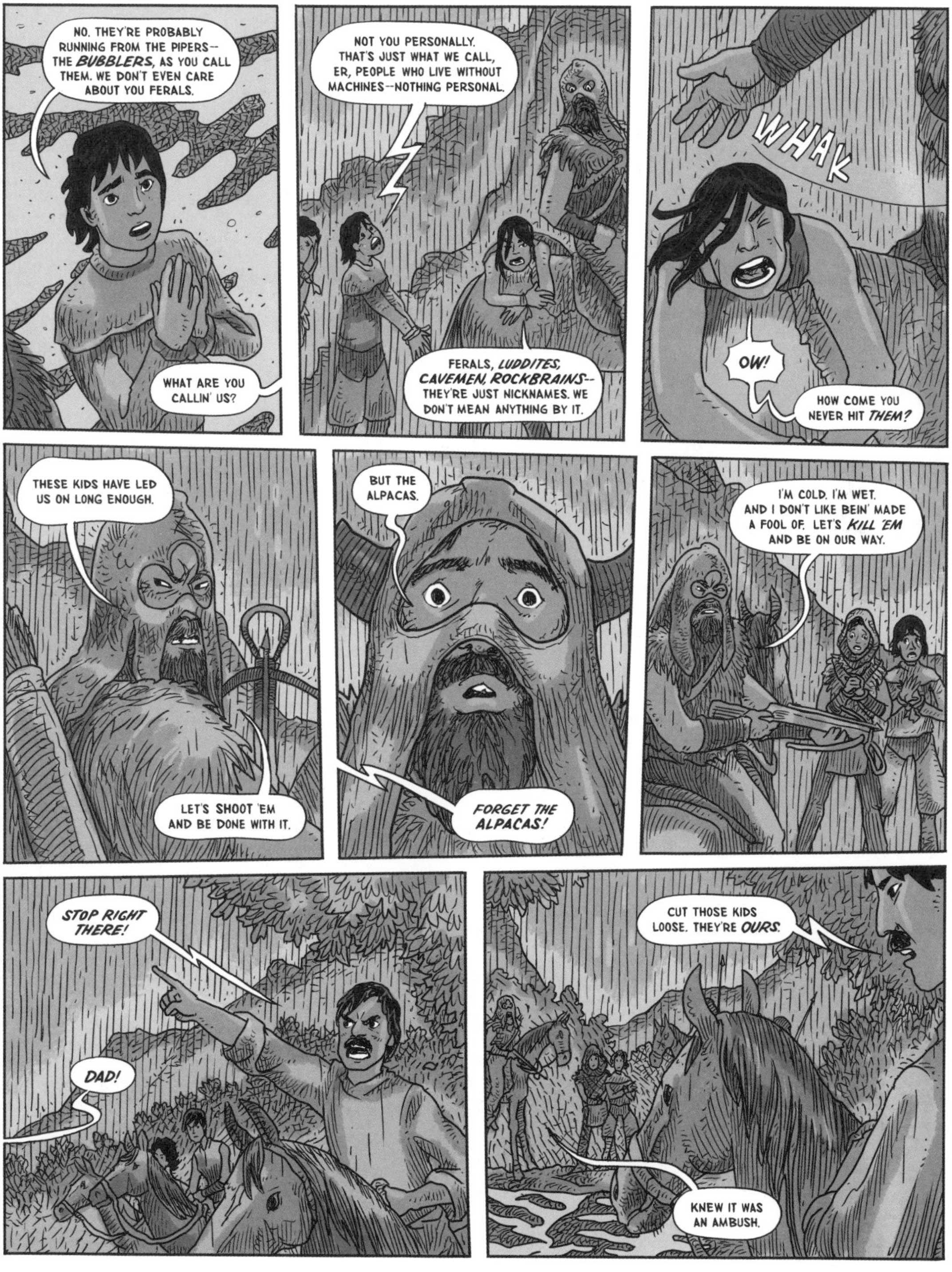
NO. THEY'RE PROBABLY RUNNING FROM THE PIPERS-- THE *BUBBLERS*, AS YOU CALL THEM. WE DON'T EVEN CARE ABOUT YOU FERALS.
WHAT ARE YOU CALLIN' US?
NOT YOU PERSONALLY. THAT'S JUST WHAT WE CALL, ER, PEOPLE WHO LIVE WITHOUT MACHINES--NOTHING PERSONAL.
FERALS, *LUDDITES*, *CAVEMEN*, *ROCKBRAINS*-- THEY'RE JUST NICKNAMES. WE DON'T MEAN ANYTHING BY IT.
WHAK
OW!
HOW COME YOU NEVER HIT *THEM?*
THESE KIDS HAVE LED US ON LONG ENOUGH.
LET'S SHOOT 'EM AND BE DONE WITH IT.
BUT THE ALPACAS.
FORGET THE ALPACAS!
I'M COLD. I'M WET. AND I DON'T LIKE BEIN' MADE A FOOL OF. LET'S *KILL 'EM* AND BE ON OUR WAY.
STOP RIGHT THERE!
DAD!
CUT THOSE KIDS LOOSE. THEY'RE *OURS*.
KNEW IT WAS AN AMBUSH.

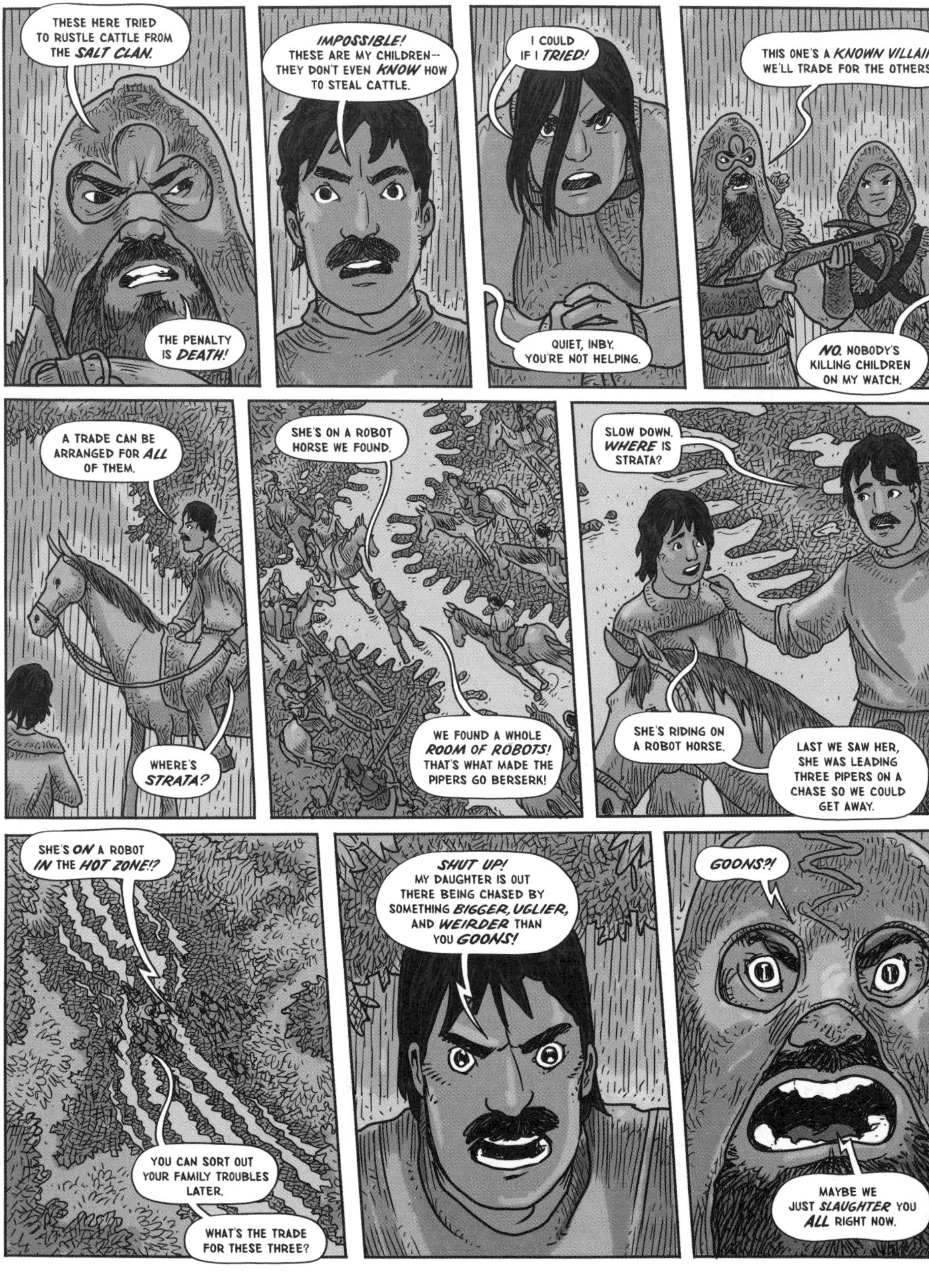
THESE HERE TRIED TO RUSTLE CATTLE FROM THE SALT CLAN.
THE PENALTY IS DEATH!
IMPOSSIBLE! THESE ARE MY CHILDREN-- THEY DON'T EVEN KNOW HOW TO STEAL CATTLE.
I COULD IF I TRIED!
QUIET, INBY. YOU'RE NOT HELPING.
THIS ONE'S A KNOWN VILLAIN. WE'LL TRADE FOR THE OTHERS.
NO. NOBODY'S KILLING CHILDREN ON MY WATCH.
A TRADE CAN BE ARRANGED FOR ALL OF THEM.
WHERE'S STRATA?
SHE'S ON A ROBOT HORSE WE FOUND.
WE FOUND A WHOLE ROOM OF ROBOTS! THAT'S WHAT MADE THE PIPERS GO BERSERK!
SLOW DOWN. WHERE IS STRATA?
SHE'S RIDING ON A ROBOT HORSE.
LAST WE SAW HER, SHE WAS LEADING THREE PIPERS ON A CHASE SO WE COULD GET AWAY.
SHE'S ON A ROBOT IN THE HOT ZONE!?
YOU CAN SORT OUT YOUR FAMILY TROUBLES LATER.
WHAT'S THE TRADE FOR THESE THREE?
SHUT UP! MY DAUGHTER IS OUT THERE BEING CHASED BY SOMETHING BIGGER, UGLIER, AND WEIRDER THAN YOU GOONS!
GOONS?!
MAYBE WE JUST SLAUGHTER YOU ALL RIGHT NOW.

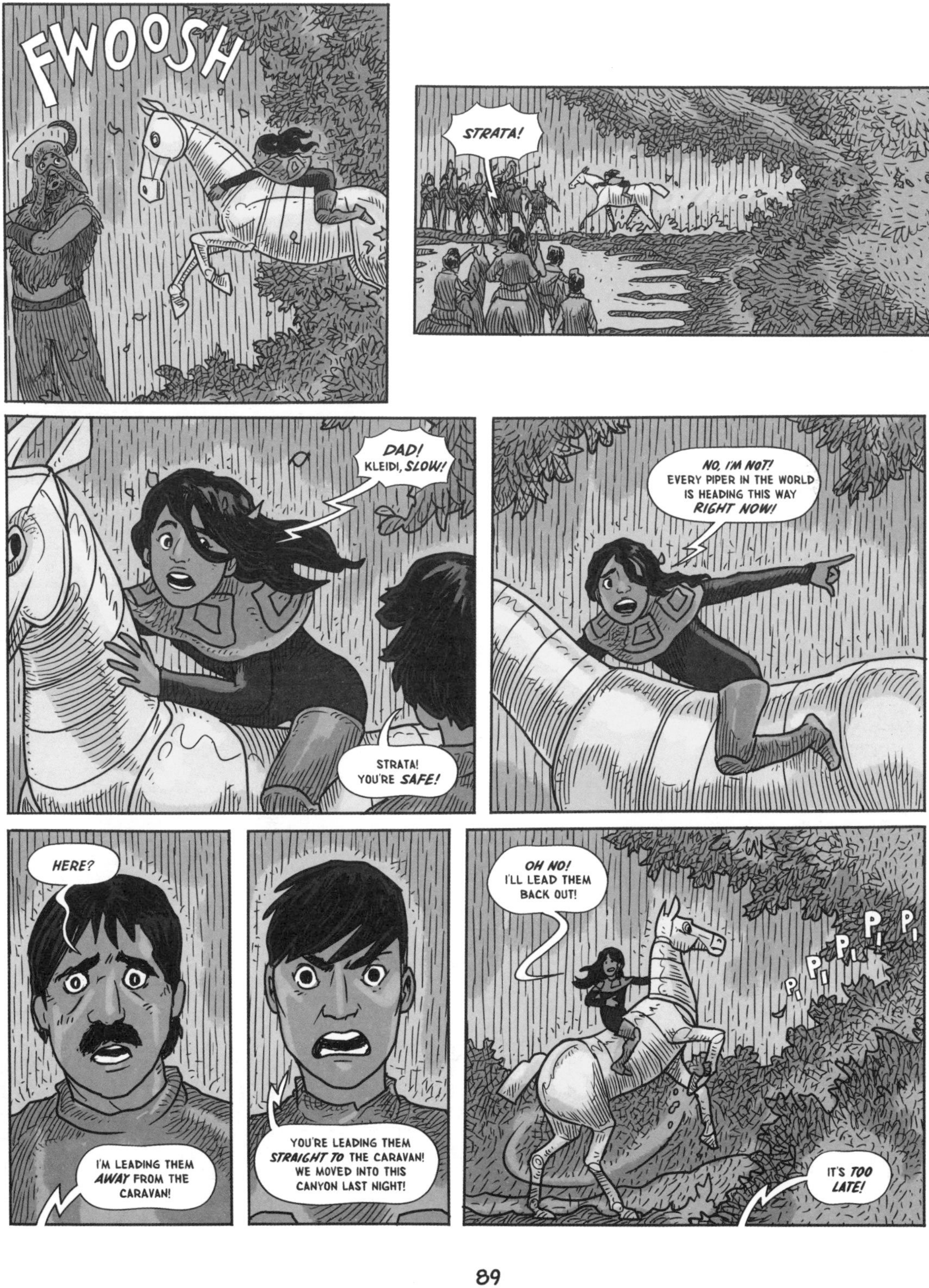
FWOOSH
STRATA!
DAD!
KLEIDI, SLOW!
STRATA!
YOU'RE SAFE!
NO, I'M NOT!
EVERY PIPER IN THE WORLD
IS HEADING THIS WAY
RIGHT NOW!
HERE?
I'M LEADING THEM
AWAY FROM THE
CARAVAN!
YOU'RE LEADING THEM
STRAIGHT TO THE CARAVAN!
WE MOVED INTO THIS
CANYON LAST NIGHT!
OH NO!
I'LL LEAD THEM
BACK OUT!
PI PI PI PI PI PI PI
IT'S TOO
LATE!

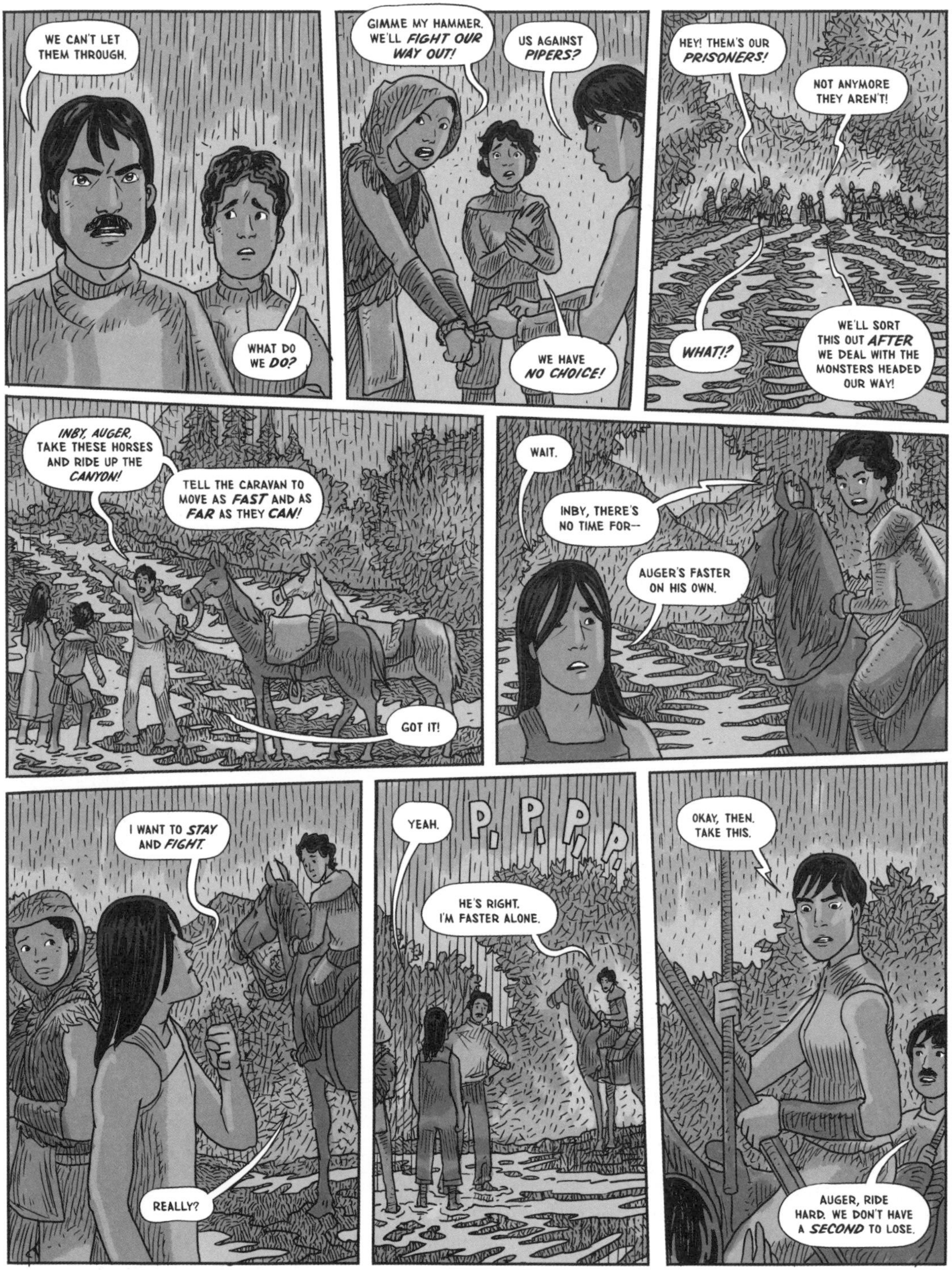
WE CAN'T LET THEM THROUGH.
WHAT DO WE DO?
GIMME MY HAMMER. WE'LL FIGHT OUR WAY OUT!
US AGAINST PIPERS?
WE HAVE NO CHOICE!
HEY! THEM'S OUR PRISONERS!
NOT ANYMORE THEY AREN'T!
WHAT!?
WE'LL SORT THIS OUT AFTER WE DEAL WITH THE MONSTERS HEADED OUR WAY!
INBY, AUGER, TAKE THESE HORSES AND RIDE UP THE CANYON!
TELL THE CARAVAN TO MOVE AS FAST AND AS FAR AS THEY CAN!
GOT IT!
WAIT.
INBY, THERE'S NO TIME FOR--
AUGER'S FASTER ON HIS OWN.
I WANT TO STAY AND FIGHT.
REALLY?
YEAH.
P P P P
HE'S RIGHT. I'M FASTER ALONE.
OKAY, THEN. TAKE THIS.
AUGER, RIDE HARD. WE DON'T HAVE A SECOND TO LOSE.

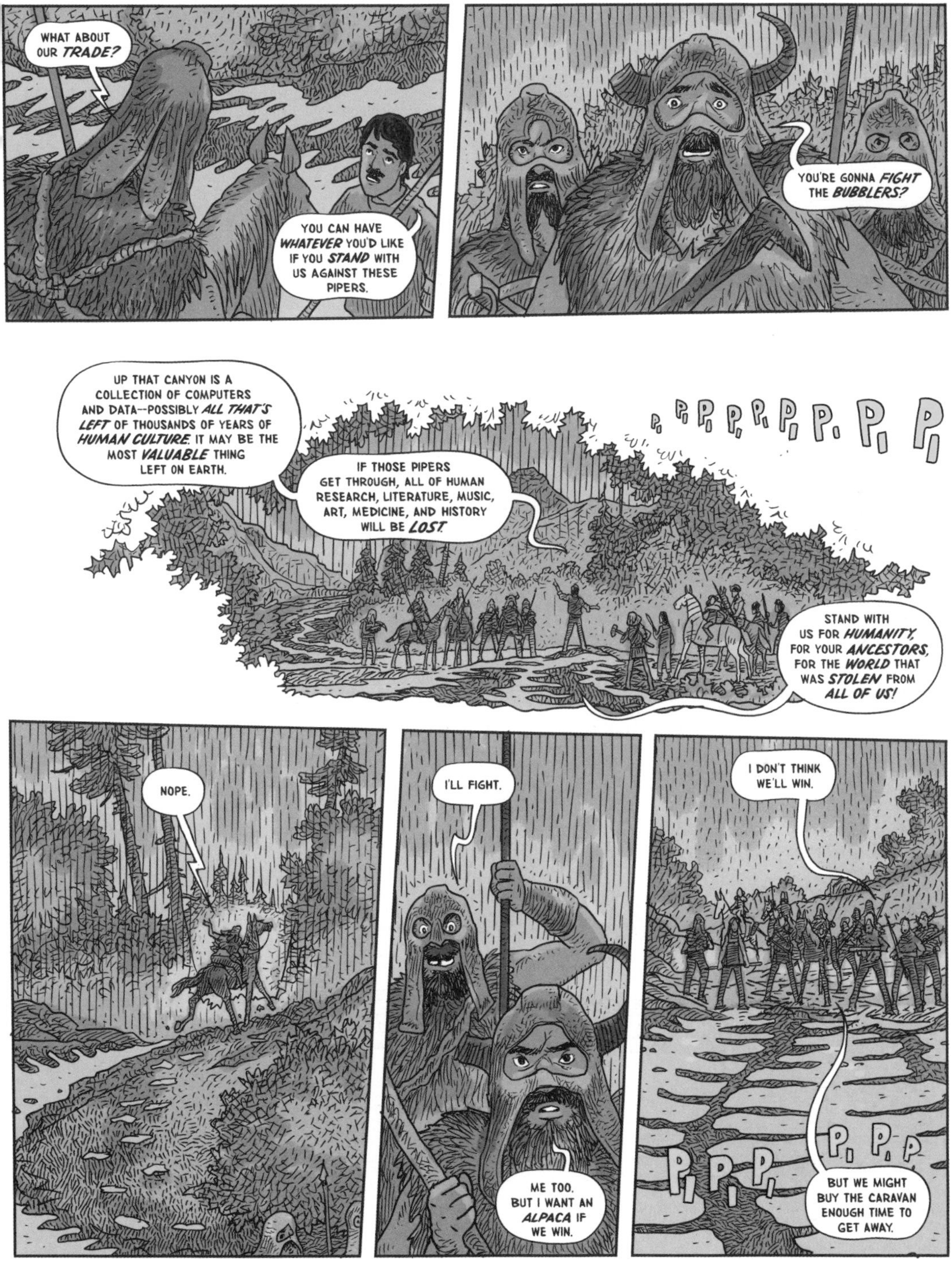

WHAT ABOUT OUR TRADE?
YOU CAN HAVE WHATEVER YOU'D LIKE IF YOU STAND WITH US AGAINST THESE PIPERS.
YOU'RE GONNA FIGHT THE BUBBLERS?
UP THAT CANYON IS A COLLECTION OF COMPUTERS AND DATA--POSSIBLY ALL THAT'S LEFT OF THOUSANDS OF YEARS OF HUMAN CULTURE. IT MAY BE THE MOST VALUABLE THING LEFT ON EARTH.
IF THOSE PIPERS GET THROUGH, ALL OF HUMAN RESEARCH, LITERATURE, MUSIC, ART, MEDICINE, AND HISTORY WILL BE LOST.
STAND WITH US FOR HUMANITY, FOR YOUR ANCESTORS, FOR THE WORLD THAT WAS STOLEN FROM ALL OF US!
NOPE.
I'LL FIGHT.
ME TOO. BUT I WANT AN ALPACA IF WE WIN.
I DON'T THINK WE'LL WIN.
BUT WE MIGHT BUY THE CARAVAN ENOUGH TIME TO GET AWAY.

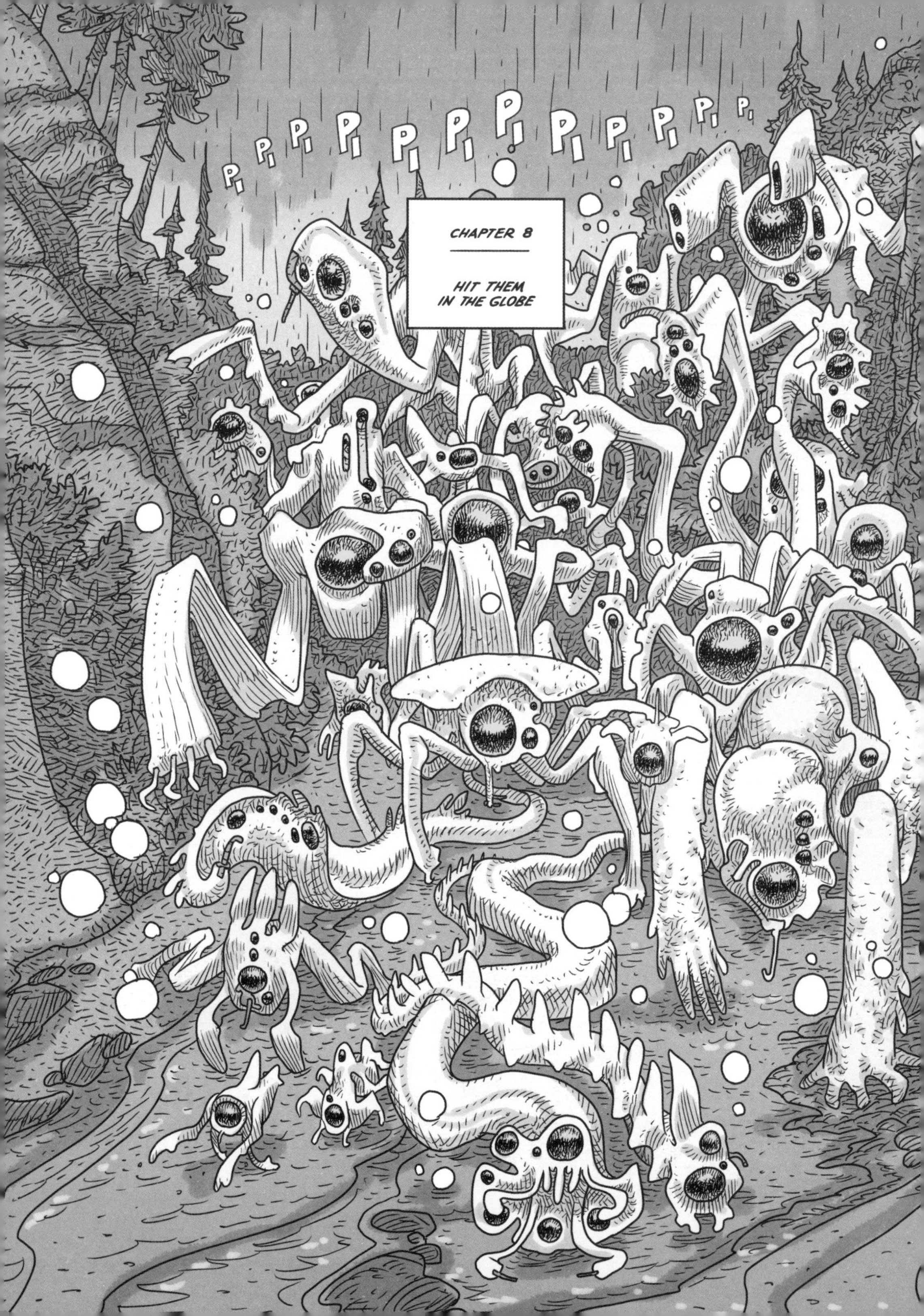
PI PI PI PI PI PI PI PI PI PI PI PI PI PI
CHAPTER 8
HIT THEM IN THE GLOBE

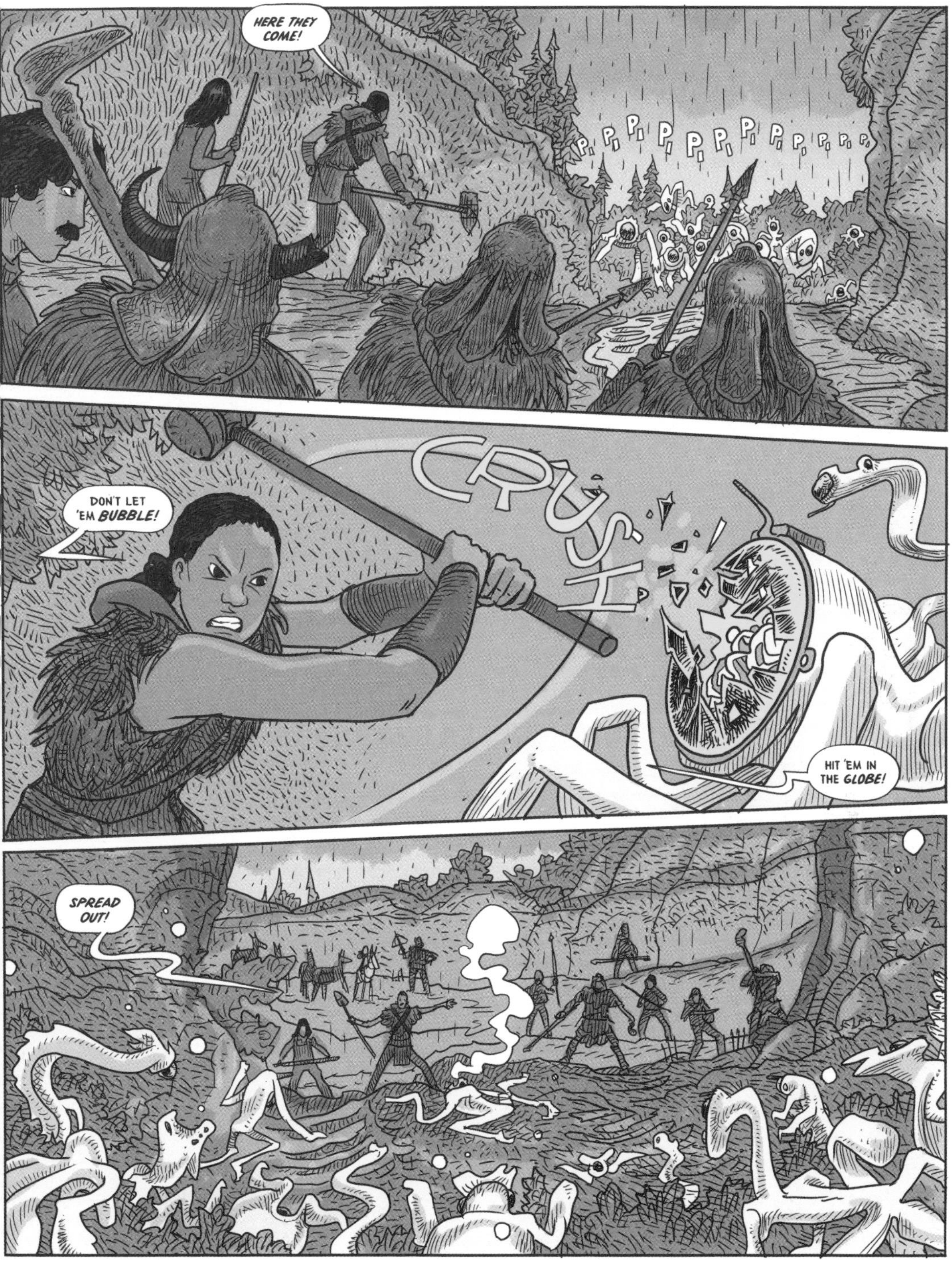
HERE THEY COME!
P P P P P P P P P P P P P P
DON'T LET 'EM BUBBLE!
CRUSH
HIT 'EM IN THE GLOBE!
SPREAD OUT!

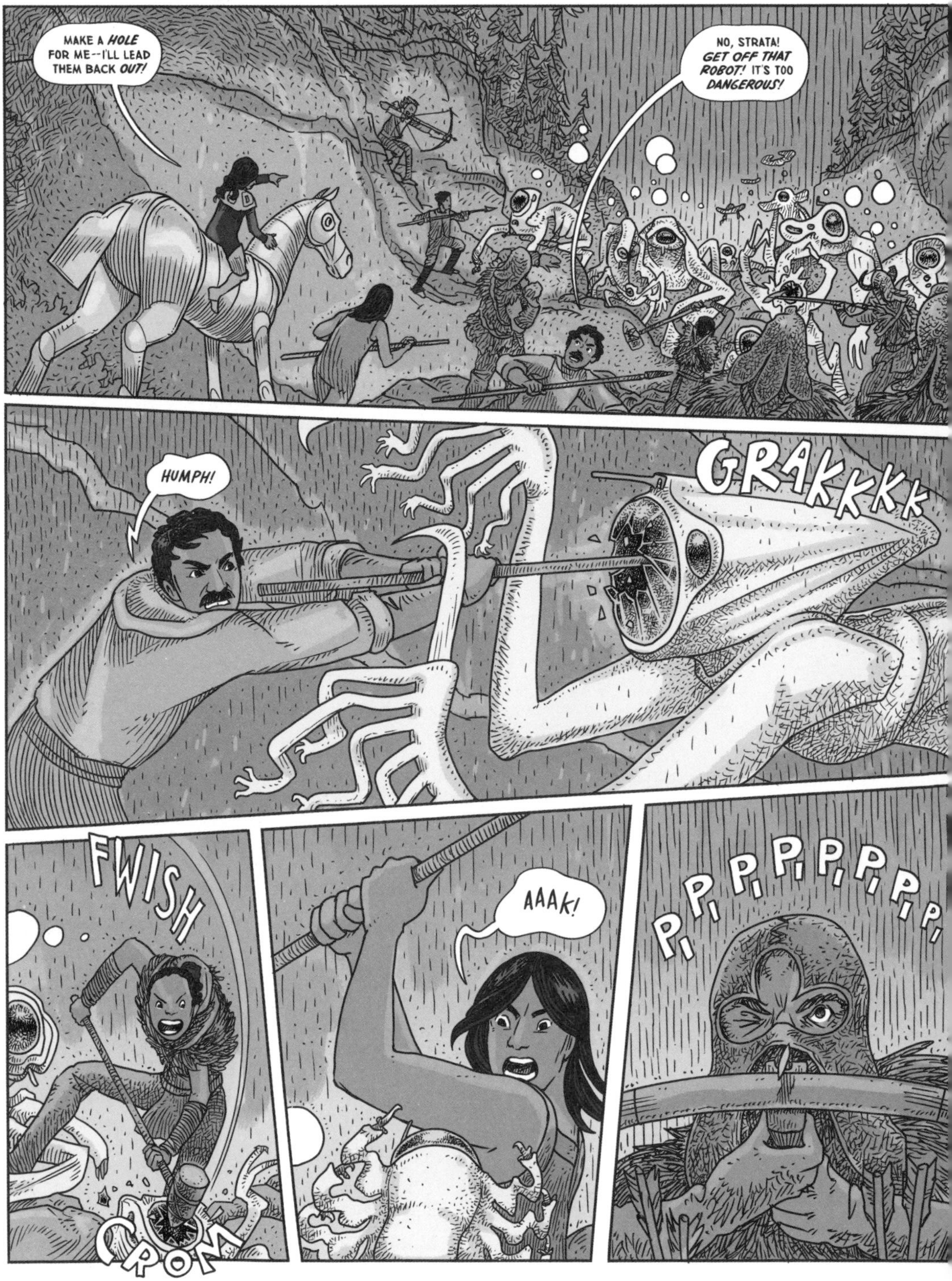
MAKE A HOLE FOR ME--I'LL LEAD THEM BACK OUT!
NO, STRATA! GET OFF THAT ROBOT! IT'S TOO DANGEROUS!
HUMPH!
GRAKKKK
FWISH
CROM
AAAK!
P, P, P, P, P, P, P, P, P, P,

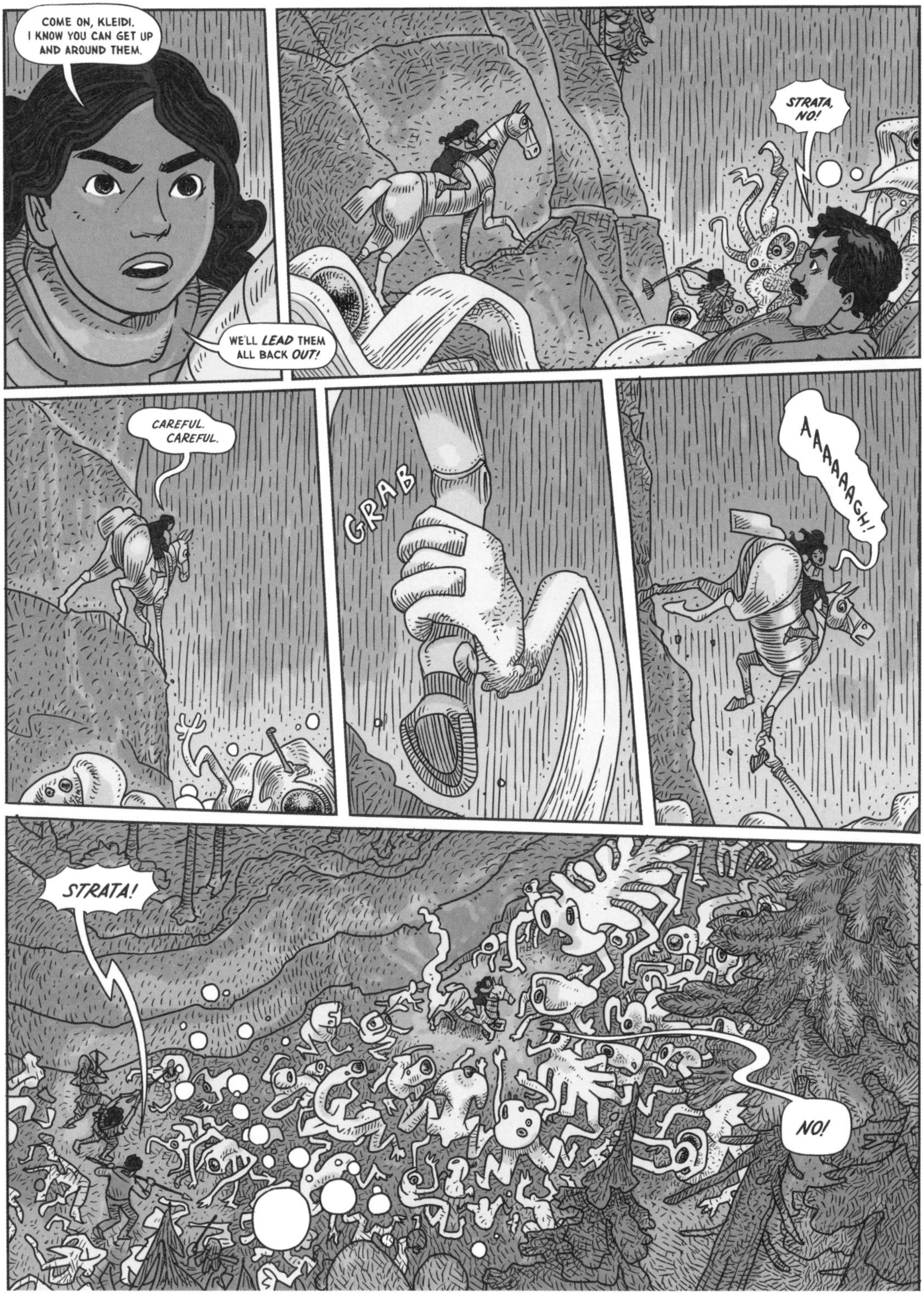
COME ON, KLEIDI. I KNOW YOU CAN GET UP AND AROUND THEM.
WE'LL *LEAD* THEM ALL BACK *OUT!*
STRATA, NO!
CAREFUL. CAREFUL.
GRAB
AAAAAAAGH!
STRATA!
NO!

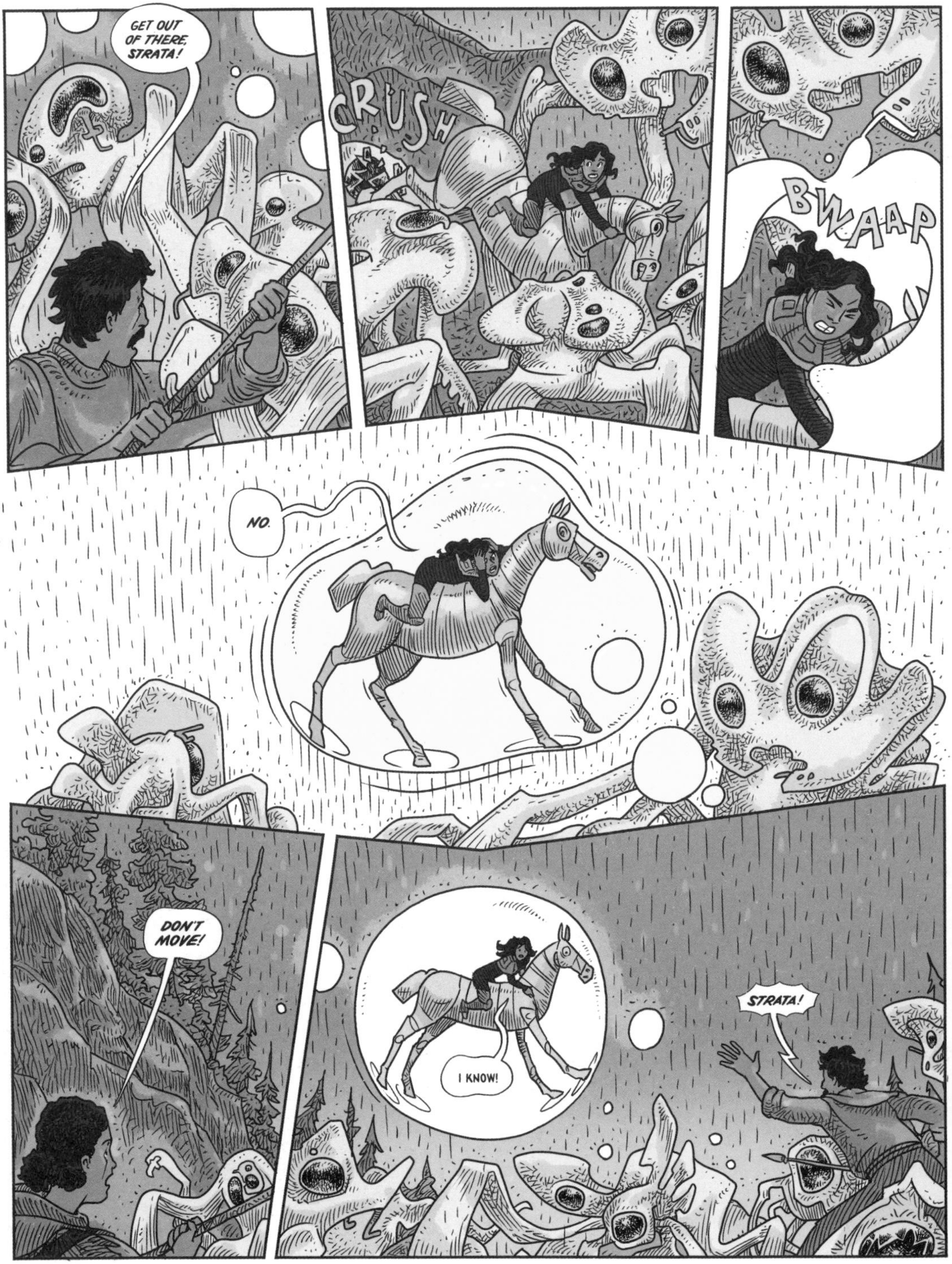
GET OUT OF THERE, STRATA!
CRUSH
BWAAP
NO.
DON'T MOVE!
I KNOW!
STRATA!

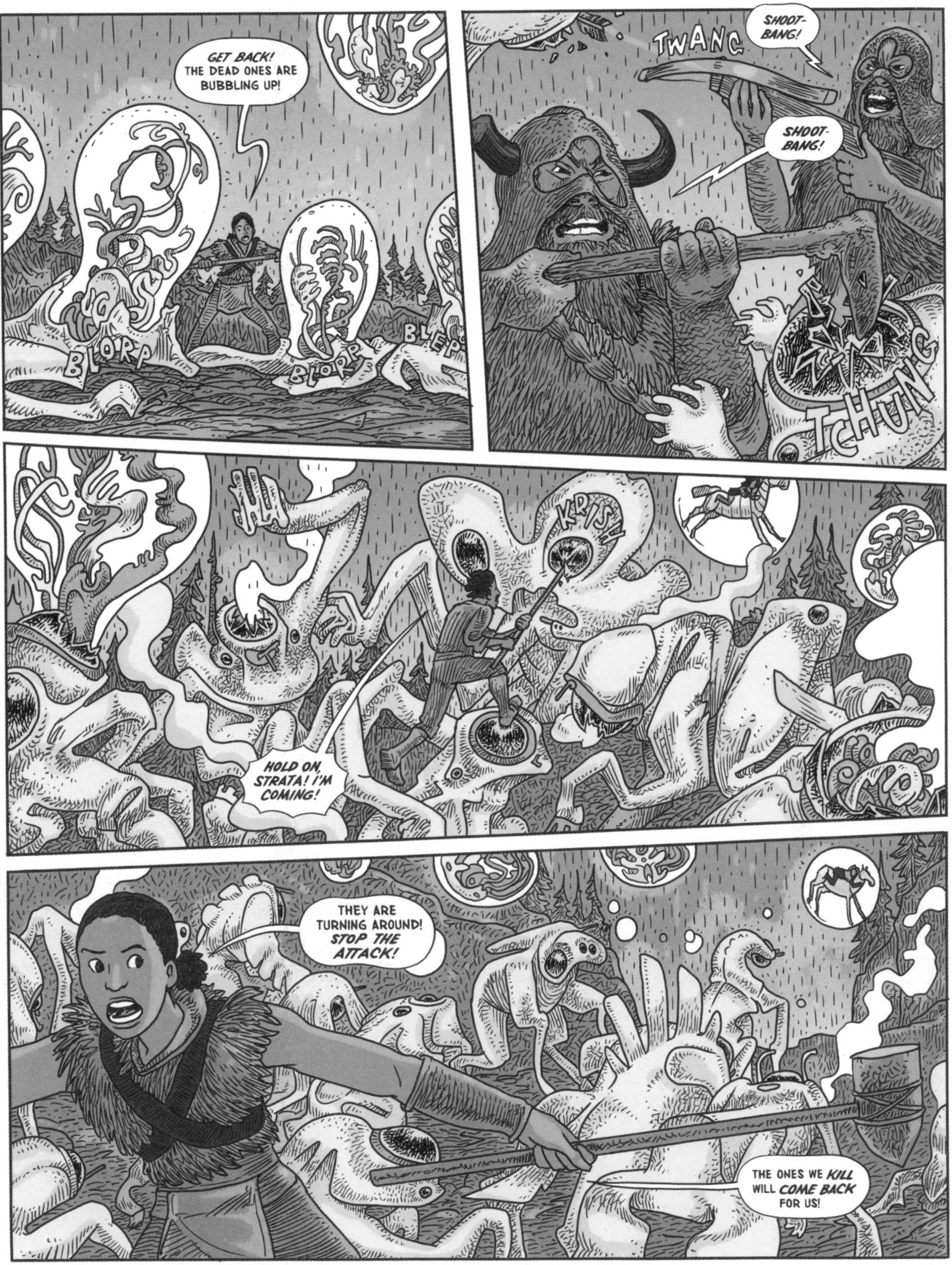
GET BACK! THE DEAD ONES ARE BUBBLING UP!
BLORP
BLORP
BLEP
TWANG
SHOOT-BANG!
SHOOT-BANG!
TCHUNG
KRISH
HOLD ON, STRATA! I'M COMING!
THEY ARE TURNING AROUND! STOP THE ATTACK!
THE ONES WE KILL WILL COME BACK FOR US!

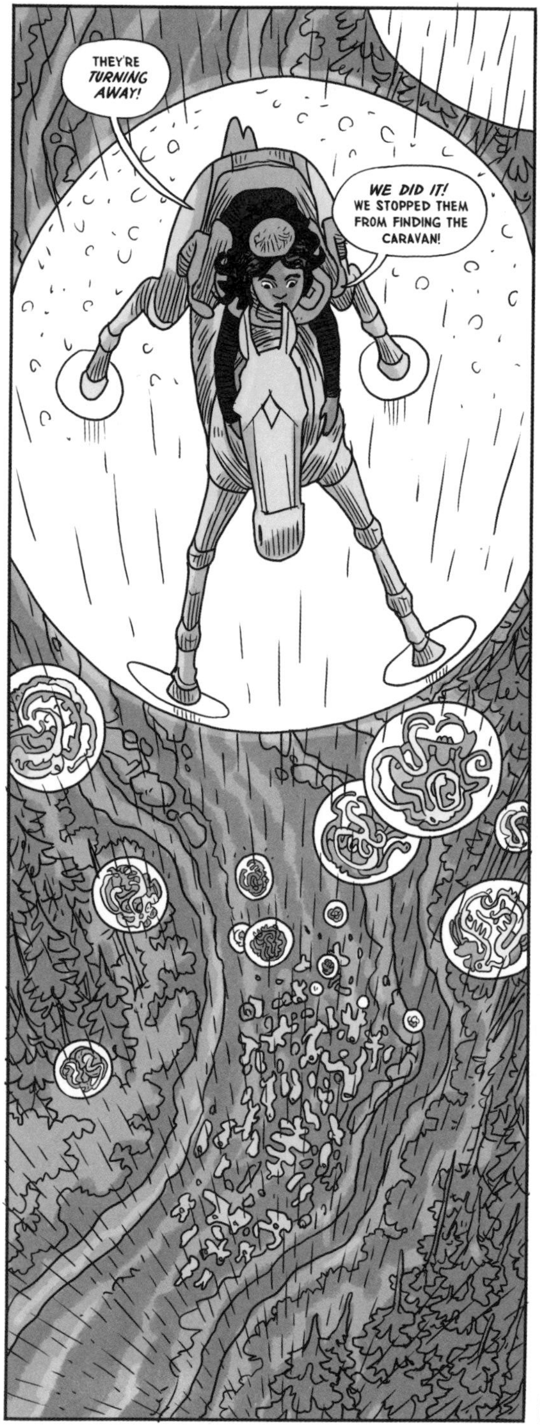
THEY'RE *TURNING AWAY!*
WE DID IT! WE STOPPED THEM FROM FINDING THE CARAVAN!

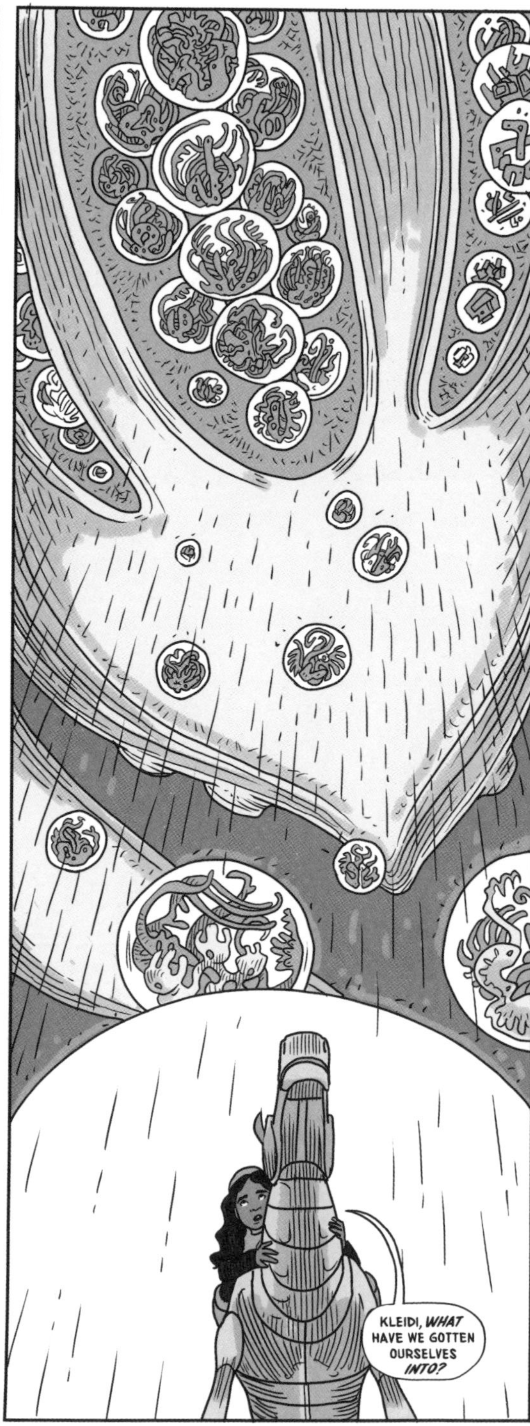
KLEIDI, *WHAT* HAVE WE GOTTEN OURSELVES *INTO?*

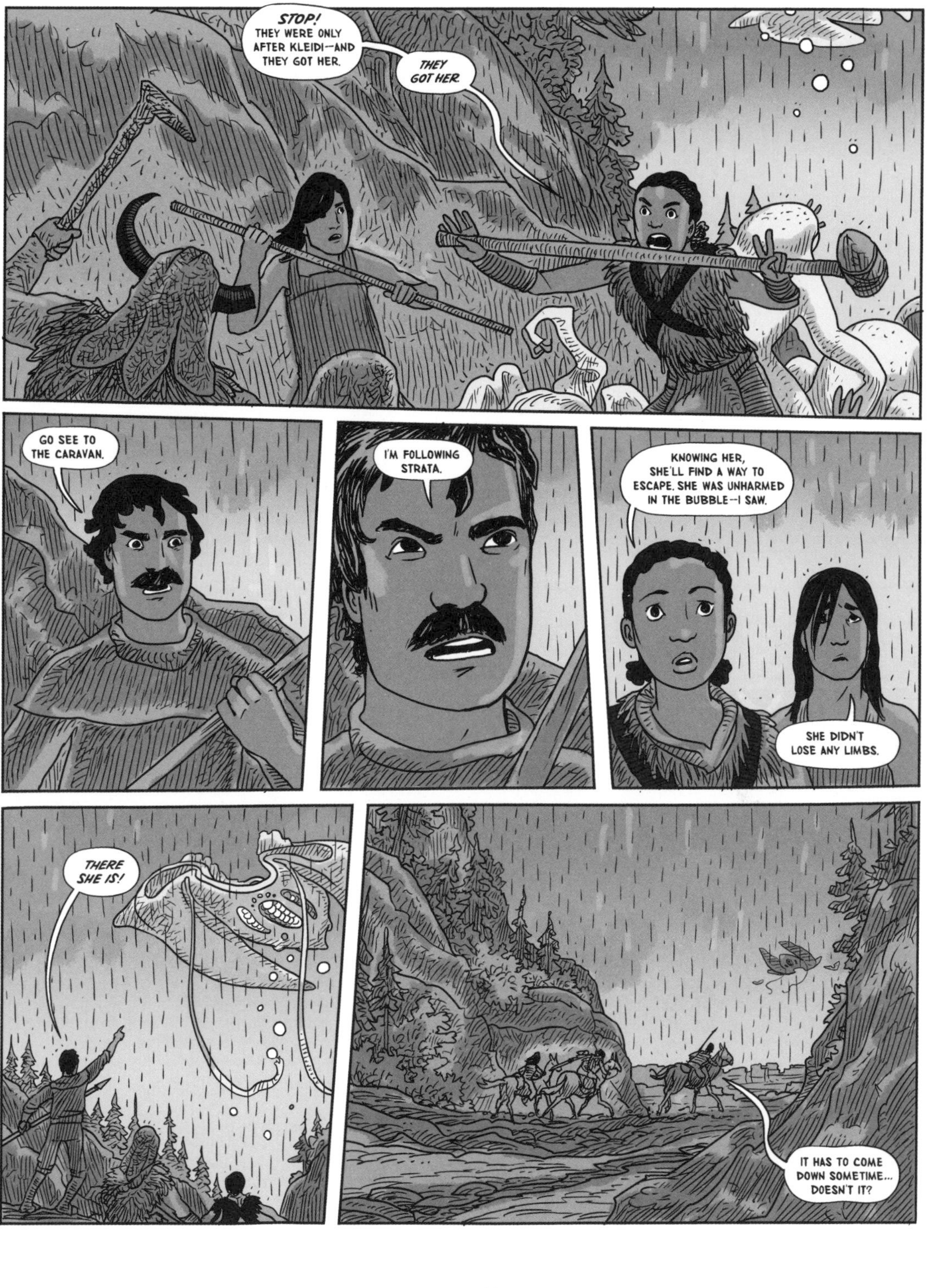
STOP! THEY WERE ONLY AFTER KLEIDI--AND THEY GOT HER.
THEY GOT HER.
GO SEE TO THE CARAVAN.
I'M FOLLOWING STRATA.
KNOWING HER, SHE'LL FIND A WAY TO ESCAPE. SHE WAS UNHARMED IN THE BUBBLE--I SAW.
SHE DIDN'T LOSE ANY LIMBS.
THERE SHE IS!
IT HAS TO COME DOWN SOMETIME... DOESN'T IT?

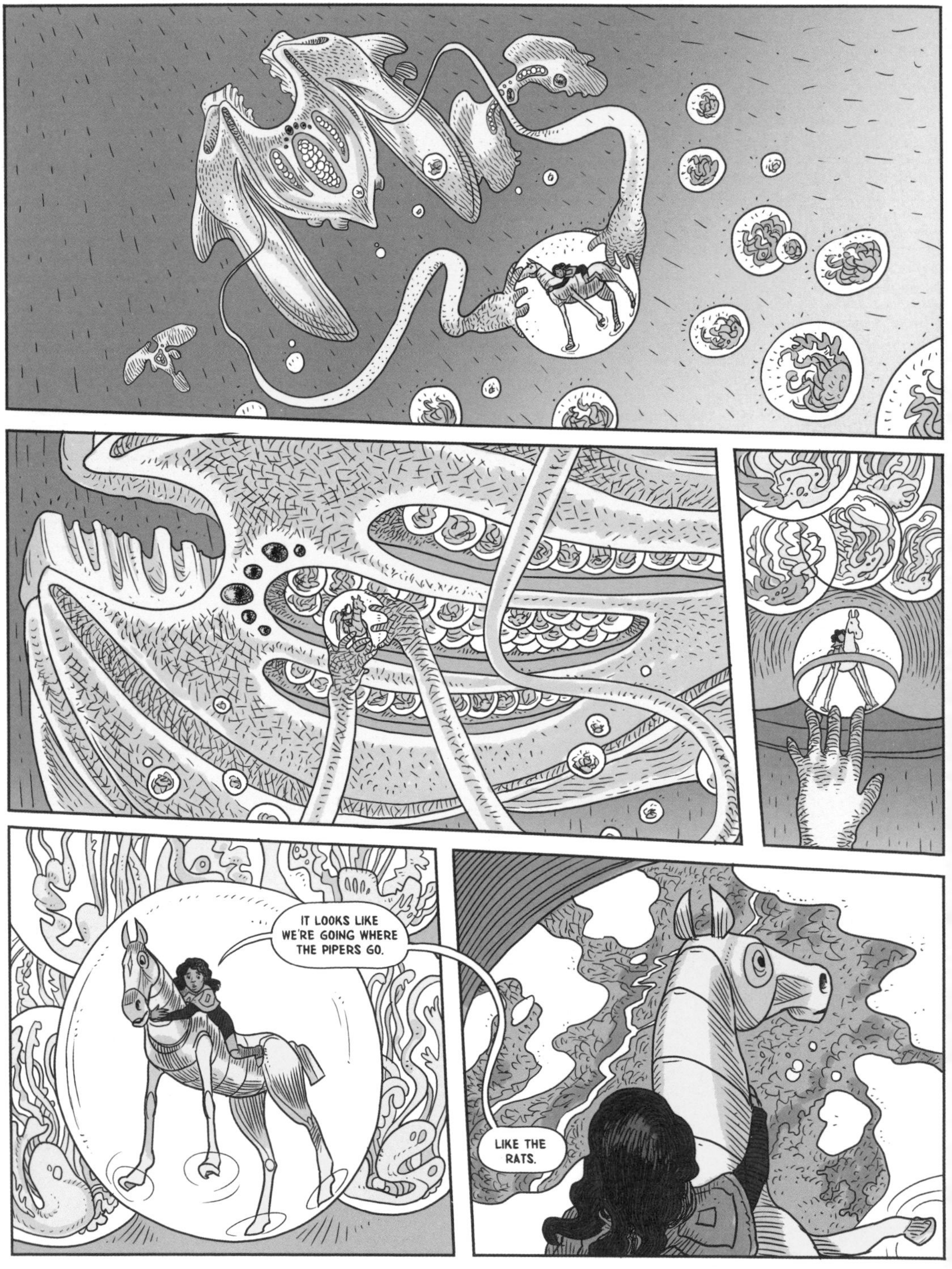
IT LOOKS LIKE WE'RE GOING WHERE THE PIPERS GO.
LIKE THE RATS.

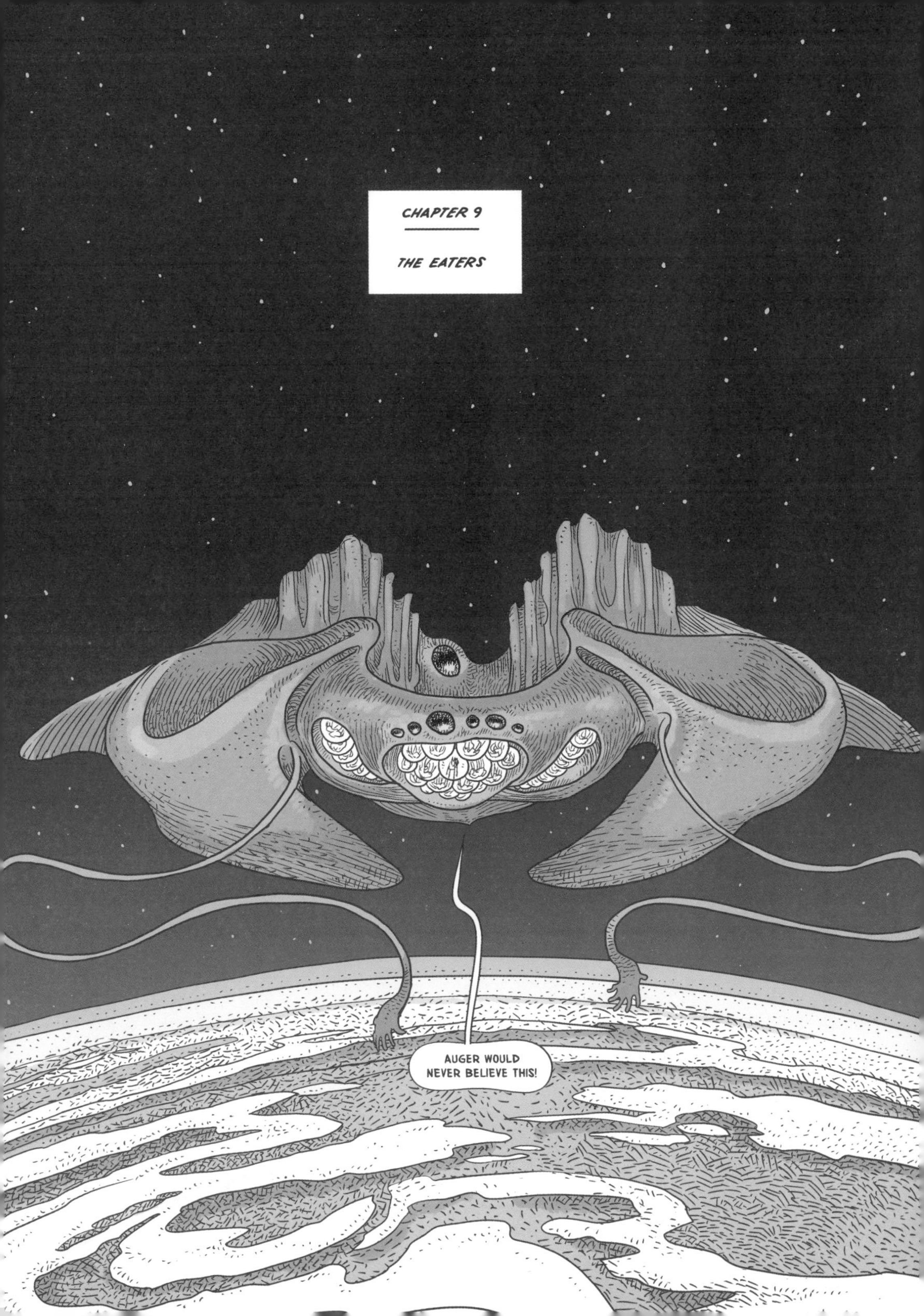
CHAPTER 9
THE EATERS
AUGER WOULD NEVER BELIEVE THIS!

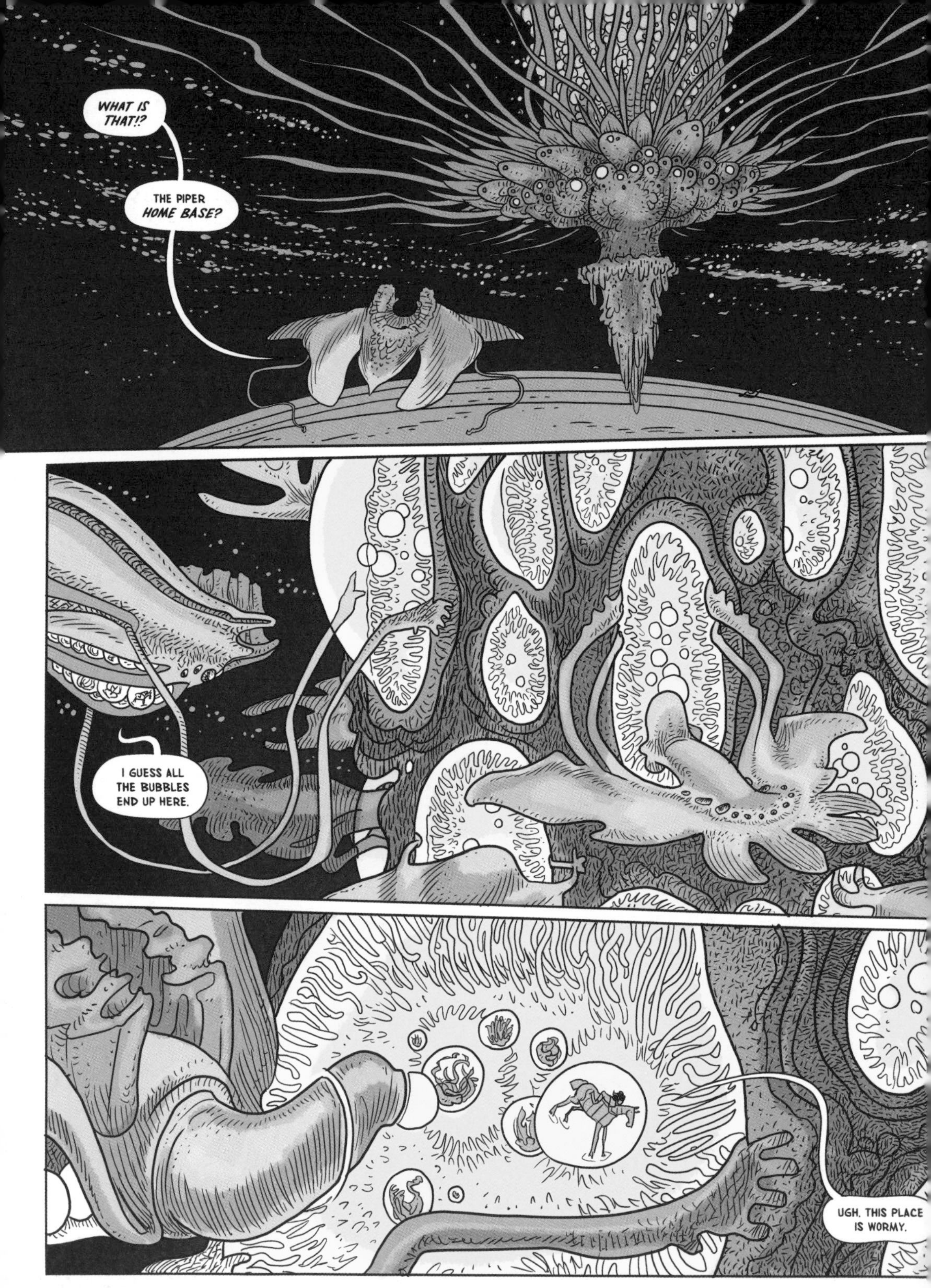
WHAT IS THAT!?
THE PIPER HOME BASE?
I GUESS ALL THE BUBBLES END UP HERE.
UGH. THIS PLACE IS WORMY.

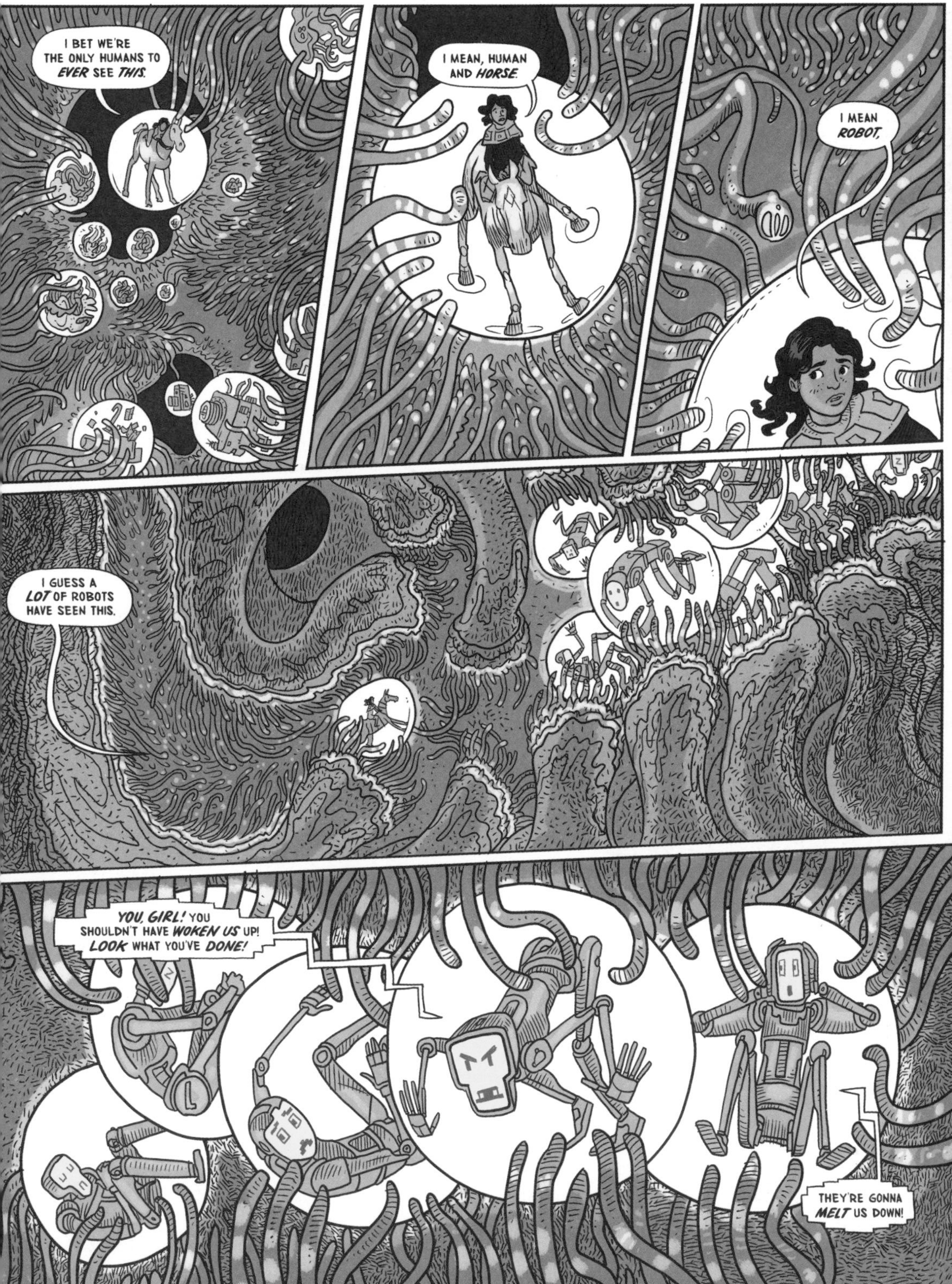
I BET WE'RE THE ONLY HUMANS TO *EVER* SEE *THIS*.
I MEAN, HUMAN AND *HORSE*.
I MEAN *ROBOT*,
I GUESS A *LOT* OF ROBOTS HAVE SEEN THIS.
YOU, GIRL! YOU SHOULDN'T HAVE *WOKEN US* UP! *LOOK* WHAT YOU'VE *DONE!*
THEY'RE GONNA *MELT* US DOWN!

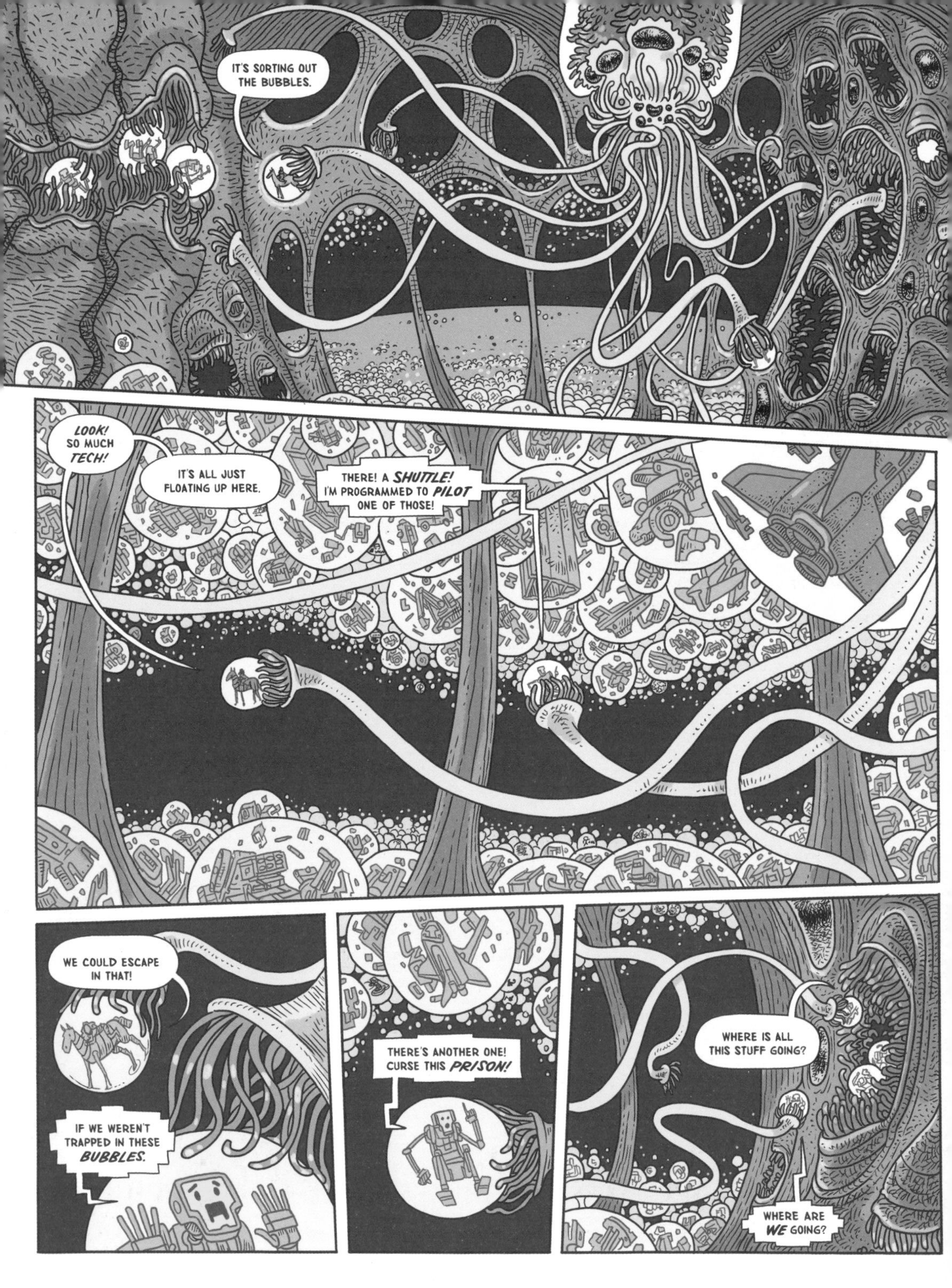

IT'S SORTING OUT THE BUBBLES.
LOOK! SO MUCH *TECH!*
IT'S ALL JUST FLOATING UP HERE.
THERE! A *SHUTTLE!* I'M PROGRAMMED TO *PILOT* ONE OF THOSE!
WE COULD ESCAPE IN THAT!
IF WE WEREN'T TRAPPED IN THESE *BUBBLES.*
THERE'S ANOTHER ONE! CURSE THIS *PRISON!*
WHERE IS ALL THIS STUFF GOING?
WHERE ARE *WE* GOING?

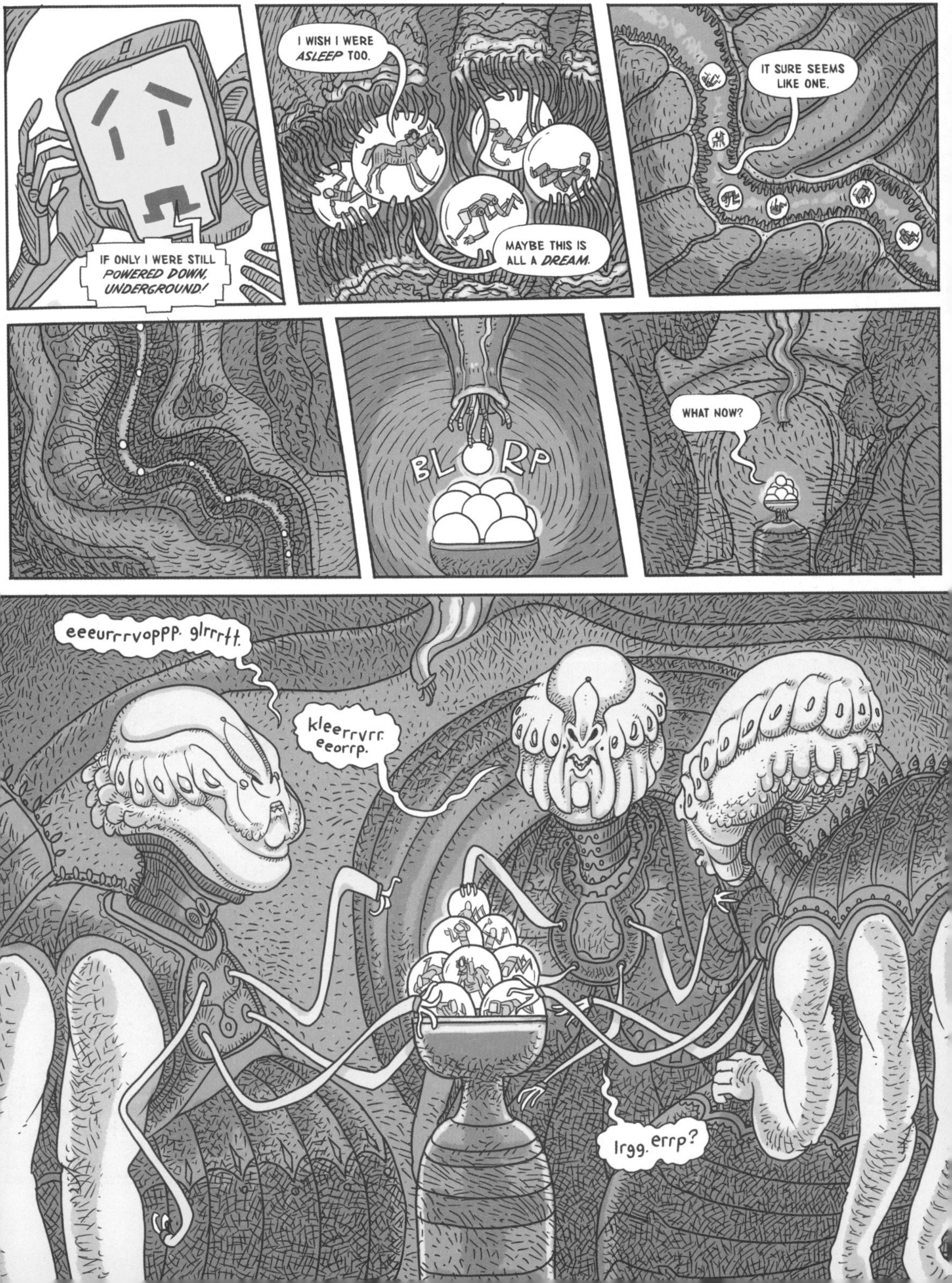
IF ONLY I WERE STILL POWERED DOWN, UNDERGROUND!
I WISH I WERE ASLEEP TOO.
MAYBE THIS IS ALL A DREAM.
IT SURE SEEMS LIKE ONE.
BLORP
WHAT NOW?
eeeurrrvoppp. glrrrtt.
kleerrvrr. eeorrp.
lrgg. errp?

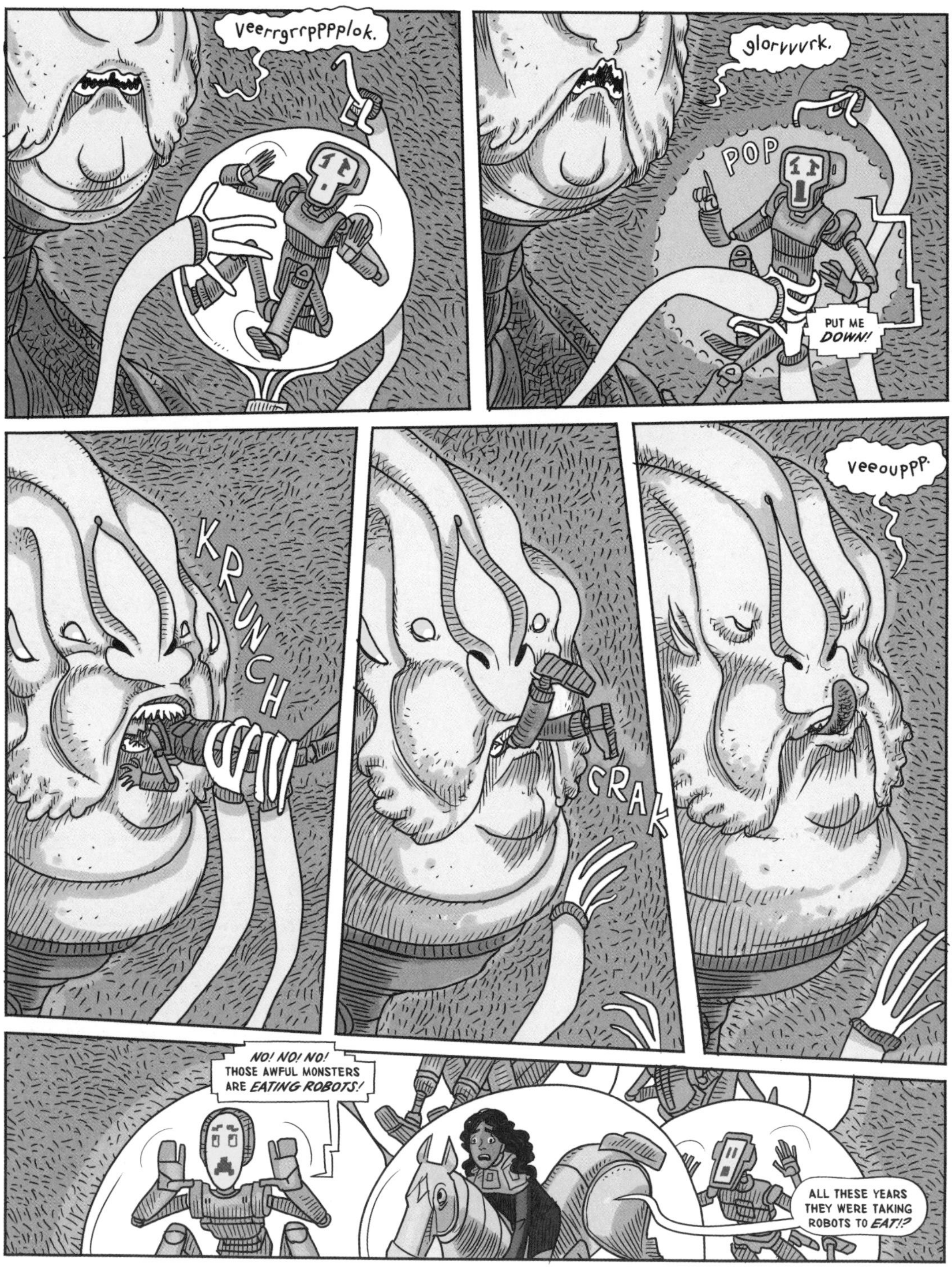
veerrgrrpppplok.
glorvvvrk.
POP
PUT ME DOWN!
KRUNCH
CRAK
veeouppp.
NO! NO! NO! THOSE AWFUL MONSTERS ARE EATING ROBOTS!
ALL THESE YEARS THEY WERE TAKING ROBOTS TO EAT!?

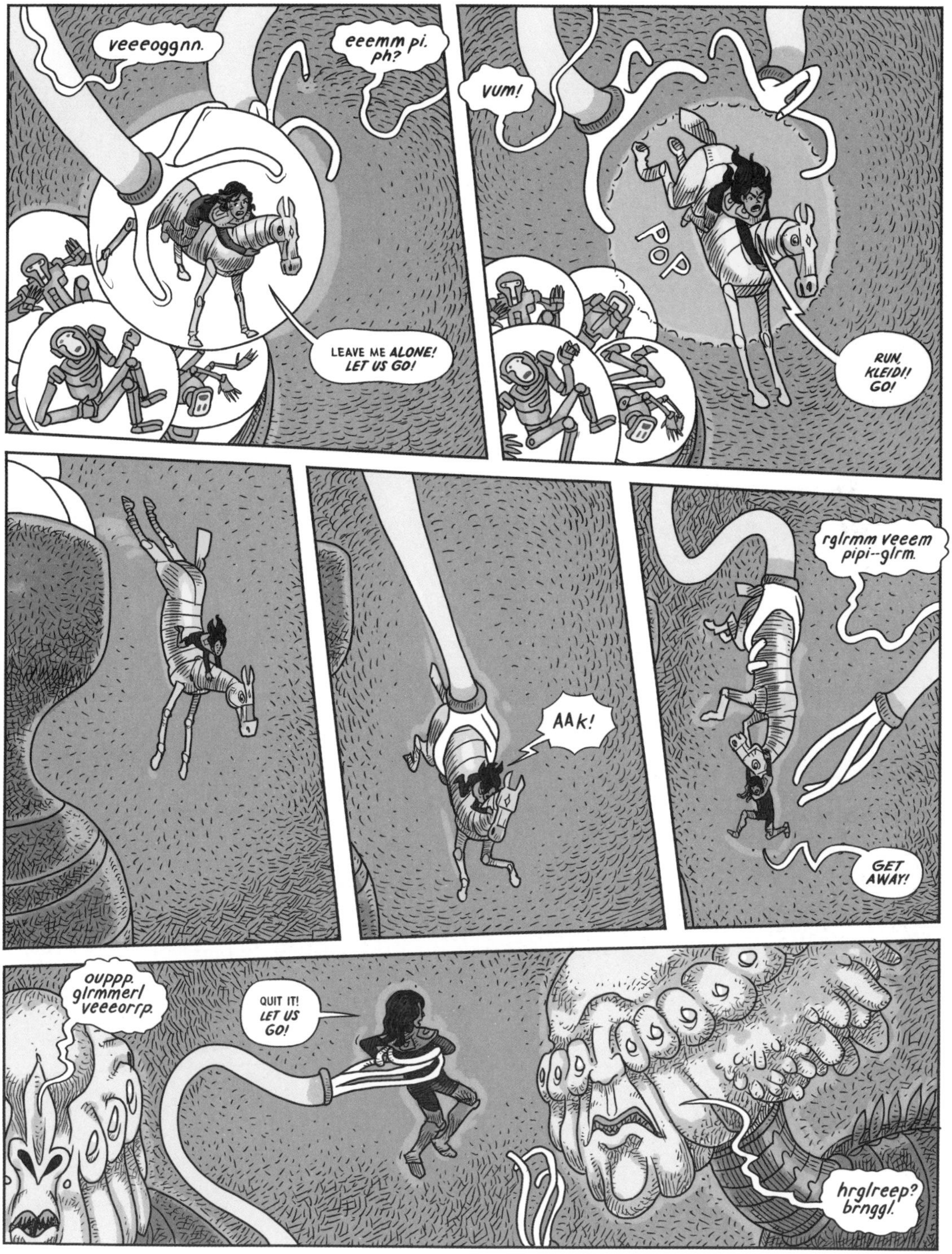

veeeoggnn.
eeemm pi. ph?
LEAVE ME ALONE! LET US GO!
VUM!
POP
RUN, KLEIDI! GO!
AAK!
rglrmm veeem pipi--glrm.
GET AWAY!
ouppp. glrmmerl veeeorrp.
QUIT IT! LET US GO!
hrglreep? brnggl.

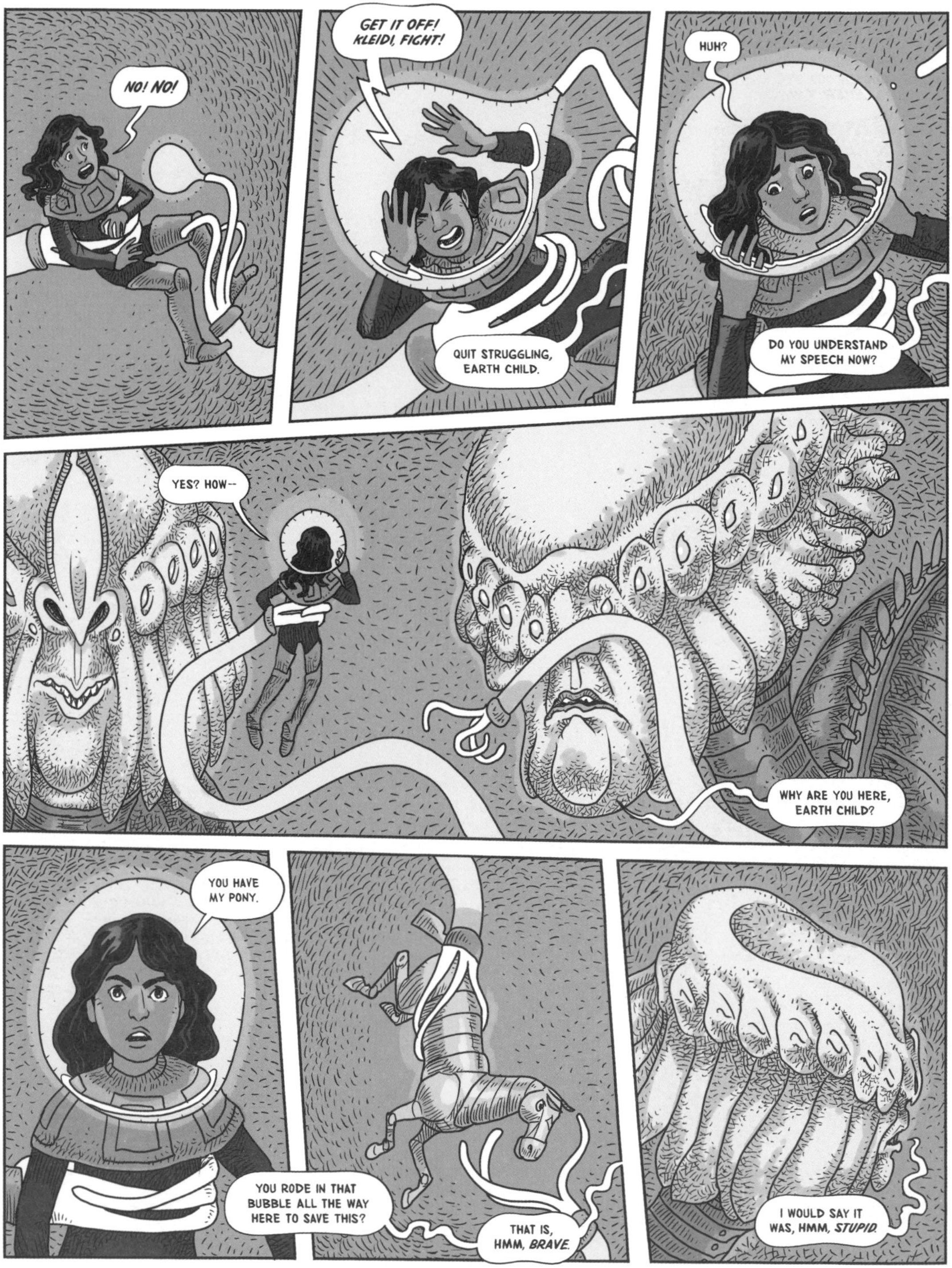
NO! NO!
GET IT OFF! KLEIDI, FIGHT!
QUIT STRUGGLING, EARTH CHILD.
HUH?
DO YOU UNDERSTAND MY SPEECH NOW?
YES? HOW--
WHY ARE YOU HERE, EARTH CHILD?
YOU HAVE MY PONY.
YOU RODE IN THAT BUBBLE ALL THE WAY HERE TO SAVE THIS?
THAT IS, HMM, BRAVE.
I WOULD SAY IT WAS, HMM, STUPID.

WHO *ARE* YOU? WHAT'S *GOING ON* HERE? WHY ARE YOU *STEALING* EVERYTHING?

HOW *TIRESOME.*

CRUNCH

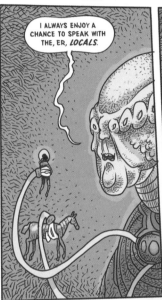

I ALWAYS ENJOY A CHANCE TO SPEAK WITH THE, ER, *LOCALS.*

I DON'T.

YOUR QUESTIONS ARE CONCISE.

TELL ME CHILD, DO YOUR PEOPLE STILL HAVE A WRITTEN LANGUAGE?

YES, WE--

CRUNCH

COULD YOU *PLEASE* STOP DOING THAT!?

I'M *HUNGRY.* DO *YOU* STOP EATING WHEN *YOU* ARE HUNGRY?

YOU *EAT* ROBOTS?

I THINK WE'VE ESTABLISHED THAT.

WE WILL EAT A GOOD MANY *MORE* THINGS BEFORE WE'RE DONE WITH THIS PLANET.

TO ANSWER YOUR QUESTIONS, WE ARE HERE TO *HARVEST* THIS PLANET.

THERE ARE THINGS HERE THAT WE WANT, SO WE ARE TAKING THEM.

BUT, THIS IS *OUR* PLANET--

IT'S YOUR PLANET ONLY IF YOU ARE STRONG ENOUGH TO *DEFEND* IT.

YOU AREN'T.

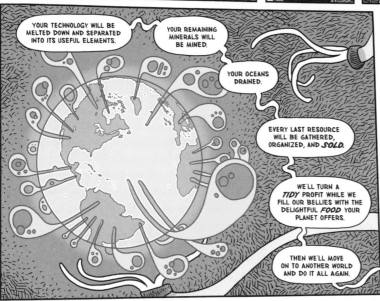

YOUR TECHNOLOGY WILL BE MELTED DOWN AND SEPARATED INTO ITS USEFUL ELEMENTS.

YOUR REMAINING MINERALS WILL BE MINED.

YOUR OCEANS DRAINED.

EVERY LAST RESOURCE WILL BE GATHERED, ORGANIZED, AND *SOLD.*

WE'LL TURN A *TIDY* PROFIT WHILE WE FILL OUR BELLIES WITH THE DELIGHTFUL *FOOD* YOUR PLANET OFFERS.

THEN WE'LL MOVE ON TO ANOTHER WORLD AND DO IT ALL AGAIN.

SO YOU CAME TO *STEAL* OUR METAL, *EAT* ALL OF OUR ROBOTS, AND *LEAVE?*

NO, NO, YOUR ROBOTS, AS *TASTY* AS THEY ARE, ARE JUST THE *BEGINNING.*

YOU SEE, IT'S *INTELLIGENCE* WE FEED ON.

YOUR *THINKING MACHINES* ARE A PERFECT FIRST COURSE.

WHAT'S THE *SECOND* COURSE?

OH, MY SWEET LITTLE EARTH CHILD,

YOU ARE.

110

EEEEK!

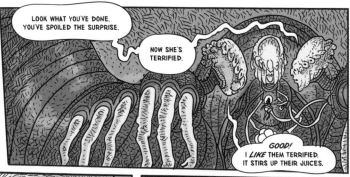

LOOK WHAT YOU'VE DONE. YOU'VE SPOILED THE SURPRISE.

NOW SHE'S TERRIFIED.

GOOD! I *LIKE* THEM TERRIFIED. IT STIRS UP THEIR JUICES.

FEAR NOT, CHILD. IT WILL ALL BE OVER QUICKLY.

WE'RE QUITE GOOD AT OUR JOB. WE'VE EATEN OUR WAY THROUGH *COUNTLESS* PLANETS.

WE'VE CONSUMED BILLIONS OF SCARED CHILDREN.

AND WHAT AN *HONOR*-- YOU WILL BE THE *FIRST* HUMAN ON THIS PLANET TO BE EATEN.

BUT CERTAINLY NOT THE *LAST*.

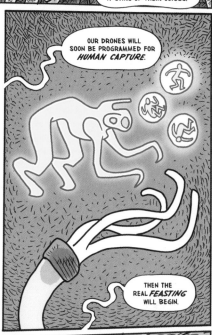

OUR DRONES WILL SOON BE PROGRAMMED FOR *HUMAN CAPTURE*.

THEN THE REAL *FEASTING* WILL BEGIN.

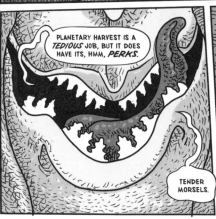

PLANETARY HARVEST IS A *TEDIOUS* JOB, BUT IT DOES HAVE ITS, HMM, *PERKS*.

TENDER MORSELS.

LET ME GO.

OH, IT'S *TOO LATE* FOR THAT.

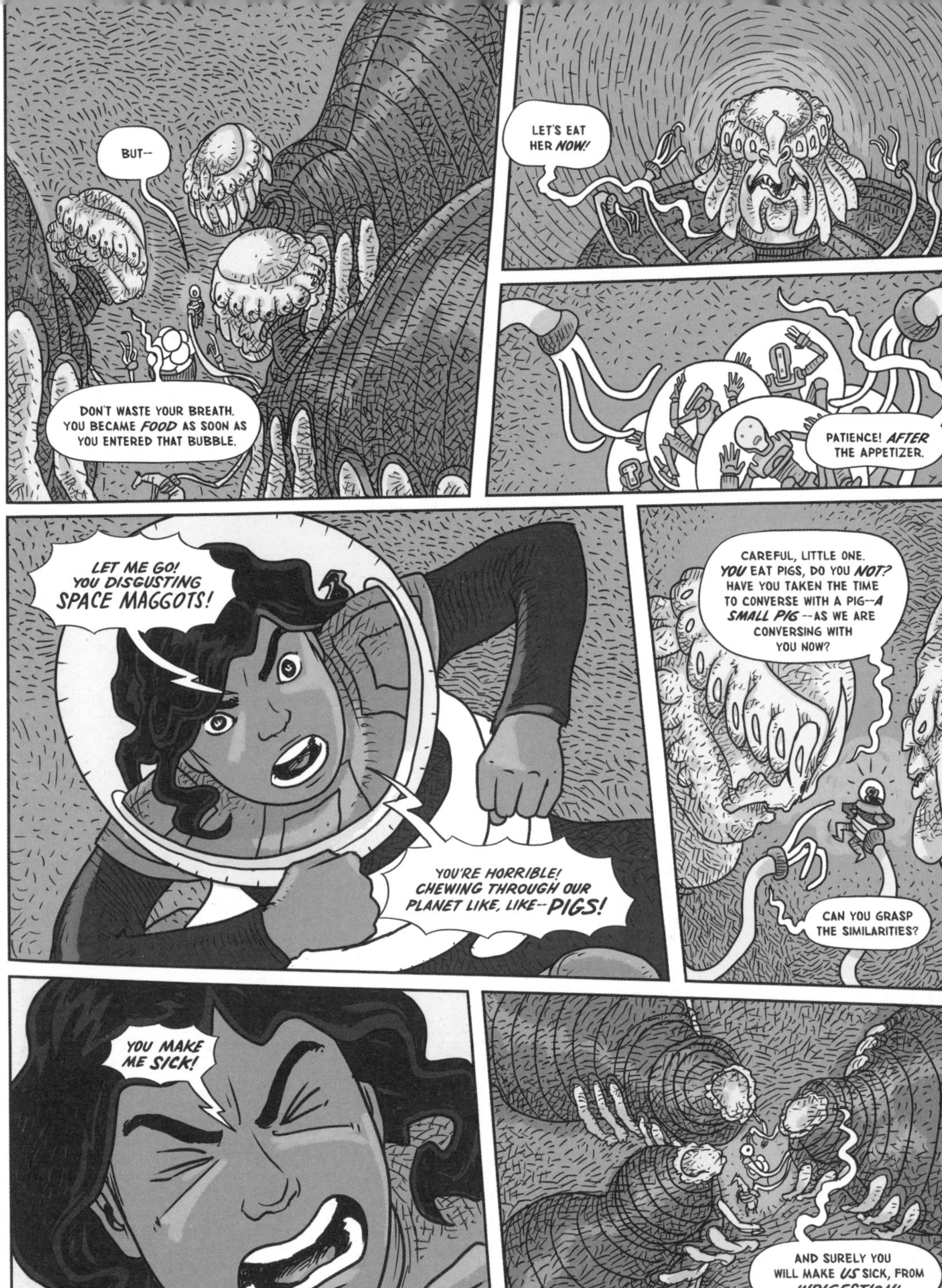
BUT--
LET'S EAT HER NOW!
DON'T WASTE YOUR BREATH. YOU BECAME FOOD AS SOON AS YOU ENTERED THAT BUBBLE.
PATIENCE! AFTER THE APPETIZER.
LET ME GO! YOU DISGUSTING SPACE MAGGOTS!
YOU'RE HORRIBLE! CHEWING THROUGH OUR PLANET LIKE, LIKE--PIGS!
CAREFUL, LITTLE ONE. YOU EAT PIGS, DO YOU NOT? HAVE YOU TAKEN THE TIME TO CONVERSE WITH A PIG--A SMALL PIG--AS WE ARE CONVERSING WITH YOU NOW?
CAN YOU GRASP THE SIMILARITIES?
YOU MAKE ME SICK!
AND SURELY YOU WILL MAKE US SICK, FROM INDIGESTION!

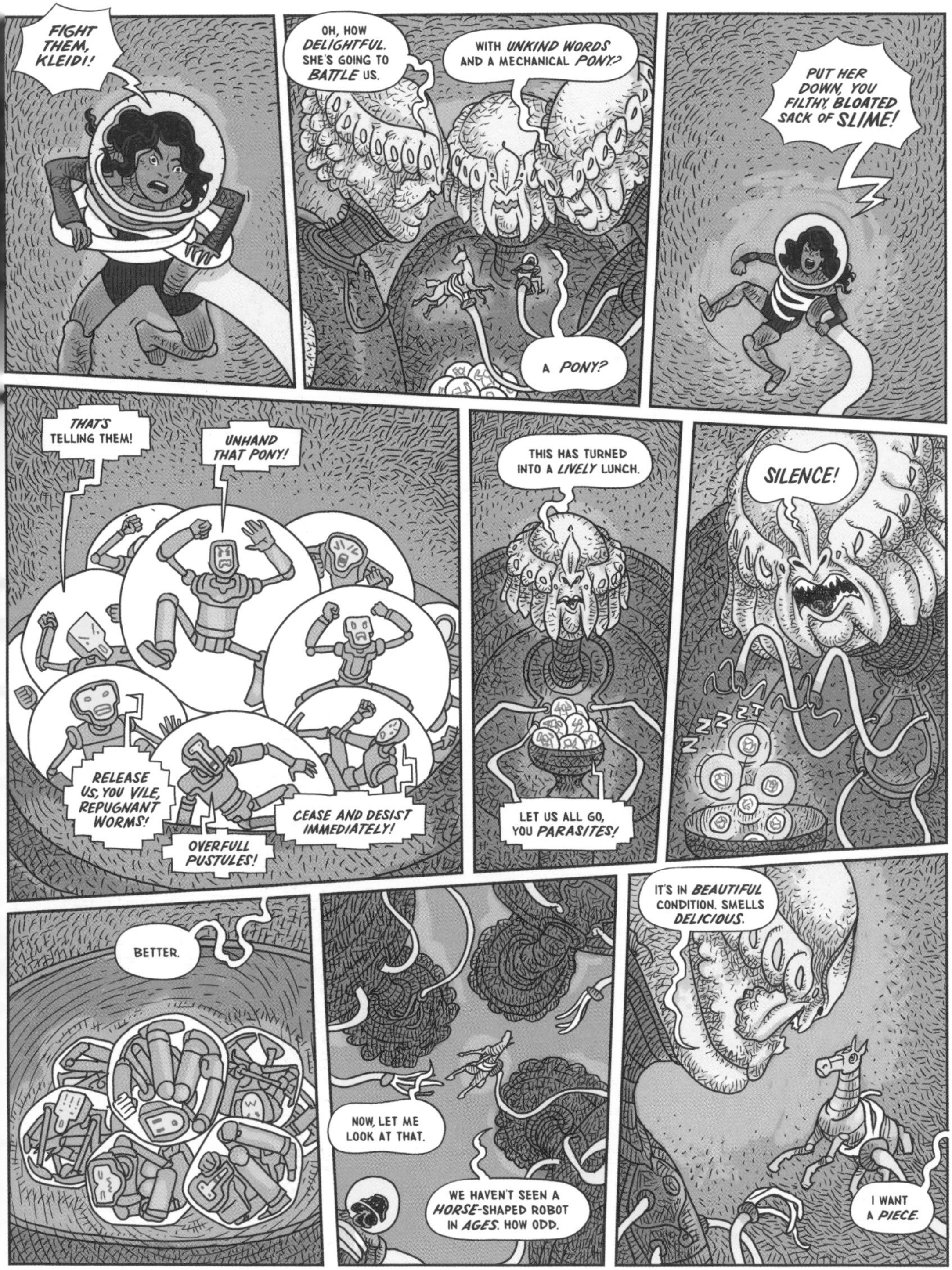
FIGHT THEM, KLEIDI!
OH, HOW DELIGHTFUL. SHE'S GOING TO BATTLE US.
WITH UNKIND WORDS AND A MECHANICAL PONY?
A PONY?
PUT HER DOWN, YOU FILTHY, BLOATED SACK OF SLIME!
THAT'S TELLING THEM!
UNHAND THAT PONY!
RELEASE US, YOU VILE, REPUGNANT WORMS!
OVERFULL PUSTULES!
CEASE AND DESIST IMMEDIATELY!
THIS HAS TURNED INTO A LIVELY LUNCH.
LET US ALL GO, YOU PARASITES!
SILENCE!
ZZZZT
BETTER.
NOW, LET ME LOOK AT THAT.
WE HAVEN'T SEEN A HORSE-SHAPED ROBOT IN AGES. HOW ODD.
IT'S IN BEAUTIFUL CONDITION. SMELLS DELICIOUS.
I WANT A PIECE.

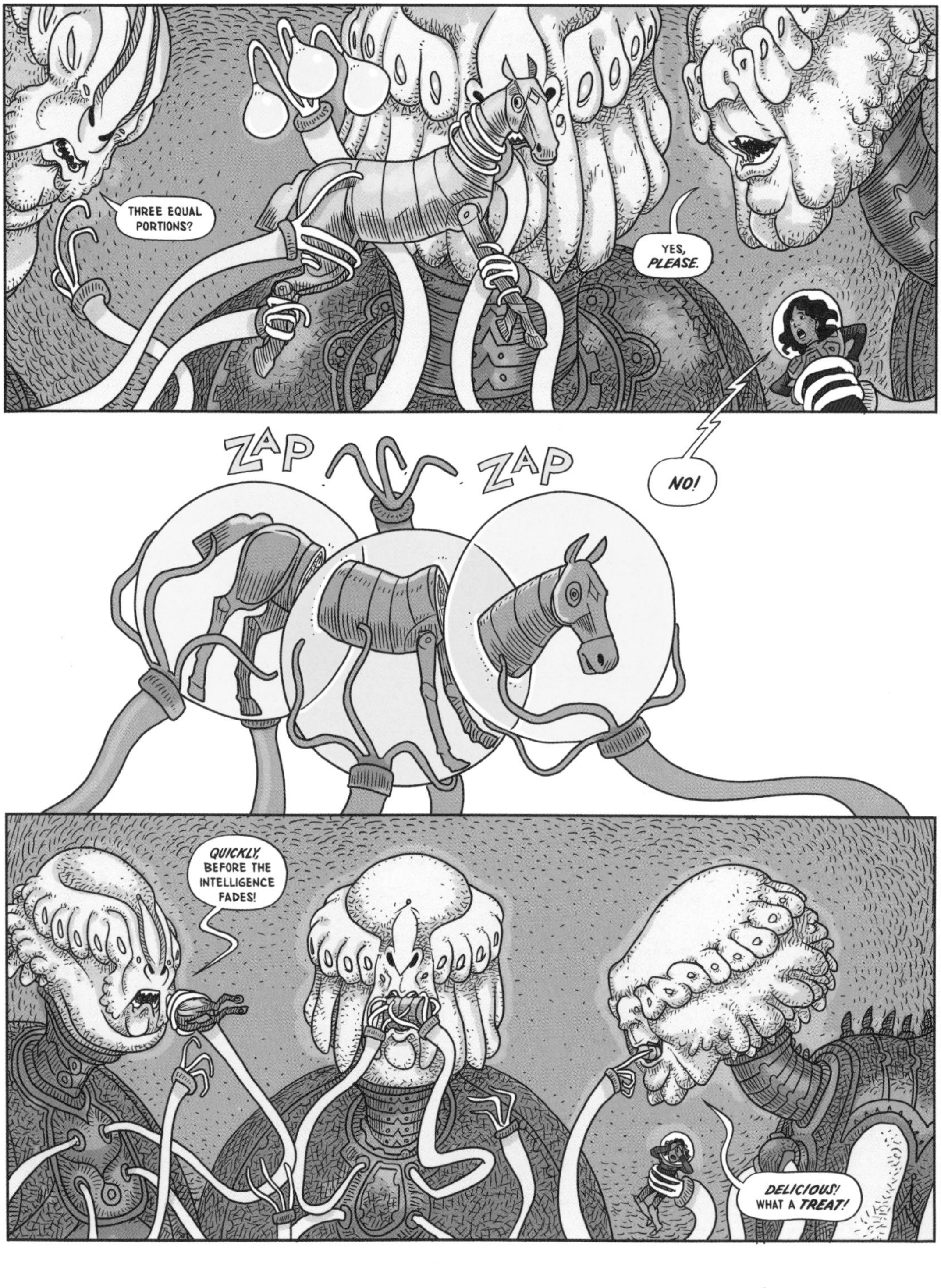
THREE EQUAL PORTIONS?
YES, *PLEASE.*
ZAP
ZAP
NO!
QUICKLY, BEFORE THE INTELLIGENCE FADES!
DELICIOUS! WHAT A *TREAT!*

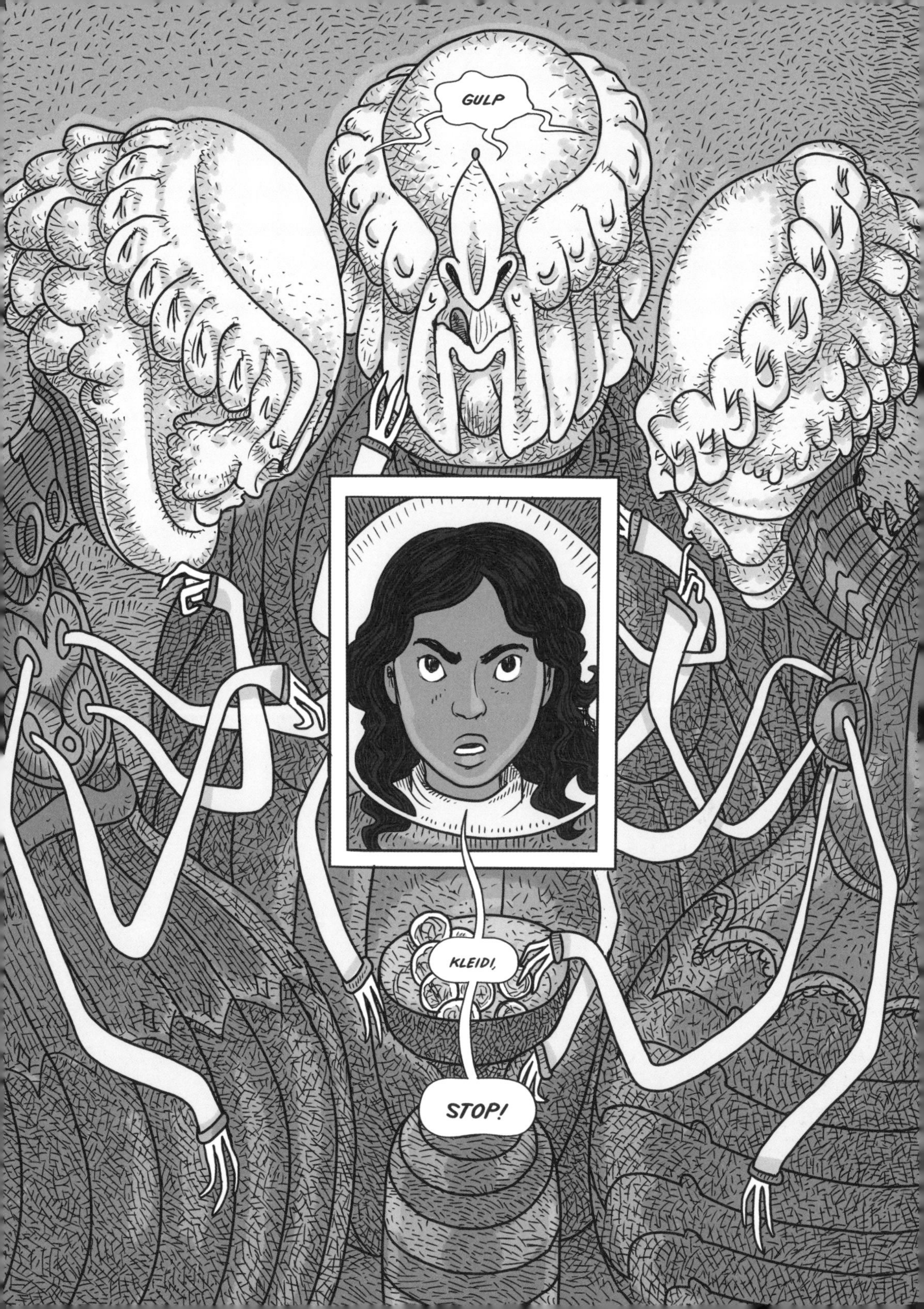
GULP
KLEIDI,
STOP!

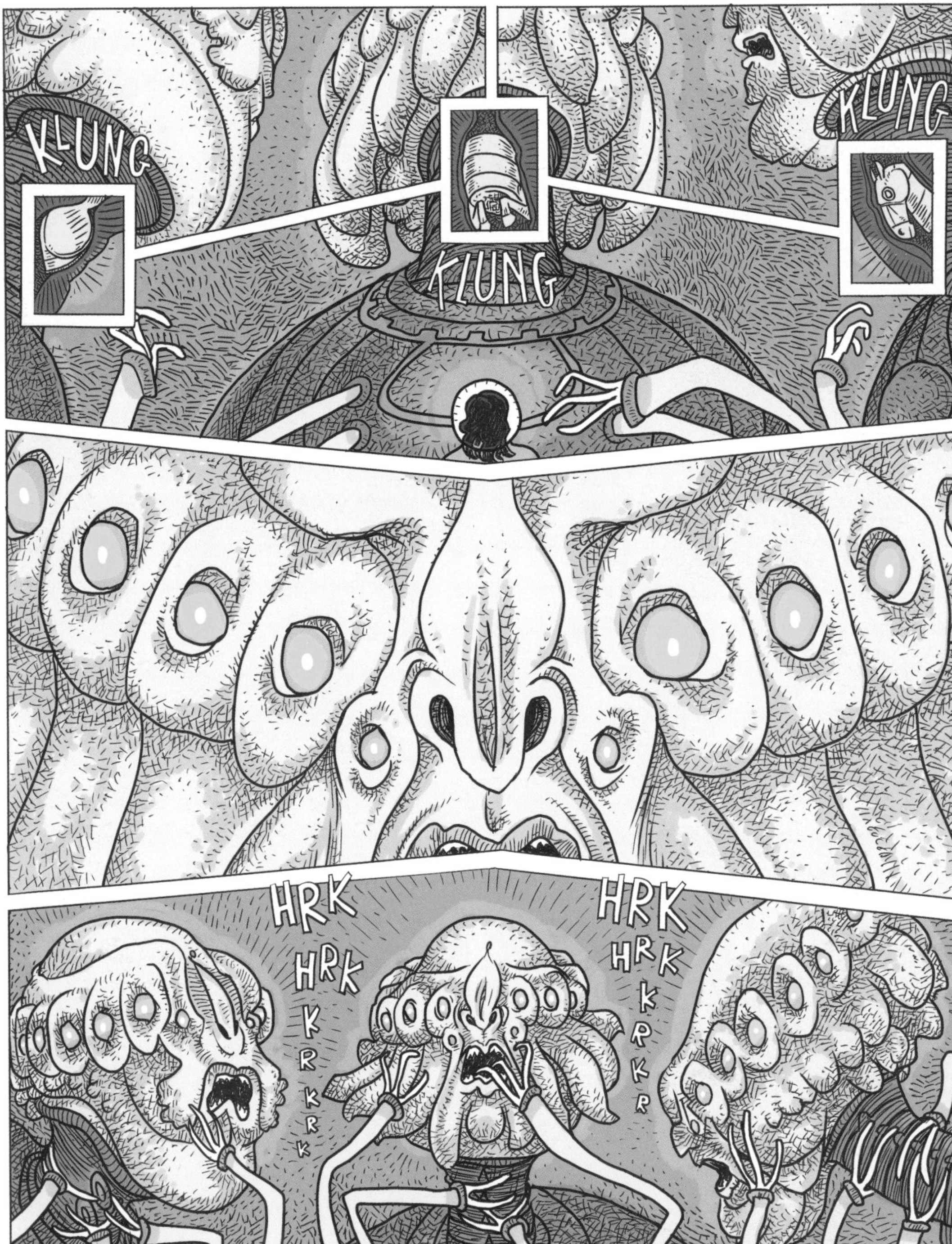
KLUNG
KLUNG
KLUNG
HRK
HRK
HRK
HRK
KRKRK
KRKRKR

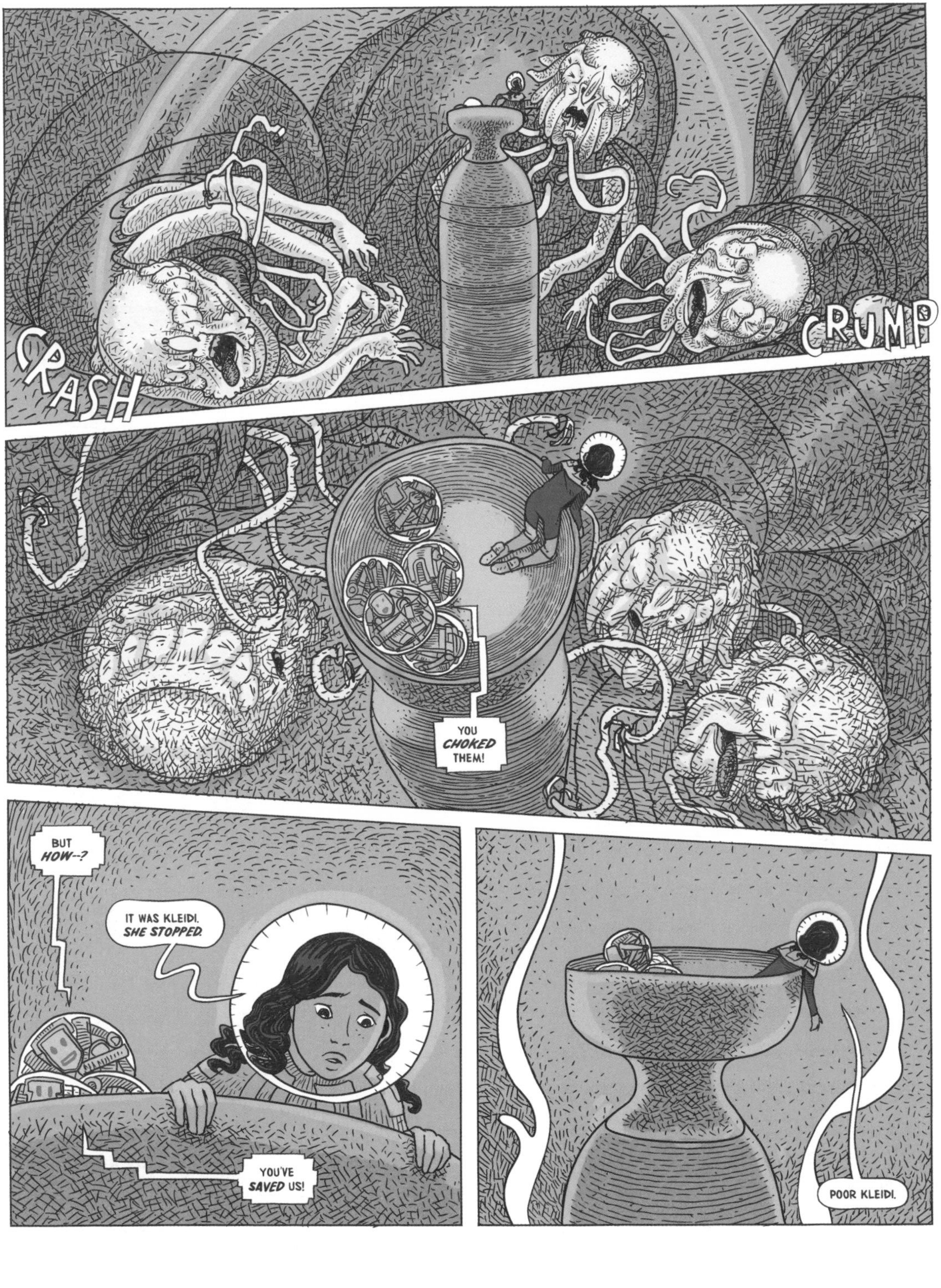
CRASH
CRUMP
YOU CHOKED THEM!
BUT HOW--?
IT WAS KLEIDI. SHE STOPPED.
YOU'VE SAVED US!
POOR KLEIDI.

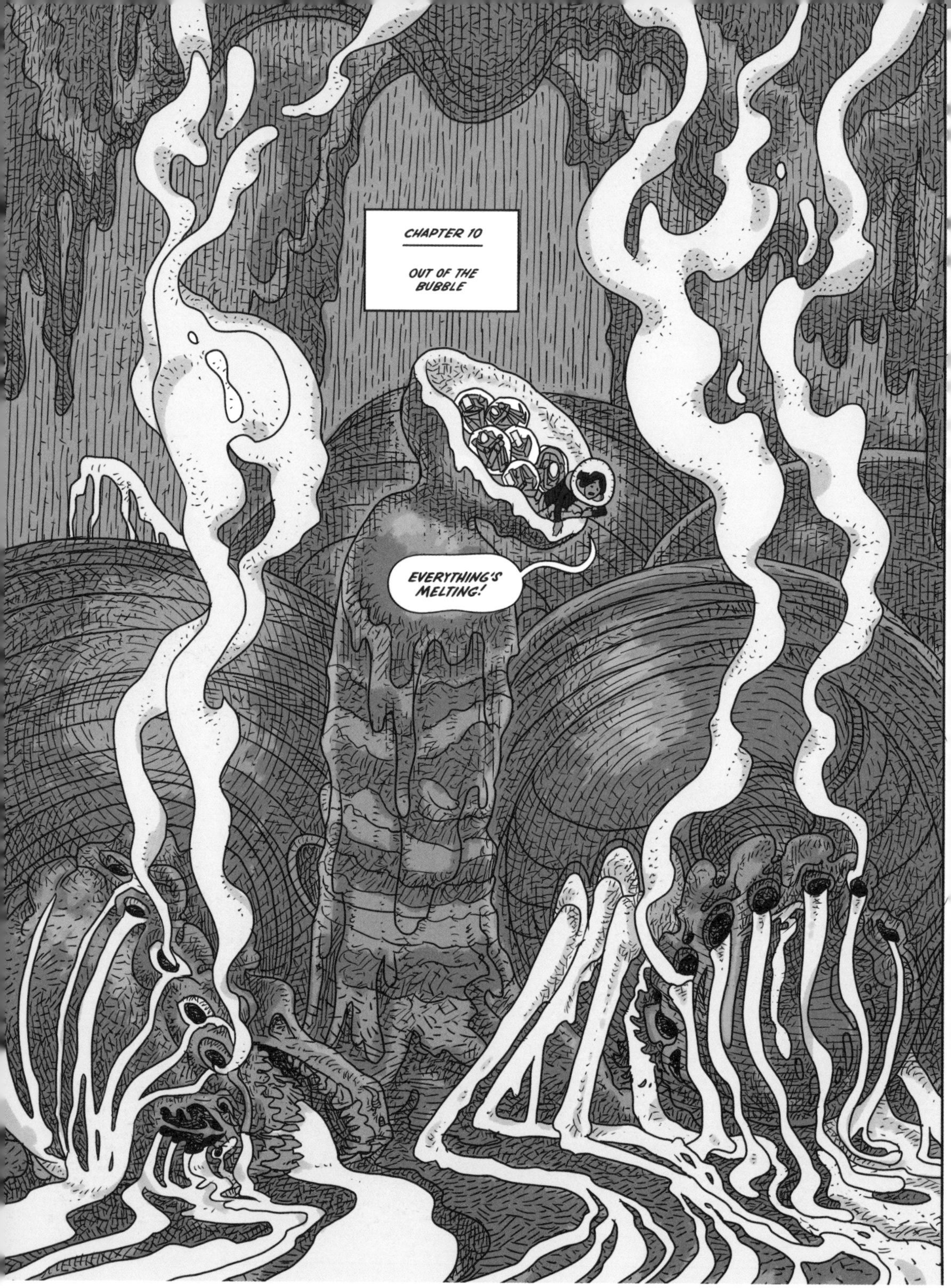
CHAPTER 10
OUT OF THE BUBBLE
EVERYTHING'S MELTING!

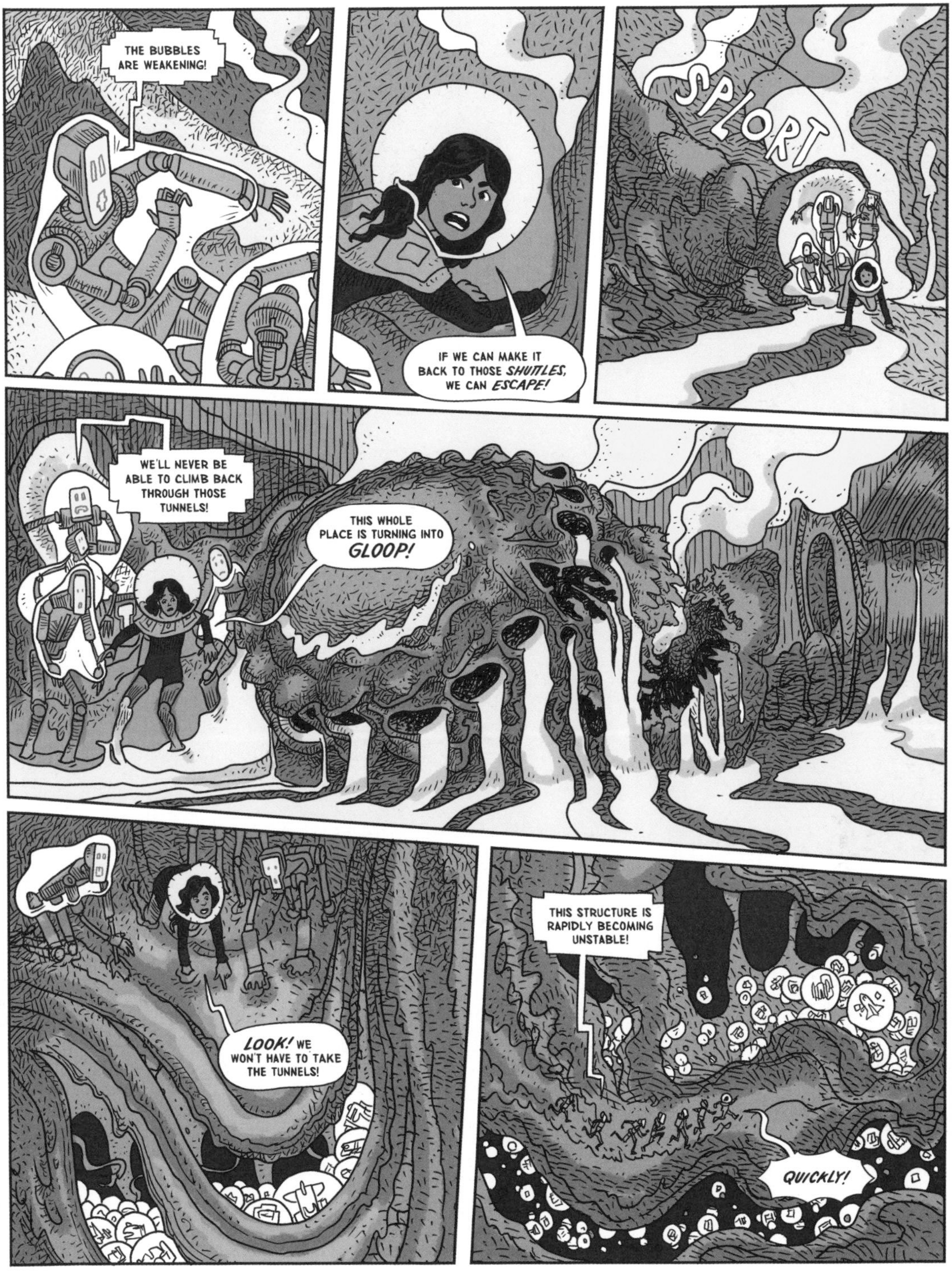
THE BUBBLES ARE WEAKENING!
IF WE CAN MAKE IT BACK TO THOSE *SHUTTLES*, WE CAN *ESCAPE*!
SPLORT
WE'LL NEVER BE ABLE TO CLIMB BACK THROUGH THOSE TUNNELS!
THIS WHOLE PLACE IS TURNING INTO *GLOOP!*
LOOK! WE WON'T HAVE TO TAKE THE TUNNELS!
THIS STRUCTURE IS RAPIDLY BECOMING UNSTABLE!
QUICKLY!

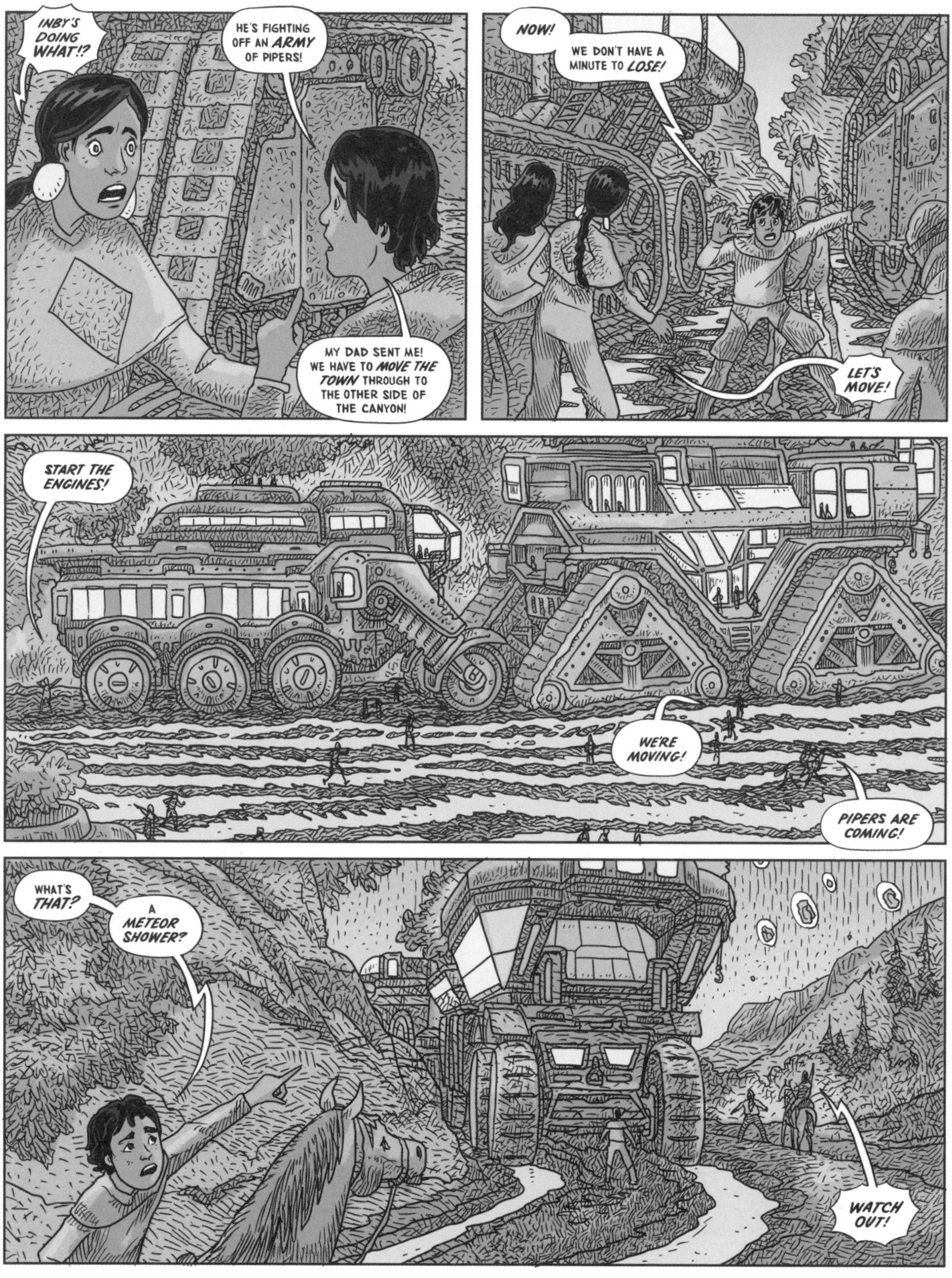

INBY'S DOING WHAT!?
HE'S FIGHTING OFF AN ARMY OF PIPERS!
MY DAD SENT ME! WE HAVE TO MOVE THE TOWN THROUGH TO THE OTHER SIDE OF THE CANYON!
NOW!
WE DON'T HAVE A MINUTE TO LOSE!
LET'S MOVE!
START THE ENGINES!
WE'RE MOVING!
PIPERS ARE COMING!
WHAT'S THAT?
A METEOR SHOWER?
WATCH OUT!

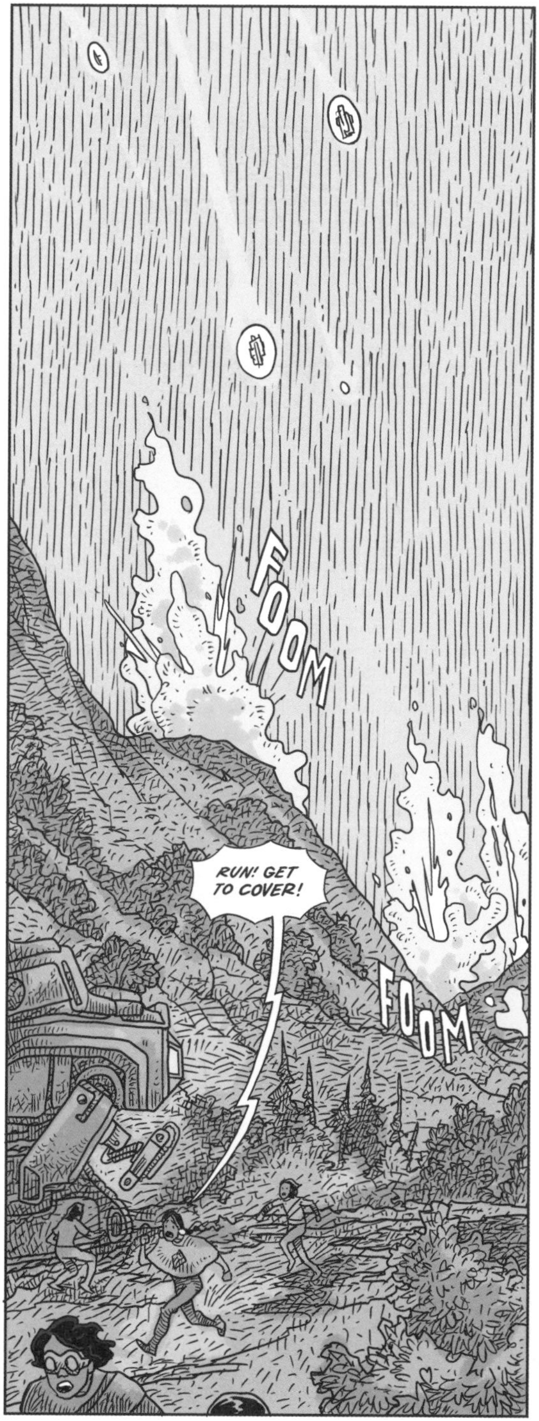
FOOM
RUN! GET TO COVER!
FOOM

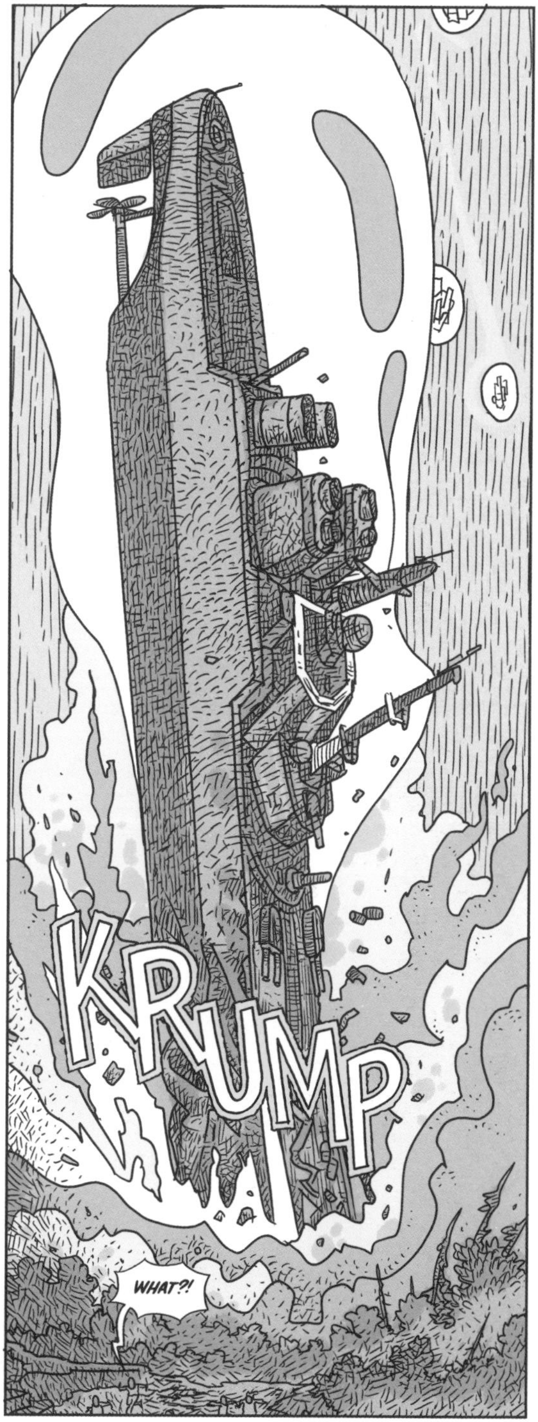
KRUMP
WHAT?!

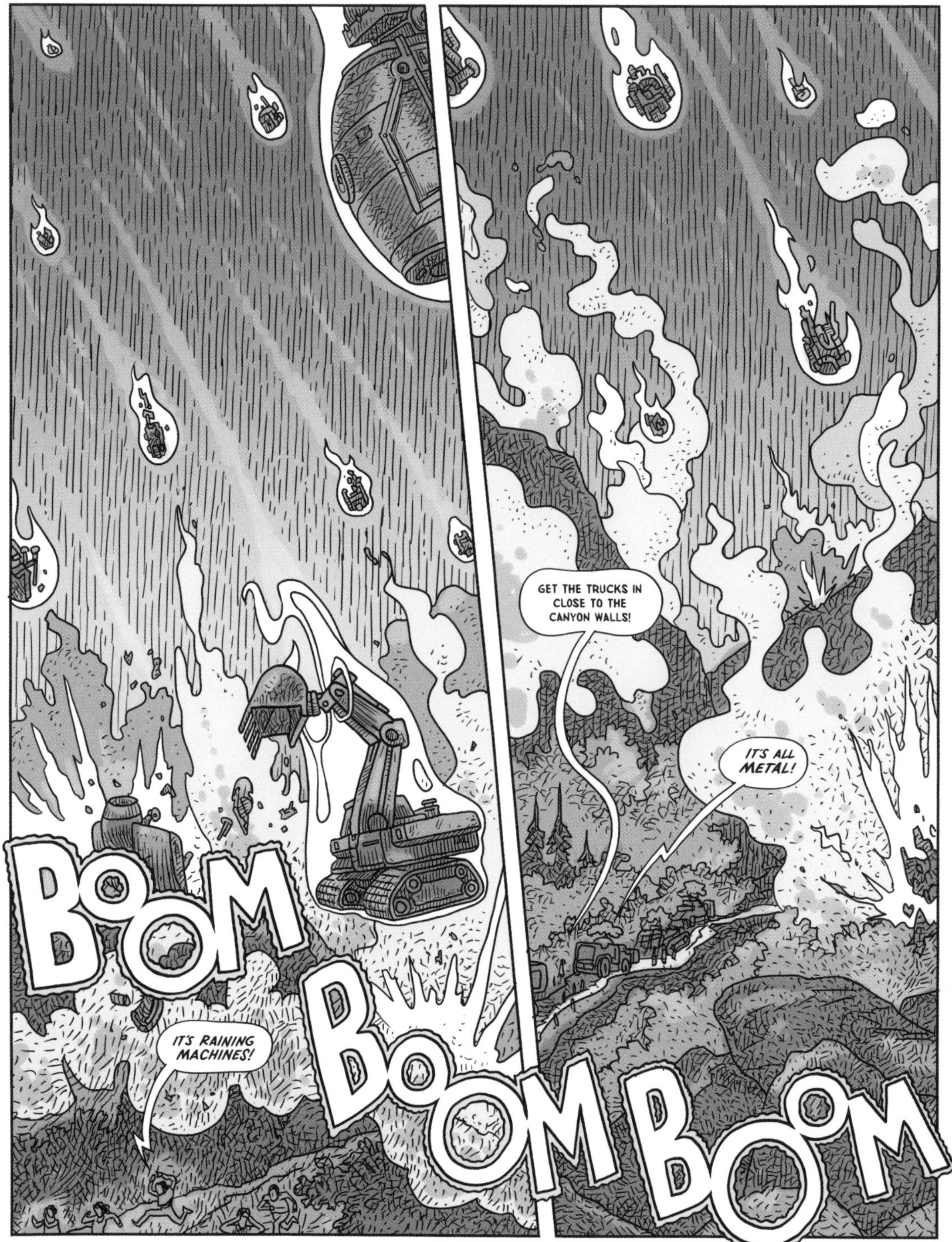
BOOM
IT'S RAINING MACHINES!
BOOM
GET THE TRUCKS IN CLOSE TO THE CANYON WALLS!
IT'S ALL METAL!
BOOM

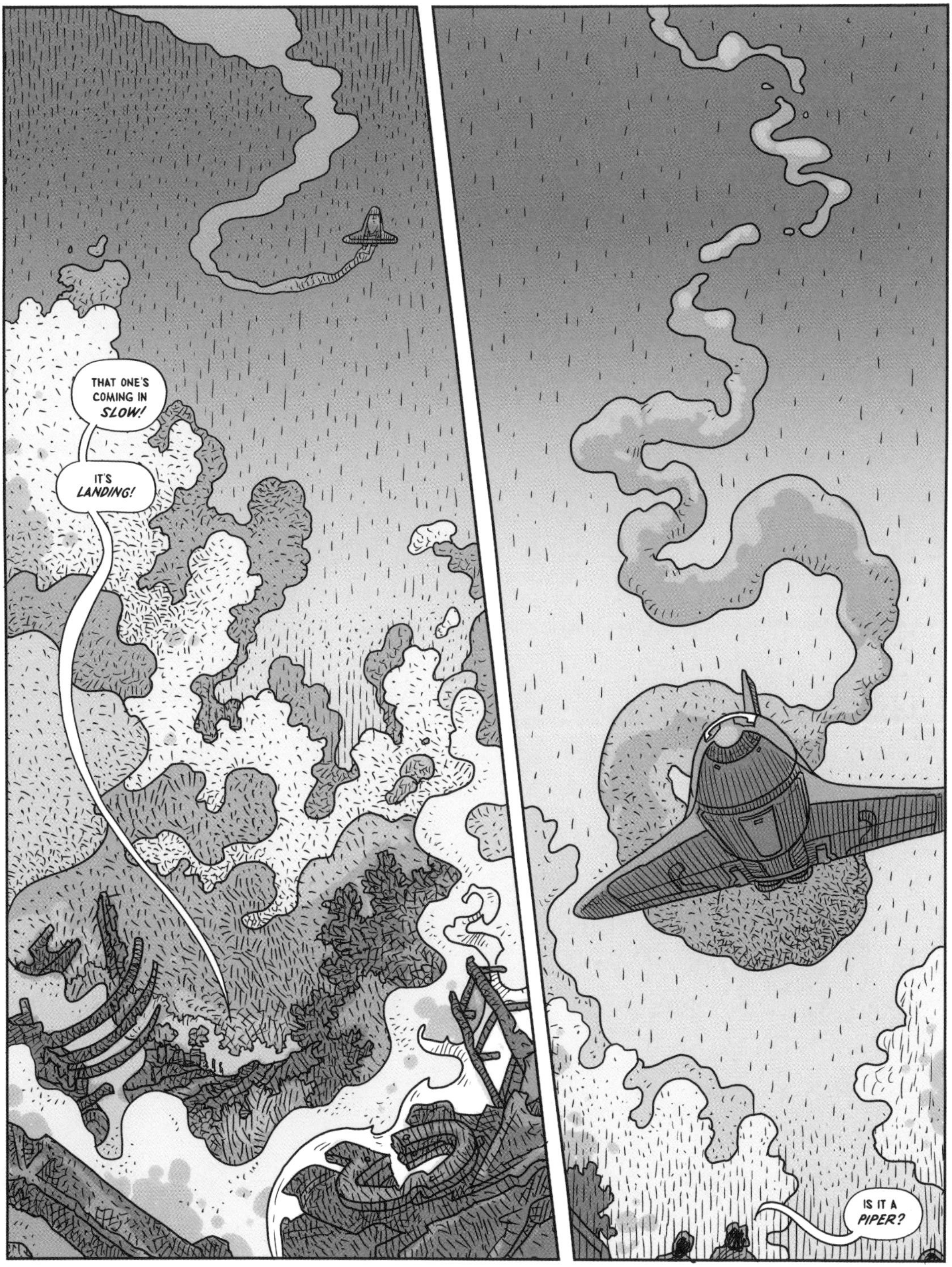
THAT ONE'S COMING IN SLOW!
IT'S LANDING!
IS IT A PIPER?

WHAT IS IT?

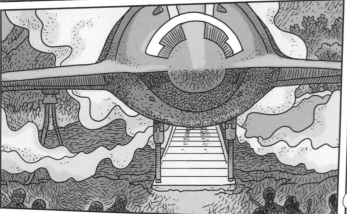

STRATA?

IS THAT REALLY *HER*?

IT IS!

HOW DID YOU— *WHERE* DID YOU— WHAT'S *GOING ON!?*

IT'S OVER.

THE PIPERS ARE ALL DEAD— REALLY *DEAD*.

SHE SAVED US ALL! SHE STOPPED THE PIPERS FOR GOOD!

IT WASN'T ME. IT WAS *KLEIDI!*

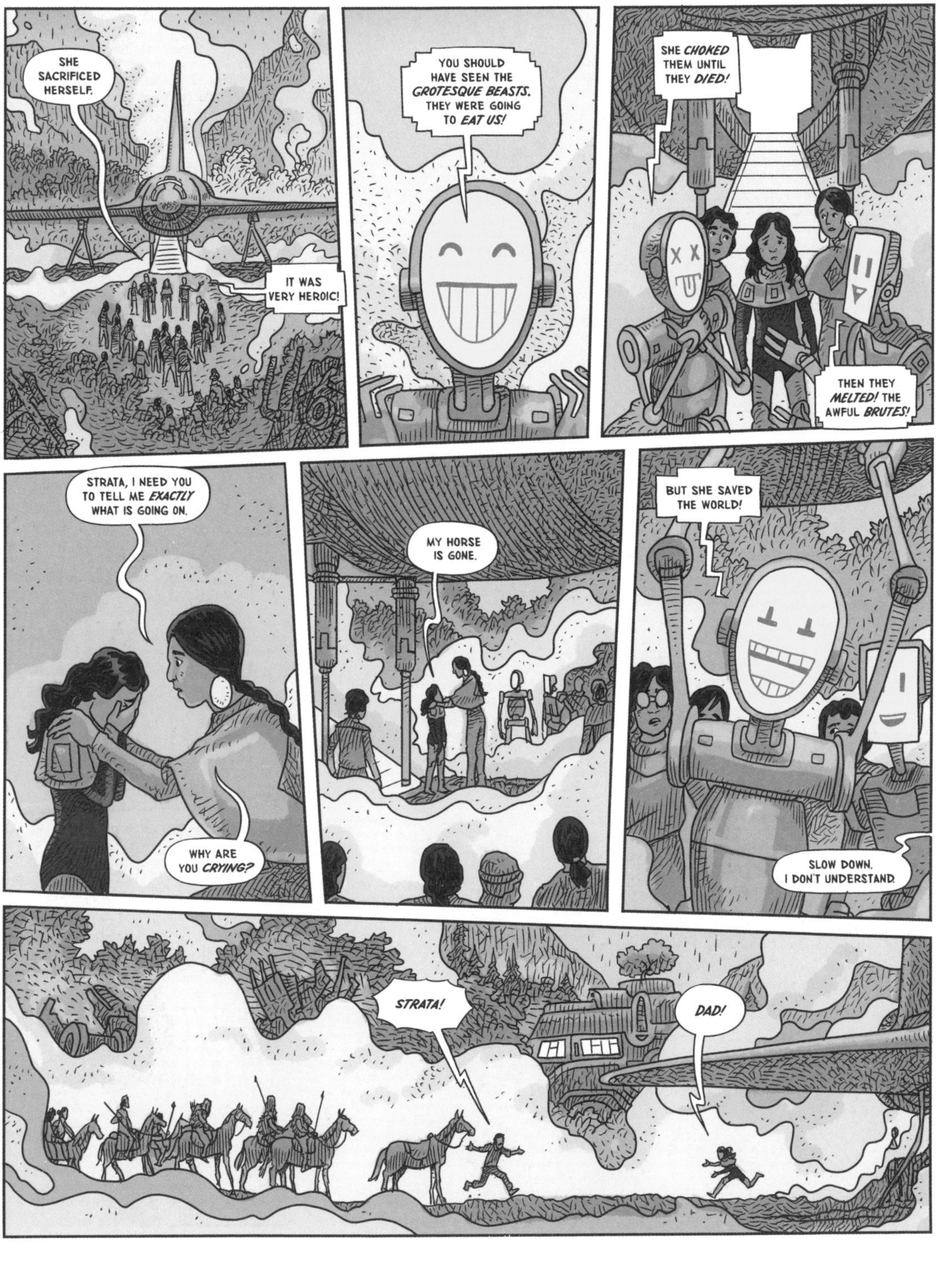
SHE SACRIFICED HERSELF.
IT WAS VERY HEROIC!
YOU SHOULD HAVE SEEN THE GROTESQUE BEASTS. THEY WERE GOING TO EAT US!
SHE CHOKED THEM UNTIL THEY DIED!
THEN THEY MELTED! THE AWFUL BRUTES!
STRATA, I NEED YOU TO TELL ME EXACTLY WHAT IS GOING ON.
WHY ARE YOU CRYING?
MY HORSE IS GONE.
BUT SHE SAVED THE WORLD!
SLOW DOWN. I DON'T UNDERSTAND.
STRATA!
DAD!

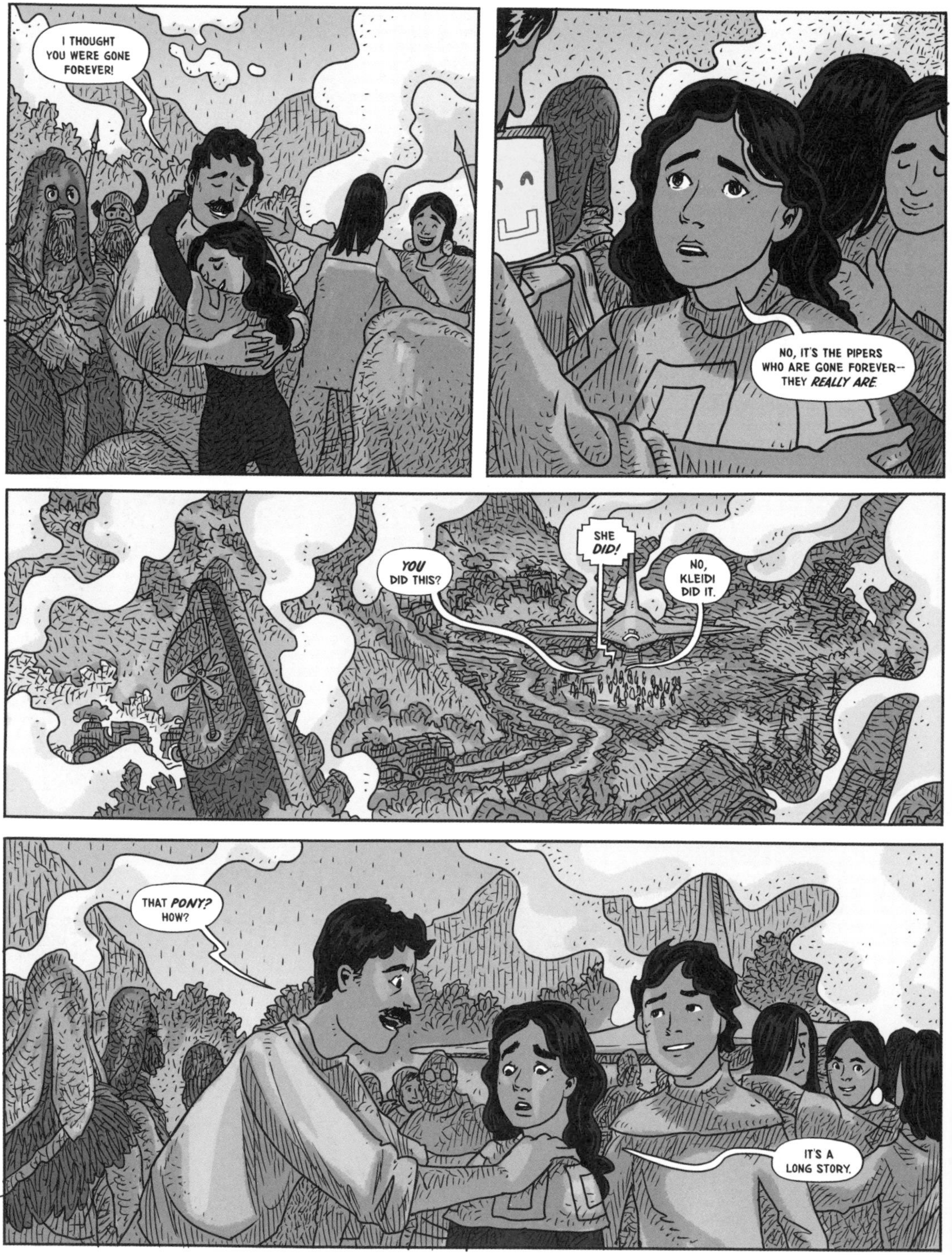

I THOUGHT YOU WERE GONE FOREVER!
NO, IT'S THE PIPERS WHO ARE GONE FOREVER-- THEY *REALLY ARE.*
YOU DID THIS?
SHE *DID!*
NO, KLEIDI DID IT.
THAT *PONY?* HOW?
IT'S A LONG STORY.

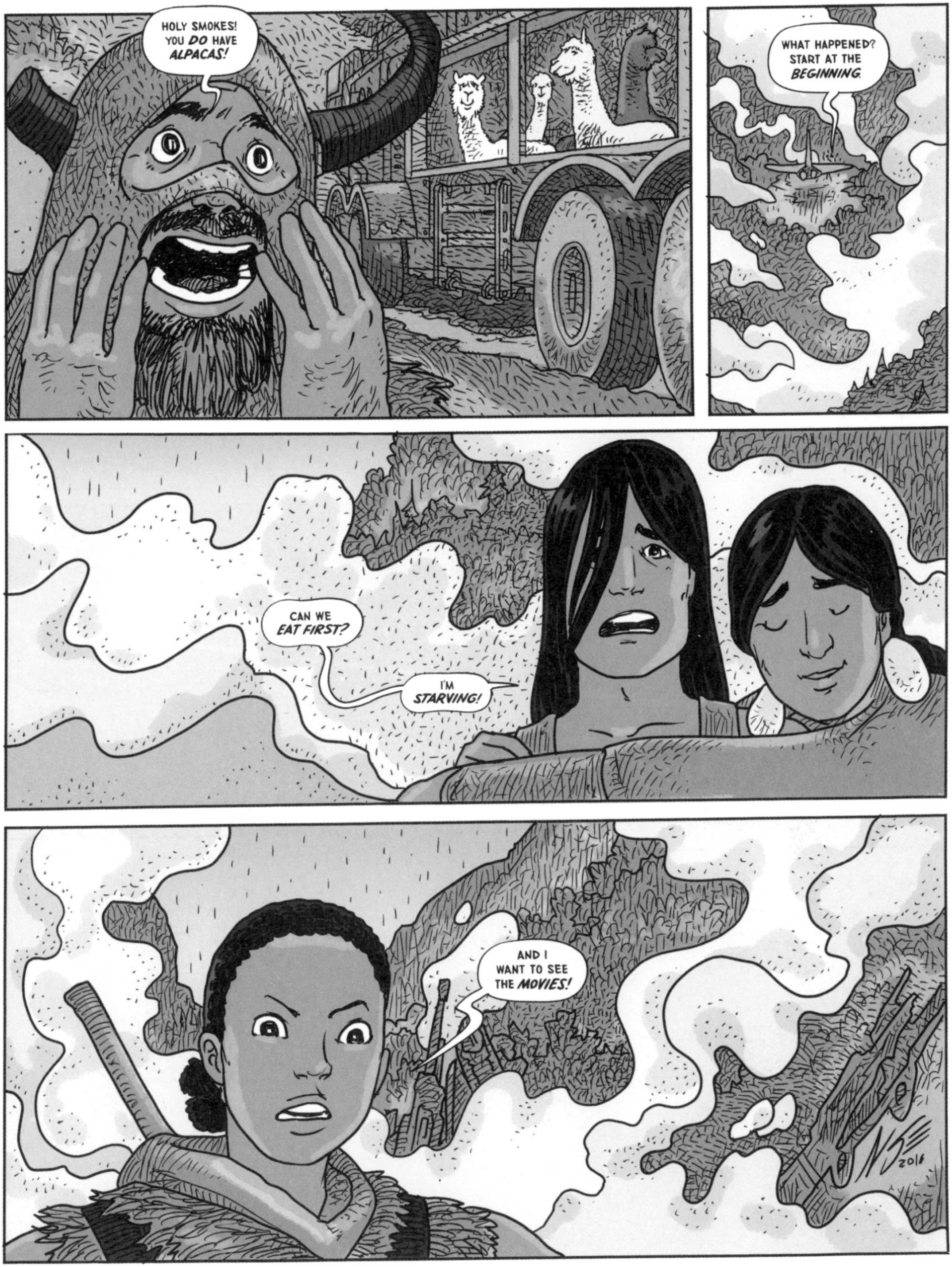
HOLY SMOKES! YOU DO HAVE ALPACAS!
WHAT HAPPENED? START AT THE BEGINNING.
CAN WE EAT FIRST?
I'M STARVING!
AND I WANT TO SEE THE MOVIES!
2016

THE END

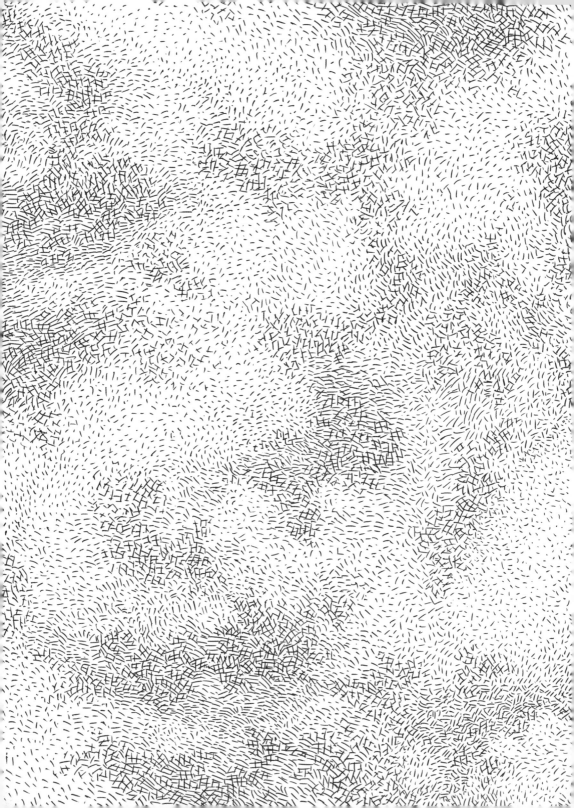

NATHAN HALE IS THE AUTHOR AND ILLUSTRATOR OF THE #1 *NEW YORK TIMES*
BESTSELLING SERIES HAZARDOUS TALES, GRAPHIC NOVELS ON AMERICAN HISTORY.

ONE TRICK PONY IS THE NINTH GRAPHIC NOVEL ILLUSTRATED BY NATHAN HALE.
HE CREATED THE ILLUSTRATIONS FOR THE FAIRY TALE EPIC *RAPUNZEL'S REVENGE* AND ITS
SEQUEL *CALAMITY JACK*, WRITTEN BY SHANNON AND DEAN HALE (NO RELATION).

HE LIVES IN UTAH. VISIT WWW.NATHANHALEAUTHOR.COM FOR MORE.

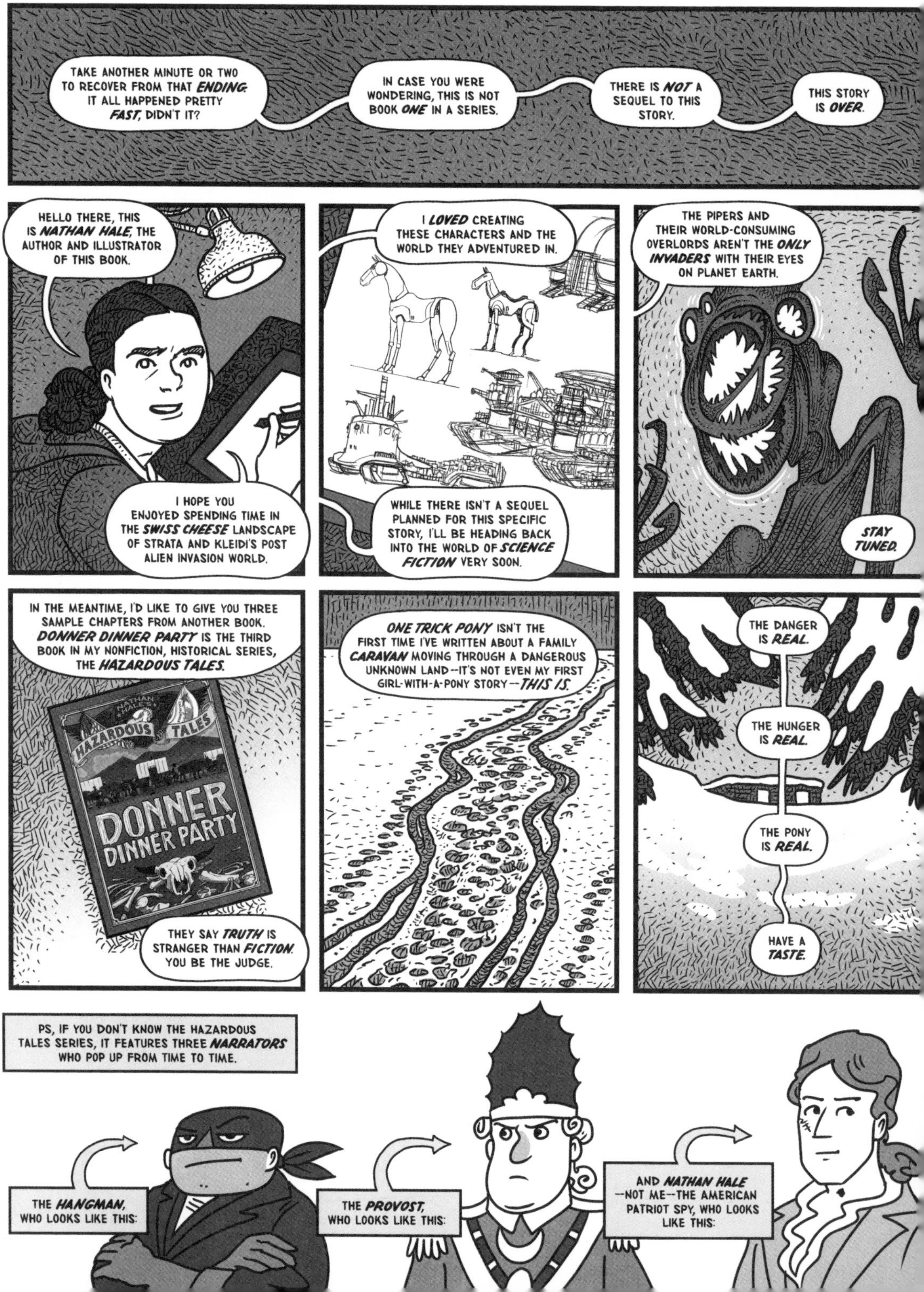

TAKE ANOTHER MINUTE OR TWO TO RECOVER FROM THAT ENDING. IT ALL HAPPENED PRETTY FAST, DIDN'T IT?
IN CASE YOU WERE WONDERING, THIS IS NOT BOOK ONE IN A SERIES.
THERE IS NOT A SEQUEL TO THIS STORY.
THIS STORY IS OVER.
HELLO THERE, THIS IS NATHAN HALE, THE AUTHOR AND ILLUSTRATOR OF THIS BOOK.
I HOPE YOU ENJOYED SPENDING TIME IN THE SWISS CHEESE LANDSCAPE OF STRATA AND KLEIDI'S POST ALIEN INVASION WORLD.
I LOVED CREATING THESE CHARACTERS AND THE WORLD THEY ADVENTURED IN.
WHILE THERE ISN'T A SEQUEL PLANNED FOR THIS SPECIFIC STORY, I'LL BE HEADING BACK INTO THE WORLD OF SCIENCE FICTION VERY SOON.
THE PIPERS AND THEIR WORLD-CONSUMING OVERLORDS AREN'T THE ONLY INVADERS WITH THEIR EYES ON PLANET EARTH.
STAY TUNED.
IN THE MEANTIME, I'D LIKE TO GIVE YOU THREE SAMPLE CHAPTERS FROM ANOTHER BOOK. DONNER DINNER PARTY IS THE THIRD BOOK IN MY NONFICTION, HISTORICAL SERIES, THE HAZARDOUS TALES.
NATHAN HALE'S HAZARDOUS TALES
DONNER DINNER PARTY
THEY SAY TRUTH IS STRANGER THAN FICTION. YOU BE THE JUDGE.
ONE TRICK PONY ISN'T THE FIRST TIME I'VE WRITTEN ABOUT A FAMILY CARAVAN MOVING THROUGH A DANGEROUS UNKNOWN LAND--IT'S NOT EVEN MY FIRST GIRL-WITH-A-PONY STORY--THIS IS.
THE DANGER IS REAL.
THE HUNGER IS REAL.
THE PONY IS REAL.
HAVE A TASTE.
PS, IF YOU DON'T KNOW THE HAZARDOUS TALES SERIES, IT FEATURES THREE NARRATORS WHO POP UP FROM TIME TO TIME.
THE HANGMAN, WHO LOOKS LIKE THIS:
THE PROVOST, WHO LOOKS LIKE THIS:
AND NATHAN HALE --NOT ME--THE AMERICAN PATRIOT SPY, WHO LOOKS LIKE THIS:

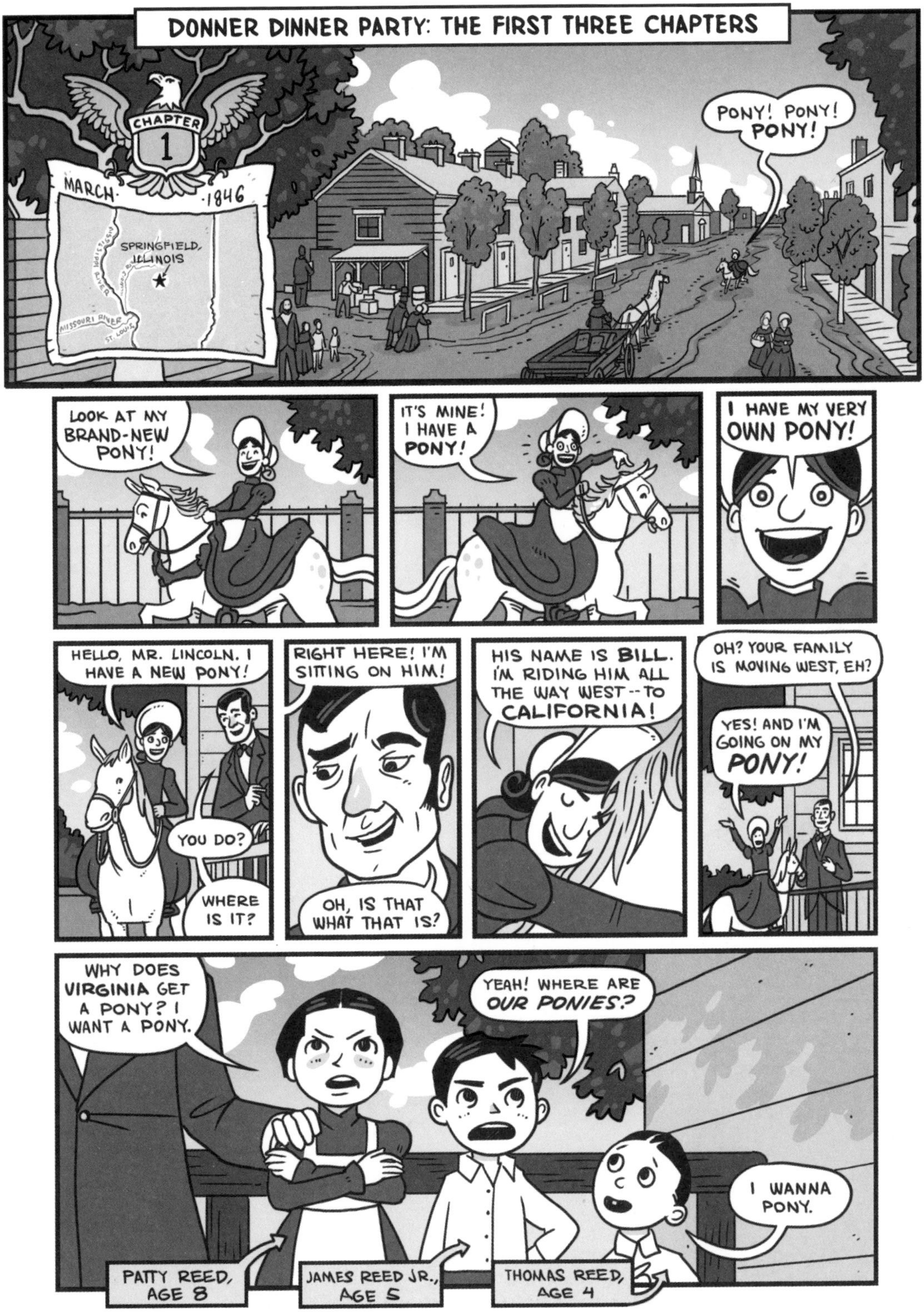
DONNER DINNER PARTY: THE FIRST THREE CHAPTERS
CHAPTER 1
MARCH · 1846
SPRINGFIELD, ILLINOIS
MISSISSIPPI RIVER
MISSOURI RIVER
ST. LOUIS
PONY! PONY! PONY!
LOOK AT MY BRAND-NEW PONY!
IT'S MINE! I HAVE A PONY!
I HAVE MY VERY OWN PONY!
HELLO, MR. LINCOLN. I HAVE A NEW PONY!
YOU DO?
WHERE IS IT?
RIGHT HERE! I'M SITTING ON HIM!
OH, IS THAT WHAT THAT IS?
HIS NAME IS BILL. I'M RIDING HIM ALL THE WAY WEST--TO CALIFORNIA!
OH? YOUR FAMILY IS MOVING WEST, EH?
YES! AND I'M GOING ON MY PONY!
WHY DOES VIRGINIA GET A PONY? I WANT A PONY.
YEAH! WHERE ARE OUR PONIES?
I WANNA PONY.
PATTY REED, AGE 8
JAMES REED JR., AGE 5
THOMAS REED, AGE 4

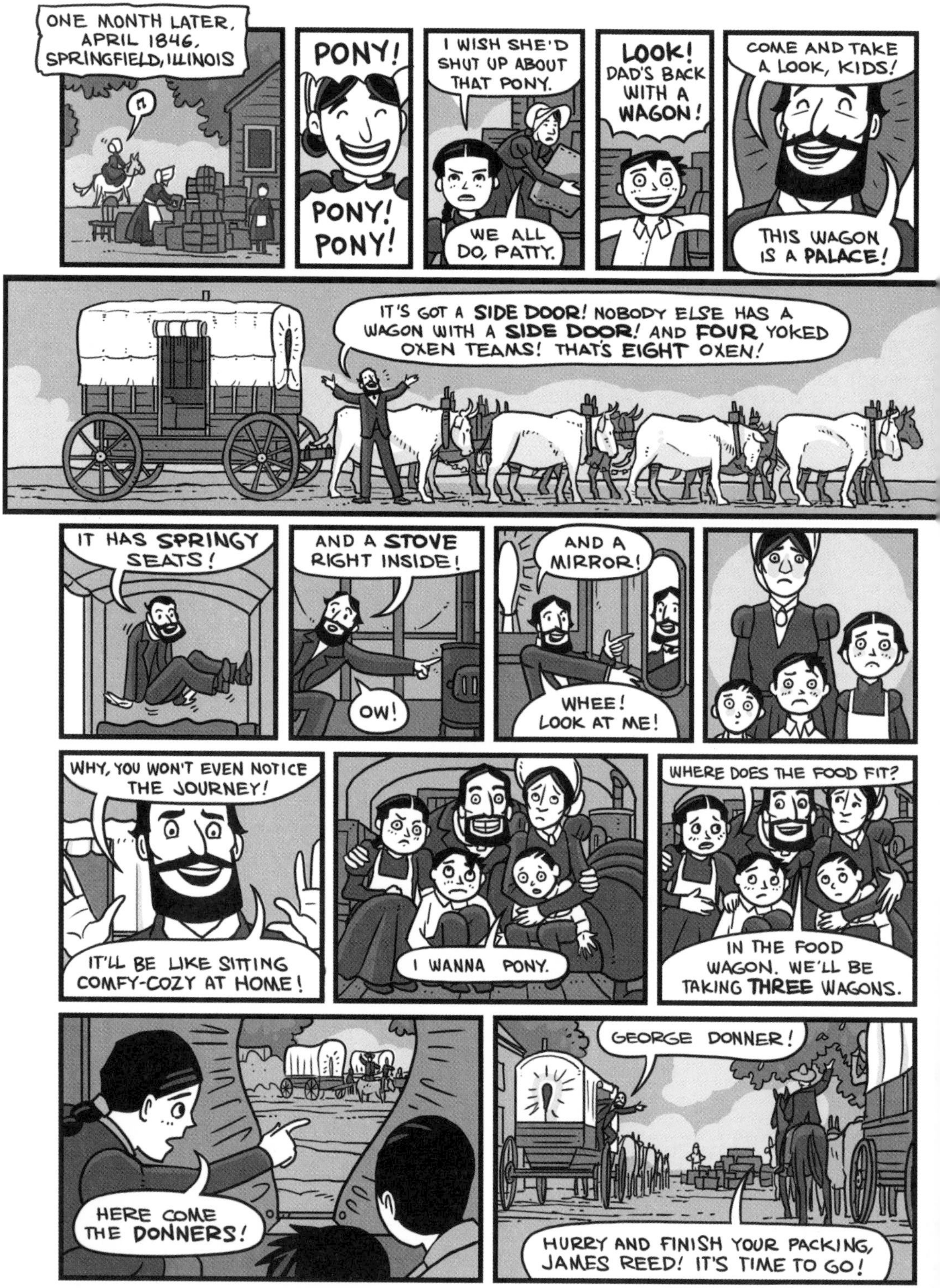
ONE MONTH LATER, APRIL 1846, SPRINGFIELD, ILLINOIS
PONY!
PONY! PONY!
I WISH SHE'D SHUT UP ABOUT THAT PONY.
WE ALL DO, PATTY.
LOOK! DAD'S BACK WITH A WAGON!
COME AND TAKE A LOOK, KIDS!
THIS WAGON IS A PALACE!
IT'S GOT A SIDE DOOR! NOBODY ELSE HAS A WAGON WITH A SIDE DOOR! AND FOUR YOKED OXEN TEAMS! THAT'S EIGHT OXEN!
IT HAS SPRINGY SEATS!
AND A STOVE RIGHT INSIDE!
OW!
AND A MIRROR!
WHEE! LOOK AT ME!
WHY, YOU WON'T EVEN NOTICE THE JOURNEY!
IT'LL BE LIKE SITTING COMFY-COZY AT HOME!
I WANNA PONY.
WHERE DOES THE FOOD FIT?
IN THE FOOD WAGON. WE'LL BE TAKING THREE WAGONS.
HERE COME THE DONNERS!
GEORGE DONNER!
HURRY AND FINISH YOUR PACKING, JAMES REED! IT'S TIME TO GO!

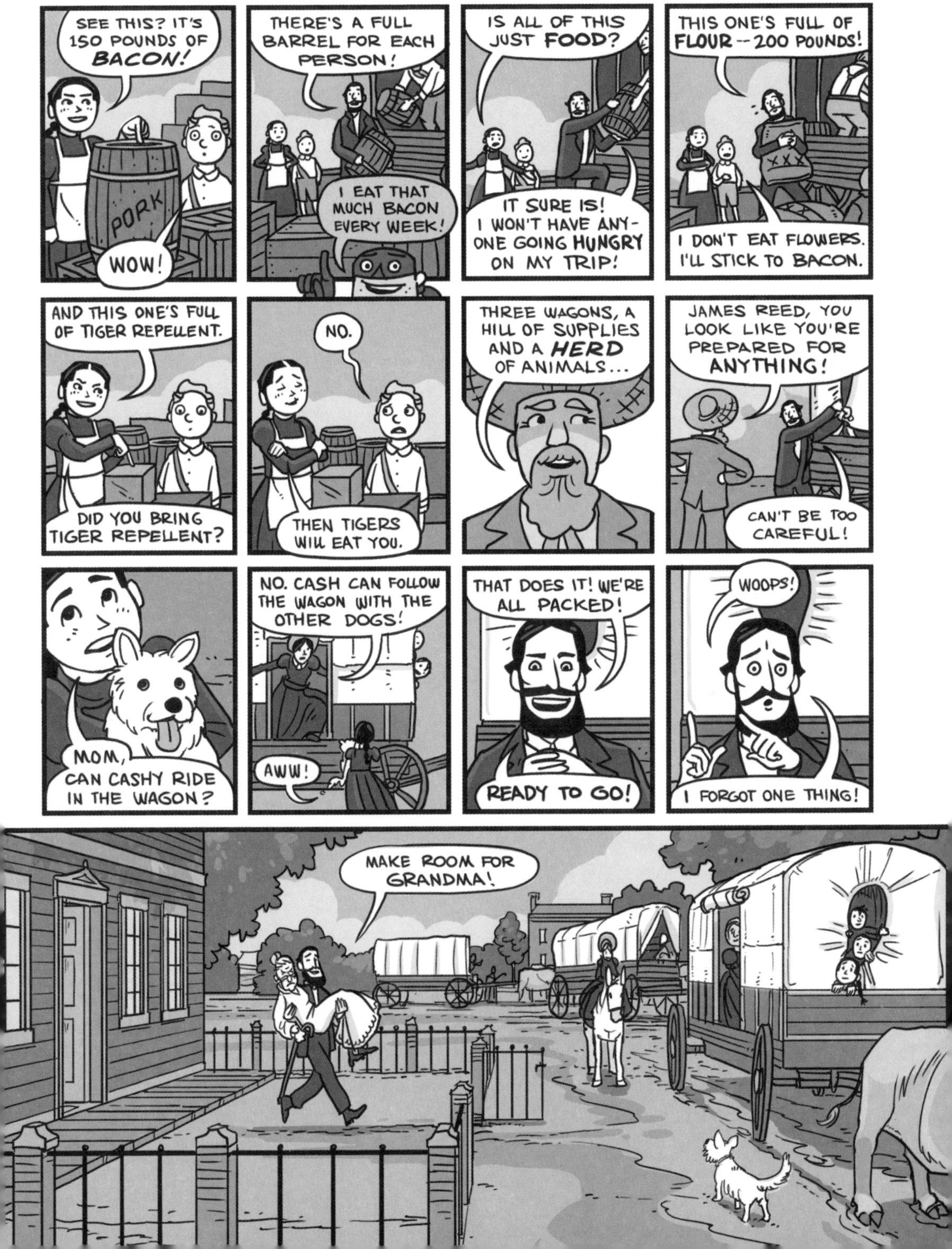
SEE THIS? IT'S 150 POUNDS OF BACON!
WOW!
THERE'S A FULL BARREL FOR EACH PERSON!
I EAT THAT MUCH BACON EVERY WEEK!
IS ALL OF THIS JUST FOOD?
IT SURE IS! I WON'T HAVE ANY-ONE GOING HUNGRY ON MY TRIP!
THIS ONE'S FULL OF FLOUR--200 POUNDS!
I DON'T EAT FLOWERS. I'LL STICK TO BACON.
AND THIS ONE'S FULL OF TIGER REPELLENT.
DID YOU BRING TIGER REPELLENT?
NO.
THEN TIGERS WILL EAT YOU.
THREE WAGONS, A HILL OF SUPPLIES AND A HERD OF ANIMALS...
JAMES REED, YOU LOOK LIKE YOU'RE PREPARED FOR ANYTHING!
CAN'T BE TOO CAREFUL!
MOM, CAN CASHY RIDE IN THE WAGON?
NO. CASH CAN FOLLOW THE WAGON WITH THE OTHER DOGS!
AWW!
THAT DOES IT! WE'RE ALL PACKED!
READY TO GO!
WOOPS!
I FORGOT ONE THING!
MAKE ROOM FOR GRANDMA!
PORK

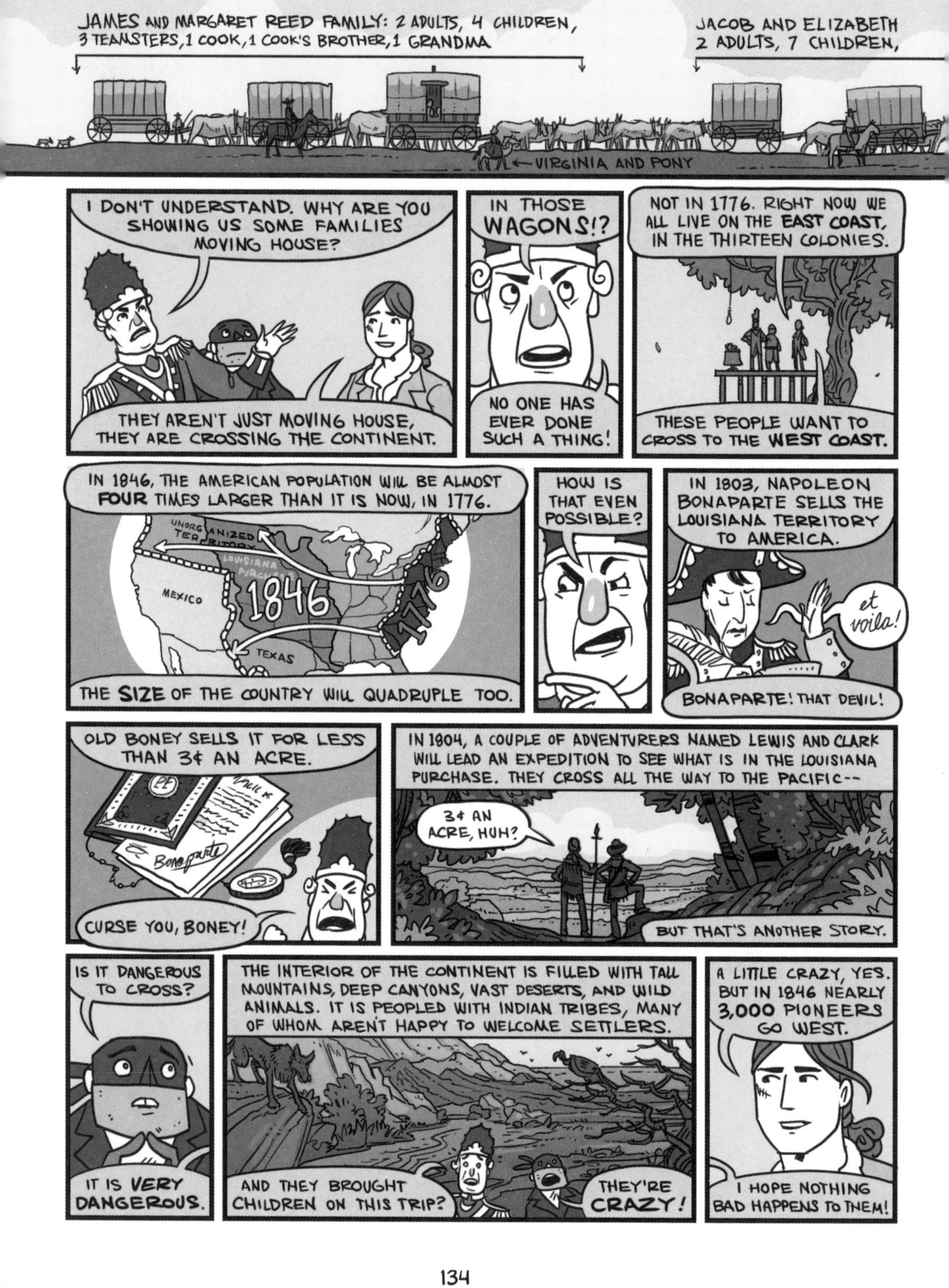

JAMES AND MARGARET REED FAMILY: 2 ADULTS, 4 CHILDREN, 3 TEAMSTERS, 1 COOK, 1 COOK'S BROTHER, 1 GRANDMA
JACOB AND ELIZABETH 2 ADULTS, 7 CHILDREN,
← VIRGINIA AND PONY
I DON'T UNDERSTAND. WHY ARE YOU SHOWING US SOME FAMILIES MOVING HOUSE?
THEY AREN'T JUST MOVING HOUSE, THEY ARE CROSSING THE CONTINENT.
IN THOSE WAGONS!?
NO ONE HAS EVER DONE SUCH A THING!
NOT IN 1776. RIGHT NOW WE ALL LIVE ON THE EAST COAST, IN THE THIRTEEN COLONIES.
THESE PEOPLE WANT TO CROSS TO THE WEST COAST.
IN 1846, THE AMERICAN POPULATION WILL BE ALMOST FOUR TIMES LARGER THAN IT IS NOW, IN 1776.
UNORGANIZED TERRITORY
LOUISIANA PURCHASE
MEXICO
1846
1776
TEXAS
THE SIZE OF THE COUNTRY WILL QUADRUPLE TOO.
HOW IS THAT EVEN POSSIBLE?
IN 1803, NAPOLEON BONAPARTE SELLS THE LOUISIANA TERRITORY TO AMERICA.
et voila!
BONAPARTE! THAT DEVIL!
OLD BONEY SELLS IT FOR LESS THAN 3¢ AN ACRE.
Bonaparte
CURSE YOU, BONEY!
IN 1804, A COUPLE OF ADVENTURERS NAMED LEWIS AND CLARK WILL LEAD AN EXPEDITION TO SEE WHAT IS IN THE LOUISIANA PURCHASE. THEY CROSS ALL THE WAY TO THE PACIFIC--
3¢ AN ACRE, HUH?
BUT THAT'S ANOTHER STORY.
IS IT DANGEROUS TO CROSS?
IT IS VERY DANGEROUS.
THE INTERIOR OF THE CONTINENT IS FILLED WITH TALL MOUNTAINS, DEEP CANYONS, VAST DESERTS, AND WILD ANIMALS. IT IS PEOPLED WITH INDIAN TRIBES, MANY OF WHOM AREN'T HAPPY TO WELCOME SETTLERS.
AND THEY BROUGHT CHILDREN ON THIS TRIP?
THEY'RE CRAZY!
A LITTLE CRAZY, YES. BUT IN 1846 NEARLY 3,000 PIONEERS GO WEST.
I HOPE NOTHING BAD HAPPENS TO THEM!

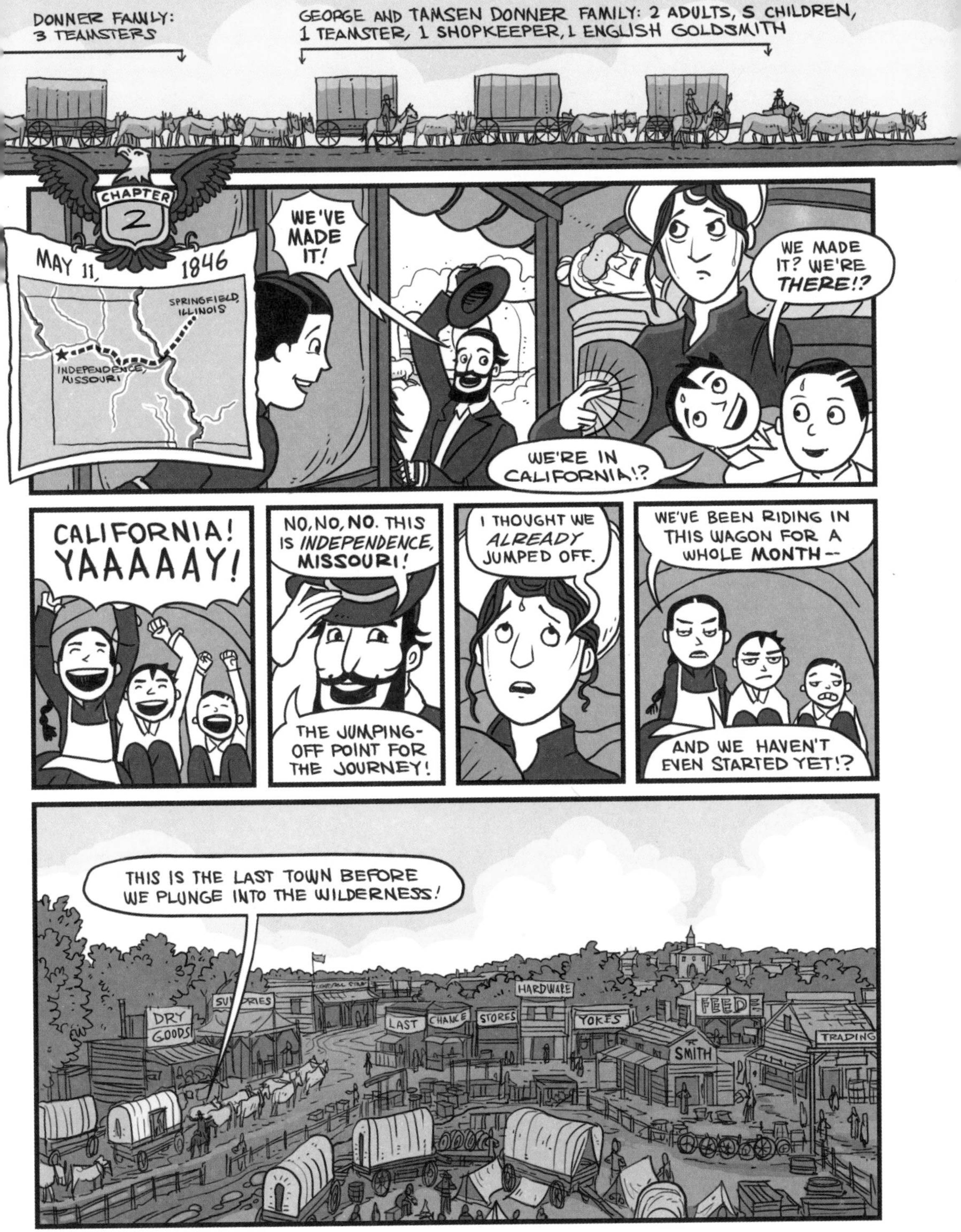
DONNER FAMILY: 3 TEAMSTERS
GEORGE AND TAMSEN DONNER FAMILY: 2 ADULTS, 5 CHILDREN, 1 TEAMSTER, 1 SHOPKEEPER, 1 ENGLISH GOLDSMITH
CHAPTER 2
MAY 11, 1846
SPRINGFIELD, ILLINOIS
INDEPENDENCE, MISSOURI
WE'VE MADE IT!
WE MADE IT? WE'RE THERE!?
WE'RE IN CALIFORNIA!?
CALIFORNIA! YAAAAAY!
NO, NO, NO. THIS IS INDEPENDENCE, MISSOURI!
THE JUMPING-OFF POINT FOR THE JOURNEY!
I THOUGHT WE ALREADY JUMPED OFF.
WE'VE BEEN RIDING IN THIS WAGON FOR A WHOLE MONTH--
AND WE HAVEN'T EVEN STARTED YET!?
THIS IS THE LAST TOWN BEFORE WE PLUNGE INTO THE WILDERNESS!
DRY GOODS
HARDWARE
LAST CHANCE STORES
YOKES
FEED
SMITH
TRADING

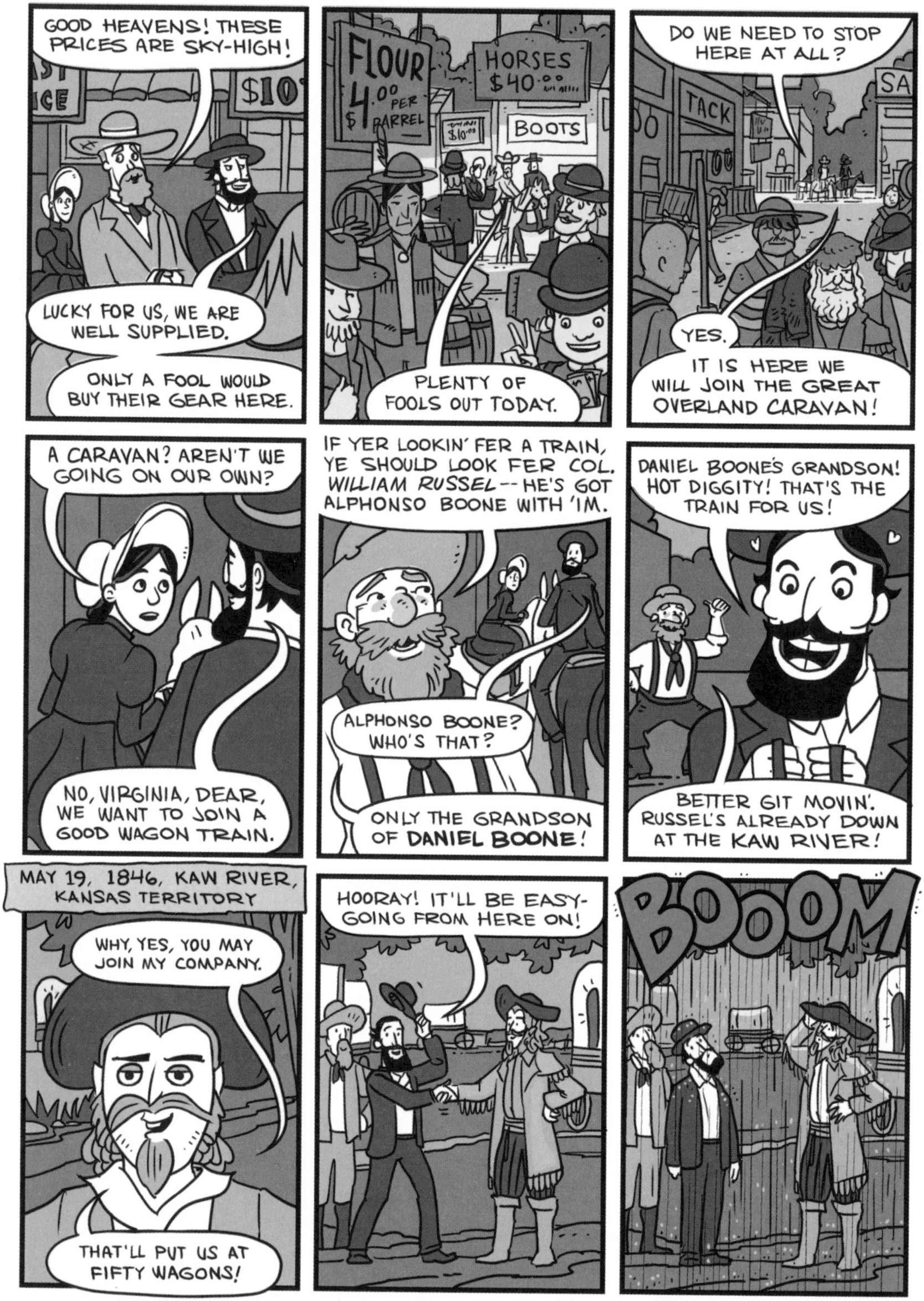
GOOD HEAVENS! THESE PRICES ARE SKY-HIGH!
LUCKY FOR US, WE ARE WELL SUPPLIED.
ONLY A FOOL WOULD BUY THEIR GEAR HERE.
FLOUR $4.00 PER BARREL
HORSES $40.00
BOOTS
PLENTY OF FOOLS OUT TODAY.
DO WE NEED TO STOP HERE AT ALL?
TACK
YES.
IT IS HERE WE WILL JOIN THE GREAT OVERLAND CARAVAN!
A CARAVAN? AREN'T WE GOING ON OUR OWN?
NO, VIRGINIA, DEAR, WE WANT TO JOIN A GOOD WAGON TRAIN.
IF YER LOOKIN' FER A TRAIN, YE SHOULD LOOK FER COL. *WILLIAM RUSSEL*--HE'S GOT ALPHONSO BOONE WITH 'IM.
ALPHONSO BOONE? WHO'S THAT?
ONLY THE GRANDSON OF **DANIEL BOONE**!
DANIEL BOONE'S GRANDSON! HOT DIGGITY! THAT'S THE TRAIN FOR US!
BETTER GIT MOVIN'. RUSSEL'S ALREADY DOWN AT THE KAW RIVER!
MAY 19, 1846, KAW RIVER, KANSAS TERRITORY
WHY, YES, YOU MAY JOIN MY COMPANY.
THAT'LL PUT US AT FIFTY WAGONS!
HOORAY! IT'LL BE EASY-GOING FROM HERE ON!
BOOOM

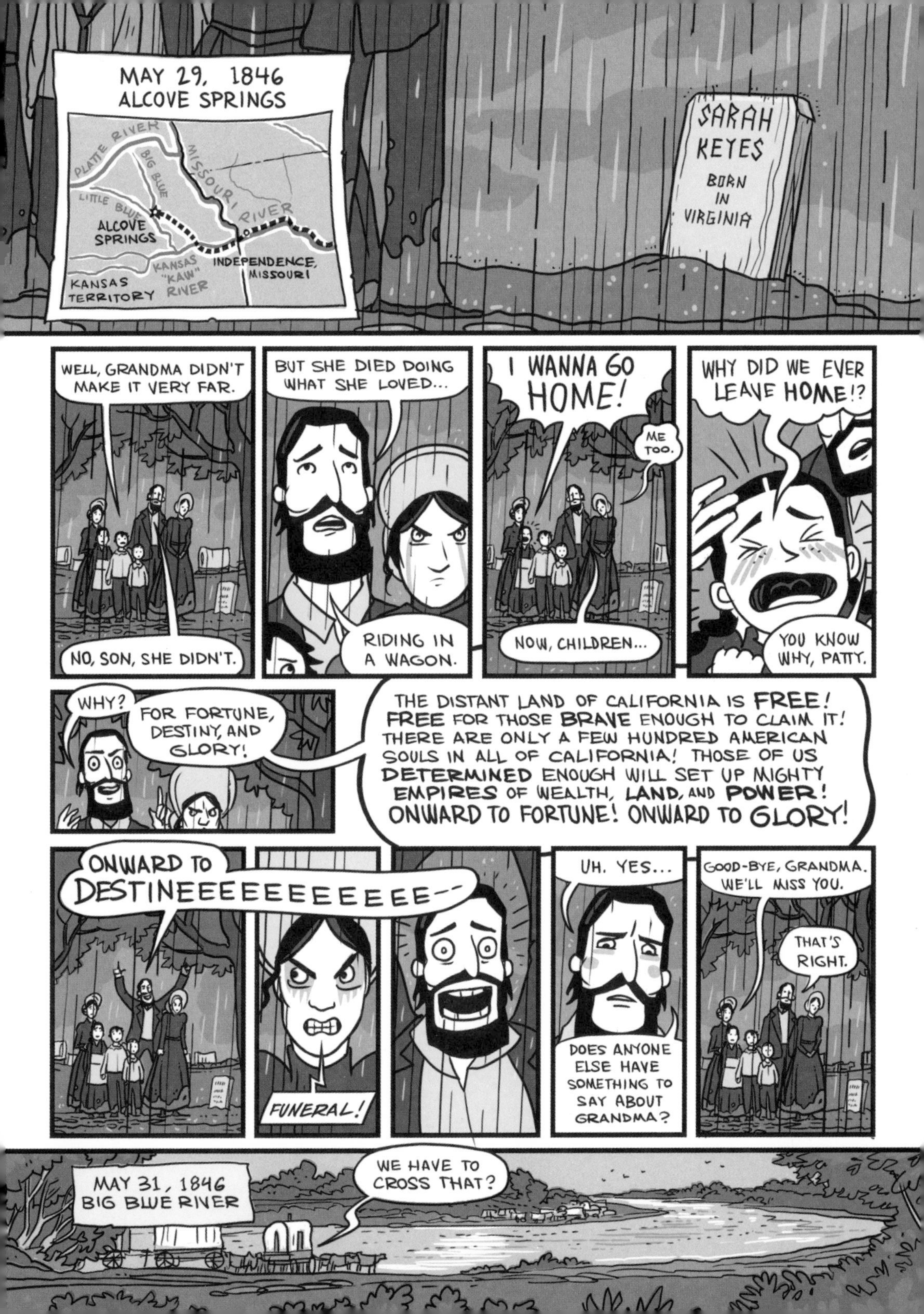
MAY 29, 1846
ALCOVE SPRINGS
PLATTE RIVER
BIG BLUE
MISSOURI RIVER
LITTLE BLUE
ALCOVE SPRINGS
KANSAS "KAW" RIVER
INDEPENDENCE, MISSOURI
KANSAS TERRITORY
SARAH KEYES
BORN IN VIRGINIA
WELL, GRANDMA DIDN'T MAKE IT VERY FAR.
NO, SON, SHE DIDN'T.
BUT SHE DIED DOING WHAT SHE LOVED...
RIDING IN A WAGON.
I WANNA GO HOME!
ME TOO.
NOW, CHILDREN...
WHY DID WE EVER LEAVE HOME!?
YOU KNOW WHY, PATTY.
WHY?
FOR FORTUNE, DESTINY, AND GLORY!
THE DISTANT LAND OF CALIFORNIA IS FREE! FREE FOR THOSE BRAVE ENOUGH TO CLAIM IT! THERE ARE ONLY A FEW HUNDRED AMERICAN SOULS IN ALL OF CALIFORNIA! THOSE OF US DETERMINED ENOUGH WILL SET UP MIGHTY EMPIRES OF WEALTH, LAND, AND POWER! ONWARD TO FORTUNE! ONWARD TO GLORY!
ONWARD TO DESTINEEEEEEEEEEEEE--
FUNERAL!
UH. YES...
DOES ANYONE ELSE HAVE SOMETHING TO SAY ABOUT GRANDMA?
GOOD-BYE, GRANDMA. WE'LL MISS YOU.
THAT'S RIGHT.
MAY 31, 1846
BIG BLUE RIVER
WE HAVE TO CROSS THAT?

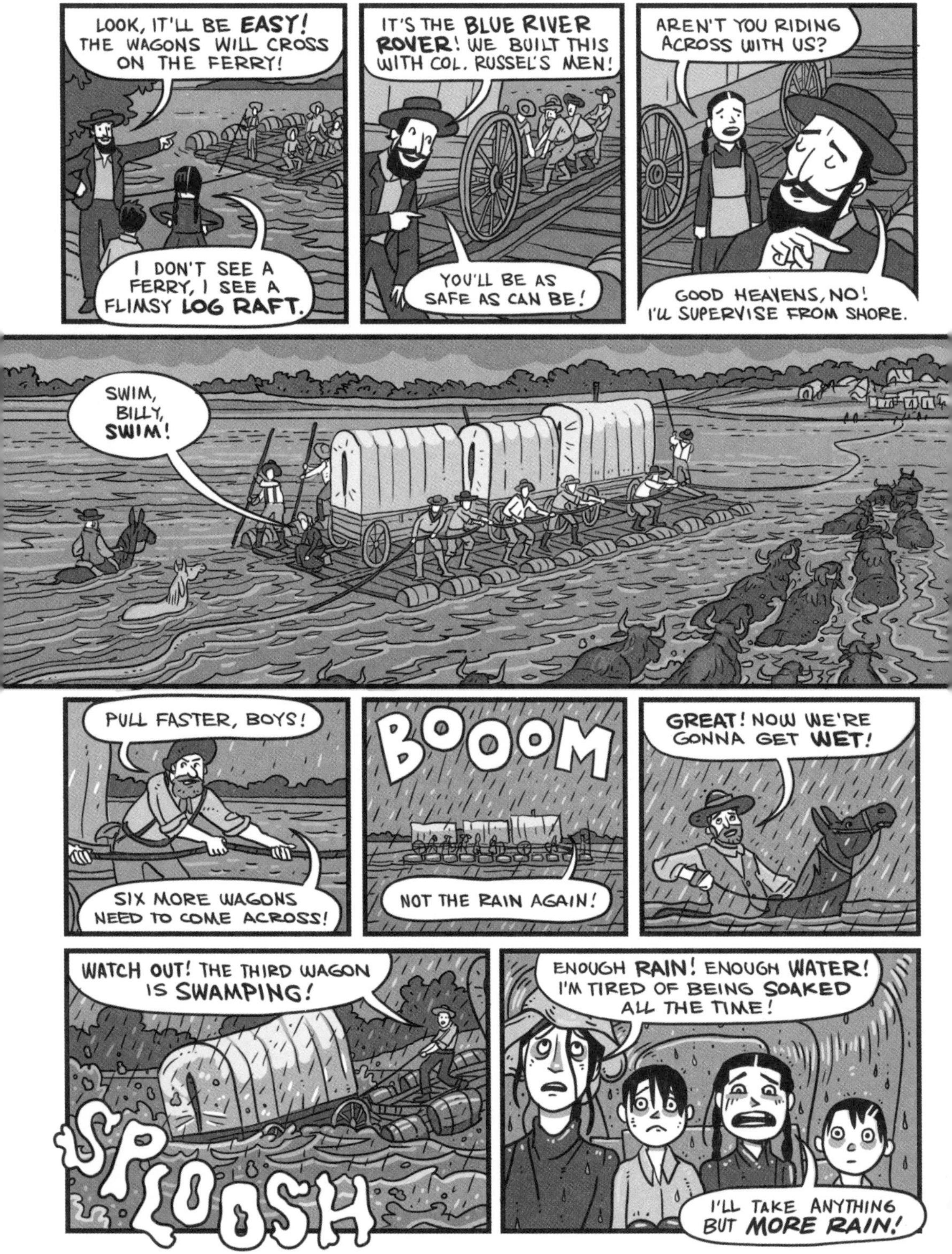
LOOK, IT'LL BE EASY! THE WAGONS WILL CROSS ON THE FERRY!
I DON'T SEE A FERRY, I SEE A FLIMSY LOG RAFT.
IT'S THE BLUE RIVER ROVER! WE BUILT THIS WITH COL. RUSSEL'S MEN!
YOU'LL BE AS SAFE AS CAN BE!
AREN'T YOU RIDING ACROSS WITH US?
GOOD HEAVENS, NO! I'LL SUPERVISE FROM SHORE.
SWIM, BILLY, SWIM!
PULL FASTER, BOYS!
SIX MORE WAGONS NEED TO COME ACROSS!
BOOOM
NOT THE RAIN AGAIN!
GREAT! NOW WE'RE GONNA GET WET!
WATCH OUT! THE THIRD WAGON IS SWAMPING!
SPLOOSH
ENOUGH RAIN! ENOUGH WATER! I'M TIRED OF BEING SOAKED ALL THE TIME!
I'LL TAKE ANYTHING BUT MORE RAIN!

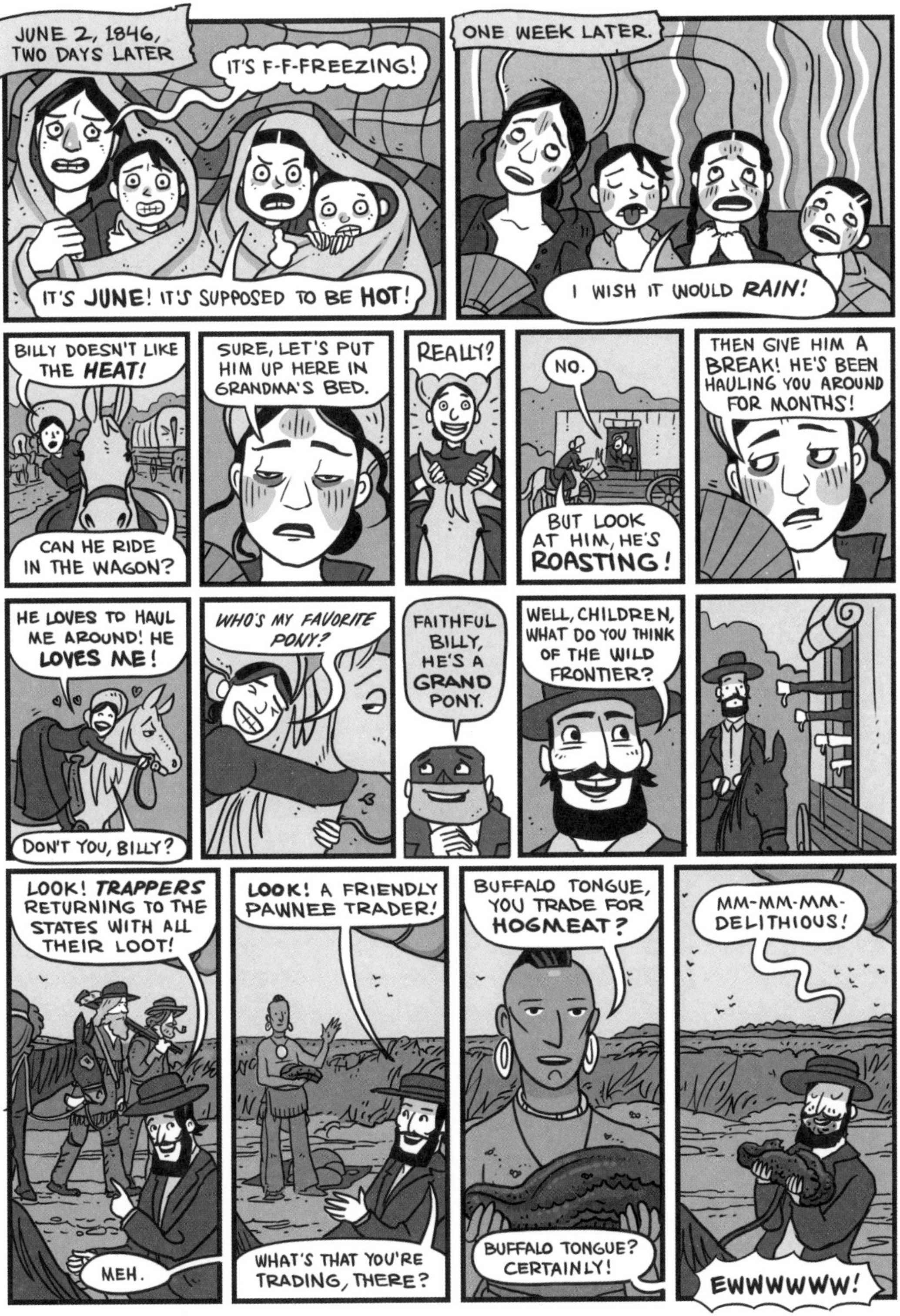
JUNE 2, 1846, TWO DAYS LATER
IT'S F-F-FREEZING!
IT'S JUNE! IT'S SUPPOSED TO BE HOT!
ONE WEEK LATER.
I WISH IT WOULD RAIN!
BILLY DOESN'T LIKE THE HEAT!
CAN HE RIDE IN THE WAGON?
SURE, LET'S PUT HIM UP HERE IN GRANDMA'S BED.
REALLY?
NO.
BUT LOOK AT HIM, HE'S ROASTING!
THEN GIVE HIM A BREAK! HE'S BEEN HAULING YOU AROUND FOR MONTHS!
HE LOVES TO HAUL ME AROUND! HE LOVES ME!
DON'T YOU, BILLY?
WHO'S MY FAVORITE PONY?
FAITHFUL BILLY, HE'S A GRAND PONY.
WELL, CHILDREN, WHAT DO YOU THINK OF THE WILD FRONTIER?
LOOK! TRAPPERS RETURNING TO THE STATES WITH ALL THEIR LOOT!
MEH.
LOOK! A FRIENDLY PAWNEE TRADER!
WHAT'S THAT YOU'RE TRADING, THERE?
BUFFALO TONGUE, YOU TRADE FOR HOGMEAT?
BUFFALO TONGUE? CERTAINLY!
MM-MM-MM-DELITHIOUS!
EWWWWWW!

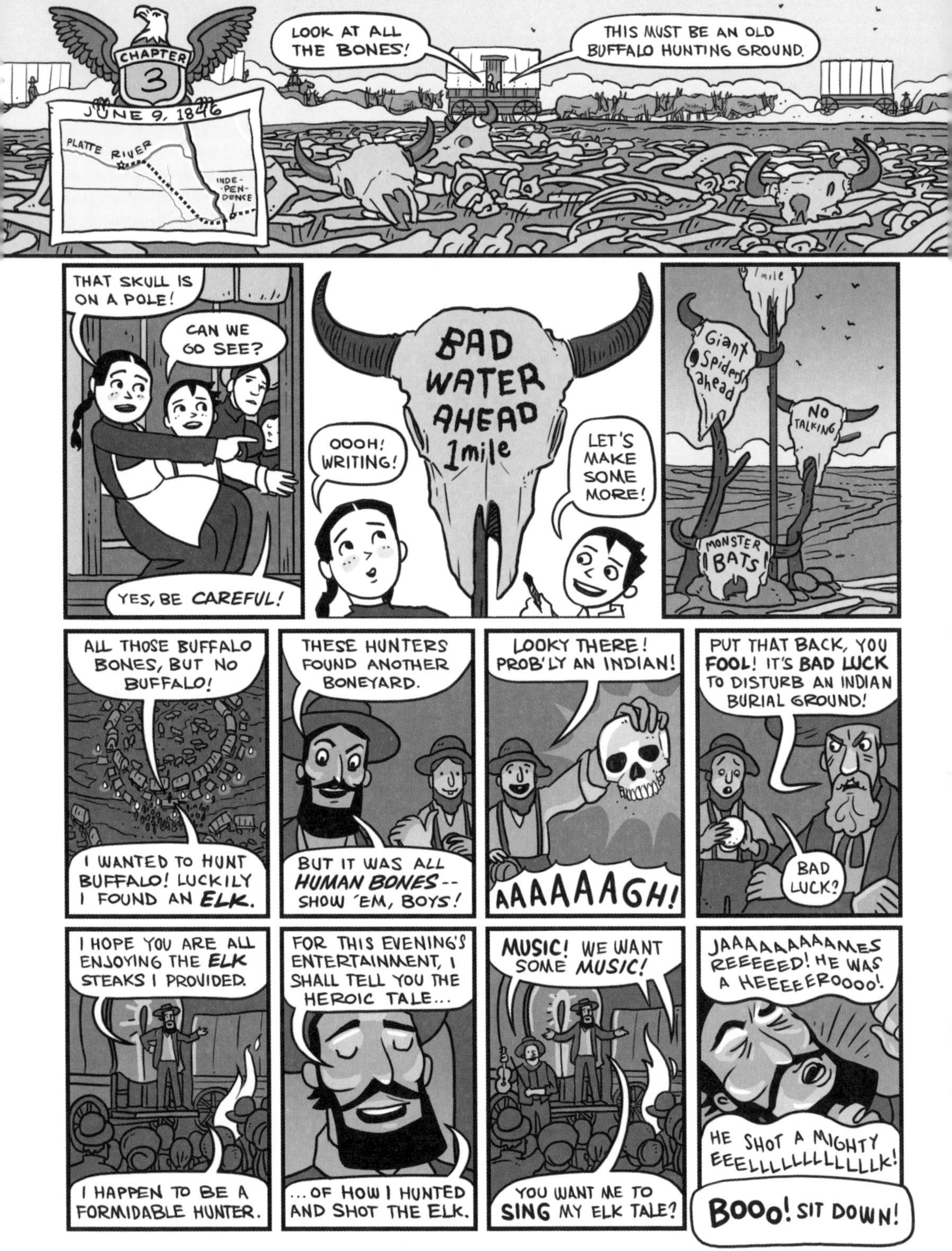
CHAPTER 3
JUNE 9, 1846
PLATTE RIVER
INDE-PEN-DENCE
LOOK AT ALL THE BONES!
THIS MUST BE AN OLD BUFFALO HUNTING GROUND.
THAT SKULL IS ON A POLE!
CAN WE GO SEE?
YES, BE CAREFUL!
BAD WATER AHEAD 1mile
OOOH! WRITING!
LET'S MAKE SOME MORE!
1mile
Giant Spiders ahead
NO TALKING
MONSTER BATS
ALL THOSE BUFFALO BONES, BUT NO BUFFALO!
I WANTED TO HUNT BUFFALO! LUCKILY I FOUND AN ELK.
THESE HUNTERS FOUND ANOTHER BONEYARD.
BUT IT WAS ALL HUMAN BONES-- SHOW 'EM, BOYS!
LOOKY THERE! PROB'LY AN INDIAN!
AAAAAAGH!
PUT THAT BACK, YOU FOOL! IT'S BAD LUCK TO DISTURB AN INDIAN BURIAL GROUND!
BAD LUCK?
I HOPE YOU ARE ALL ENJOYING THE ELK STEAKS I PROVIDED.
I HAPPEN TO BE A FORMIDABLE HUNTER.
FOR THIS EVENING'S ENTERTAINMENT, I SHALL TELL YOU THE HEROIC TALE...
...OF HOW I HUNTED AND SHOT THE ELK.
MUSIC! WE WANT SOME MUSIC!
YOU WANT ME TO SING MY ELK TALE?
JAAAAAAAAAMES REEEEED! HE WAS A HEEEEEROOOO!
HE SHOT A MIGHTY EEELLLLLLLLLLLLK!
BOOO! SIT DOWN!

THANK YOU, THANK YOU! NOW I'D LIKE TO DISCUSS MY TWO FAVORITE WORDS.

"JAMES REED!"

SHORT CUT!

"SHORTCUT" IS ONE WORD.

I'VE BEEN THROUGH THIS BOOK SEVERAL TIMES.

THE EMIGRANTS' GUIDE TO OREGON AND CALIFORNIA . . . LANSFORD W. HASTINGS

I'VE FOUND A WAY TO SAVE US **400 MILES** OF TRAVEL! HOW WOULD YOU ALL LIKE *THAT!?*

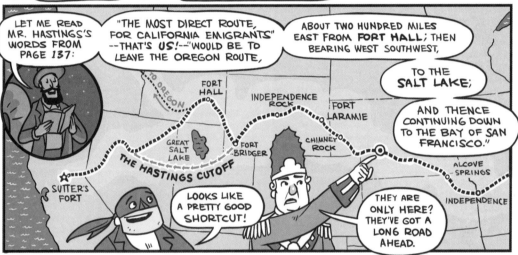

LET ME READ MR. HASTINGS'S WORDS FROM PAGE 137:

"THE MOST DIRECT ROUTE, FOR CALIFORNIA EMIGRANTS" --THAT'S *US!*--"WOULD BE TO LEAVE THE OREGON ROUTE,

ABOUT TWO HUNDRED MILES EAST FROM **FORT HALL**; THEN BEARING WEST SOUTHWEST,

TO THE **SALT LAKE**;

AND THENCE CONTINUING DOWN TO THE BAY OF SAN FRANCISCO."

TO OREGON

FORT HALL

INDEPENDENCE ROCK

FORT LARAMIE

GREAT SALT LAKE

FORT BRIDGER

CHIMNEY ROCK

THE HASTINGS CUTOFF

SUTTER'S FORT

ALCOVE SPRINGS

INDEPENDENCE

LOOKS LIKE A PRETTY GOOD SHORTCUT!

THEY ARE ONLY HERE? THEY'VE GOT A LONG ROAD AHEAD.

IMAGINE *THAT!* LEAVING THE OREGON TRAIL--

SHAVING **FOUR HUNDRED** MILES OFF!

NO MORE WAGON TRAIN **DUST!**

NO MORE FIGHTING FOR GOOD CAMP-SITES!

IT'S ALL RIGHT HERE IN THIS BOOK--*THE HASTINGS CUTOFF!*

HOORAY! HOORAY FOR THE HASTINGS CUTOFF!

HOORAY FOR THE **SHORTCUT!**

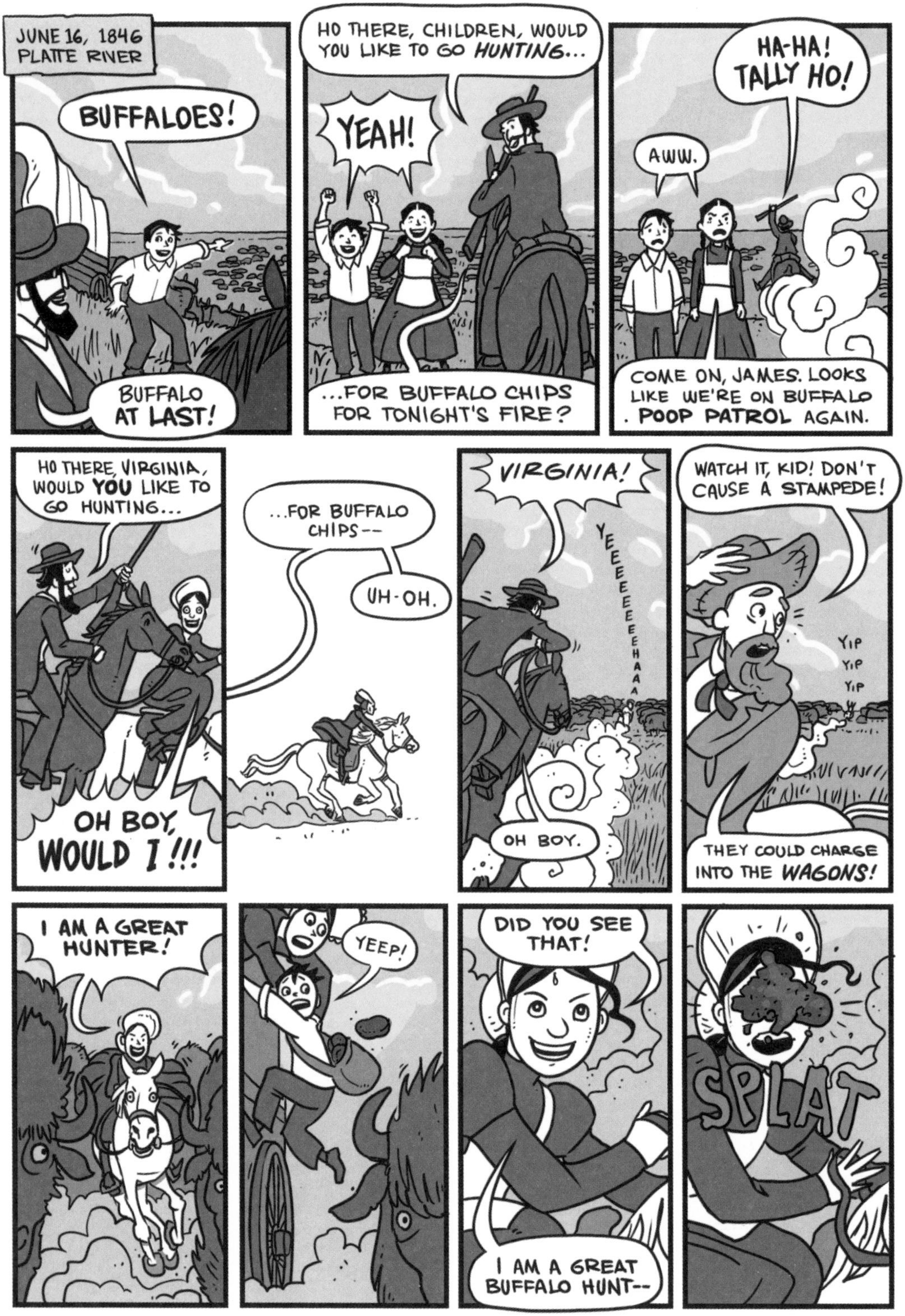
JUNE 16, 1846
PLATTE RIVER
BUFFALOES!
BUFFALO AT LAST!
HO THERE, CHILDREN, WOULD YOU LIKE TO GO HUNTING...
YEAH!
...FOR BUFFALO CHIPS FOR TONIGHT'S FIRE?
HA-HA! TALLY HO!
AWW.
COME ON, JAMES. LOOKS LIKE WE'RE ON BUFFALO POOP PATROL AGAIN.
HO THERE, VIRGINIA, WOULD YOU LIKE TO GO HUNTING...
OH BOY, WOULD I!!!
...FOR BUFFALO CHIPS--
UH-OH.
VIRGINIA!
YEEEEEEEEEEHAAA
OH BOY.
WATCH IT, KID! DON'T CAUSE A STAMPEDE!
YIP
YIP
YIP
THEY COULD CHARGE INTO THE WAGONS!
I AM A GREAT HUNTER!
YEEP!
DID YOU SEE THAT!
I AM A GREAT BUFFALO HUNT--
SPLAT

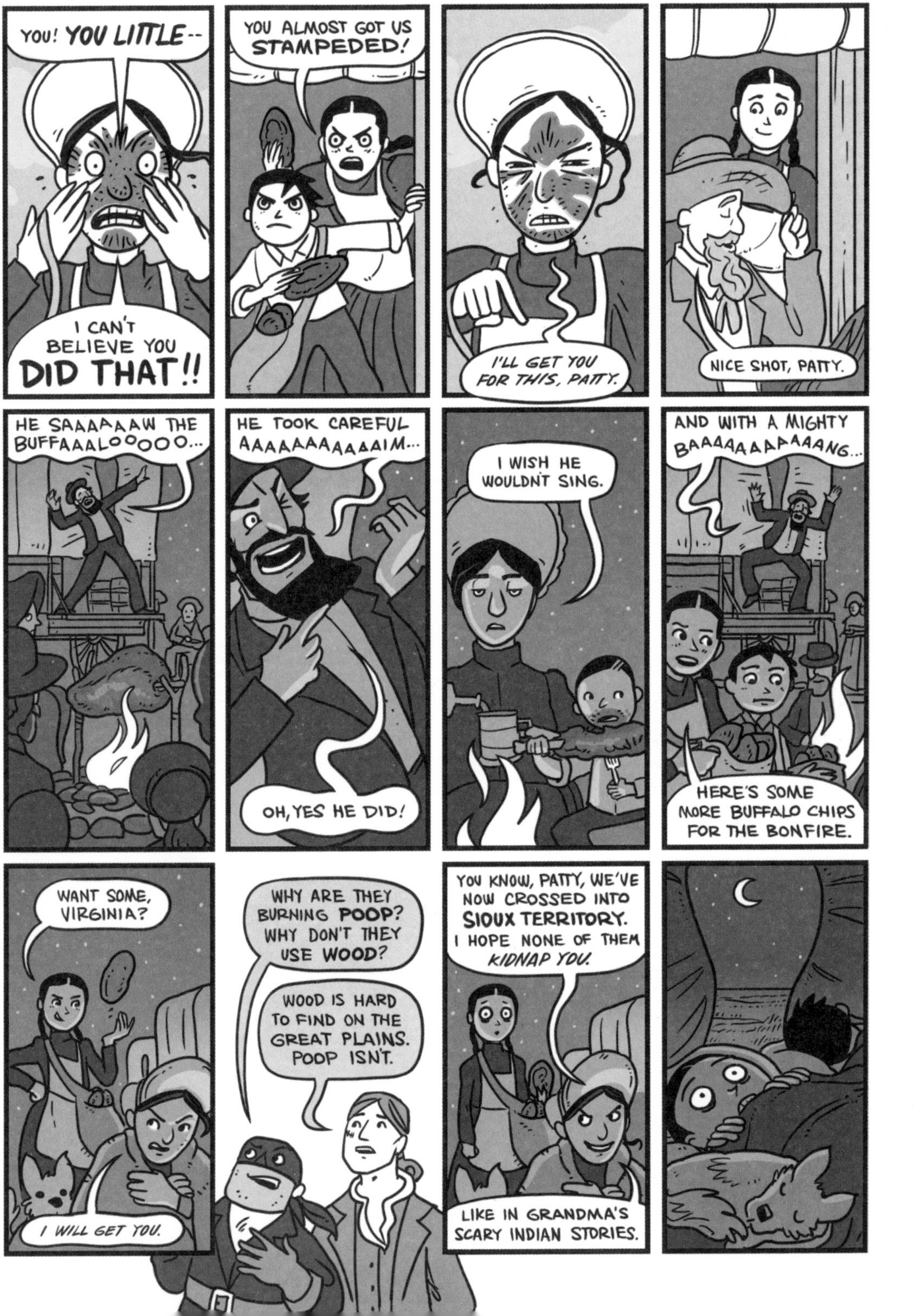
YOU! YOU LITTLE--
I CAN'T BELIEVE YOU DID THAT!!
YOU ALMOST GOT US STAMPEDED!
I'LL GET YOU FOR THIS, PATTY.
NICE SHOT, PATTY.
HE SAAAAAAW THE BUFFAAALOOOOO...
HE TOOK CAREFUL AAAAAAAAAAAIM...
OH, YES HE DID!
I WISH HE WOULDN'T SING.
AND WITH A MIGHTY BAAAAAAAAAAANG...
HERE'S SOME MORE BUFFALO CHIPS FOR THE BONFIRE.
WANT SOME, VIRGINIA?
I WILL GET YOU.
WHY ARE THEY BURNING POOP? WHY DON'T THEY USE WOOD?
WOOD IS HARD TO FIND ON THE GREAT PLAINS. POOP ISN'T.
YOU KNOW, PATTY, WE'VE NOW CROSSED INTO SIOUX TERRITORY. I HOPE NONE OF THEM KIDNAP YOU.
LIKE IN GRANDMA'S SCARY INDIAN STORIES.

READ THE COMPLETE CATASTROPHIC ADVENTURE IN *DONNER DINNER PARTY,* BOOK THREE IN

NATHAN HALE'S HAZARDOUS TALES

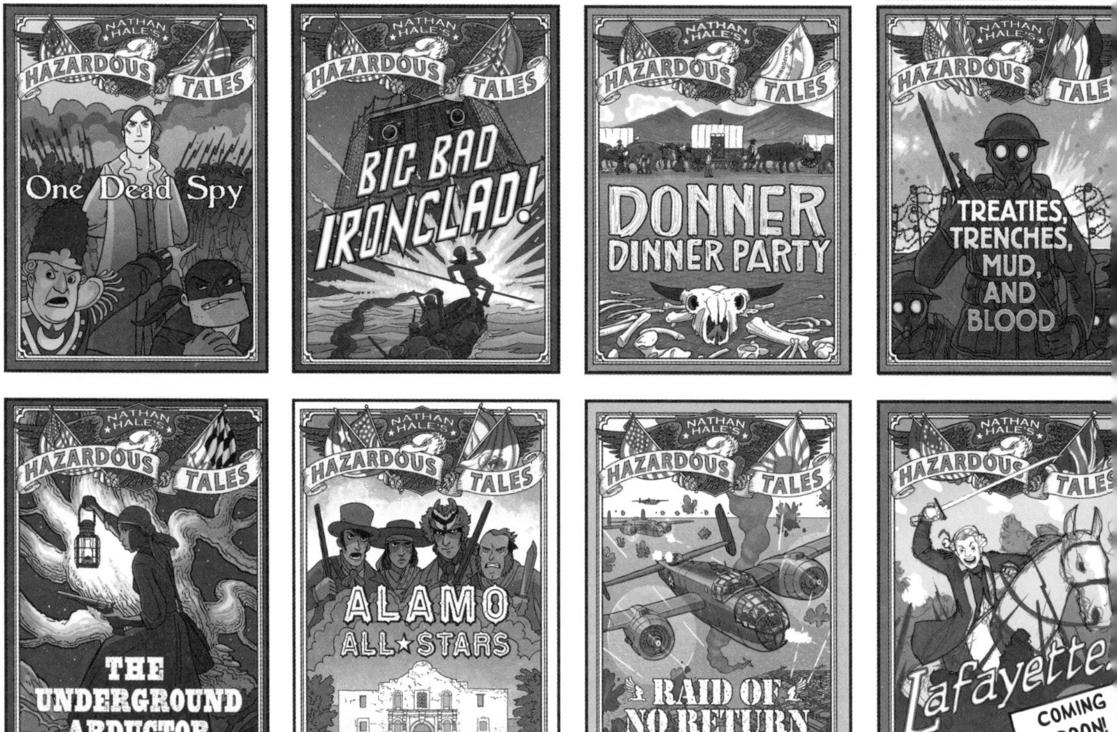
NATHAN HALE'S HAZARDOUS TALES
One Dead Spy
NATHAN HALE'S HAZARDOUS TALES
BIG BAD IRONCLAD!
NATHAN HALE'S HAZARDOUS TALES
DONNER DINNER PARTY
NATHAN HALE'S HAZARDOUS TALES
TREATIES, TRENCHES, MUD, AND BLOOD
NATHAN HALE'S HAZARDOUS TALES
THE UNDERGROUND ABDUCTOR
NATHAN HALE'S HAZARDOUS TALES
ALAMO ALL★STARS
NATHAN HALE'S HAZARDOUS TALES
RAID OF NO RETURN
NATHAN HALE'S HAZARDOUS TALES
Lafayette!
COMING SOON!

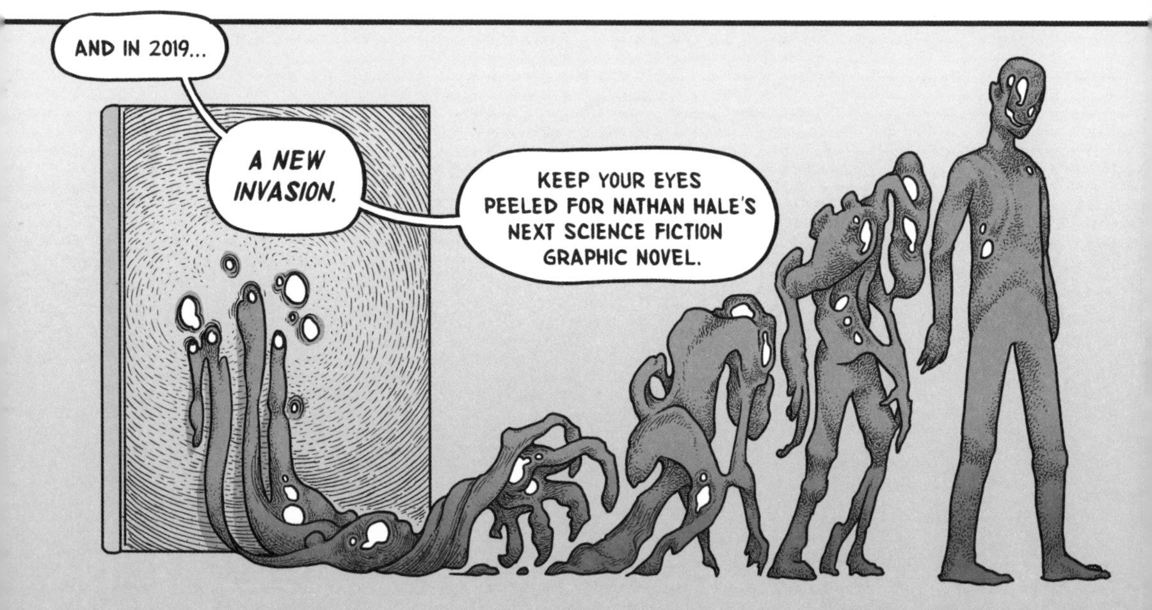
AND IN 2019...
A NEW INVASION.
KEEP YOUR EYES PEELED FOR NATHAN HALE'S NEXT SCIENCE FICTION GRAPHIC NOVEL.